PRIORITY SUSPECT

A Tiffany Chanler Novel

Suzanne Eglington

A woman is like a tea bag. You never know how strong it is until it's in hot water.

—ELEANOR ROOSEVELT

Priority Suspect Copyright © 2021 by Suzanne Eglington. All Rights Reserved.

All rights reserved. No part of this book may be reproduced in any form or by any electronic or mechanical means including information storage and retrieval systems, without permission in writing from the author. The only exception is by a reviewer, who may quote short excerpts in a review.

Cover designed by Suzanne Eglington

This book is a work of fiction. Names, characters, places, and incidents either are products of the author's imagination or are used fictitiously. Any resemblance to actual persons, living or dead, events, or locales is entirely coincidental.

Suzanne Eglington
Visit my website at www.suzanneeglington.online
www.suzeglington.com

Edits by Edwards Editing

Printed in the United States of America

First Printing: May 2020
Independently Published

ISBN-9798647123152

ASIN- B088TYNW87

Suzanne Eglington

ACKNOWLEDGEMENTS

Thanks go out to my family and friends who understand writing is becoming my passion and forgive and understand my absence. In the 2020 year of COVID-19 and pandemic viruses, I hope everyone keeps cautious and safe.

For my readers who post reviews for me, send me feedback, and help get my name out as an author: thank you. You are solid gold.

PRIORITY SUSPECT

CHAPTER ONE

I will not give up. Not today, bolt. Victory will be mine. The irritation in Greg's voice should have made me stop, but I almost had it.

"Tiffany, detective wants to have a word with you."

I growled back, my body pressed against the grill, feet planted, focusing my energy. "Come on, you son of a... grrr..." I leaned into it. Snap! It gave way, smashing my knuckles against the engine block.

"Ah! ERRRR.... Ouch! Ouch! Ouch!" Jumping back, I walked in a circle, shaking my hands in pain to even out the throbbing of my fingers.

I checked over the damage. Nothing serious, no broken skin. I then shifted my gaze to the stranger standing next to Greg.

Both men surveyed my injured hand. The detective's face was scrunched up in empathy as he sucked in a breath from a frown and clenched teeth, and my eyes darted down again to see some slight swelling. I wiggled my fingers just in case. Dang, that hurt.

The cop stepped closer as I straightened, grabbing a rag hanging over the radiator and wiping my hands carefully to avoid my fresh injury. I needed ice so they wouldn't swell more. I was meeting Andy later at the gun range, and I needed my trigger finger. I would get an ear-full if I couldn't shoot today because of carelessness.

As I inspected the section close to where my knuckles hit, the cop empathized. "I know the pain. No blood. That's a good sign." Glancing up again, I saw that he wore a cheap, navy blue suit coat. Apparently, there was no woman in his life. He was clean-shaven with black hair, and the drugstore cologne stank from here. I nodded, acknowledging. "Detective, is it?"

"Diaz. Detective Diaz, Miss Chanler." His eyes focused on my grease-stained hands as he returned my nod with politeness. Greg grabbed my hand, not caring about dirt. "Ouch! Careful." I resisted, growling at him.

He inspected my injury. "I'll get the ice, kid. You owe me a bolt." He peered into my eyes with a look that let me know he would give me privacy for as long as it took him to walk to the ice machine and back. I gave a slight nod of understanding. He released my hand, turning in the direction of the ice machine, and waddled away.

"Miss Chanler, I'll cut right to the reason for my visit. Do you know a guy named Lee Reardon?"

I stood a little taller. I hadn't been expecting to hear that name. *Yes, I know that maggot!* screamed the voice inside my head. I glanced toward Greg, seeing him fill a plastic bag with ice. He was watching me right back. Greg didn't go for visitors in his garage. Especially cops.

My attention turned back to the man who wanted to learn something about Reardon. "Why are you asking?"

"A case about him landed on my desk."

Good, I hope one of the girls is suing him. Molesting bastard.

"What's this have to do with me?"

"Nothing, I hope, Miss Chanler. We seized back files, and it shows you saw him." Detective Diaz pulled a small notepad from his pocket, flipping it open. "Six months ago. Is that right?"

"Yes, that's about right. Needed to get cleared to come back to work and his agency conducted the questionnaire."

"Cleared? For what?"

I knew he also knew why. "Are we going to play this game, detective? I figure you are not walking in here blind."

He surveyed the shop. "Organ donor transportation service. Never in my life would I have guessed how much trouble you guys could be."

"Glad we overachieve by your expectations. Just remember, we're the good guys. We deliver second chances. Don't mock us." My fingers were throbbing and his cologne was giving me a headache. It was time to get rid of him. "Apparently, when we are part of a crime scene, the company covers its ass by making sure our mental health is passable."

"I read about that robbery. State took over the investigation, though. They sealed it pretty quickly. Never learned the outcome."

"They got away."

He cracked a smile. "I can see why you need clearing. Insurance companies rule the world."

"You understand clearance, right… being a cop?"

"So, you're working in the garage now? They take you off transport?"

"I'm on light duty temporarily. That last holdup got me a bullet through my leg. I'll be back driving in a week. Meantime, I do this for fun."

His eyes scanned down, then up. I wasn't sure he realized how obvious that was. Greg returned and handed me the ice bag.

"Fun? You work in this garage for fun? Are you single, Miss Chanler? Because there's a dozen fellas I can think of who would label you the perfect woman."

"Not single."

He looked over his notes, raising an eyebrow. "I'm not surprised. All the good ones are taken."

Greg didn't like him anymore. "Mister, I don't care who you are. Tiffany is working and you have taken up enough of her time. Finish, because it's time for you to leave."

He closed his notepad. "Almost done. Sorry, I didn't mean to offend."

"No offense taken." I replied.

"Anything unusual happen with your appointment that day?"

I didn't want to get into it, especially in front of Greg. I wasn't sure where he was going with this. If they seized his files, then I was only one small fish in the big sea of shit for him. "The guy's a dirtbag. I noticed it the moment I saw him. He reeked of sleaze. Tried to pass himself off as a legit psychologist. I called him out on it. He didn't appreciate that."

Detective Diaz flipped his notepad open again, jotted something.

"Is that it?"

"Pretty much."

"Okay, thank you for your time, Miss Chanler. If I have more questions, is there another way I can reach you?"

"Here is fine. But I am usually inside recording reports."

He glanced around. "Will do." He flipped his notepad closed, tucking it back in his pocket as he took one last glance around the garage.

Greg pointed, "That way."

Detective Diaz nodded again, walking away.

"What's that about?" Greg was not in the least worried about my privacy.

I lifted the ice-filled bag off my knuckles. The swelling was already going down.

"He just asked about that guy who cleared me from that first accident a while back."

"Hmmm. Why?"

"Didn't say."

"Hmmm, okay. Wrap this up and call it a day. Leg's holding steady. You'll be back driving soon."

"Let's hope so. I hate logging reports." The only thing left was the damn running test. I still needed to shave off a few minutes, but then they'd have to put me back in my ambulance. The rumor was Mr. Donovan wanted to keep me on desk duty. That was not going to happen.

For the past two months I had played nice with the brass. Time was up. My light duty restrictions were about to be lifted. If it hadn't been for Greg and this garage, I would have been going out of my mind.

Greg closed the hood of the ambulance. "Have you met the new recruits?"

"Not yet. Chris knows two of them. One she couldn't stand on the force. We seem to attract ex-troopers. Why is that?"

Greg frowned. "Already trained. Donovan can put them right to work. Experienced, working part-time. Win-win for the company. One guy is a former prison guard. Not good with people, I hear."

"Great. Well, I guess it's better than hiring candidates like Taylor. She was an epic fail."

"Her lawsuit is the reason he looked into stronger players."

"I told him not to hire her. She failed the training. That alone should have raised a red flag that she wasn't qualified. Guess he's going in a better direction. From a business perspective, he's right. Everything you listed is an asset."

"They are a bunch of cowboys. Watch yourself."

"I hear Michael is working with one."

"Hmmm. Yes, The Polack. That's the bad egg."

"Excuse me? The Polack?"

"That's what he calls himself."

"What is he, a gangster?"

Greg chuckled. "You could be right." He leaned on the hood, reaching to inspect my hand again. "Thanks for your help, kid."

"If it wasn't for you letting me hang out in here, I'd be miserable."

"You keep my overhead low. My numbers look good because of the work you do."

"At least someone likes me hanging out. I'm sure I will ruffle feathers when I'm back driving."

"Yeah, be ready for that."

I cleaned up and headed to Andy's place, needing to change and check in on Kitten before I met him at the range. I pulled around the corner. There was a white Ford sedan with government plates parked in my spot. I pulled in next to it. There was no one in the car, so I texted Andy. My phone lit up immediately. He was calling.

"Hel.."

"Tiffany, go! Get out of there! Right now. Drive to your condo. Right now!!! Move, move, move!"

My heart jumped, racing, making me lightheaded. "What? Why?"

The alarm in his voice shook my core, raising goosebumps across my arms. A shiver ran up my back. He never sounded alarmed.

"Who is here, Andy?!"

"Tiffany, damn it! For once in your life, listen to me! Get out of there NOW!"

He was yelling in a tone of voice I'd never heard from him.

I threw my car in reverse, squealing tires and all, while I spun my Lexus around to make a fast getaway. No one emerged from around the building in my rearview mirror. Were they inside? Was this car just parked, and no one was there?

I was moving and gaining distance away from the warehouse. He was swearing on the other end of the phone. "Andy! Who's car? Who was that?"

"Get to the condo. I'll be there as soon as I can."

"Is Kitten safe?"

"Yes! Get to the condo, stay put!"

He hung up as I white-knuckled my way back to my place. Who was there? Why were they there?

We hadn't been at my place in a month. I didn't dare stop at the mini-mart I drove past. He had told me to go straight home and wait. My condo seemed cramped compared to Andy's warehouse. I opened the back doors for fresh air, fidgeting just to do something at this point.

Time crept by. My mind made up horrible scenarios. Was that a hitman? Was Andy in danger? Who does he have contact with in the government? He had been active in the military for seventeen years. He still was. Could it be someone who wanted his freelance services. Someone dangerous?

I needed to keep busy. Andy was not returning my texts. I went through my clothes, pulling out my uniforms. Between takeout and Andy's cooking, everything had been fitting tight. I tried on my uniform. It, too, was uncomfortable. Ugh, I had to crash-diet or order a size larger. The bullet wound to my leg interfered with everything in my life. My workout regimen, my eating habits, my job. This slow process of getting back to where I should be was torture. Even grappling was restricted to light duty, but progressing.

I squatted, attempting to stretch the material. Damn it. I was going to have to lose ten pounds in two weeks. I moped in front of the mirror as I saw the start of a muffin top. And, on top of everything else, someone had invaded my home-life with Andy, leaving me with only one option: stay here and wait.

Chills ran down my spine. The thought hit me like a punch in the head. My ears muffled all the sound around me like I was underwater. *What if it's a woman? What if it's an old girlfriend?! Ugh!* I grabbed my phone and texted him. *Who the fuck is keeping me from coming home?!* Now I absolutely needed to lose weight! I stripped out of my uniform and slipped on the heaviest cotton workout clothes I could find, then started jumping rope. Sweat poured down my back and legs, drenching me twenty minutes in.

That bitch was going to pay. From the sound of his voice, she was probably a psycho. Game on. I could take her. I was more or less sure of that. I needed to show Andy that I could take care of myself no matter who showed up from his history. I needed to shower and put on something sexy. Andy needed reminding that I was the only woman. No one was going to come between us.

Everything in the fridge was spoiled. It took ten minutes to clean out, scrubbing the shelves off and washing out the drawers. Not enough time had lapsed. I kept looking at my phone. I didn't dare leave here in case Andy arrived. He still wasn't returning my texts, and I felt nauseated.

Soup. Good, I found a can of chicken noodle soup. I should have been at the range with him right then, but instead I was stuck here heating soup. Visions of him shooting whoever was messing up our plans right now filled my thoughts with mild satisfaction. I glanced down at the camisole I was wearing and suddenly it seemed ridiculous. I changed into a comfortable T-shirt instead.

My shopping network channel separated $600 from me. Andy wouldn't be happy about that, but this was his fault for making me a prisoner in my condo while he dealt with whomever the hell was at the warehouse. As I was waiting to finish my next transaction, I heard the door open.

I hung up, jumping off the couch, anxiety rattling my every nerve. Andy was finally here. Kitten meowed in her crate as he closed the door behind him, setting the crate on the floor and letting her out. She looked around and ran to my bedroom. She loved hiding out under the bed since she didn't get to do that at the warehouse. Andy's bed sat right on the floor. No frame.

I was in front of him now, impatient for news, looking at his expression. "Well?"

He took hold of my arms. "Thank you for following orders."

"Who was it?"

"I need you to hang here a few days."

"What? Why?"

"It will bother me as well, being away from you."

"Where are you going to be?"

"Just realize this arrangement is temporary. Few days, tops."

"Andy! Who is it?" I backed away from his hold. This person was still there and was staying. Even worse. He was staying not with me. but with???

He looked conflicted. I'd never seen this expression on him. He looked guilty. *He's downright guilty! It has to be a fucking woman, and she's staying in my house. I am the one not allowed over.*

"You'd better tell me who or I'm driving there right now!"

He sighed, struggling with the words.

"Andy!" I stomped my foot, clenching my fists. This was unfair, and my patience was wearing thin. He looked everywhere around the room except at me. I was not letting him get away with this. "So help me God!"

He cleared his throat. "It's my mother."

My heart plummeted. My hand instinctively massaged my throat, which had begun to tighten. I needed to sit. I was starting to feel weak. "What? What did you just say?"

"My mother is here. She's staying a few days and then she will go."

That's who it is? His mother? I fled his place and I'm in lockdown in my condo because his mother's *here?*

No longer weak, I now felt numb. My body felt as if it were vibrating. I stared down at my hand to see if I was shaking. No, just feeling very strange.

"I don't get it." *He didn't want me to meet his mother?* The numbness gave way to a tingling sensation. Blood rushed through my veins with searing heat. I was breaking out in a hot sweat. I could sense my face burning. "Get the fuck out of here."

"Tiffany, wait. My mother is…. She's different. I don't want you to meet her just yet. Not right now. This isn't a social visit."

My heart pounded against my chest. "So… what is this?"

"She is here because I fucked up. I need to straighten some stuff out."

"I don't get to see you because your mother is in town?"

He stepped into me and I stepped back. He was not getting away with this crap.

"I need a few days, then we will be back on track."

An idea hit me and I again felt weaker. I put a hand on the end table to steady myself. "Are you ashamed of me?"

He didn't care about me needing space between us as he grabbed my arms, holding me in place. "No! Never let that thought in your head, even for a second. There's something I have to work out with her alone. You will meet her. Just not right now."

I felt like I could summon fire in my breath. *I will not kiss him no matter what he says.* But Andy didn't care about that either as he pressed his lips against mine, extinguishing my burning heart, forcing me to respond by kissing him back. When he released some of his tight grip, he leaned in, searching my eyes. "Only a few days, babe. It's just as hard on me."

I didn't answer as he let go and told me he would text me soon. He turned, leaving swiftly, not allowing me to protest anymore and shutting my condo door behind him.

I despised his mother already.

CHAPTER TWO

It was my scheduled day off and I was waking up alone. I still had Kitten, at least. She sprawled out on Andy's side of the bed.

Mrs. McMillan suddenly proved to be an excellent motivator. Screw light duty. I was back to training with a vengeance. With every spare hour, I pushed myself to do more.

I made a checklist of things to tend to while Andy was with… her. My hairdresser fit me in, neatening my style and lightening the blonde. I'd gotten soft, comfortable even. His mother's visit just proved it was time for me to toughen the hell back up. Love sucked. Andy sucked.

Leaving the hairdresser's, I felt my phone vibrate. Speak of the devil, he was calling. "Yes?"

"Hi babe, how are you doing?"

"Fine."

"Good. Can you meet me on the range tomorrow morning?"

"You don't have to. Your mother is more important."

"Babe, come on. Don't do this."

"I'm sure she wants to be with you."

"She probably does, but I am not in the mood to listen to her critiquing my shooting."

What? Critique Andy? He was the master shooter. "What does that mean? Why would she critique you? What qualifies her to do that?"

"She taught me."

"What?"

"She continued my education when my dad died."

"I don't understand, Andy."

"Will you meet me?"

My heart felt heavy. I missed him. "I'll see if I am available. I have to check my schedule."

I heard him grunt. We both knew I was doing this on purpose.

"I miss you, Tiff."

I caved. He was the only person who could give meaning to those words. "I don't like your mother."

He chuckled softly. "Few people do."

Oh. I didn't expect that. "So, what's her deal?"

"It's complicated."

"Then I want a full explanation tomorrow."

He sighed. "If you lose the word 'full' in this demand, I can accommodate somewhat of an explanation."

"Fine. As long as it's something."

"See you tomorrow, babe."

I ended the call without saying goodbye. It tore at me, but he was stupid for keeping me away. My phone vibrated again. I assumed it was him calling me out for not saying goodbye. Instead, it was Audrey.

"First you leave the company and now it's forever and I still don't hear from you?"

"It's been three days."

"It's been an eternity. What are you doing right now?"

"Well, I just left the hairdresser."

"Okay, meet me for dinner? I have news."

"Where?"

"Depot."

"Oh, the new place?"

"Yes. No jeans."

"Oh, come on."

"No jeans!"

"Fine. What time?"

"Six."

Another call came in. "All right, see you at six. Gotta go, Hannah is calling." I ended Audrey's call and switched to Hannah's. "Where have you been?"

"Hi, I know, I know. How about tomorrow after work?"

"I'm at the steakhouse tomorrow working the bar."

"Four o'clock?"

"That's fine. Plan on a few hours."

"I will. I'm all yours."

"Is everything okay, Tiff?"

"Yes, why?"

"Just haven't seen a lot of you. Nor heard from you."

"Sorry about that. Just been working this damn leg so I can get back on my driving shift."

"You are still trying for that? I thought things were going well at your father's company."

"Wow, it has been a while since we spoke. I hated being in the office."

"Oh please. You were flying out to Michigan every other week."

"Yeah, well, I learned about the new engine, snagged an amazing quarter-billion-dollar contract, and now it's time to get back to my real job."

"How did your father take that? You two were finally making progress as a team."

"He's fine. It's the contract that was important. He got what he wanted, I got what I wanted, we are good. Actually, I think he is just as glad that I left. We have distinct ways of how each of us approach things. He was getting riled up by some of my changes."

"What? Okay, well, tell me tomorrow. Quickly, what's with your leg?"

"I still have to run and pass a timed mile."

"You drive. Why do you need to run a timed mile?"

Finally, someone who understood. "Exactly! It's so dumb." Hannah got this. Why didn't everyone else?

"Okay, we'll talk about that tomorrow, too. Love you."

"Love you, too, Hannah. See you tomorrow."

* * *

I should have been more careful when allowing Audrey to pick the restaurant. This could be a disaster.

I took in a big breath opening the doors. People were sitting on cushioned benches, waiting. I figured it would be busy on a Saturday. I was sure the recent grand opening and streak of good weather also had something to do with it. None of the people waiting were Audrey. I checked the time on my phone. I was right on time. Perhaps, I thought, she got delayed at the office.

I stepped up to the hostess cursing her seating chart and glancing around the entrance and checking the time. She tapped on podium ignoring me. A waiter interrupted, complaining about clearing tables was not his job. She snapped back with equal venom, again, without paying any attention to me, the customer.

This was going to take a while. I looked around the restaurant. My phone buzzed. It was Audrey telling me where she was sitting. I abandoned the hostess standing in everyone's way and saw her put her arm up to catch my attention. With the hostess and waiter still arguing, I took the liberty of walking past them and seating myself. New restaurant, new trend, same old crowd. Audrey continued waving as though I hadn't seen her. I walked quicker.

I glared for her to stop, then glanced around to see how many people were now watching her waving like an idiot. *Oh no!* There, across the room, sat Reese and her bitch cousin at a table several rows back. *Damn it.* They were the last people I wanted to see tonight. I stopped in my tracks. There was

Blake, walking from the bar toward them. *Crap!* I looked back to Audrey, who was still waving. I scurried closer to our table. "Stop waving! People are staring."

She laughed. "I like to wave. Do you want to see my impersonation of the Queen's wave?" She raised her hand halfway up her body, slightly turning her hand in one direction then the other. "Nailed it, right?"

"Please stop. Blake is over there." She jolted forward, scanning the restaurant, eyes shifting from one person to the next. Her voice sounded excited. "The man you knocked out at the gala?"

"Yes, and Mandy is with him." Audrey stretched her neck as far as it would go, weaving it left and right for a better angle, reaching halfway out of her seat as she strained to see them. She recognized Mandy instantly. "Oh, there's that little gold digger. She looks thinner in person than on camera. Pretty. I can see why Richard caved. Let's go say hello."

She was drawing more attention to us. I leaned in, grabbing her arm to make her sit down. "Are you crazy? I don't want them to find out I'm here. And don't remind me about that tramp and my father." She sat, looking at my hair first, then leaned over, examining down to my feet and back up. "I said no jeans. I can't take you anywhere."

"Well, I am wearing $800 shoes that go perfectly with my jeans, so the shoes cancel out the jeans. I am perfectly acceptable."

Audrey glared into my eyes, narrowing hers, pressing her lips into a thin line. She peeked under the table to see my shoes. "Cute shoes. I like them. I will forgive the jeans."

The waiter stopped at our table, picking up her empty glass and replacing it with a full one.

I pointed to the tall drinking glass with a skewer of fruit submerged in it. "What is that?" She waved me off, ordering the waiter, "Bring one for her, thank you." He nodded briefly, waiting for any objection before he walked away. I reached over suspiciously, grabbing the glass, bringing it right to my nose as I sniffed, then tasted. "This is alcohol!"

She dismissed me with her hand again. "Yes. Nothing gets by you. You are wasted as an armed guard."

"Audrey! Are you insane? Do you want to die?" Now I was the one attracting attention.

"Oh, big deal. I am allowed a little." She reached for the glass, taking it from my hand.

I looked side to side. How could she! I couldn't react the way I wanted to without causing a big scene. I leaned in, grabbing the edge of the table. I felt my face getting hot.

The entire hijacking scene played out in my head. I had hidden her liver in the steel reinforced tube that Danny made. I remembered every detail. The back door to my ambulance being ripped open, Taylor's hysteria, the fog hanging heavy like a scene from a scary movie, and the terrifying uncertainty of who was on the other side. My heart raced. I could almost feel the icy touch of the frozen organ. I let go of the table as I remembered Taylor's screams. I clamped my teeth together and spoke so only Audrey could hear what I was saying. "I took a bullet for you. I might have lost my life protecting your new liver. I risked everything so you were able to recover."

"I know, darling. That's why I love you."

"This is what nearly killed you. I can't believe you can be so reckless. You can't drink. Don't do this, Audrey. Especially in front of me." I pulled the drink from her hand and placed it out of her reach.

"Tiffany, it's fine. Doctor says I can have a little. I asked. Besides, this liver will outlive me at my age. It's fine, really. Stop making such a fuss. I will live life to the fullest this time around. It was a combination of other factors, by the way. Let's not forget the stress of running your father's highly successful company."

I was fuming. How could this be? She was making more excuses?

I was the killjoy now. She tried to turn it around, but I watched as her eyes kept moving back to the drink. "Enough lectures. Big news. After thirty-five years of waiting for this guy to ask me out... I have a date tomorrow night."

"I can't accept that you are drinking."

She huffed. "Fine! I don't like water. Order me a cola when he comes back."

How could she think this would be okay? The pressure was building inside of me. First Andy's mother, and now this. Our waiter walked back, setting the drink in front of me. Audrey watched my refusal as he stopped, hand still on cocktail, looking confused as I instructed him to put both glasses back on his tray. I reassured him by saying I would pay for both, then changed our drinking order to one water with lemon slices and one cola.

Audrey frowned. She was not used to being told no. She was sulking with a tight face, letting me have my way for now. I thanked the waiter again as he took the drinks away. "Now I am happy. Who's the guy?"

Audrey monitored Blake, giving me updates when they moved to the bar. I checked my phone, but there was no word from Andy. I couldn't even tell him I was having dinner with a friend without sounding like I was rubbing it in his face. Andy's mother needed to leave and soon. I didn't care for this one bit. It was wrong of him to keep me away. This wasn't normal.

"What's wrong, Tiff?"

I looked up. "Besides you destroying your liver for a second time and in front of me?"

The zinger drew an instant look of disapproval from Audrey. "I did nothing wrong. I am an adult who can make my own choices. If I want to have a mild cocktail, I can."

"You were about to have your second mild cocktail. Or were you going on number three?"

"That's enough. Blake seems to enjoy himself. He's not a bad-looking guy. What happened between you two that you dislike him so much?"

I looked down at my phone again. Nothing.

"Tiffany?"

I raised my head. "He forced himself on me against my will when I was sixteen."

Her face softened, bringing her right hand to her chest. Audrey leaned in, reaching for my hand. "I'm sorry, Tiffany."

"I'm over it. But, man, did that feel good knocking him out."

"I can see the justice in that."

I twisted my head to see where they were hanging out. "I used to get nervous around him. Now I don't, but I also don't want to interact with him if possible. Karma has a way of evening out the score."

Audrey lowered her menu. "Let's not talk about karma."

I would give this place two years, at the most. Hannah's restaurants were far better. No competition here, for sure. This was an average restaurant serving small portions, overpriced food, and slow service. I had experienced enough and was ready to leave.

I asked Audrey to join me for a walk, but Agent Lanski stuck around to do some of her own special investigating by eavesdropping. Blake and the others didn't know her, so she was free to walk among them without suspicion. Audrey was the biggest snoop, and she loved spying on people.

I kept my back to the bar as much as possible as I made my way to the front entrance without the Montgomery family knowing I was ever there. I sneaked a peek around a pillar in the waiting area, seeing that their threesome had grown by a few men who looked familiar.

It wasn't hard to watch them. They called attention to themselves with exaggerated body animation and loud voices. I studied them for a few seconds and again felt relief that my father had ended it with Mandy before the affair turned into the biggest mistake of his life. She was pretty – I had to give her that – and probably great in bed. Women like her thrived on being sexually talented. It was how they got rich men to do everything for them. Half the women I knew growing up used to brag and swap stories about that particular tactic. From the looks of Mandy, who was leaning into one of the men and tossing her head back with laughter, she was fishing for company tonight.

Audrey snagged an empty seat right next to Blake as she observed him a little too obviously. Audrey was right, Blake was easy on the eyes. I flexed my hand, releasing the tension from the fist I'd unconsciously made.

The hostess at the podium was still agitated, arguing over the seating chart with a waitress in front of all the waiting guests. There was no warm, fuzzy goodbye for me as I turned toward the door, walking past them and straight out.

I fished my keys and phone from my bag, pushing the button to unlock my Lexus, which sat next to the curb. Sliding in, I paused for a moment, watching the restaurant doors. There were still no messages on my phone. Still thinking about Andy's mother, I called mine to see if she was home.

CHAPTER THREE

The building that I had called home for so long felt sterile. My footsteps sounded strangely amplified as they echoed throughout the grand entrance. The evening-shift desk attendants acknowledged me without checking my credentials. Unfamiliar faces. I didn't recognize any of them. That was fine. If I didn't have an elevator key, I couldn't get far.

It had been a while since I stopped by to visit. Mother said they changed ownership of this place. She didn't prefer the new owners – they were foreign – and even mentioned moving out in one of our conversations. I could see her point of view. It wasn't the same warm welcome here with the updated colors presenting a modern industrial look. My father's company had conveyed warmth in the lobby, even with a pair of engines displayed as a main focal point.

Mother was waiting, holding her door open. In my entire life, this had never happened – not during my childhood or when company was expected. Not even when the lobby called to say someone was on the way. She never waited by the door. But here she stood, door ajar, watching my approach.

"Well, what a pleasant surprise," she said, looking past me as she spoke. "Are you alone?"

"I just ate dinner with Audrey. Did you know she's drinking?"

Mother tilted her head, as if she didn't understand. "Drinking? I'm not sure what you mean by that, Tiffany. Please explain."

"I mean, I met her at that new restaurant downtown. It sucks. Don't waste your money. When I found her sitting at a table, she was finishing one cocktail and ordered another."

Mother still looked confused. "Is she restricted from alcohol?"

That was a trigger. *Did my mother ask that?* "Are you kidding me? She destroyed her liver from alcohol. It nearly killed me getting her new one to her."

Mother motioned to the sofa. "Tiffany, come sit. I see your point. Audrey is older. She has faced death. I am sure she's just being social and…"

I shot up out of my seat. "And? No excuse. There is no excuse!"

Mother stood, holding her hand out. "Tiffany, I am not making an excuse. I realize you don't see this the way Audrey does, but you have to remember it is her life. How she lives it from here is her choice. I don't think you should upset yourself over this."

That was it. I was done listening to this crap. "Where is Father?"

"In Michigan. He will be home in a few nights. Would you like to talk to him? I think he is out of his meeting now."

"No." It was stupid of me to come.

Mother changed the topic. "How is Hannah doing with her wedding plans?"

I looked down at my phone. "I am meeting her tomorrow to go over things."

Mother smiled. "Please tell her to reach out to me if she needs help. This is my passion. I love planning events and I'm able to show her how to keep on schedule with a few different techniques that might help."

I stared at her gentle smile. She was sincere about Hannah, but I was still irritated about Audrey. She was probably drinking at the bar right now. How could Mother excuse her like that? My life was altered trying to save hers. I still hadn't even returned to my route yet.

"Tiffany, would you care for a glass of orange juice or water?" Mother must have been watching the television when I arrived. It was on, with the volume muted. It was one of those cooking challenges. I pointed. "No, all set. You should enter one of those."

She adjusted, looking at the program. "Oh, goodness no. I could never work under that pressure in front of a television camera. I would be too embarrassed."

I heard water running in the hall bathroom. I turned my head, getting out of my seat again as I started to walk toward it.

"Is someone here?"

Mother answered in a tone that sounded like she had already told me, but she hadn't. "Jordan is staying in your room for a few days."

"Your substitute chauffeur?"

"Yes, he has rodent problems in his apartment building and called to ask if I knew of anywhere he could stay for a few nights while they exterminate. With your father out of town, I thought he could stay in your room."

I stopped advancing. "Does Father know he's here?"

Her face hardened as my throat tightened. "Yes, Tiffany. He was in on the decision."

I needed to leave. I didn't want to know about this arrangement.

"Whatever, none of my business. I have to go."

"Tiffany!" She reached for my arm. "It's just a favor."

I tugged loose. "I have to go. I'll call you later."

"Tiffany?" She called after me, only I didn't turn this time. I just kept heading for the door until I pulled it closed.

Driving home, my phone glowed. It was Father calling. *Damn it!* I didn't want to talk to him. "Hello?"

"Tiffany, your mother called quite upset."

"I don't care what either of you do. I saw your ex-girlfriend tonight. She's still here."

"Tiffany!"

"Oh, and Audrey's drinking again."

"What?!"

Finally, someone who understood. "I was having dinner with her tonight. When I arrived she was swapping out one drink for another."

"After you nearly lost your life? This is unacceptable."

"That's what I thought, but Mother brushed it off and said it was her life and her decision."

"She said that?"

"Yes."

"Okay, Tiffany. I have to go. Please call your mother and apologize."

"Bye." I ended the call.

My mood did not improve. I arrived home to find a van parked in front of the entrance, where someone had propped the doors open. This was a secure building. I moved a box to close the door. A woman called from behind me. "Hey, leave that open."

I turned. She was around my age, walking toward me down the steps. "It's against the rules to leave these doors open. This is a secured building."

She met me on the landing. "I'm moving in. I have no help, and it's saving me time. This place isn't in a dangerous neighborhood. What's the worry?"

"No worries. That's the way we want to keep it. Door stays closed. Moving in? I wasn't aware of a vacancy."

"Who are you? Building security?"

"My family owns this building. Who are you?"

"Great. I'm moving into my mother's place."

"What's the name?"

"What's it to you?"

This girl sported an attitude. She looked like trouble. "Your mother is free to have whoever she wants in here. There are no restrictions. Only rules. One rule is to make sure this door is locked at all times. We allow only those who have keys or their guests."

"Christopherson. Her last name was Christopherson. Don't bother trying to reach her unless you have contacts beyond the grave. Besides, I only have a few more boxes."

"Your mother is deceased?"

"You catch on quick. I can see nothing gets by you. Don't worry. As soon as I can get back on my feet I'll sell her place and be out of here."

"Sorry to learn of your mother. Wendy Christopherson? I didn't realize she was sick."

"Thanks, not a shocker though, been a few years coming. She was too far down the list for a kidney and not popular enough for social media to take pity on her."

"Still... um, do you have a key?"

"I have my key, and a copy of the will. Do you need to see it?"

Wow, what a bitch. Then again I suppose it's how I'd react if I were in her place. She was going to be living here. Time to play nice.

"Look, sorry about coming across so blunt. Do you need help with the boxes? I can access a handcart and open the side door."

"No, I only have three boxes left. I can do it. But if you want to help, stay right here. Security at this place is a pain in the ass."

"I'm not so sure. There might come a time when you are grateful for these rules. What's your name?"

"Robin."

"I'm Tiffany."

She openly scanned my body. "You don't look like a Tiffany. More like a Karen."

"I'll let my mother know."

As soon as she brought the last box through, she informed me, "This is the last one. I'm all set."

I gestured toward her as she headed up the stairs. "You can't leave the truck there."

She laughed and, turning her head, loudly replied. "I wouldn't dream of blocking the entrance. God forbid an emergency take place in the next ten minutes. No, no, no, I don't want that on my conscience. I'll move it in a minute."

* * *

I walked through the door to loud protests from Kitten, who quieted to watch as I cut up the rest of my overcooked steak and set it down for her. She loved meat, noshing on the chunks, growling for me to stay away. It was hilarious. She was my little panther.

All I did was toss and turn in bed. It was day two without sleeping next to Andy. Nothing was the way I liked it. I tried searching for his mother on the internet but could only find his father's name.

Andy's father was a sniper, Marine Corps. Top man for essentially a decade. I found records from the Wimbledon Cup. I had never even realized it existed. There was no fooling around with this guy. His record was impressive, judging from what I had learned from Andy about the technical side of shooting.

I sat up in bed upon finding one photo of a younger Andy with his parents.

Andy could have been an exact clone of his father. The resemblance was alarming. I enlarged the photo as much as I could on my phone. *This is how Andy looks now.* His mother's appearance was plain, but attractive. Her expression looked like it could peel paint from a wall. Suddenly, I wasn't sure I even wanted to meet her anymore. There were no warm, fuzzy feelings coming from her in this picture.

I found a brief obituary. His father died when Andy was around fifteen. There was no mention of Andy or his mother, which seemed strange. He was almost fifty years old when he passed. I did the math. He must have started a family late. *Only a few years younger than Andy is now.* I considered a moment. *Yeah. Given the chance, I would have a baby with Andy.*

It would give me a chance to be the kind of mother I always wished I'd had. I'd have a little buddy to hang out with when Andy left on assignments for days at a time. I wondered if he wanted kids. Now would be a good time. He wasn't getting any younger, and I was young enough that if we decided to I'd still have plenty of time to give junior a sibling. I smiled at the idea of a mini-Andy running around.

I couldn't stop thinking about what it would be like if we had a child. I could do it mostly on my own. I could do this. I could be a good mother. I would have to give up my job or cut back to part time. I could give up work and stay home like Mother did. Hang out with Hannah, wait for Andy to come home.... No, I didn't think I could give up working. That was my freedom.

The skin around my bullet wound started twitching. I rubbed it as Kitten sprawled out on Andy's side of the bed before rolling into a new position and purring in satisfaction. Now my leg began cramping, forcing me to get up.

I walked it off, heading to the kitchen to make coffee. I held my breath, hoping he may have snuck back and filled the coffee pot for me. I pulled the lid open. Nope. I was stuck making my own coffee.

This was war. I wanted my boyfriend back. I put on makeup and my best-fitting T-shirt to look good. I was meeting Andy on the range. It had now been two full days since Mommy Dearest arrived. I was going to make sure he was missing me. All of me.

Nacho walked out of the one-man station, manning the security gate. He smiled upon seeing my car. "Miss Tiffany, always good seeing you here."

His smile was infectious as I greeted him. I always enjoyed seeing him on duty. He was pretty tempting to the eyes and had good manners, too. I was finally becoming comfortable calling him by his nickname. "I'm meeting Andy. Do you know which range?"

"McMillan reserved the ninth hole. Looks like you're playing with big toys today. Wish I could join you."

"You should ask him sometime. I'm sure he won't mind, Nacho."

"Oh, hell no. I just want to see you shoot, miss. Overheard a rumor you were getting good. Perhaps you should enter competitions."

I laughed. "Right, like Wimbledon? I don't think so. Have a long way to go."

He leaned his hand on the roof of my car. "Wimbledon, nah. That's for guys like your fella. I was thinking amateur stuff. Get your feet wet, see what it's about. You understand..." he leaned down closer, "competition shooting is a whole other beast to tackle. You might enjoy it. Think about it. We don't have enough women in the sport and, with McMillan's coaching, you have a shot at putting your name on the books."

That was something to consider. "Hmm, maybe. I'll talk to Andy. Thanks."

Nacho straightened up, touching his chest. "It'll give me something to talk to the fellas about. Been getting boring around here."

I rolled my eyes. "Then you should tell Andy to bring his mother while she visits."

Nacho's expression changed from friendly to serious. "Agnes McMillan is here?" His eyes bored into mine, looking concerned.

"Yes, arrived two days ago."

He raked his hand through his hair and looked at the landscape over the roof of my car. His eyes came back down to meet my gaze. "How long is she here for?"

"No idea."

"No idea? She didn't give you the details?"

"She didn't give me anything. I haven't met her."

"You haven't met her?"

"No, not yet. Almost, though. She showed up unannounced. Andy sent me away as soon as I called him to complain that there was a mystery car in my spot. Why is that? Why did he do that?"

Nacho inhaled deep, slowly letting it go. "Just... I don't know. Not my place to say. Avoid her if you can. That's my recommendation." He tapped my car. "I'm sure he's waiting for you, Tiff. Probably looking at his watch wondering where you are. Go. Remember what I said about competing. I think you will like it."

I turned, looking straight ahead as the gate opened, then back to him to catch his reaction. He picked up his handheld device and talked as I drove through.

Perfect, even Nacho knew Andy's mother. And he seemed uneasy upon hearing she was here. Andy was going to tell me what was up, no matter what. This was ridiculous.

Quickly, I smoothed on a tinted lip gloss and checked my hair in the rearview mirror. Andy was a hundred or so feet from me, and I exited the car confidently before walking toward him. He fiddled with his rifle, but I could tell he was watching me approach. I stopped four feet from him, shading the sunlight with my hand. I didn't want to put on my sunglasses yet. I went to the trouble this morning of putting on makeup to look like I wasn't wearing makeup. The subtle color made my eyes pop.

He glanced up. "Get your hair done, babe?"

I shrugged as if it was no big deal. "Yup."

"Looks pretty."

Good, I had gotten his attention. "Thanks. How's Mother?"

"Not too happy at the moment."

"Why is that?"

"I fucked up a job that cost her money and a client."

"You work with her?"

"Occasionally."

"What does she do?"

"Government contracting."

"Like what? Stuff like my father?"

"No, not quite."

"What does that mean, Andy?"

"She controls people."

"I don't get it. Controls people? You don't do that. You assess risk."

He looked back down at the rifle. "That's one way to look at it."

"What, am I wrong?"

"No, babe, you nailed it." He glanced back up, placing the rifle in its case before stepping closer. "I miss you. This is hard on me, too." He held my arms. "Damn, woman, you are all I want. All I think about."

I stared straight into his eyes. "I am not the one keeping us apart. Ask Mommy if she will let you come over."

Sighing, dropping his shoulders as he let go of the tension he was holding, he leaned his head to mine, touching foreheads. "I will straighten this out. It won't be an issue between us again."

Was he kidding me? "This is all you, you're keeping us apart!"

He was cracking. He wanted to kiss me. I could see and feel his conflict. I wanted the same, to kiss him and wrap my arms around him. I missed his touch, his scent, everything. There were only inches between us now. His aroma scrambled my thoughts, making me separate my lips to breathe through my mouth instead, so I held strong. He needed to learn that I came first. I should be the one he was with. He was causing our separation because of his mother! He was with her at night instead of me.

I angled my head and looked over the table to see his inventory. I brought us back to business. "What's the lesson of the day, McMillan? Oh, Nacho suggested I enter a few competitions."

His entire disposition changed, as if wiping a chalkboard clean.

"Competitive shooting? Is that something that interests you?"

I nodded, stepping back for more separation. "Yes. I think I would like to try."

He smiled. "Takes a lot of practice. Hours on the range, discipline."

"I already do all of that."

"You must buy your own guns. They have to be in your name."

"I don't see a problem. Besides, you have a gun range. Oh, that's right. I'm only allowed there when your mother isn't around."

"Tiffany, enough." He turned, walking toward the table. "I can get you started. Competition shooting is a whole other mindset. You will start as a nobody. I won't be able to go with you to competitions. You have to do it on your own."

My heart sank at this lack of support, then rage erupted. It was because of his mother! "Why? Why won't you be able to go with me?"

"Family name. If I show up, people find out you are with me, there will be unfair judgment as soon as you step on range. You don't want that in your head. Trust me. I lived it."

His family was really starting to piss me off. Even his name came with complications. To say it fueled my aggression in shooting for the day would have been true. I fired the worst shots I had ever attempted. His talking down to me wasn't helping matters, either. After thirty minutes of trading insults, Andy shut me down. He didn't want to waste the ammunition if I wasn't taking this seriously. That made it so much worse between us.

I stormed off the range without saying goodbye, and he let me leave without trying to stop me. Terrible choice once again, Mr. McMillan!

CHAPTER FOUR

I drove with tunnel vision, thinking about the fight with Andy all the way to my grappling class. My instructor caught sight of me as I arrived and told me not to change, but instead to wait in his office.

Ten minutes of waiting bought me enough time to calm down. That lasted until he walked in and sat in the chair next to me, looking sympathetic, like he truly cared. He asked what was wrong, and that was all it took. I caved, giving myself permission to let the emotions flood out. Tears spilled from my eyes, streaming down my face, as I spluttered about gun competitions, Andy's mother, worries about the running test, getting back to driving, this stupid bullet injury, Audrey's drinking and that I had gained weight!

He looked worried, wide-eyed, clearly not used to dealing with women's emotions. He paused, and his expression slowly changed. He spoke like Mildred would have. "Life isn't fair, and you deal with things you can change and not the things you cannot." Half of my issues dissolved as I listened to his calm, soothing voice. He made me write down a list of the things I had control over.

My weight, training to pass that mile, and practice shooting for competition. He even suggested I join a gun club and make my own connections. The whole point of entering competition shooting was so Andy and I could be together. It was something we both liked. Another reason to spend time together. It only backfired because of his family's stupid reputation in competitive shooting. It was something else I would have to do alone, or maybe Michael would agree to come along. He was always asking me if I needed his support. I figured this might be a great activity for the two of us, especially if Andy didn't want to support me.

I suddenly realized I hadn't seen or called Mildred in months. I missed her.

I missed all my friends, making me realize Andy's mother's visit was just what I needed to get my life back on track.

I headed to the garage. No text from Andy. He must have known I was angry, or his mother was busy changing his diaper. Greg was only in for a few hours today. I liked quiet weekends in the garage. Greg and I worked together on an engine, talking about life. He questioned why I wanted to get back to driving and offered a full-time position working for him. That wouldn't satisfy me. I enjoyed coming in when I wanted to, not because I had to. I loved the adventure of the unknown, delivering the donor organs from hospital to hospital.

I cracked a smile. "You can barely put up with me part-time. Besides, will you really be so easygoing when paying me throws off your budget?"

He laughed it off, watching something over my shoulder. "Speaking of trouble." I turned. There was Michael walking toward us. Greg grumbled under his breath, telling me to finish up and get out of there. Michael stopped by my side. "Understand you're joining us soon."

I turned back to my engine and focused on my work. "Yes, that's right."

"Tiffany, are you sure you're ready?"

"Yup, I need to be back. I'm going stir-crazy in the office. I'm not cut out for desk duty."

"Your mother disagrees. You started that new lean-production method. Priscilla said you have saved the company thousands upon thousands."

"I didn't realize you still spoke with Mother." It was odd that he kept in contact with her. "Besides, it's no big deal. I just trimmed the fat on a lot of wasted steps. Also, it wasn't all my idea. Audrey and I hashed out the problems. I just pointed out things managers were not paying much attention to."

He stepped closer and his face softened. "Well, it's what makes a good team. I don't understand why you are choosing this over your father's company."

I struggled, tightening the oil cap. Michael watched, waiting for me to finish. He stepped back as I dropped the hood and collected the surrounding mess. He was still waiting.

"Speaking of excellent teams, are you going to come back and ride with me? Or are you still having your hissy fit?"

"They want me to take over Kyle's bus permanently. I'll be on the same shift, but I think I would like my own ambulance now. I kind of liked being boss these last few months. I don't want to fight with you anymore and we can still talk. Best of both worlds right now. You'll be my line mate."

"All right. I will miss having you ride shotgun, but I guess that would be best."

"Me, too." He looked down. I recognized this expression. He was holding back. He wanted to talk. Instead, he let out an amused grunt and shook his head. He cracked a grin, showing me his cocky side. "Let me know if you want to meet at the challenge course. I can motivate you. You're probably off your game still with the injury and there's not much time left to practice."

This was fun. Michael was trying to rile me up. "My game is just fine. Andy's been training with me."

"Figures, well, tell your boyfriend I say hi." I shook my head slightly as I watched Michael turn and walk away, whistling to himself as he headed back out the doors.

I scrubbed up better than I usually did. Hannah would have a fit if I showed up at the bar looking unpresentable. I fiddled with my hair a bit and drove to the other side of the city.

Hannah was wiping down the bar and making sure everything was in order. A few customers sat at the other end. One of her staff placed a brown takeout bag on the counter. Hannah smiled, joking with Judy, then thanked her. I had almost reached the bar unnoticed when Judy called out my name in greeting. Hannah's head turned. I stomped my foot at being discovered, swinging my right arm across my body as I snapped my fingers. "Damn it, almost snuck up on you."

"We need to talk wedding. How long do I have you for?"

I glanced at my phone. "Five minutes."

"Good." She recognized I was kidding.

"Still having it here?"

"Glad you brought it up." She whispered, leaning in and looking around.

I slid onto the barstool, sat up straighter and whispered back to her.

"Really? Not having it here?"

"I want to get married outside, in a garden. Here, look. I found a few botanical gardens only an hour or so away. We can still bring in catering, so the food part isn't an issue. Look, isn't this beautiful?"

"Very nice. What does George think?"

"He's worried about the weather."

"There are always tents."

"I'm not sure about tents. I think they're a little tacky."

"They have amazing event tents. Nothing tacky about them."

"Says the woman who would get married at a gun range."

I laughed. "Yes, I would. I like that idea."

"Figures."

"Well, if you don't like a tent, how about the hotel where Mother hosted my birthday party? Surely you can flower up a room enough to have the best of both worlds."

"Yeah, but then food becomes an issue again. Besides, it takes away from the ambiance I want to create. It's not the same."

"Then keep looking for a place with a nice garden and a function hall you can bring food to, or just put it off another year."

"I don't want to put it off another year."

"Hey, what about one of those destination weddings?"

"We talked about that. It would exclude too many people we want attending. We can't afford an entire weekend event. People work. Besides, we don't have that kind of money. George wants to buy a house. The neighborhoods we are looking at will keep us both working overtime at this rate. His priority is a simple wedding and to save our money for a better house."

"How about you buy the house with a nice garden and have it there. Problem solved! I am a genius."

"No. You are impossible!"

"Okay, that's the limit on my suggestions, then."

Hannah bent down, pulling out a stack of magazines and dropping them in front of me. Wedding magazines. Tons of wedding magazines. "We need to shop for dresses. Now. Decide in a week. I need all of this ready in less than five months."

"Ugh! Without a new venue? Is that even possible?"

"Oh stop. Worst-case scenario, we have it here as planned. Look through these, tell me if you like anything. I'll be right back."

Hannah walked over to check on her customers as I thumbed through the first few bridal magazines rather quickly.

I stopped on one page. The wedding dress caught my eye. Wow, this was something I'd wear. It was simple with a little lace entwined at the sides and the same lace accenting the bottom trim. It was shown in soft ivory satin. I envisioned myself in this dress. This might be the dress I would marry Andy in.

"That would look good on you. Lucky guy." I slammed the magazine shut, startled, looking up to my right at the guy who had spoken. He smiled and looked down, meeting my eyes. He stood solidly, had grey-black hair with a little curl to it. Neatly groomed facial hair covered around his mouth and chin. His hands were more greased than mine, and I detected the familiar scents of a garage.

Hannah called out to him as she walked back toward us, taking his eye contact away from me and onto her. "I thought that order was for you. You must be on a pretty good job to be working today. Five days in a row now. Steak tips and mashed potatoes. You're getting predictable, sir."

He grinned quickly, and it was gone, just like Andy does with me. The smell of truck grease kept me watching him as he pulled his wallet from his work pants. "You guys cook how I like."

I leaned back a little, trying to peek casually from my seat and not get caught reading the back of his shirt as he leaned over the bar to hand the money to Hannah. She took it and picked up the bag, placing it in front of him, then made his change.

She turned, looking back and making friendly conversation. "I'm glad you like our food and thank you for your business. Have you ever stayed for a meal here?"

He reached for his change on the bar. "No, I'm not in the area, usually. Got this pain-in-the-balls job going that is taking me longer than expected. The guy on the jobsite recommended this place." He shuffled his money around and isolated a ten-dollar bill, separating it from his change. "This is for the bride's drink. Congratulations."

He was back to making eye contact with me, and his smile held a little longer. I quickly tilted my head down, considering the flush in my cheeks.

"Bride?" Hannah looked down at all the wedding magazines in front of me, snickering. "Oh, I am the bride, this is my maid of honor." He threw down another ten dollars. There was a pleasant sound to his voice. "Ladies, next round is my treat."

Hannah beamed. "Thank you. That is so nice of you." I looked back up to him. He winked at me, turning while carrying his bag away. My eyes and head followed until he faded around the corner.

Hannah was right in my face. "He's cute, right? Dirty, but cute. And that was so nice of him. What do you want, Tiff?"

I straightened back around to Hannah. "Iced coffee."

She nodded. "Me, too. Excellent choice." Hannah kept chatting as she made our drinks. "That's funny, he thought you were getting married. If he only knew your thoughts about marriage."

I quickly shuffled the magazines to hide the one I saw my wedding dress in. "What an idiot."

She placed our iced coffees across from one another. "Cheers, my dear." We clinked glasses. "Did you see anything you liked?"

"I'll wear whatever you want me to. And if it's too frilly I will make alterations."

Hannah scowled. "I know this about you. It's why I want to see what you like, so I have an idea how to dress everyone."

"How many again?"

"Eleven bridesmaids and four flower girls."

I snorted mid-sip, sending coffee dripping down my chin. She handed me a napkin. "I know, the altar will be crowded. Between his sisters and my family we cannot help it."

"We have plenty of time, Hannah. Priscilla is the party-planning queen. She can probably find you that picture-perfect venue you want. Why don't you draft her? She even instructed me to tell you that she's here for whatever she can do to help. Besides, I suck at this. Think of her as picking up my slack."

Hannah fidgeted, biting her lower lip. My eyes widened, reaching for her hand.

"Hannah? She would love to help you."

She dropped her shoulders and exhaled. "I know, but George and I don't have the budget she is used to."

"So?"

"I know how carried away she gets. My parents are gifting all the food, my dress, and the use of one of our restaurants. They won't pay for something that they can already provide."

"If she finds out you wanted her help, but didn't ask, then she will be mad. Do you want Priscilla mad at you? Besides, she will probably offer to pay if she gets out of hand. Mother loves this crap. Call her."

"Okay, look. I don't know how to say this, so here goes. I know she will pay for it, but that is money that should go to your wedding someday. It's not right. She's your mother and should do this for you. Not me."

I stood up, holding my hands out. I knew where she's going with this. "Stop, Hannah, come on. I am not the white, frilly wedding type. It will never happen that way. You were right about the gun range. I am totally into that style of wedding. Mother and I even joked about a campfire and a bucket of beer being the perfect wedding for me."

"Tiffany, I can't. It would also make my parents feel bad."

"Hannah, they don't have to find out. You would be doing me a great favor by recruiting Mother. She'll get to put on her once-in-a-lifetime, dream wedding. The one she always wanted for me. You'll be the fairytale bride you've always wanted to be, and no one has to know about the financial cost or where it comes from. Trust me. Let her go over the top, then tell her you can't afford it, and about that thing you just said about your parents? Trust me, it will all be hush-hush. There, everyone happy."

"I don't want to use your mother like that."

"Then make her an honorary grandmother when you have babies. It will not happen in my lifetime. I don't think Andy wants kids. Besides, he is too much of a baby himself. You are her only source for this stuff. Well, besides Michael."

"You don't even want kids, Tiff? And what about Michael?"

"I like my cat. She's enough of a brat for me. Priscilla and Michael talk. They have their own secret friendship."

"You can't blame her for that. She loves Michael. Just because you moved on with Andy doesn't mean she has to give him up. Michael is very good to Priscilla."

"So is Jordan."

"Who's Jordan?"

"Her substitute driver. Been staying in my room while they fumigate his apartment."

"Maybe Priscilla likes the company of younger men." She wiggled her brows.

"Gross! Stop that."

"I'm just saying, your mother is an attractive woman. It would serve your father right if she evened the score."

This conversation was rubbing me the wrong way. "I'll be right back. Gotta use the ladies' room."

I checked my phone. Nothing from Andy.

Hannah asked again how long I was staying when I returned. I confidently answered that I'd be there until she got sick of me. Her smile widened and she spread the magazines out in front of me. "Do you want to see what I think would look beautiful on you?"

"Oh, good god. Fine."

CHAPTER FIVE

I didn't want to see Andy, especially after yesterday. Not to mention his mother was still there. There would be no making myself look pretty today. After gun practice was my mile run. I didn't even want to brush my teeth. Anything I could do to keep him away from me seemed like an outstanding idea.

If only I had the nerve to show up unkempt. Tank top, shorts, with my range pants and T-shirt layered on top worked. The weatherman said it would be a warm, sunny day. Spring was catching us early, and I loved the warmth that came with it.

Andy picked me up. I met him outside. No need for him to come in. We didn't say much on the ride over. He set up our guns, with me ignoring him as best I could. I checked my phone for distraction as Andy called my name. He was ready.

I reached to take the rifle from him. As soon as my fingers touched it, it felt off. It was much lighter than the ones we had been shooting. It looked legit at first glance until I turned it over and heard beads rattle around inside. What the....

"Is this a paintball gun?" I dropped my arm to my side. All these hours spent training the past few weeks, and we end it like this.

His face lifted, staring into my eyes. "Yes."

I felt my eyebrow raise. Was he kidding me? "And why are we playing with toys?"

His tone was irritated. "Because you have a scheduled exercise in less than two weeks, provided you pass your run."

"Yeah, but those exercises are a joke. I don't need to train in paintball shooting."

"Yes, you do. Especially with the three retired troopers they hired in your absence."

"Oh, come on. Chris said this is playground work for them. Do you really think they will take this stupid exercise seriously?"

He stopped unloading his bag and angled his head to stare back into my eyes. He was dead serious. "You stick a cap gun in the hand of a retired professional serving twenty-five plus years on the force, and he will bring every experience from his training to any battlefield. Stop mocking this because it's only a paintball gun. You'll be surprised how deadly this is."

My inner voice confirmed how stupid this was and I shook my head. I brought my arm up and held the gun like it was a toy, which I was certain it was. "I heard I will beat them on my run even with my bum leg."

Andy ignored what I said. "Tiffany, come here. I want to show you a few advantages."

He held out a bag of paint pellets. They were all red. "What? I don't get to pick my color?" My attitude was met with a look of disappointment.

"Lesson one: when you use a gun like this, always load red pellets."

"Because?"

"Because red represents blood, and it works on the psychology of the person you hit. You may realize it's only paint, but somewhere deep in the nervous system, it registers that you have been shot. The body reacts the same whether it's paint or a real bullet."

"Okay, red, I get it." The sun was just at the right angle, making me squint. I touched the top of my head. Dang it. I forgot my sunglasses in the car.

He reached out, touching my arm. "Second, get it out of your head that this is a toy. Used effectively, you can inflict serious damage. This is a weapon, Tiffany. Your attitude will get you hurt."

"What, is someone going to shoot my eye out?" Now I really wish I'd thought about making sure I brought my sunglasses.

Mr. Safety handed me clear eye protection, grumbling just enough for me to hear how unhappy he was about my comment.

He changed attitude to Mister Military Business. "I'm going in the building. You have thirty attempts to land a single shot on me."

Well, wasn't he all-powerful and mighty? "You don't think I can?"

His half-smirk ignited an instant fight in me. "Sorry, I didn't know I sounded so obvious."

My blood boiled, with my inner voice cursing him. I purposely narrowed my eyes, pressing my lips together as I tightened my grip around the fill cap, twisting it shut. My mouth was already ahead of my brain.

"Really! You think I can't land a shot on you?" I pressed my shoulders back and puffed up my chest. *How dare he!* "Well, if you are so sure, mister, how about a bet?"

"I don't bet. You know that."

I shot out my hand for him to stop. "Andy, how about if little ole me manages to shoot you, you stay over tonight, and we watch TV together? That is unless Mommy disapproves?"

"Tiffany, it's not like that. She's only here for business temporarily. Who knows when I will see her again?"

"I don't care how long she is here for. She can move in with you. I am kind of liking the entire bed to myself again. Well, except for Kitten. She's been sleeping on the other side of the bed."

"My side of the bed?"

"The empty side of the bed, so it's now her side. Oh, and I choose what we watch."

He frowned. "Shopping? Cop shows? No, thank you."

"Wait!"

He turned away again and stopped. He was giving me at least the courtesy of listening. "And if I don't, I will do anything you want, no complaints."

Andy stared hard into my eyes. "Anything?"

I nodded yes, holding firm. I repeated to let him know the sky's the limit. "Anything!"

He grinned only quickly before he lost his amusement. I knew he would take the bait. "Does it count for only tonight? Or can I use it whenever I want?"

I chuckled. "Hmm, okay, you can use it whenever you want, I guess. But only once, and there has to be an expiration date, like three months or something."

"That's a deal, woman. Stay here. As soon as I enter the building, you may advance."

I yelled so he could hear me. "I am glad you are sleeping over tonight. Good choice because I was thinking about dumping your ass. No woman likes a mommy's boy." My taunts got no reaction from him.

My heart was racing for different reasons. I inhaled deep, slowing down my newly brewing anxiety, and watched him disappear into the building. *I must win.* His mother needed to know I was important. Important enough that he chose me for a night while she was here.

If I couldn't meet her, then she would at least know that I was in his life. It would be her turn to wait for a night. Besides, it had been too long since we chilled out and cuddled. Not being with him because she was here was wearing on me.

He was inside. This was my cue. I scanned the windows. It would be just like him to shoot me on approach. I moved slowly, poking my head into the entrance just enough to see no immediate danger. I stepped forward.

Okay, nothing. He wanted to play cat and mouse. I knew this psychology of his. I was safe for a few yards inside, then all bets were off. It was time to play. I looked around, scoping out different spots for cover. Most likely he was watching me from up on the next floor.

I, too, gained an advantage knowing the layout of this building. Andy ran many mock drills using this and both our places when we first officially became a couple. He enjoyed teaching me war games, and I liked playing with him.

I studied every corner in this building shell, first for the obvious. I concentrated on what I was hearing. When you block enough out, it's amazing what you can tune into. There was no sign or noise from him. He was holding his spot secure. I could almost picture him and how he would position himself, waiting for the perfect moment to reveal.

Ever so slowly, I stalked deeper into the building, keeping the rifle ready at my hip. I knew this position wasn't favored, but it allowed me to shoot freely, and sometimes at an angle he didn't expect, which could land the shot to make tonight happen.

Regardless of this exercise, I started shaking a little. Adrenalin was leaving my body. *Crunch!* Damn, I didn't see those small rocks as the sand scraped, grinding against the concrete under my boots. Surely that was loud enough to give away where I was.

I crept along, deciding which direction to go in. *Son of a....* I scurried behind the closest pillar, the side of my head stinging from the paintball's direct hit. "Ouch!" Red paint dripped down behind my ear. I smeared it away. "Damn it! This better come out of my hair!" I stared at the red on my hand, knowing my hair would be stained for a while. Another paintball stung my shoulder.

I didn't look at the hit, but it throbbed along with my head. Quickly glancing in the direction it came from, I changed my position as another splat hit the wall. I was right. He was positioned at two o'clock. I wasn't safe here. And he was on the second floor.

My heart was racing again as I glanced around, looking for options to get to the next floor. Based on where Andy was, both sets of staircases would leave me wide open for him to pelt me. Sometimes you just had to choose and run into danger.

So help me, he was going to be mine tonight. No mothers allowed. *I got this!*

I snuck up the stairs, rifle ready. Four hits, one after another, landed on the still-healing bullet wound on my leg. I dropped my gun in pain and grabbed the wound. "Damn it! Not fair!" I picked the gun up, bringing it butted against my shoulder. "Not the leg, okay?! I have to pass my run."

He revealed himself to shoot my leg again. "Ouch!" I ducked behind a wall, hissing between clenched teeth. "I hate you!"

I could hear him snicker. "All is fair in love and war, babe."

"Yeah, well, you suck!" I rubbed my leg to quell the stinging.

"And you can't object to anything I buy on TV!"

He was clearly amused. "I won't have to, because it will not happen."

"Oh yeah, that's right. Mommy has you on a curfew."

I bumped my head back against the wall, with the ache in my leg spreading. *Don't let him win, don't let him win. Come on, you've got this.* I looked down at all the red. Andy was right. I was flashing back to the night they shot me. *Snap out of it. This is paint, and he has decades of training. Think!*

I had trained in these drills with him. I looked around. Okay, yes, each room connected. I remembered this one training session when he was on the other side of the door. This room was equipped with side-entrance doors, opening room to room, by the windows.

Struggling to get up, I called out. "No more shooting my leg. It really hurts." There, maybe he would think for a minute. "They won't let me back on shift if I don't pass the mile run." No response. "And if I can't be back on my rounds, I will be very unhappy. I am not going back to my father's company and I don't want to be stuck doing dispatch or paperwork." I tapped the door open wider, looking around at my surroundings.

Just as I stepped through the door, there he was, standing still, watching me, reaching his arm toward me in a sign of truce. His eyes were wide, concentrating on the hits he made to my leg.

"Sorry, I shouldn't have hit you in the leg. You okay, babe?"

I opened fire horizontally, below his rib cage. "Yes! Yes! Yes! You and the TV are all mine tonight!" I shot his leg twice for additional satisfaction.

He looked down at his shirt. "We were in a timeout."

I laughed. "I don't think so, buddy. I never asked for a timeout. What was it you said, 'All is fair in love and war?'"

Ha! Bet those words tasted like vinegar now. Happy, happy me. He watched as I jumped around, proud in the moment. My last victory hop made me stop to rub my leg.

He asked again. "Are you okay?"

"No! You suck. But I will let you rub my leg tonight on the couch while we watch television together." He knelt and took hold of my leg, rubbing and pressing his thumb over the paint where he shot. "Ouch!" I tried pulling away, but he held me.

"Stand still. Let me fix this."

I wiggled some more, trying to stand still, but what he was pressing hurt like hell. "Ouch! Stop it! I'll be fine."

He looked up at me. "Okay, enough training for today. Let's end it with your mile run on the course."

I dropped the paintball gun to my side. "No, thank you. I would rather not."

"Come on, Tiffany. Work through it. I will follow behind through the woods."

"Why don't you run next to me, then? Do this together?"

"With my way you won't know where I am. It will add another layer to your psychology."

I huffed out. "I don't need another layer of guessing with you. I'm already tapped out."

"Come on. One mile and we go back to the condo. I'll fill the bath for you."

My heart fluttered, I loved it when he made romantic boyfriend gestures. I looked at the path of red paint across his chest. He looked down. "Nice trigger finger. I'm glad you didn't stop."

"You taught me not to."

"Then I am glad you pay attention sometimes."

"Sometimes what you say makes sense."

"I wish you listened more."

CHAPTER SIX

I stripped down to my running tank and shorts. The red pellets had stained right through to my skin. My hair would probably be splotchy red for a while. Andy filled up my paint gun with clear pellets. I watched, picking up one that had spilled out.

"What is this?" I squished it between my fingers, unable to suppress the temptation.

"Water pellets."

"What do you need these for?" I enjoyed squishing them, popping a few more.

"Pelting you in the ass when you slow down."

"What?"

He grinned, tightening the cap. "I'll give you eleven minutes to finish." He slung his gun over his back, aiming mine at me.

"You will not shoot me with those!"

"Yes, yes I will." He stepped toward me. "Let me try to wash some of this red away."

My hands shot out in warning, trying to hold him back. "Don't you dare!" My heart raced as I backed away quickly.

"You better get moving, babe. I'm right behind you."

"Andy!" He was serious. I turned and ran.

"Three, two..."

My run began inside the challenge course. My quadriceps hurt almost immediately, but the ache was bearable. I slowed to a stop as I decided which path around the climbing walls would be shortest. A sharp sting hit my buttocks.

A bee? "Son of a bee– " Another hit. It was wet. It wasn't a bee; it was my bastard boyfriend pelting me to keep me moving. I raised my middle finger. I was sure that he saw it.

I fell into a rhythm and was making solid progress, ignoring the ache in my thigh. The pain wasn't going anywhere, but I was making good time. Still time to aim for a nine-minute mile. If I could do this, no one could stop me from returning to my shift. I kept a decent pace as I approached the rope grid deep in the course. Two soldiers were standing there, talking. I smelled trouble.

The one facing me hit the other's arm and he turned to watch. An uneasy feeling washed over me.

One of the men walked in my direction. "Hey there, you lost, little lady?" he cackled.

"No."

They both picked up their pace, closing in. "Well, you are a fine, fit woman. Haven't seen you around before." They surveyed my body.

My heart jumped into my throat. They were not stopping to make friendly conversation. They were now purposely blocking my path. I darted to the right and they moved to cut me off. The situation was getting worse.

"I'm getting in a run. Get out of my way, you're messing up my time."

Lefty smiled "Messing up your time? You military? What's with all the red stains?"

"None of your business. Move."

"Move? What do we got here, Jimmy? She's a bossy, pretty thing, isn't she? I bet your bark is worse than your bite. I would sure like to know that bite, though. Bet it gets real good."

My heartbeat echoed in my ears. They were staring at my chest. I was in trouble. I sized them up. *Never show fear.* I glared at them, already clenching my fist.

"Get the hell out of my way."

Lefty lost his smile, stepping closer. My plan of action was to watch his movement, take out his knee. My weight shifted.

The one named Jimmy answered. "Really? 'Hell' is a strong word, but you can do better. Like 'fuck.' Get the fuck out of my way. I like the word 'fuck,'" he gazed down at my body. "I like your type. This is going to be fun. You are on my property, lady. You need to earn your privileges here."

I stepped back to get better footing for my forward motion. This was going to happen. They wanted to hurt me.

He leaned in and my weight shifted back on my left to kick. His hand reached immediately to his forehead. "Ow, what the fuck?!" The color red was splattered across the center of his forehead. I pivoted toward the woods and back. *Andy!* I had forgotten he was following me.

Now Jimmy's buddy was mimicking him. Both had been shot with red paint, which dripped down as more shots pelted their faces seconds apart. I backed away. A shot flew in Jimmy's mouth, and he coughed and gagged, grabbing his throat.

Several more headshots landed on each before Jimmy was on the ground. Lefty ducked and bobbed in every direction. I looked around for my mercenary but couldn't see him. "I told you to get the hell out of my way."

"Fucking bitch!" Jimmy yelled as he scrambled behind a tree.

I ran around them, putting as much distance between us as possible. The adrenaline left my body fast and I felt weak, but I didn't stop.

That was too close of a call. In all my time training here, I had never experienced something like this. I wasn't prepared, and I was so glad Andy had followed me. I was sure this wasn't the end of those two.

I didn't make my time, not even close. Andy stood waiting at the one-mile opening. I slowed down to a walk, wet-haired, breathing heavy. I leaned over, ready to puke. The shock of the experience finally washed over me. Dry heaves rippled my stomach as my body shook.

MPs in a jeep approached. They reached us and Andy asked for a blanket. The passenger jumped to the rear of the jeep and handed Andy an army blanket, which he wrapped around me.

"Is she okay?" The dark-haired guy was younger. Tall and thin, a few years from now he would be a force to be reckoned with.

"Shock. She'll be fine. Did you find them?"

"Sir, we located and apprehended the perpetrators. We'll handle it from here. I am sorry for the harassment. We will address this. Angel Wings has reserved the course for Friday and we will make sure it's cleared."

Tears spilled out. *No! This is ridiculous. I don't cry!* Quickly wiping them away, I cleared my throat to try to regain composure.

"Thank you." I thought about Jordan staying at my mother's house as a distraction. "Thank you." I repeated more confidently. That stopped the waterworks.

He nodded at me, saluting Andy. "Major McMillan." My stomach flip-flopped. They recognized Andy. He dismissed the MP, observing me.

"What?"

"You."

"I don't get what you are saying?"

"Thank you, Andy."

"Come on, Tiff, let's get all this behind us."

We both heard Kitten screaming from the other side of the door. Andy bent over, scooping her up.

"Hungry? Little monster." She purred loud, rubbing her face against his abs, dangling limp in his hold as he brought her over to the food dish. He knew where everything was kept, even though we hadn't spent much time here. Kitten purred, happy to see him. "Tiff, do you want me to fill the tub for you?"

I slid my bag under the side table, rising up straight, looking in the bathroom's direction.

"I'm gonna take a shower. See how much paint I can get out of my hair."

He smirked. "Sorry about that."

Yeah right. I scrunched my eyebrows. "Sure you are."

He walked toward me. "I need your laptop."

"Bedroom."

As I turned, he reached for my arm. "Are you sure you're okay? I've never seen you fall apart like that."

I almost didn't want to answer him. I had no idea why I was being so emotional lately. I made up an excuse. "My leg hurts, but it is what it is. Thanks for being there."

"They're lucky I was only armed with paint guns." The expression in his eyes changed.

This man was so confusing. "Why? Would you have shot them?" His expression hardened.

"Yes."

I knew he meant it. Andy would have shot those men. Nothing in me doubted him for a second. I could feel certainty in his icy response. He was still angry, but it was because of them, not from having to come home with me.

The formerly red stain in my hair now shone in a light-pink tint, giving a little edge to the blonde. I kind of liked it.

There was my boyfriend, sitting on the couch and talking on the phone. He typed on my computer while Kitten sprawled out next to it on the coffee table. I smiled. This was my family. He noticed me watching and he spoke, still typing.

"How was the shower, babe?"

I wore my silk bathrobe, with my hair wrapped up in a towel. "Good. Are you still on the phone?"

"No, all set. Paint come out?"

"Most of it."

"What do you want for dinner?"

My stomach growled on cue. "Hadn't thought about it. I still haven't been shopping. Been eating out the past few days."

"With who?" Suddenly, his tone made me realize I had his full attention. Wasn't this change a little interesting?

"The girls."

"Did you have fun?" He tried recovering from his abrupt question.

"Hmmm, Audrey's drinking, Hannah is deep in wedding mode."

"I'm not expected to be part of that, am I?"

Ouch! My heart sank.

"You're expected to be my date! If that's what you're asking."

"Calm down, woman. That's not what I am asking. Making sure I'm not part of the wedding party, with you being maid of honor."

"No, you are not part of the wedding party. I think George's single friend is best man, though. So, if you can't make it, I will be taken care of."

"Single?"

I cracked a smile. I realized that would get him.

"Kidding. She told me who, but I forgot."

"Why don't you get dressed and get something to eat."

"Okay, give me a moment."

We were taking his car. He held his keys in one hand and touched the other to my lower back, guiding me down the hallway. As we walked around the corner, music from a second-floor apartment grew louder. Andy heard it, too.

One of my neighbors, walking in our direction, shook her head. She looked at me before her eyes darted to where the noise was coming from.

"New girl isn't used to having neighbors, I guess."

I disagreed. "Just inconsiderate. We will handle this." Andy followed me to the second floor, and I banged on her door. Nothing. I banged again. The older gentleman who lived across from her opened his door.

"No one answering?"

I shook my head. "No."

He held up his index finger. "Hang on, this worked last night."

And he disappeared for a moment. I looked at Andy.

"This one will be trouble. I already talked to her about leaving the front door open. Her mother passed away, and she inherited this place."

"I can kick the door in."

"Not yet. Let's see what Mr. Brooks' solution is."

Mr. Brooks came back with a cast iron pan, drawing an amused look from Andy.

"Good choice." Andy took the pan and banged it against the door. The music stopped, and he banged again. Robin yelled that she was coming, and the door opened. She looked right at me. "Oh, great, the cops."

Mr. Brooks glared. "You have neighbors, you realize. We don't like listening to your music. Your mother was a good, quiet woman. You are here a few days and already causing problems."

I held my hand up because she looked ready to fight right back.

"Look, I don't know where you lived before, but we are considerate of each other. You either need to figure out how to fit in or put this place up for sale. It will sell fast and you will get a good price. I'm sure it's worth more than you're thinking and you can move into somewhere that is more suitable. Win-win for all of us."

She stood there, arms folded. She looked at Andy. "What? Nothing from you?"

He handed Mr. Brooks back his skillet. "She said what needs to be said."

"This is a fucking retirement home. Fine, I will keep the music down. Now leave me alone."

She stepped back and shut the door. Mr. Brooks shook his head.

"Now I understand Wendy's complaints about that ungrateful child. I hope she sells the place." He disappeared back inside his condo.

Andy asked me her name as though he had recognized her. The name clearly meant nothing to him, though, and he walked with me out the door.

"Why are we at a grocery store?"

He looked confused. "To pick up food."

"I figured we'd get takeout."

"Food is cheaper here. Besides, you can stock up so you don't have to keep going out."

My eyebrows shot up. "Stock up? How long am I at the condo for?"

He shrugged. "Couple more days, possibly a week."

I turned angrily toward him. "Two days, you said. She's here for more days! What the hell? She's staying all week now?"

He looked surprised by my reaction. "I don't know. I didn't ask. She said she may be here longer when I hung up."

"You know what, I'm not hungry anymore. Take me home. Drop me off. You can go back to mommy."

"Tiffany?"

"Bring me home!"

I was so mad I could spit fire. He pulled back into my parking space and followed me inside. I turned to him when we reached the building's entrance. "You can go." I pointed back toward his car.

He ignored me. "I'm staying." He walked right past me and, after using his own key, held the door open for me to walk through. Part of me wanted to turn around and leave, and the other part was confused that he insisted on staying.

Being angry at Andy made me realize how small my place was. He ignored me, too, making some soup he found in the cabinet. I turned on the TV, staring into it, not paying any attention to what was on the screen. He came around with two bowls and a package of crackers, placing the bowls on the coffee table before pulling two spoons from his back pocket.

"Tiffany, I don't understand why you are so upset. Please explain this to me."

I didn't know where to start. Thoughts swirled in my head, each one fighting to be first out my mouth. "I don't understand why you are keeping your mother and I apart."

"She is complicated."

"That is not an answer. So are my parents, but I don't keep you from them. Even Mother expected you to be with me when I showed up the other night."

He leaned forward, rubbing his scalp.

"Okay." He sat up and turned to face me. "I've never wanted anyone in my life like you are. It's been my mother and me since my father was killed."

"I'm your first girlfriend?"

"No, I didn't say that. Just none have ever stuck."

"Why, because of your mother?"

"Partly."

"Does your mother run your life?"

"No. She does not run my life. But when she is around, she wants my attention."

"I can be around when your mother isn't. Do you recognize how crazy that sounds?"

He softened. "That sounds bad. No, my mother is... I don't even know how to word this.... She knows about you."

I relaxed some. "Well, at least that's a good thing, I guess."

"No, it's not. Okay, I can explain this, at least. I did a job she was involved in and it turned out bad. I fucked up."

"Job? You said she works on contracts for the government. How's it possible you cross paths?"

He looked at me with an eyebrow raised. We sat silent for a moment.

"Forget about it, Tiff. The less I say, the better."

I didn't get it. He was shutting down again.

"Andy, I don't understand."

He stood up, grabbing his phone as it lit up.

"She lost a client because of me. It cost her millions. She is here for me to reassure her it won't happen again. I have to take this call. Be right back."

Is that why he was gone so much a few months back? He was freelancing for her? I overheard him say, "No, I won't be back tonight," before he closed my bedroom door. *I'm not offended. He wanted privacy. I will give it to him. Besides, he's staying, and that is most likely his mother again.*

CHAPTER SEVEN

Andy left early the next morning. I wanted to get up with him, but he convinced me to sleep a little while longer. It was the day we logged reports in. Michael stopped in to see me. Chris also came by. She was excited about me coming back and offered to run with me in the afternoon after her shift ended. I liked that idea. I could ask her more about the new guys.

I texted Andy to let him know, and he informed me that he wouldn't be able to see me tonight. Whatever. I wasn't too upset about Mommy anymore. He proved to me that he was torn, and I knew I was the only woman in his life to make it this far.

Michael found out about our run and asked to join. I didn't even mind that. It was good to run with my crew. Michael supplied the motivation and it surprised me to find that despite Chris being on the heavier side I was the unfit one. This woman could run. Michael even helped me when my leg cramped up. The two of them made me push myself. I let Michael massage and stretch my leg, while Chris gave me some helpful advice about working through an injury.

Upon returning to my condo, I didn't recognize the car in Andy's spot. I hoped it wasn't the new girl. She was getting on my nerves. Even so, I couldn't blame her for this mix-up. Visitors often parked in my spots because they were so close to the entrance, even though they were each marked with a reserved sign.

I exited my Lexus to find a slender woman walking toward me in a business suit, holding a briefcase. I figured it must be her car.

"Excuse me, can I help you?" I offered. She was less than ten feet from me when she removed her sunglasses. Sharply, confidently, she said, "Tiffany Chanler. I want a word with you. I am Agnes McMillan."

Mildred, my godmother, had nothing on this woman. There must have been some private Agnes McMillan boot camp for dominant women that I didn't know about. She instantly made me feel guilty and ashamed even though I'd done nothing wrong.

I suddenly understood why Andy wanted to keep us separate. I could see who he inherited some of his controlling traits from. He inherited her attitude, plus her eyes.

I regretted the way I looked. I should have been more presentable. This was our first official meeting. I couldn't imagine what she was thinking about me, fresh from a run and messy looking.

"Mrs. McMillan, nice to meet you."

"Sinner!" She glared into my eyes accusingly, pointing her finger in my face.

"What?"

"Slut!"

I took a few steps back and put my hand over my pounding, wounded heart. She immediately stepped closer, following me, not allowing any distance between us. She was right in my face.

"Either you leave him, or I will see he finds out the truth!"

"Truth? What? What are you talking about?"

"You are not good enough for my Andrew!"

"What? I don't understand?"

"I know your type. You spread your legs, smile and invite everyone in. Dirty whore!"

She just called me a whore, a slut, and a sinner.

"Mrs. McMillan, please."

"Do not speak my name with that filth in your mouth."

I felt three feet tall. She was towering over me. All my muscles constricted.

"He will break free from your foul attempt to trap him."

"You can't be serious. What is this?"

"I will make him see his wrongdoing, dirty slattern." She marched passed me to her car.

"I … I …" I stammered, watching her walk. She came to a stop and slowly turned.

"You cost me. You will feel the same shame."

"What?"

"You leave him."

"I can't."

"Then you will suffer."

She opened her car door, started the engine, and zoomed out of the lot.

Anxiety covered my arms with goosebumps and me chest tightened enough to bring both my hands against it, leaving me wondering whether I was having a muscle spasm or heart attack. *Oh no, I am going to throw up.* I leaned over. Nothing came up. My chest constricted, my stomach knotted, and I heaved air in and out through my mouth. Everything felt as if it was caving in at my chest. I thought I must have been having a panic attack. My body was covered in a sheen of sweat.

I had seen this happen to Mother when I was younger. I remembered it as clear as yesterday. I needed water, fast. I dropped to my knees and ripped open the zipper on my bag. *Water's going to help. Water's going to help.* Reciting the assurance to myself, I pulled everything out and grabbed hold of the bottle.

My hands shook as I worked open the bottled and chugged as much as I could. Water spilled down both sides of my face and soaked my shirt as I swallowed through the tightening in my throat. *Water is helping. This is working.*

A car pulled into the lot and drove past as my hands, working on autopilot, quickly gathered my stuff. I realized I was in a vulnerable situation. What if she came back? I gathered my belongings and ran inside my complex. Still shaking, I tried and finally succeeded at inserting the key in my door. I closed it forcefully behind me and locked it.

Never had I suffered feeling out of control. First yesterday at the mile and now this? What the hell was going on with me?

I was safe, leaning against the door. Easing down to the floor, I sat there pushing my bag with my foot.

His mother is insane. No wonder he didn't want me to meet her. Totally on his side now. Why did she keep calling me horrendous names? What's with all the holy roller talk? I needed to text Andy what had happened. I grabbed my phone, hesitating.

I found his name right away. *What do I tell him? Your mother was here threatening me, insulting me, putting me down? I had to tell him. He was going to find out.* I wasn't even sure where he was or whether his phone would have reception. He had been vague about where he'd be today.

I texted. *Your mother was just here.* I read it again to make sure this was how I wanted to start this conversation. I hit send.

My phone lit up in my hand. It was Andy. I held back tears.

"What happened!" He demanded.

He asked about every detail, down to the car she was driving. When he was satisfied with what I had told him, he calmed down. "Tiffany, I will fix this. I want you to stay in tonight. Will you do that for me? I need to know exactly where you are."

"Why, what's going on, Andy? Why is your mother so psycho?"

"I told you, because of something I did. She lost a big client. She's embarrassed."

"Embarrassed? What the hell?! She is insane! Ten times scarier than Mildred on her worst day."

"Just stay put, okay? I'll take care of this, I promise. I gotta go, but I will contact you."

"Okay."

As soon as I hung up, I felt exhausted. It was like the life had just drained out of me. Kitten was observing from across the room. She still hadn't come over to greet me. I understood her caution, as I explained, "Grandma on daddy's side is a lunatic, Kitten. We must stay on our game with her."

Oh, shoot. I forgot to tell him she demanded I leave him. Well, that would be another story for him to deal with. Besides, he sounded pissed off enough. He didn't need to hear that, too.

If there had ever been a reason to turn to some kind of crutch, this was it. I showered instead. Michael was texting, complimenting me on the outstanding job I did running. He was inquiring about my leg. He cared. He always cared, making me realize I'd been hard on him for the past six months.

I needed to tear down this stupid wall I had built between us. I texted back. *Thank you, it's better. First run I completed not in throbbing pain.* I looked at my text. He deserved more. Michael deserved so much more.

My cupboards were still bare. Damn, I regretted not going in that grocery store now. My last can of soup and peanut butter crackers would have to be dinner tonight. Tomorrow I needed to stop by my mini-mart, whether or not I wanted to. Andy's mother was unpredictable. She knew where I lived, and I needed to prepare for being here a few more days.

I looked up Agnes McMillan again. The same family picture I had found earlier now sent shivers down my spine. I thought about how Nacho reacted upon hearing she was here. His peculiar response now made complete sense.

It was almost nine o'clock when Hannah texted two pictures of wedding dresses. Both were stunning. I liked the second one. She sent three possible bridesmaids' dresses to go with that one. I liked the simple one. She sent a bunch of heart emojis and said that was my maid of honor dress in violet. Her colors would be white, grey and violet. It would be a very nice color palette for August. I encouraged her to contact my mother again.

Hannah insisted I stop by tomorrow, making me promise. I reminded her that I had to run after work, so it would have to be after that. She seemed satisfied with that answer.

I awoke to a loud crash from inside my condo and leapt out of bed from a dead sleep. My heart raced as I remembered I only stored Andy's paintball guns here. The lights were still on; I had fallen asleep with everything on. Kitten walked into the bedroom casually, so I at least knew no one else was in the condo.

I grabbed a paintball gun just in case and rounded the bedroom door. What I found were pieces of my ceramic bowl and the variety of treasures it had held – lip balm, old keys, and more stuff I'd collected and didn't know where to put – scattered on the floor. Kitten had knocked it off. I placed the paintball gun on the table and carefully stepped around the mess as I fetched the broom and dustpan. Kitten listened listlessly to an entire lecture as I cleaned up her destruction and then checked my phone.

Still nothing from Andy, and it was nearing midnight. A sound caught my ear outside my back patio doors. Was someone out there? I walked toward them and pulled back the curtain slightly, peeking around. I turned on the outside light. My heart leapt in my throat. Yes, there was someone out there. They were walking in the back entrances. I shook it off, assuming it must be a resident. They opened the locked door.

Why am I so damn jumpy? I closed the curtains so no one could see in, flipping the side light on in the living room. I needed to calm down. Instead, I spun around as I heard someone at my door. I saw the knob turn and I again grabbed the paintball gun. This was it. I was ready to fire.

Kitten ran toward the door as I tried to sweep her away with my foot, giving enough time for Andy to poke his head in.

"Jesus Christ!" I dropped the gun to my side, nearly ready to throw it at him. He stared at me, acknowledging the state I was in.

"Sorry, babe. I figured you'd be sleeping."

"I was until Kitten knocked my bowl off the table a few minutes ago. Then I saw someone out back, and now you walk in." He walked to the back door.

"I came in the front. Man or woman?"

"Out back? I think a man. But they used a key because they walked right in."

"That means nothing. I'll be right back. Stay here."

My nerves were frazzled. I wanted to go with him. Who was he looking for? Twenty minutes later he was back. "I saw nothing out of the usual."

"I wasn't expecting you to. They used a key. Did you get to talk to your mother?"

"No, she wouldn't answer her phone. She must have left. You were probably her last stop before heading out of town."

"Great. Does she do stuff like that often?"

"She won't stay mad for long. This will blow over and everything will be back to normal."

"New rule with your mother: she has to announce herself before she comes to town."

"I'll mention that. We are staying here a few days, then back to the warehouse."

"That's fine."

"Come on, let's go to bed. It's been a long day."

CHAPTER EIGHT

In the morning, Andy and I woke up together. I informed him of my work plans, just as I had before his mother came to visit, and told him I'd be getting in a run with Chris and Michael. He grumbled when I spoke Michael's name. I told him Michael would be taking over Kyle's truck and I would most likely have Chris as my new co-pilot.

He seemed somewhat content with the news, but I wasn't entirely sure. We left together which was nice. We walked to my car and kissed. His lips lingered softly, with his hand pressed gently against my back. I loved those kisses. I had missed those kisses.

Today, there was the pleasure of meeting Pete Marshall, one of the troopers from the last round of hires. He reminded me of Kyle, only in big-boy pants. This guy didn't have the resentment for me that Kyle did. Pete seemed to like me, or at least like the view of me, because he was all smiles, chatting while I logged reports. Michael waked in and, within minutes of listening, stopped our conversation. "She has a boyfriend, buddy."

Pete looked from Michael to me. "Yeah? I have a wife. What's that got to do with anything?" Michael turned his attention to me. "Tiff, are we still running after this shift?"

I straightened up. "Yes, if that's okay. I've got to keep pushing through until Friday."

Pete looked at me, shaking his finger. "Ah, I get it. You're the girl who got shot."

I nodded. "Yup, and now I'm ready to get back into it."

He chuckled. "Why does this place make you run? It's a delivery service."

I jumped up and pointed to him. "My thoughts exactly! It's stupid. Besides, running is useless when you have donor organs to protect and you're in a box."

Michael interrupted. "Insurance reasons. I looked it up. They don't want you to blame them for other factors that come with being less physically active."

"There's the voice of reason, always a killjoy, squashing a good rant." I laughed to make sure Michael realized I was only joking.

Michael smiled. "See you at the end of shift, Tiff."

"Okay, careful out there."

Pete stood up, grabbing his clipboard. "Time for me to get moving. Hey, I'm good at running. Be happy to give you motivation."

"Thanks, that's nice of you."

He walked out, tapping the frame of my door, stopping to talk to Chris just outside in the hall. She popped her head in. "Meet Pete?"

"Yes, I like him. Seems like a good guy."

"He's a sweetheart. Told me he offered to help run."

"Yes, he did, as a matter of fact."

"Don't do it. The man runs marathons for fun."

She grinned at the shocked look on my face.

"He doesn't look like a marathon runner."

"Don't let the pot belly fool you. He will probably run back for us after he finishes Friday."

"Great. He's one of those."

She tapped the doorframe. "See you after shift."

Just before lunch, Mr. Donovan walked in, specifically to talk with me. All I picked up was, "Valuable employee, never had someone as good as you in the office." I squashed all ideas of continuing office duty.

I made sure he knew that if I was not transitioning back to my driving post, then I was leaving to collect five times my pay here as a department manager for my father's company. He abruptly dropped the hints and let me know he was bringing Kyle back, giving him dispatch.

I hadn't seen Kyle since the accident. A bullet had passed straight in and out of my upper leg muscle. It touched no bone. Kyle lost his left arm during the holdup. He had since been given a prosthetic.

Driving was out for him with this company's strict policies. But dispatch and scheduling were just pushing a bunch of buttons and making phone calls. No problem there. I knew Michael had visited him a few times. They kept in touch. I found out he didn't blame me for what happened, but still, we never liked each other from the first day I started. It was going to be awkward here again with him back.

I looked down at my vibrating cell. It was Andy, texting to tell me to pick up a few days' worth of food for the condo. That had me making up a shopping list in my head between filing reports. I loved sharing household chores with my boyfriend. Next it was Father calling, most likely, I assumed, to invite us to dinner. "Hello, Father."

"We have an emergency meeting. I need you to come to the office. How soon can you get here?"

The hair on the back of my neck stood, tingling. "What happened?"

"Tiffany, just get here."

"I'm working." I looked at my watch. "I have three more hours."

"I need you here."

I looked around. I was only doing paperwork. I could come back and finish. "Okay, I'll be there as soon as I can."

I texted Hannah that something had come up and I would call her later. I found Mr. Donovan and assured him I would be back to finish. I then texted Michael to let him know I had to leave. He called me. "Everything alright, Tiff?"

"No, my father just called an emergency meeting. I have to go."

"That sounds serious. You want me to stop by after?"

"No, but can you tell Chris I have to cancel?"

"Don't worry about us. I will run with her. It's not for a few hours, anyway. You might be back by then."

"I have to come back and finish logging the reports."

"Call me if you need some help. I can stay later."

"Thanks, Michael, I will."

I gathered my bag and drove straight to Henshaw Logistics' corporate building. Security waved me in as I darted past people glued to their phones in the lobby. I grabbed the first elevator when one of the employees exited. I held his arm. "What's going on?"

"I'm not sure but it's a mess. Let me know as soon as you find out."

People were scrambling about my father's office floor, workers calling back and forth in the hallway about contact and some arguing with each other. I headed straight for the boardroom, having to back myself against the wall as employees ran past. There was Audrey, leaning over another worker, throwing her pen down in front of him, asking him about any signs, any hints. She sharply tilted her head toward me. My father stood up.

"Tiffany." Audrey looked from my father to me.

"Fucking mess this is! We lost the green engine contract!"

I was almost sitting when that news made me shoot right back up.

"What? How?"

Audrey surveyed the entire board. "Well, someone wasn't paying attention to the fucking signs. You all complain that I am too controlling, I never let you take charge of a project." She slammed her hand on the table. "This is fucking why! I give you some leeway and you lose a two-hundred-million-dollar contract!"

This was my project. I helped secure the government contract. I felt ill. This was devastating to the company. I was the one who convinced my father this was the way to go. Audrey zeroed in on four employees.

"You should've seen this coming. There must have been something to tip you off." My father took a call leaving the room. Everyone's face expressed guilt. Audrey typed something on her computer. "Our fucking stock just fell! How did this get out so fast? Who is the *fucking leak?*"

I wasn't quite sure what was going on. "Will we be able to recover?"

She looked over her computer for a second, then met my eyes. "Not unless you have another buyer in your pocket."

This was bad. I walked out to find Father. He pressed his phone to hang up.

"Is it really this bad? I mean, you can recover, right?"

He shook his head. "Once you lose a government contract, they blacklist you. Private sector doesn't have the program allowances the government can skirt around. This is bad, Tiffany." He turned toward the window. "Perhaps it's time I retired. Your mother and I've been talking about it. She wants to move."

"What? Move? I guess a new building would be a pleasant change. She said she doesn't like your new property owner."

"I'm not referring to in town. I am saying move, move. Across the country."

I gasped, "What?"

"I could do some consulting on the side. Priscilla always wanted a lake house. Washington State would be ideal. Plenty of young entrepreneurs looking for direction out there."

My brain tried to keep up with what he was saying. "Move? Across the country? A lake house? That's hours away – by plane! Where am I going to go?"

He put a hand on my shoulder. "Tiffany, you have your entire life ahead of you. You have the job you want, your condo. Now a fella. You'll be fine."

"But you can't move. All your connections, work. Everything is right here."

"Mother and I have been playing this game a long time now. It's tiring. You were smart to follow your own path. Besides, it might be nice to live somewhere new. I have connections on the West Coast. Old college friend has an offshoring shipping company. He's been asking me to come aboard for the last decade. Maybe this is the sign I needed to make the change."

"Sign you needed? Mother doesn't drive. How is she supposed to get around? What about her Wednesday luncheons? What about Mildred!"

"We will figure it out. Maybe it's time to open her event-planning business. I'll be her chauffeur."

"No! No, this is crazy! You can't leave. What will happen to Audrey?" We both turned to hear Audrey yelling again. People fled the boardroom scared. One woman was in tears. Audrey continued to berate them. Upon walking back in, Audrey barked orders to Father about whom to call next. He picked up his phone, agreeing with her. Mother was walking in, watching people leave, and reaching her arms toward me.

"What happened?"

I couldn't believe what I was seeing. My family's company was crashing in front of me. There went my safety net. I needed to get out of here. There was nothing I could do about this disaster falling down around me. Hannah was calling as I sat in my car looking out the windshield. The building looked so peaceful on the outside.

"What is going on? Are you okay, Tiffany? I am hearing all kinds of crazy reports that your father's company is crashing."

Sigh. "Well, that didn't take long to get around."

"What's happening, Tiff? Do you need me?"

"Nothing anyone can do now. Government pulled out of the green engine contract. I should have stayed at my father's company. This is all my fault. I should've seen this through."

"Oh, Tiffany, don't blame yourself. Your father pays good employees to do their jobs."

"It should have been me helping to oversee it. I convinced him this was the way to go."

"Tiffany, stop right there. You didn't control this outcome."

"I should have stayed."

Andy texted. He was going to be late and I shouldn't worry about dinner. I couldn't eat if I tried. My stomach was in knots. I had to return to work, like it or not. This was my job. This was my only source of income for the future. I would secure it.

Michael and Chris returned from their run to find me logging reports. Michael spoke first. "Everything all right, Tiffany?"

I shook my head. "Father's company crashed." He stepped closer.

"What? What happened?"

I repeated, "Father's company crashed." He sat next to me. "Yeah, got that, but how?"

"That new green motor I convinced him to invest in? The quarter-billion-dollar contract I helped land? Government pulled out. We lost it all."

"What does that mean for the future of Henshaw?"

"Not sure. Father talked about retiring, moving to Washington State, and buying a lake house."

"Washington? That's on the other side of the country."

"I know Michael. I realize where Washington is. I have to finish these."

He reached out and patted my shoulder. "Okay, Tiff, I understand. I'm here for you. You know that, right?"

I nodded. "Yes, I appreciate it. Thank you, Michael."

He hesitated. Then stood up and walked out. Chris caught my attention.

"Hey, Tiff. If there is anything, I can do?" I looked over my right shoulder. I hadn't noticed she was listening.

"Thanks."

That was all I could say. Mildred's name lit up my phone.

"Tiffany, be over at your parents' home in one hour." I was nearly done and it was almost seven o'clock.

"Okay," I agreed. I texted Andy that I was stopping by my parents' and there was bad news.

No return message. That was odd. I even specifically said bad news. Usually, he called me. He must be in a low-reception area. He had better be in one. I needed him for support.

I arrived to find Audrey and Mildred on their computers, my mother on the phone, my father on the phone, father's secretary on her computer, and a few people I vaguely recognized. The energy in the room was dismal. Mother spread out food for anyone who could eat.

That was not the case. Liquid was the only thing flowing. Alcohol was the meal for most. Audrey had a bottle of vodka in front of her. I marched right over and she stood up to confront me.

"Touch that and you will lose your arm." She was dead serious.

"I can't watch this. You drinking is disturbing."

"Maybe I wouldn't be drinking if you stayed with the company, Tiffany!"

My father quickly arrived at my side.

"Audrey, this isn't her fault."

"Well, it's sure as hell not my fault! Maybe if she stayed instead of slinking back to her stupid delivery service, this wouldn't have happened."

That was it, the final straw.

"You are fucking alive because of my delivery service, you drunk."

Now both my parents were between us, Mildred ordering me to go get something to eat. I turned to Mildred now, softening her stare. I nodded, understanding this cue. Mother explained that we were all on edge and should take a step back. This was nobody's fault, and these things happened without explanation. I poured a glass of water. That was all I could stomach at the moment. I looked at my phone, still nothing from Andy.

Nine o'clock and Henshaw Logistics' stock plummeted to twelve dollars a share. Father was on the phone to the manufacturers. I knew insurance would cover a slight amount. I was trying to think of other ways we could sell the engines.

We could always partner with our competitors, but that would still only cover a third of what that government contract held. The alternative plan was to see if we could collaborate with other shipping companies and make it a global environmental campaign to help reduce air pollution. Partnering with all our competitors to buy and install these engines for the good of the air-breathing world? It could work.

Audrey was drunk, now chain-smoking to add to my irritation. She stood up.

"Richard, I want this company. I will buy you and Priscilla out for half what the shares are right now. I refuse to bail you out again. If I do this, then it will be for me. Not you."

I stopped the conversation, telling them about my fresh angle. Everyone looked from me to Audrey.

My father stared at my mother.

"Tiffany, the idea is excellent. There'd be a lot of work involved. Mother and I will talk it over tonight. Audrey, we will give you our answer in the morning. We all have had a long, stressful night."

"No. I want your answer now."

"Audrey, I know if anyone could rebuild this company it would be you. I know our answer. I just want to make sure we are all thinking clearly. Please stay tonight and we will talk about this in the morning over breakfast. You can have Tiffany's room." My father looked to me, backtracking his invitation, "Unless you are staying, Tiffany?"

"No, it's time for me to go, as a matter of fact." I walked to Audrey. "I am sorry I let you down. Please stay and get some rest. Talk in the morning, okay?"

Audrey deflated. "Oh, Tiffany! I'm sorry I shouted at you. This isn't your fault. Well, maybe a little. I love you. I'm sorry I said those mean things. I am grateful for everything you have done for me. I'm not hiring you back, though. Okay, but I love you." She turned. "I'll take her room; we will talk in the morning."

She said good night to everyone, unplugging her computer, stamping out her cigarettes, and sliding the vodka bottle off the table before walking toward my bedroom.

I hoped Jordan was out because Audrey was going in. My mother excused herself, following Audrey with a few bottles of water in her hand.

"Audrey dearest, let me get you some nightwear that will fit."

Father walked to me. "I will call you tomorrow. That is an outstanding idea if everyone comes on board."

Mildred packed up. "Tiffany I will walk out with you." She then called her car to alert them she would be down in fifteen minutes.

I walked out with Mildred. She turned toward me in the elevator. "I am always here for you, Tiffany."

"What?" That was out of the blue.

"If your parents move to the West Coast. They've been talking about it since you graduated. This is the perfect opportunity."

"I don't want to talk about it."

"You will still have me here. Besides, I've practically raised you. Where have you been, anyway? You used to call me and now that you are in a relationship, nothing. No phone calls, no lunches. You don't even drop by the office."

"I know, sorry. I will do better about visiting and calling. Hey, do you recognize a tenant by the name of Wendy Christopherson in my building?"

Mildred dropped her shoulders. "I've already found out about the miserable offspring. I'm sure you can handle her."

"I can, but what's the daughter's deal?"

"Hardship. The girl has not had a peaceful life."

"How old is she?"

"Young twenties."

"Really? I thought she was more my age."

"Like I said, not a peaceful life, from my understanding."

"I think our whole building wants her to just sell and get out."

"The last unit sold for $350,000. That was a year ago."

"The two bedrooms in the back corner?"

"Yes, there is no reason the Christopherson unit would sell for any less."

"I'll tell her. That information might tempt her."

Mildred pulled out a plain, brown folder, handing it to me. "Is this the real estate info?"

"No. I've been doing some of my own investigating into your fellow." I gripped the folder. I didn't understand why she would do such a thing. "Tiffany. Stop looking so shocked. Like I said before, I have raised you like my daughter. I look out for my family."

"When? Why? Why would you do this?"

"What do you know about him, Tiffany? I mean truthfully?"

The elevator reached the lobby. I wanted to open the file, but not here.

"Tuck that someplace safe. People get defensive when they find out you have been checking up on them."

"Mildred, when did you do this? Why?"

She turned, directly facing me.

"Because your mother didn't have the balls to, and we have been suspicious since you have become close with him. Look, I know he works for the same company, but your last hijacking raised concerns. Have you even read the report on it?"

I hadn't. I knew I should have. Andy and I had been too busy becoming a couple. I trusted that he'd read it over and everything was fine.

"I haven't had the chance to. We've been busy."

She nodded, knowing my answer already.

"Do yourself a favor. Knowledge is power. Read this stuff. I have a copy of the report. Come see me. You need to read."

I looked down at the folder. "Just tell me. What's in here?"

"Tiffany, I know you better than you know yourself. Nothing I say will change your mind. You need to decide for yourself if any of the information I gathered is of any use to you. Read it, don't read it. It's up to you. But I could never forgive myself if I held this information and didn't pass it on to you."

"Does Mother have a copy of this?"

"No, you are a big girl now. You make your own decisions. It's your life, child. You left your father's company for the job you love. With love comes risk. Your heart is not the only thing at stake there."

"I didn't leave father's company. I was only there temporarily while my leg healed. Never left Angel Wings. That was never my intention. I was clear about that right along."

"Tiffany, like I said, your life, your rules. That's just some help to keep your head on straight as you go."

"Whatever! Look, I'm tired. You are tired. It's been a stressful day. I'll look these over when I have time. I would say thank you, but I think this is an invasion of privacy."

"Yes, not unlike the ones you mounted by spying on your father's mistress." *Gasp!*

"You know about that?"

"Audrey had a field day with those. They led to some important information about the connection of Blake Montgomery and the Rivera fellow. Information we would never have had access to unless you spied on her." She pointed to the folder. "That might come in handy if you know about it." I looked down again as she turned. "Good night, Tiffany."

Her heels echoed across the lobby as she walked away from me. There I stood, staring at a secret file on my boyfriend, then looking at my phone. It was ten-thirty and still nothing from him. I walked toward the parking garage doors, fed up with the absence and called him. Four rings before he picked up.

"Tiffany, are you okay?" He sounded as if I had just woken him up.

"Where are you?"

"Home. Is everything okay now? Are you on your way?"

What the hell! He was home with no return texts?

"Did you get any of my texts?"

"Yes, I just figured you would tell me if you needed me to come to you, or you'd tell me about what happened when you got home."

Grrr! "I'm on my way."

"Okay, babe, be safe. See you soon."

I was so going to read this file. Not once did he text me that he was home. Nothing about this man made any sense. Maybe Mildred found out something that made sense about him.

He did not greet me at the door. My condo was dark, quiet as I walked in.

"Andy?" My heart pounded against my chest.

He answered from the bedroom. "In here." I marched angrily to the bedroom.

"How long have you been home?" I turned the light on and gasped. There were scratches on his arm, and gauze taped to his right cheek. I rushed to his side touching his shoulder, assessing his condition, the damage to him.

His answer was calm. "About an hour before you called."

"Andy what happened to you?"

"Got jumped. I'm fine."

"Where? How? Is this a cut?"

"Yes, blade caught me."

"Andy!"

"I'm fine, Tiffany. Guys I did business with in the past turned on me. It happens. They lost money. People don't like losing money. Comes with the game. There are no guarantees. It was nothing personal."

I wanted to fix him, protect him, take care of him. "Nothing personal? This looks personal to me. Can I do anything?"

"Yes, come to bed."

I wasn't sure what he meant by that, but I remembered some of the hits I had received, whether in training or on the streets growing up, looking for trouble on my own. I came home banged up and Mother would sleep next to me, quiet, not saying a word. As angered as she was by my sneaking out, she would lie next to me until I was up the next morning. It was a comfort no matter how much I was rebelling. I did the same for Andy. I stripped off and slid in next to him, staying close enough that he could feel my warmth but giving him distance because I didn't know the full damage yet.

"Good night, babe." He whispered.

"I love you." I replied.

"Love you, Tiffany."

He said it out loud and my heart exploded in love. A tear spilled over, running along my nose. I didn't dare move. Nothing could change the bond between us now. Andy was my future, and I was going to fight anyone who came between us – even Mildred if she tried to turn me away from him.

CHAPTER NINE

I woke up tucked against my mercenary. As banged up as he was, there was one part of him still working just fine.

Shoot. I was employed and late for work. I used the excuse of my father's emergency yesterday. No one seemed to mind. Michael and Chris wouldn't be in until the end of my shift. At least, that's what I thought until Michael walked in at ten.

"A little early there, Michael?"

"Checking up on you. Are you okay? I can help with the reports." He handed me a cup of coffee and a bag of jelly donuts from Lou's diner.

"I'll take the coffee but remove the donuts. I have gained weight. My uniforms are tight."

"Doesn't show. You look good, Tiff."

"I don't feel good. I feel fat."

He chuckled. "Okay, more jelly donuts for me then."

We both turned, hearing the familiar voice. My heart pounded. Cold sweat covered my body. This was it. Nowhere to go. It was going to happen right now. Kyle rounded the corner with Donovan. My eyes went straight to his shoulder. He stared at me. "Hey," he spoke softly, almost sympathetically. "How's the leg, Tiffany?"

I looked down at my brace. "Of no consequence compared to your arm." He looked, raising his prosthesis.

"I'm bionic now. Don't even try winning at arm wrestling. No chance whatsoever."

"See nothing has changed. That's good, I guess."

He nervously laughed. "A lot has changed. I just rolled with it. Bitching and crying don't help. Just gets you pity. Had enough of that shit to last the rest of my life."

"You coming back, Kyle?"

"Yup, your new voice of radio central. At least I finally get to tell you what to do and there is nothing you can do about it."

I frowned. "I can always turn off the radio."

Donovan interjected. "Not in my company. Kyle, hang around here for a bit. Tiffany will bring you up to date. Michael?"

Michael snapped his head toward Donovan. "Yes, sir?"

"Come with me for a moment. I want to talk with you."

"Sir, I'm not officially here. My shift doesn't start for three hours yet."

"Then you shouldn't be here bothering the help."

He stood up. "I . . . I . . ."

"Michael, this way."

Michael glanced over at me. I shrugged. No big deal. I could update Kyle on what'd been happening.

We talked, saying everything we could except about the accident. Finally, Kyle put it out there.

"Tiffany, shit happens. This didn't happen because of you. I am alive because of you. You are really good at what you do. I'm sorry I never recognized that before."

This was too strange. I couldn't deal with this right now. Not on top of all the other stuff happening in my life. "Kyle, you would have done the same. Just forget about it."

He chuckled. "Yeah? I'm not so sure. I'm not sure I would have done the same, Tiffany. God, I hated you. But I don't anymore. I will take care of you on my end. I promise."

I shook my head. All was right between us now. He declared he would have let me die, maybe. . . . I thought as much. "I still think you're an asshole."

He chuckled. "Good, now that we have that straightened out, you will still have to take orders from me. Just know, I have your best interests in mind. If you can understand that, then we will get along."

I narrowed my eyes at him. "Jackass."

He grinned widely. "Bitch."

I grinned, knowing Kyle and I would be just fine moving forward.

We both turned, hearing a voice accompanied by heavy footsteps approaching. This tall, very solid, older guy rounded the corner holding a stack of paperwork. He stopped in the door frame wearing an Angel Wings uniform, observing the both of us as he stepped in. Now he was staring at my chest.

"You must be the princess they've warned me about." Kyle snickered as the man turned, observing Kyle's arm. "And you are the moron who got his arm blown off." Kyle leaped out of his seat nearly faster than I could catch his good arm. The man just stood there, eyes narrowing. "I can see why you were the weak link." Kyle looked back at me to let go.

I spoke through my clenched teeth just so he would hear. "Don't. It's just words." He calmed down enough for me to know he would not retaliate.

Donovan and Michael were now behind the man. Donovan walked past with no reaction. Obviously, he hadn't heard what this man had said.

"Tiffany, this is Bartek Wojcik."

Bartek spoke up proudly. "Call me Polack."

Kyle shook his head, stepping toward him in sarcasm. "With pleasure, Polack."

I answered, "Interesting nickname."

Donovan was clearly uncomfortable calling him by his requested username. "Mr. Wojcik is one of our newest recruits." Michael walked past him, stopping to stand next to me.

"Tiffany is one of our drivers. Kyle is coming back, taking over dispatch and scheduling, right?"

Kyle finally took his eyes off the intruder. "Yes, get used to hearing my commands." He turned again, speaking right to Polack, who challenged him by not missing a beat.

"Our radio personality? Hope you are entertaining." Wow, did this guy have an attitude.

Kyle fired back, "Coming at you with the latest orders."

The Polack laughed. "This ought to be good. Here is my paperwork. Do I give them to this secretary or the emcee?" Michael had enough.

"She's not a secretary. One of the best drivers here."

This guy just stared at my chest again. "I doubt that still holds with the crew just hired. Average at best. She looks like she would be worried about chipping a nail."

That was it. Michael put his hand on my shoulder, stopping me. Kyle turned to block me. Kyle spoke out, "Get this jerk out of here. Seriously, Donovan, did you have to scrape the bottom of the trooper rejects?"

Polack laughed. "I'm not a statie. Retired prison guard."

Kyle over-emphasized turning to him. "Well, that makes much more sense. Staties probably rejected you, and the prison system takes anyone. What did they offer you, early retirement?"

He placed his paperwork down, losing his grin. Kyle struck a nerve there. The Polack turned and walked out. We all turned to Donovan. I asked it first.

"What the fuck were you thinking?"

He looked from me to Michael to Kyle and back at me.

"He's just a little rough around the edges. He will ease in. Big, trained, part-time. He's what we need to change the image of this place. Too many hijackings last year. I don't want to be the target anymore. As I am sure none of you do either."

"But him?" I questioned Donovan's choice.

"Like I said, just rough around the edges. He will be fine."

"Who do you have him paired with?"

"Allen."

I breathed a little easier. Allen liked everything safe and in order. I bet he would like this goon riding with him.

Kyle, Michael, and I were all on the same side with our opinion of this new employee. We had never agreed on anything before – not until now. If Polack stayed with Allen, we were all set. Kyle would have to deal with him a few shifts a week, but from the sound of it, outside of the guy teasing about the radio, that was all he would have to put up with.

Andy was texting. He would be away tonight. My heart leaped at the thought of the state of him. He was banged up. He should be home resting. I tried to convince him to give it one more night. He answered back that there was no room for rest now, followed by orders to stay in the condo tonight. Tomorrow we were back living in the warehouse.

At least we were getting back on track after his mother's visit. *Horrible woman.* I wondered if there was any information on her in Mildred's file.

My parents were unavailable. I expected they were working out the details with Audrey. Hannah was the only one answering, and she wanted to know everything. I agreed to have dinner at the bar to fill her in after my grappling class.

When I walked in the door, my instructor announced today was strictly cardio. I smiled. This was because I had a meltdown in his office a few days ago. He was trying to help, without making it obvious he was helping.

I pushed myself so hard that I had to wear my leg brace at dinner. The thing helped, but it made me walk weird.

I was limping to the bar when a deep voice close behind me insisted I had better fix that walk before the wedding. His scent perfumed the air around my neck, reaching my nose, igniting a heat deep in my belly. My head turned, looking over my shoulder. It was him. The guy who had bought Hannah and I drinks the other night.

"Still here?" He was now standing next to me.

"They delayed the part I needed. Another day and I should be done. What did you do to your leg?" He pointed to the brace.

"Took a bullet about six months back."

He stopped the both of us with his hand. "Took a bullet?"

"I work for an organ donor transplant service. We got hijacked."

"You're the girl?"

"Excuse me?"

"I read about that. What the hell you doing that kind of work for?"

"Because I love it?"

"Hmm. You should be on the cover of one of those magazines from the other day."

I laughed. "I don't think so. That's not me."

He looked me over again. "You have trouble written all over you."

"Capital T, mister."

I smiled as we walked on, nearing the bar. Hannah arrived from the kitchen with his order. She quickly glanced to the both of us, giving me a slight smile.

"Missed you a few days."

"Didn't have the right parts."

"Well, you are back now. We forgive you."

"Job's almost done."

"I can't say I am happy about that. Enjoyed seeing you come in here."

"I'll be back. Not sure when."

"Maybe I can even greet you by name the next time. I'm Hannah, this is Tiffany."

He grinned. "Tiffany is it? Definitely trouble. I'm Doug."

Hannah smiled. "Well, you have Tiffany figured out. Nice to meet you, Doug."

"Thanks for feeding me the last week or so."

"Like I said, we appreciate your business."

He turned to me. "If I didn't need to get out of here, I would ask you to sit with me for dinner."

I was instantly grinning, maybe blushing a little as well. "If I didn't have a boyfriend, then maybe I would have dinner with you."

He waved his hand away. "I don't care that you have a boyfriend. He's not here, but I have to get out of here. Nice to meet you, ladies. Until the next time."

He picked up his bag, nodded to Hannah, then to me before turning and walking away. Hannah leaned in.

"He liked you."

I straightened back, taking the seat at the bar next to the pickup area. "Doesn't matter. Andy is all I want."

"How is he? I mean, I don't see you, then it's twice in one week. Everything all right between you both?"

"Yes and getting better every day."

"That's good. I'm happy for you, Tiff. Tell me everything that is going on with your family. The rumor is unbelievable. Wait, I've just got to cash them out and take those people's order. Everything, Tiffany. I mean it."

Between customers, she had as much information as I did. By the time I was ready to leave, she had sorted her feelings out about the wedding.

"That's it. I will call Priscilla. If they move to Washington, I will never see her again. I'll deal with whatever comes. I will ask her for help. It will give me time with her. I love your mother."

I reassured her with a smile and put my hand over hers. "She will love that." Hannah nodded with mixed emotions. I was sure the expression she was showing was because of the possibility of my parents moving to the West Coast.

I arrived back home with a takeout box of steak shavings Hannah had packed for kitten. Spoiled little kitty loved the food, growling for me to keep away while she ate. I sat with my head back on the couch, thinking about my day. Kyle was back. We were on unfamiliar terms. Donovan had hired an asshole to change the image of our company. My parents were possibly moving to Washington state. My boyfriend was somewhere doing business, still roughed up from last night. And I had a file on him that Mildred had put together. *Hmm. Now's a good as time as any to look through it.*

I pulled a good-size stack of papers with photos from my bag, placing the folder on my coffee table and spreading them out. Each small pile was individually paper-clipped. There was a photo of him with his father at a gun range. Andy looked about ten at the time, belly down with a big rifle against his cheek. His father was standing with his boot on Andy's back. Looked like he was pushing him down. He looked just like his father. I touched the photograph. Our son would be amazing.

The argument outside my back door made me look up, but it stopped as I picked up a few papers. All the awards Andy had accomplished were pinned next to his father and mother's. I looked at all of hers. Best female marksman for seven years in a row. Holy crow, she was good. The McMillan family cleaned house for years. Then it jumped five years, only showing Andy's records. For the next ten years he ranked in the top five. They listed him as Army and Marines. I wasn't sure what this other group of letters meant.

I heard arguing again, enough to make me put down the papers and turn on my back light. I pushed the curtain back some. No sound. I peered around. Someone was heading toward the back entrance and someone else toward the parking strip. The person headed toward the doorway stopped at the entrance landing.

She yelled, "You're a fucking asshole! Don't come here again!" That was clearly Robin. She was running up the steps and inside. I opened my door. The guy hopped in a light-colored van, not responding.

Kitten thought the door being open was an invitation to explore as she ran past my feet into the night.

"No, no, no, no. Not here kitten." I scooped her up, turning back to my patio. "Tomorrow you can run around at Daddy's. Sorry." I closed the door and locked it, letting her down, as I turned my attention back to the file.

The only thing I had gotten out of the papers was how good Andy was at shooting. I already knew that. That was why he was teaching me. No information on his mother and nothing I hadn't already looked up on my own about his father.

There was a picture of him standing with his mother, receiving some medal. Wasn't recent, possibly ten years ago. She still looked the same. I could hear her calling me a slut right from the photo, making me bury it in the pile while I collected all the papers and stuffed them back in the envelope.

I was tired. I texted Andy that I was heading to bed and I missed him. I hoped he was all right. He immediately returned my text, telling me to meet him at the south range for eight o'clock and be prepared to get a run in. I sighed with relief. He was okay.

I slept on his side of the bed but was excited about my morning, so I got up early enough to give myself a little extra time to look good for him. Layers were the way to go this morning, what with it starting off cool then forecast to get warm. I told kitten we were moving back this afternoon and closed the door tight, concentrating on my man. I was going to kiss him this morning. I didn't care who was around.

The base was active. Training weekend for them. "War games," as Andy called it. Just as I exited my car, he walked toward me. His bandage was off. Nasty looking cut. The closer he got, the angrier I became. *Who would do this to him?* I went to examine it.

"No big deal, Tiff. Let it go." Perhaps there was someone here watching us, and he didn't want the fuss.

"Can I kiss you?"

He answered that question with a full-on, mouth-open, tongue-swirling kiss, leaving my head spinning and me a little breathless.

"How do you feel?"

"Like I was stuck in a drum and rolled down a hill."

"That is very specific. Done that before?"

He gave me a sharp glance. That answered my question. Today it was about close contact. He wanted me ready for next Friday. We were a week away now. He showed me a neat trick, trapping the opponent's finger on the trigger. We practiced for more than an hour until I got it right. By noon, my training was over, and my fingers hurt. He was running with me. As banged up as he was, I still had to catch up to run by his side. This man was a machine. Praising me after for how well I did almost seemed like an insult.

I followed him back to the condo because we were moving. He packed up food and walked around, making sure everything was secure. I coaxed Kitten into her crate as I told him about the argument last night in the back area between Robin and some guy. He checked the door and stopped at the coffee table, picking up the folder.

"Tiffany?"

I looked up from my bags. "Yes?" My eyes went straight to the envelope that held his information. He slid the documents out. I stepped toward him. "I had nothing to do with that. Mildred's been spying on you. She gave that to me a few nights ago, and I only opened it yesterday." He met my eyes and pulled the contents out completely. He looked everything over.

I moved in front of him. "There is nothing in there that I don't already know." He pulled the photo of him with his father's boot on his back from the paperclip. He studied it.

"I was nine here. Dad said I was an inchworm. Every time I would shoot on my belly I would squirm up. He had to hold his foot on me to get me out of the habit."

My heart fluttered, thinking about Andy as a little inchworm. How his father's voice must have sounded. How his little voice sounded at that age.

"I swear, this wasn't me. The only reason it's on the table is curiosity about any information on your mother. That would be the only thing I am guilty of, and I can barely find anything on her. She is a ghost."

He skimmed the paperwork. "Yes, she is. I don't blame you for being curious about her. I would have done the same if your mother treated me like she did with you."

Relief washed over me. "I'm sorry I didn't show this to you."

He was done flipping through the papers. "It's okay, Tiffany. These are all public records. There is nothing here you could not find on your own."

"Will you tell me more about your mother?"

"Yes, and in time you can ask her yourself."

I stepped back. "The woman called me a slut. She hates me, Andy. I don't think she will be talking about herself to me anytime soon."

"Well, she will have to eventually."

That sentence had so much promise in it. I didn't think I could love him more.

He loaded my car with what we were transferring to the warehouse. I made sure there was nothing in the fridge this time and that we had plenty of stuff in the cabinets that wouldn't expire. He picked up Kitten's crate, and we walked out together. Robin was walking in, head down.

"Hi, Robin. Heard you arguing with someone last night. Everything okay?"

She lifted her head to reveal a blackening eye. "Would you just leave me the fuck alone!" She darted up the stairs and we heard her slam the door shut.

Andy shook his head. "Babe, come on. None of our business." That was hard for me to swallow. If she was in trouble, then we all needed to know who was coming in and out of here. He put Kitten on his front seat and kissed me before he closed my door.

Following behind Andy made me think about Hannah's wedding magazines. I wanted to find out who made that dress I loved. Hopefully, I would recognize the cover at the store.

Was it a recent magazine? I remembered she had been collecting them for a while. I had to get my hands on those magazines and find that dress.

We settled back into his place. I wanted to wash every room and clean the bedding to remove his mother's memory from here. Andy cooked for us that night. I cleaned the bathroom and got the bedding done.

When we finished, he pulled out an ammo box. It was not full of bullets. It was filled with his memories. There we were at the table as he shared his childhood with me. His mother had taken her husband's death very hard.

Right up until Andy went into the military, she was by his side, taking over her husband's training. Only she did not allow for any mistakes. She was harder on him than anyone. She secured a position in the government when he went in and she climbed rank quickly.

Soon she was responsible for hiring and training special units. She clashed with too many other personnel and moved to the contract division, securing anything from land to weapons. It was the weapons department that drew her special attention. She became difficult there, and they moved her to the future of the military, making it a desirable choice for a lifelong career.

He loved his mother. I needed to make sure he understood my support of that from here on out. If he needed to keep us at a distance, then I would respect it and not act like I did the first go-around. She had issues, and I was here to stay.

We were lying in bed and he announced that he had to be on base all day tomorrow until late. He was in charge of some war games. This was my opportunity to get my hands on the maker of that wedding dress. I was off-duty but logged reports until I was sure Hannah was at work. She was grabbing shifts to help pay for the possible new wedding venue or house if they couldn't find a new venue.

* * *

Got in four hours logging reports. Monday was going to be a breeze in here. Hannah was happy to see me. I told her there was a dress I remembered that I really liked but didn't know which book it was in. She plunked all the magazines in front of me.

"This I have to see."

Brunch at Hannah's restaurant drew a guaranteed crowd. George walked in at one o'clock, heading to his shift, and she packed him dinner. We greeted each other with affection. He was perfect for her. I didn't realize how much I really liked him. He asked about my leg and gave me the scientific explanation, blah, blah, blah. . . . It sounded good, but I didn't understand a damn thing he was saying. Another hour spent flipping through the magazines and getting down to the final two had me anxious. Hannah was at my side now, looking at the other magazines as we drank coffee. She nudged me.

"You know what, Tiff?"

"What?"

"I picture you in this dress someday if you ever get married."

I was nose-deep, concentrating on the pages I was flipping through. She held it up for me to look at.

"It's perfect, simple, elegant. This would be beautiful on you." I glanced.

"It's nice." Her hand slipped and turned a few more pages. *There!* There was my dress. I grabbed the magazine. "You are right. Do you mind if I borrow this one?"

Her head jerked back. "Of course, help yourself. You okay?"

"I can't find that maid of honor dress. These are all starting to look the same. I like the dress you picked out. Let's go with that." I pulled out twenty dollars. "Here, for the food and coffee. I have to go. I'll get this back to you."

"Tiffany? Take your money. Here." She stuffed it back in my pocket. "I'm meeting Priscilla tomorrow. Want to come?"

"Oh geez, I can't. Training. My run is Friday. Got a lot to do before I start back driving. You are in expert hands, though. Glad you called her."

I could not get out of there quick enough. There were so many cars on the road. *Ugh!* I just wanted to get back to my place and look at my dress. How could I have missed it in that book?

My mother was calling.

"I am calling to see if you and Andrew are free Tuesday night for dinner."

"Andy has a lot going on this week."

"Then how about you? We have a lot to go over. Your father and I have decided to sell Audrey the business."

My heart sank a little. This meant they would move across the country. "I might be, but I have to train. My running test is Friday. I have to pass. This is my only job."

"I understand. You realize this sell-out won't leave you penniless. You will still have a good safety net. We made sure of that since you were a baby."

"I'll be there. Seven o'clock work?"

"It does, dear. I have more news. Hannah asked me to help her. Although I think it was because of your nudging."

"She wanted to ask you, but she was having difficulty asking. She doesn't want her parents to feel like you are stepping on their toes."

"I know how to step gently."

"I know you do. That's what I reminded her. That's why you are seeing her tomorrow."

"She told you?"

"She invited me. But this is a good thing, Mother. I really don't have a lot of time for what she needs me to do so you take my place, and it will help me, too."

"You have never been one to get excited about a glorious party."

I chuckled. "You have enough excitement about parties for all of us, Mother."

"That's another thing we will talk about. Your father wants me to open an event planning company."

"I know that, too. It's about time."

"Did you know in Washington state?"

"Yup."

"Why am I just finding all this out?"

"It was just everyone blurting out ideas when I arrived at the emergency meeting. Father covered a few things on his mind. I didn't take what he said as anything more than talking out loud from frustration about what was happening."

"That makes me feel a little better."

"Have fun with Hannah. She really wants a garden wedding. I'll see you Tuesday, Mother."

"Okay, Tiffany. Bye, darling."

I had no idea when Andy would be home. I swung by my condo to pick up my uniform. They were allowing me to dress casually while on report duty, but come next Saturday morning I was back on rotation. I kept the wedding magazine here. I took a snapshot of the dress and designer. I would call tomorrow to see if they had the dress locally.

I knew Hannah kept a wedding day keepsake box. Maybe I could do that? I wasn't totally against planning my wedding. A shoebox was . . . No! Andy's handmade Tiffany box from my last birthday. I pulled it down from my closet shelf. I ripped out the page that displayed my wedding dress and folded it to fit. I smiled, placing it back on the shelf. This was so girly. Hannah would be delighted right until I confessed the hole in the side was where Andy slid his manhood in. I needed to show her this box someday. I laughed thinking about it.

CHAPTER TEN

Andy hadn't arrived home by the time I wanted to go to sleep. I checked my phone at eleven, not waiting any longer, and fell asleep. Finally, he got home, pulling me against his body. He kissed the side of my head, assuming I was sleeping. I turned into him, confirming I was awake. He kissed my lips softly.

"Tiffany, what are you doing with a guy like me?"

I touched the side of his head softly. "You are the only man I have ever fallen in love with."

His half-smile vanished in the moonlight. "I can't give you normal. Might even put you in danger. I would never forgive myself if something happened to you because of me."

I pushed him over on his back now, looking down at him.

"Train me to be safe. I don't want normal. I want you. I want us. Take me into your world. I will learn to handle anything, even your mother."

He searched deep into my eyes. Both of us seeing each other's reflection. "Then marry me."

I nodded. "Okay." And lowered to kiss him.

My phone vibrated. Andy was calling. I sat up, answering, looking around the room.

"Hey, babe, sorry I didn't make it home last night. Come to the range. Bring your running gear. Be here in an hour."

I shook my head, making sure I was awake. "You never came home?"

"No, why? Someone else intrude my bed last night?"

"No, I . . . you . . . I . . . never mind. I'll be there in an hour."

"Can you bring me coffee? Black."

"Yes."

"See you in an hour. Get moving, woman."

I sat for a moment. I touched my lips. It felt so real. It couldn't have been a dream. Kitten sprawled out on his side, rolling over and purring.

Damn it!

Today we ran with an entire platoon. These guys set the pace, and they boxed me in the middle. I had to run or get trampled. Excellent strategy. I made my nine-minute mile. Right here proved I could do it. If I messed up on Friday, it would be my fault. Andy stood waiting, proud of his idea, and I thanked him when I caught my breath. I had to push myself now.

He walked me to my car. "Tiff, I've got to do something. I'll be gone for a few days. I promise I will be back on Friday."

"What?"

"I realize this is sudden, and we are trying to get back into a routine. There is nothing routine about my life, though. You have to adjust to that. I also need you to take Kitten and spend the days I am gone back in the condo."

"You fucking kidding me?"

"I told you there would be times like this. I promise it will be better when I get back. Trust me."

I looked in every direction besides his. He stood waiting.

"Tiffany, please?"

I shifted my weight, then snapped my head around, glaring into his eyes.

"Fine!"

He tried to soften my irritation, raising his arms to rest both hands on my shoulders. "I will be back Friday, watching you pass. I need to do something."

"Are you coming back to the warehouse to pack?"

"No. I have everything I need here. Lock it up tight, okay?" I huffed. "That's my girl. This is for us, okay?" I nodded with a bigger frown. "For us," he slowly and clearly stated, tilting my chin up to look at him. I shifted my focus on his eyes again. He held my stare. He kissed me. "God help you when I get back, babe." He chuckled, turned, and trotted away.

What the hell did that mean?

I packed again, taking my clothes and Kitten. I would shop at the gas station on the way back for food like I always did. I checked everything twice, locked his door, and headed home. I settled back into my condo with Mildred's conversation playing in my head. The report from my accident that I didn't remember seeing gave me something new to occupy my mind. Picking up my phone and pressing her name, she answered on the first ring.

"Hello, Tiffany."

On the drive downtown, I stopped at my favorite pizza shop, buying a large, plain pizza for us. Mildred never ate pizza in front of anyone but me. When I arrived, there she stood, looking over a blueprint, sporting a slightly turned-up smile. She ordered her secretary that she was not to be disturbed for the next hour. I followed behind to her office and closed the door.

"Did you read those files?"

"Yes, but I already knew that stuff. Where did you find the photos? I barely find any on him or his family."

"I have my sources. I take it you want to see the accident report."

"Yes, have some pizza while I read."

She grinned. "Fair enough." Mildred went to a filing cabinet across her room and pulled out a thick folder.

"That's my accident report?"

"No. These are all your accident reports since the day you started at Angel Wings."

"Why did you keep them all?"

"You may need them someday. The top one is the latest and they continue in sequence from there." She handed me the file and opened the pizza box, pulling a slice onto a paper plate.

There were a few things circled in red.

"Why is there stuff circled?"

"I found it interesting. Easy to refer back to."

"Post-it notes, highlights?"

"I am successful for a reason."

I didn't need to read the report, just what she had marked. The photo of the bullet hole next to where my head should be. The blood from Kyle's arm splattered the entire cab. All the memories rushed back with more intensity than ever before. As I studied the penetration hole, it was amazing that Taylor didn't get hit. In through one side of the wall, clean out the other and the same for the back door. Her screams echoed in my ears. I read through Mildred's notes, viewing the pictures a second time.

Mildred ate half the pie, pushing it away from her.

"Remove this pizza. I've eaten enough."

I lifted the box automatically and placed it on the chair next to me as I continued to read, not missing a beat.

I didn't like looking at this stuff. I was aware of the risks in my job. I'd seen enough, placing the report down, arranging her papers back in order.

"I don't need to read anymore."

"Tiffany?"

"What? I mean, I get it, Mildred. I am in a high-risk job. I take chances. I realize this. I'm not quitting. This is what I do, and I like it."

"You're missing the point."

"What point?"

"You should have been dead. Look. Look at where that bullet hit."

"My ambulance swerved all over the road. I remember leaning to keep the tires on the ground. It wasn't my time."

"I don't accept that!"

"Then I don't know what to tell you."

"I think he set you up."

"Of course it was a setup. That's what hijack means, Mildred."

"I am saying your boyfriend set it up."

"What?"

She reached for the folder, spreading all the incidents out into a fan.

"From the day you two met you have been targeted, but have walked away barely touched outside of these last two."

"Are you crazy? Andy would never do that. He works for us."

As soon as I said it, I remembered that he had saved me, tying my leg to stop the bleeding and leaving with half the organ. He left with half the organ. He was working for the other side!

I wanted to puke. I needed air. Sweat covered my body. I looked wide-eyed up at Mildred.

"He is playing both sides."

I stood up. All his shooting awards flashed in my brain. That bullet was meant for me. He was going to kill me.

"Tiffany!" Mildred called, but I was already in the hallway, quickly exiting the building. The street was busy with pedestrians as I made my way through the crowd. They weren't walking quick enough. I needed to get out of here. *Where did I park?* I was walking the wrong way. I turned to head to the correct parking lot. I bumped into a guy wearing headphones as he barked at me to watch where I was going. *My car, my car. Where the hell was my car?*

I drove straight to the warehouse, cautiously walking in. Andy said he was gone and told me to move back to the condo, but was he really gone? Perhaps he was trying to get rid of me, to plot a better way of taking me out.

He did say *God help you when I get back*. There was his file with all the pictures he had shared. What was that about? Trying to get in so I wouldn't suspect anything? I looked around, went through every drawer, cabinet, everything. I found a .38 Special and released the cylinder. It was loaded and it was coming with me.

I went to the table and read everything again. I couldn't stop flashing back to the accident. I heard the bullet pass my ear. I heard it. I definitely heard that bullet. He was trying to kill me. What? Did he reconsider after he missed?

Everything, all the accidents, our first meeting, everything flooded me. I picked up a photo of him holding a trophy. He wasn't smiling. I sorted through more photos. Not one of them showed a proud look on his face. No emotion at all. I brought the picture closer. He looked right into the camera like he was looking at me. I dropped the picture. My eyes shifted to another photograph of his mother. Same emotionless expression on her face. She was staring at me as *slut* repeated in my head.

I buried the photos in the pile, stacked them all up, and stashed them in his ammo box where they came from, then took the file Mildred had compiled and locked up the place. I realized tucking the gun in the back of my pants didn't work well as I slid in my car, instantly climbing back out to remove it and place it in my center console instead. I backed out and drove off normally as I'd done so many times before. This time my heart was breaking.

I arrived back at the condo with groceries. As far as I was concerned, I was staying here even when he got back. The bastard tried to kill me. He blew Kyle's arm off, and I couldn't forgive him for that.

I stress shopped. Spent four hundred dollars, forgetting what I bought. Andy texted me. *Hi, babe. Miss you already. You did great this morning. Very proud of you.* I wanted to chuck the phone against the wall. *Now he texts me?* Right when I didn't want him to. The nerve of this guy. I decided not to answer. He had gone for days without replying to me. The same could apply now.

An hour passed. He texted again. *Babe, please text you are okay. I need to know you are safe.*

Safe? I thought. *Oh, please. So you can have another shot at me. I wonder if that is why he shot up my bullet wound.* I jumped up. *I wonder if he planted those two guys there, and that was why he hid in the woods! Bastard!*

Now my phone vibrated. He was calling. I pressed to answer.

"Hello?"

"Everything okay, Tiffany?"

"Fine, why?"

"Okay, just making sure. You didn't answer my text."

I grumbled. "How does it feel?"

"What?"

I sighed. "Nothing."

"Listen, I understand I am asking a lot but limit your activity outside the condo for a while."

"Yes, that is asking a lot. I am Hannah's maid of honor, my parents might move away, Audrey may need support, and I have to keep training for my test. I'm not in lockdown. I have shit to do and people to see."

Silence.

"Are we done?"

He cleared his throat. "I'm sorry I am not there for you. It will be different. I promise."

"Don't change for me. I'm all set."

"I'm changing for us. For our future."

Now I was silent. *Whatever* . . .

"I'll see you Friday."

"Whatever, don't rush back."

"Tiffany, what's wrong?"

"Nothing. Goodbye." I hung the phone up.

A text came through. *Love you, babe.*

I growled and tossed the phone to my left. It was almost nine and I yawned. Morning shift would come quickly. I must have been tired; not once did I wake up. I slipped on my jeans that used to be tight. All this running was beginning to reshape me. I packed my jogging stuff. It was Michael's day off, but he said he would meet me when I was done.

I pushed myself and tried to run like I had yesterday morning. It wasn't the same. I was down by three minutes. Michael still praised my progress. We walked, cooling down about a mile from the base when I asked him.

"Do you remember the night of my last hijacking?"

He turned his head with his eyebrows raised. "Of course, I have reoccurring nightmares about it. Still kicking myself for not riding with you."

I thought about that. Andy would have killed him. That's for certain. "I'm glad you didn't. See what happened to Kyle?"

"I don't think I would have lost my arm."

"No, probably your life."

"I was so angry with you. You disobeyed orders."

"I had to. You didn't see what was happening. I will again, you realize."

"I know. God help Kyle."

"I recognize you don't like Andy . . ."

"Hate the bastard."

Angling my head. "Okay, I realize you hate Andy, but do you think he would sell out the company?"

"What do you mean sell out?"

"I mean pretend he's working for Angel Wings but actually be working for the other side."

"In a fucking heartbeat. Why? You finally seeing that?"

I stopped Michael. I needed to tell someone. "He was there that night."

"Where?"

"Before you got to the scene. He wrapped my leg."

"Why didn't you say something, Tiffany? This changes everything!"

"He saved me. I probably would have bled out."

"We all thought you did that. Not that fucking numbskull."

"Did you hear me? He saved my life and Audrey's life."

"That's the other thing. Why did you only have half an organ? The hospital secured a full organ in your ambulance."

"I don't know."

"Well, don't clam up now. Get it out. I'm not going to fucking tell anyone."

Narrowing my eyes. "*I don't know!*"

"Yeah right! Go ahead and play that card. Bet he took it and sold it to the highest bidder."

"I'm sorry I even told you."

I walked quicker to get away from him. "Tiffany, wait. Sorry. I'm acting like an idiot. I didn't mean to put you in a corner. He makes me . . . defensive. You shouldn't be with him. You deserve so much better."

I chuckled. "Like you?"

He tugged my arm for us to stop. "Someday you will see, and I will be waiting."

"I've told you. Stop waiting. We will only be friends"

"That kiss in the ambulance said differently."

I turned, throwing up my hands. "Michael, that was post-accident melodrama."

"You can call it whatever you like. But you can't deny the chemistry."

I gritted my teeth. "Enough."

CHAPTER ELEVEN

Both my parents were home cooking together. They set the table for three, and mother gave last-minute orders. I walked right in wearing my street clothes.

"Hello?"

Mother was setting napkins on the table.

"Tiffany, darling. Come see my new handsome chef in the kitchen." I walked over, and there was Father in an apron.

"She put you back to work already?"

He chuckled. "I think I like cooking. Who knew?"

"I take it you are selling Audrey the company?"

Mother poured drinks for her and my father. "Yes! We have a few more details to iron out, but it's happening."

I grabbed water. "This is a good thing?"

"Miracles come in many disguises."

"Wow, okay, this is a change."

"A change we needed."

"Washington state still your destination?"

She turned optimistic. "You could come with us."

I shook my head. "Nah, I like it here. Besides, what would Mildred do if we all left?"

"Move with us, too. Anyway, that's not for another year."

"Year?"

Father turned the stove off and picked up his drink as Mother rested next to him, turning to join our conversation.

"Not a year. More like eight months, pending our finding a house we both like."

"House? Mother, houses are a lot of work. You won't be living in a carefree environment like this."

"We can hire people to do the work. Besides, who did all the cleaning and cooking in here? We didn't have a maid. It was me."

She was right. She only had a driver.

"Father going to drive you around?"

"I know how to drive, Tiffany."

"You have your license, Mother?"

"Of course I do. I enjoyed being driven around. Father is buying me a sleek sports car."

I chuckled. "What, a Porsche?"

"Oh, heavens no. Too small. A Bentley."

"A Bentley? Can you still afford that?"

They both looked at each other, insulted I had said such a thing. "What? All that talk the other day about being ruined and the stock dropping."

"We have plenty of money. Thirty-plus years of savings, building that company. Did you think it left us penniless?"

"Kind of?"

"Well, you are wrong. You have a nice nest egg, too, thanks to your parents. But you don't get it until you are thirty."

"I don't need it. Keep it for your Bentley. I'm doing just fine."

"You say that now. What if you get hijacked again and even worse next time than a bullet through your leg? Then what?"

"I will probably end up dead next time, so, again . . . I don't need it."

"Andrew would never let that happen."

I sat down into a slump. "Andrew will probably be the one pulling the trigger."

Father pulled Mother's chair out as she sat. "Did you two have a fight?"

"No."

"Well, your fellow would take a bullet for you. I can see it in his eyes, Tiffany. He loves you. I wouldn't be surprised if I got to have two weddings here before we left."

"I'm not getting married, Mother. Stick with Hannah. That's your sure bet. How did it go?"

She sat up straighter. "Fingers crossed; we may have found her venue. The only thing is we would have to move it up."

I mimicked her straightening up. "When?"

"If we get in, her wedding will be in seven weeks."

"What? Is that even possible?"

"Of course, it is. I will make sure she has everything she wants. Might be a little pressure, but it is very possible."

"She doesn't even have the dresses yet."

"I called the company that she wants her bridal party dresses from. They can guarantee them in a month. She picked her wedding dress, too. Everyone is waiting for the go-ahead."

Seven weeks? I needed to change my vacation dates.

My parents acted differently tonight. Playful and upbeat. This was a pleasant change for them. Could be that this was a minor miracle of some sort. They talked about the future with vigor. I asked about her ladies' luncheon tomorrow and she waved it off, telling me she wasn't going. *Not going!* She never missed a luncheon. She announced Mary was coming over and teaching her how to scrapbook. *Scrapbook?* I couldn't take it anymore, I had to get away from this incomprehensible black hole I had entered. The food was excellent, but now I was wondering if they had drugged me.

I drove home with my window down. I needed air. When I pulled into my parking space, there was Robin wiping her arms and throwing a bag in the dumpster. She hurried to the door as I approached. She opened it as I called to hold the door. She jumped and quickly turned her head back, looking at me. There were dark red blotches on her shirt, and she looked like she had been wrestling an alligator.

I pointed to what looked like a bloodstain.

"Are you okay?"

She pulled her sleeve down, covering her arm.

"Fuck off."

What a bitch! She darted up the stairs, slamming her door shut. I looked at the dirt that littered the entrance now and kicked it aside. *Slob.* Joe would see that in the morning and clean. When I rounded the corner to my unit, there were a dozen roses in a vase on the floor. I picked them up and heard Kitten on the other side. I brought them in. She was more curious about the flowers than about eating. I opened the card. *Love you ~Andy.* Flowers before my funeral. How nice.

Two years he couldn't say that to me and now it was all he was saying to me! I tossed the card on the table and plated Kitten her dinner from Grandma. No text from Andy tonight. I guess he realized I was mad. I tossed and turned all night. His side of the bed smelled like him. Mental note to self: wash the sheets tomorrow.

The day proved to be a breeze. I had both Michael and Chris running with me. I did better on the time. Perhaps Michael was mollycoddling me yesterday. I needed him to stop doing that. It wasn't doing me any favors. I had tomorrow left to train, and that was it. I was going to pass no problem, but I wanted to pass in the top tier – no questions asked about my injury anymore.

Thursday, after my run, I added participation in my grappling class. It felt good to get back into my regimen. All went well until I took an awkward step, a bad step that sparked pain around my wound.

"*Fuck!*"

My instructor went right to the ice machine.

"Here, Tiff, straighten your leg. Let me look." They helped me to the floor as he examined around the wound. It was muscle. I'd pulled something. He handed me a cream to put on the muscle area, telling me to ice it tonight and asked when my training test was. I looked into his eyes.

"In the morning."

I watched the reactions, everyone making sympathetic faces, except him.

"Do you want me to drive you home?"

I flexed my foot up and down. "I'm fine to drive."

He softened. "Tiffany, I'm sorry."

I shook it off as the guys helped me up. "Not your fault. This is me. All me. Pushing too much, as usual."

Andy text me at eight. *Get some sleep and I will see you on base.*

I texted back: *I pulled a muscle in my leg at grappling tonight.*

My phone lit up in my hand. "How bad?"

"I'm not sure I can run."

"I'll come to the condo first and drive you over. Tiffany, you will be able to run. I promise."

He was probably going to poison me. I didn't care, as long as I passed the test.

"Fine."

"Did you get the flowers I sent? I'm only asking because I've never done that before. Sent flowers."

"Yes, thank you."

"I'm not sure what they do at condo buildings. Did they leave them outside?"

"Joe was here. They were in front of my door when I got home. I assume he put them there. Kitten is trying to eat them. Are roses poison?" Great, another thought I hadn't flagged. He was trying to kill me *and* my cat.

"Is she actually eating them?"

"I don't think so, but she is biting them."

"I'm looking it up right now. It says the thorns can be dangerous. I asked them to remove the thorns. No sense in sending something nice then getting stabbed – seemed counterproductive. So they are safe. Says here the rose itself can cause a little gastrointestinal upset. She's fine but don't let her eat them all the same. I bought those for you, not her."

This was not a man who was going to kill me. Maybe his intention was to miss. I remembered the expression in his eyes when he was tying my leg: no regret that he'd missed the shot, if that was even him shooting. I didn't know if he was the one who'd fired the shot. What if it was someone else?

The only way I was going to find out for certain was to ask. Not over the phone. I would ask in the morning when he was here. That way I could see his facial expressions and learn the truth.

"I will stop letting her eat them. I'll see you in the morning."

"Tiffany?"

"Yes?"

"Love you."

My heart pushed through the doubt. "Love you, too."

And he hung up.

He showed up before I woke up. Coffee perfumed the condo. He walked in holding Kitten in one arm and a medical bag in the other. I sat up.

"Hey."

He kissed me first. Not a peck, but a proper kiss. One that lingered, letting me know he'd missed me the past few days.

Next, he was all business assessing my leg. He cleaned off the balm that my instructor gave me and filled a syringe with a clear liquid.

"What is that?" I asked.

He poked around my leg, and I jumped when he pressed a spot. "Stay still. This is going to hurt. I can't do anything about that."

In he went with the needle as I grabbed a pillow to my face and screamed into it. It lasted only a few seconds, but it took all my self-control not to grab that needle and throw it across the room. The pain melted away and then . . . no pain. I put the pillow down and he pulled the needle out, pressing a gauze pad to the area.

He glanced up. "Better?"

"Yes, what did you do?"

"Nerve block. You won't feel your leg. Don't do anymore than you have to today, though. Once this wears off, all the activity from today will be front and center. I'm hoping we will be home by that point."

I slipped out of bed to test it. Nothing, not one tingle of discomfort. I couldn't feel my leg either. He had me practice walking, telling me not to even think about it. Apparently, I walked awkwardly.

We arrived at the military base together in his car. He slung my duffle bag over his shoulder and walked with me up to Donovan.

"McMillan, good to see you. How have you been? Keeping busy, I presume?"

I looked from Donovan to Andy. Andy handed me the sign-in clipboard. "Yes, busy."

"If you are around tomorrow, I would like you to come and sit in on the assignment announcement. Seeing that you are here today, you can observe the recent recruits. Even though you are not working for us anymore, we might be contracting you again."

I placed the clipboard down, touching Andy's arm.

"Since when did you stop working at Angel Wings?"

He answered me first. "Eight months ago," then turned back to Donovan, "I think I can be there."

Eight months ago? That was before the last hijacking. He wasn't working for us at that point?

The look on my face must have alarmed him. He took my arm and led us away. Donovan called over.

"Good luck, Tiffany! I'll be watching you."

People started showing up, observing Andy and me.

"Why didn't you tell me you left Angel Wings?"

"I don't know. No big deal. I am a freelancer. I go where the money is."

"So, when you were there, at my last hijacking, it wasn't for Angel Wings?"

"Tiffany, this isn't the place to talk about this."

I looked around. He was right, but I was pissed off at him right now.

"I want answers. You will tell me."

He nudged me along. "Let's get you warmed up."

"I'm serious, McMillan. Answers!"

"I'll tell you what I can. Come on. This way."

CHAPTER TWELVE

As the company's attendance grew, Andy did what he did best, blending into the background. Michael arrived, walking over to Jeff and me. For me, this was a reunion to catch up with the gang working different shifts who I never got to see anymore. There was occasional banter in the garage when I went in to see my mechanics, but it was brief.

"How's the leg? Ready for this?"

I looked down at it and stood, wobbling on the one leg.

"Ready."

Michael sneered. "You can't balance for shit. What's up with that?"

I put my other leg down, about to fall over. "Tweaked it last night during grappling. Andy administered a nerve block so I could run." Michael turned to scan the area.

"Jackass here? I could use a nerve block against him."

"He's over there."

Michael spotted him, and Andy stared right back at Michael. They hated each other.

"There's the prick." He turned back to me. "Don't know what you see in that guy. Zero personality."

Jeff tapped my shoulder. "Don't push it, Tiffany. Just make it in the time allowed. Don't need you out any longer.

These new goons take some getting used to. I don't want any more of them, to tell you the truth."

"Donovan is trying to rebrand the company. That last guy, the guy who calls himself Polack, have you met him yet?" I looked over to where Michael was concentrating.

Michael waved Chris over. "Oh, I don't know. One isn't bad."

Pete jogged toward her, both making their way to our group. Jeff answered me. "Polack, yes. Everyone's heard about him. Sounds like a real dickhead."

I nodded. "That was my first impression. Kyle is starting back tomorrow." He grinned.

"Speak of the devil, I'll be right back." Kyle was signing in.

Chris and Pete were just yards away. I shaded the sunlight from my eyes.

"What's Kyle doing here?"

Michael shrugged. "Don't know."

Pete was being funny, high-stepping, asking me if I was ready, sizing me up, and offering to carry me if I needed.

Donovan announced we were running first and to change into our proper running attire. We got the twenty-minute warning to get over to the start line.

Andy walked to me. "How's the leg?"

"It's good but strange. Still can't feel it."

"Concentrate on the run. Watch your footing. I don't need you tripping and hurting yourself worse."

"Okay. I think Michael will run with me and Chris." I looked over to Kyle. "Is Kyle running?"

"I don't think so. You better get over there. Good luck, babe."

"Thanks." He kissed me right on the lips and walked away. I met my group.

Chris asked, "Is that your boyfriend?"

I nodded. "Yes."

"Private contractor, right?"

"Yes."

"Looks like one."

I grinned. "There's a specific look?"

She nodded back. "Hell yeah. He's cute in an underworld sort of way."

I chuckled. "I will let him know."

We were off. The first few steps were awkward again, but I focused on a rhythm. It was better running behind someone; it took away the effort of watching where my footing was to build on better timing. Not bad. I finished in a little more than ten minutes.

I officially passed, and Andy was there waiting at the finish line with a bottle of water in his hand. Everyone stayed, cheering all the others coming in behind. As fit as the Polack appeared, he was one of the last to finish. He didn't care. His ego most likely carried him to the finish line. Good to know I could outrun him, even with a bad leg.

Everyone suited up for the gun exercise. Donovan walked over to Andy and me. "Is it true you hurt your leg yesterday?"

Michael! Tattletale. "It's nothing. I'm good."

"This next part you have down. I wanted to make sure you could run. Looks like you proved it completely. Tiffany, go home and take care of that leg. If you are set against helping in the office, then I don't want you missing another day because of it."

"What about this training exercise? People will wonder why I skipped out. I don't want that kind of attention on me."

"Don't worry about it. You only needed to pass the run. I will handle everyone else. See you tomorrow morning for the roster." He extended his hand. "McMillan."

Andy accepted the gesture. "Tomorrow."

Donovan nodded.

Well, this was going to backfire on me. I didn't want special treatment. This was Michael's fault. Andy held my bag as I touched his arm to hold on. "I'll be right back." I marched over to Michael. "Thanks a lot." He looked up. "For what? Why aren't you changing?"

"Because you said I injured my leg yesterday and now Donovan excused me."

"What? He excuses no one."

"Correct! Your big mouth just made me different."

He looked around. Polack had overheard. "Chip a nail, princess?"

I snapped my focus around to him. "Fuck off."

I narrowed my eyes back at Michael.

"Brush it off, Tiff. I am glad he excused you. You're one of the best shots here. You don't need to prove that. You survived six hijackings and you came out better each time. I don't think many people could do what you do."

To hell with his stupid pep talk. I was fuming, and all because of his gossip. I started to head back to Andy.

"Rest the leg, Tiff. See you tomorrow." I flipped my finger up, not turning to see his reaction. I didn't like being singled out and now I was being stopped by all the guys I passed, asking where I was going. *Grrrr*.

Andy remained silent all the way home. He didn't even say anything on the walk into the condo. When he closed the front door, he asked if I wanted him to start the tub for a soak.

"Fine," I snapped and made my way to the couch.

I complained to Kitten about what had happened today, and she seemed to empathize as she kept walking under my hand, purring away. That was until Andy opened a tin of her food and she ran over to him, meowing.

Andy called out, "I think the tub is almost ready, babe. Have a soak. You will feel better for a bit. It will also help when the block wears off."

I grumbled back, still in a foul mood. I walked into the bathroom; he had placed a few magazines on the floor next to the bath. I sighed. That was nice of him. I settled in and opened my travel magazine that I had not looked at in a year. My mother bought subscriptions when I moved into my condo. She thought I would like getting fun mail once a month. It was a nice gesture. I had never opened them, but here I was, flipping through the pages.

Andy called through the door that he was going to go out and pick up some groceries, asking if I wanted anything.

I smartly replied, "New leg," but he argued he liked the current one.

I glanced down at my bullet wound and remembered Mildred's accusations about Andy trying to kill me. I had stopped thinking about it, but here he was, taking care of me again. He always took care of me. It made little sense that he would have tried to kill me.

I called out again, "Chocolate, and check how much coffee we have."

I heard him leave as I put the magazine down, resting my head back and thinking about that bullet shot through my windshield. Kitten meowed, and next came the scratching at the bathroom door. I recognized her game. She would come in here, see what she was missing, and leave.

"I'm not falling for it this time. You can wait." I talked to her as if she would understand what I was saying. She was clearly ignoring me. Now she scratched more and meowed.

There was no way she was going to let me rest. Time to get out. Maneuvering out of a tub when only one leg had feeling was interesting. I did it though. Kitten won the battle, and I opened the door to have her walk in, sniff around, and walk right back out. *Brat.* I slipped into my comfy sweats and plopped on the couch. I picked up my phone, sighing again. It was a little past noon. Everyone was probably still in the training exercise getting ready to wrap things up. I should have insisted on staying. This was stupid.

A text came through from Hannah. *Your mother is a miracle worker. We have my garden, and they have the cutest function hall on the premises. We moved the wedding up. We have seven weeks! Priscilla has everything under control. I just need you to change your time off at work. This is happening, love! Tell me when you are done with training.*

I looked at the calendar. That was the end of June. Seven weeks. I called her. "I'm home."

Hannah squealed on the phone. "I can't believe it. They had a cancelation. There was a wait list, but your mother's connections and my family's restaurant name . . . they gave it to us! George loves the place, too. This is happening, Tiff; I can't believe it! Make sure you have that week off. I don't want you to miss anything."

Hmm. "A whole week? I don't need to take a week, just the dates. Wait, what about a bridal shower?"

"Priscilla is already on that. She has the exact list of dates you need to black out."

"Wow, wow . . . so fast."

"I know. It's crazy. But you don't have to worry about anything. Your mother has it all organized. We just need you to show up. Hey, how did your run go? How's your leg?"

"I passed. Leg is fine."

"Oh good. I knew you would. Listen, I have a million things to do. Thank you for calling me. Call your mother so you can arrange the time off with the dates we need."

"Will do." I pressed the phone to hang up. Wow. Seven weeks. Donovan would not like this. I needed to tell Andy about the time-frame change. I called my mother, who was equally high-strung about the wedding score. She was already recruiting my father as she talked to me and made him recite her to-do list as she changed and added to it. I asked for the dates, but she couldn't locate them, promising me she would text them soon. She said goodbye about five times in a row, then hung up.

Let's see. I looked at the calendar on my phone. I was good with the weekends and my rotation. Depending on how the event dates played out, I wouldn't have to take many days off. This could work out as a good thing on my end, too.

Andy walked through the door carrying two bags of groceries. "Hey, beautiful. How was the bath?"

"As soon as you left, Miss Kitten was banging the door down."

He chuckled. "I almost opened the door before I left. I figured she might do that. Sorry, I'll act on it next time."

"What smells good? I'm getting hungry."

"I bought us meatball subs. One toasted, one not toasted. Which one do you want?"

"Not toasted."

He nodded, grabbing two plates and waters, bringing them over to me. *Delicious.* This was just what I needed. When we were done eating, I felt calmer. Calm enough to ask him about the bullet in my ambulance. He was about to get up and clean our area when I touched his arm to wait. He stopped, giving me his full attention.

"There is something I want to ask you."

He was relaxed and curious. "Okay, what's up?"

"That night of my last hijacking. You took half the liver. I didn't know you were working for someone else. Who hired you?"

He tensed up. Grumbled under his breath and took a moment.

"I can't tell you. Confidential. Why?"

"Because you were there. Were you working for the people hijacking me?"

He hesitated, but forced his answer out. "Yes."

My body froze. My heart skipped. He answered honestly, and I didn't really want to hear him say that.

"Did you shoot me?"

Now he turned defensive. "No!"

What about the bullet through my windshield?"

He remained silent.

My stomach tossed and twisted. I definitely felt like my lunch was going to come back up. Neither one of us said anything. He didn't move, didn't try to get away. He just sat there with a blank expression. I reworded it because now I had to know.

"Did you try to shoot me?"

"No!"

"Then who shot through my windshield?"

Silence again.

"Andy, I need to know. Mildred showed me the police report and the pictures. I need to know if that was you."

"Tiffany, I would never hurt you. I would kill for you. No one will ever get to you without having to go through me first."

I felt the release of relief, but he didn't answer my question.

"Did you shoot *at* me?"

He looked away, didn't get up though, and turned back to look me in the eye.

"I planted that shot. I had to. You were never in any danger. I knew what I was doing."

I stood up. I needed to walk around. I shook my hands out. I was going to start shaking any moment. Then the other thought barreled my brain over.

"Did you shoot Kyle?"

"I had a job to do. He is here today because you wanted him taken out but alive."

"What?!" He said it like I had ordered him to shoot Kyle. "What the hell does that mean?"

"You told me you wanted him out of the picture but not dead."

I needed to sit. My head was spinning, everything in me was confused, jumbled. When it came out, I didn't know where to start.

"I said that because I was mad at him, not as a suggestion. *Oh, honey, can you blow Kyle's arm off because I don't like him?* Do I have to watch what I say around you? Are you insane? Who does that? Oh, my mercenary boyfriend. Don't fuck with me or he will bury you. What the fuck, Andy! What's wrong with you."

He sat there listening, waiting patiently until I was done. My breathing hurt. My chest . . . I thought I was having another panic attack. I chugged my water. He handed me his, talking slow and softly, telling me to focus on the table and just breathe, slowly, in and out, in . . . and out . . . . I did. It helped. He helped, telling me he was getting up and getting something from the kitchen that would help me relax. A knife, no doubt, so he could finish the job. I focused on my breathing. I was gaining more control. He was back with a bottle of whiskey and two glasses. My eyebrows shot up. "Whiskey?"

"I bought it for when the block wears off. You will need a shot."

"Let's not use that word right now."

He poured us each a shot. "Why are you drinking?"

"You think this is a simple conversation for me? I've played this out in my head and have no idea of the outcome at this moment."

Well, that made me feel a little more at ease. He was prepared for me to ask someday. We both drank the small amounts he poured in one swallow, placing the glasses back on the coffee table. Kitten jumped on the back of the couch, sprawling out behind us as we sat in silence. It was clear that I had the floor. He waited, being very patient.

Okay. I collected my thoughts. I was ready.

"You left me half the organ. Why?"

"You had to save your friend."

"See, of course. I should have seen it then. I wondered why I only had half. We were working for two separate people. Why didn't I figure that out? Did you get into trouble for showing up with half?"

"Yes."

"Were you fired?" *Was he fired . . . why the heck did I ask that?*

"No."

"Did they question you?"

"Yes."

"What did you say?"

"Half is better than nothing."

"You said that?"

"Yes."

"What happened to the guy that shot me."

He sat there silently. Kitten was purring behind us. We both glanced back to her for a second, then looked at each other.

"Oh, what? You can tell me you shot Kyle's arm off because I didn't want him dead but you can't tell me what happened to the bastard who shot me?"

"Correct."

I needed another drink.

I must have been staring at the bottle too long. He reached for it and poured us each a small amount again. He handed me my glass. "Thanks."

When I drank, he drank.

"How could you look at Kyle today?"

"What do you mean?"

"Normal, like you never took his arm off? No one would suspect you did that to him."

"He's alive because you didn't want him dead. He's lucky to have only lost a limb. Besides, I was nice about it."

My mouth fell open. "Nice about it? What the hell does that mean?"

"The right side would have been cleaner, easier. But he is right-handed, and his life would have been even worse. I had to work hard for that left shot."

"Aargh! I don't want to know."

"Tiffany, the guy's been a bastard since day one toward you."

"He's just insecure around powerful women."

"He's an asshole."

"Just the way he expresses himself. He's harmless."

"He's an asshole."

I chuckled. "No, he's preschool. You want to see an asshole you should meet Blake Montgomery. Now that's an asshole." I quickly covered my mouth. I should not have said that. "Don't kill him . . . no wait . . . No. Don't kill him. And don't you dare touch Michael!"

Andy's expression tightened.

"I'm serious. Do not touch Michael or let anything happen to him."

"No promises."

"Andy! No!"

He poured a small amount of whiskey for himself, drank it, and placed the glass down harder than he intended. "Oops."

He stood up. "That's enough alcohol for us. Do you want a cup of coffee?"

"Yes, please." He cleared everything away. I sat back, thinking about the last hijacking, what I remembered from it. He saved me.

CHAPTER THIRTEEN

He stood in front of me with coffees and the bag of chocolate he'd bought. I stared at the bag. It was my favorite dark chocolate. I watched him. This man was not going to kill me. He knew how I liked my coffee, my favorite chocolate. He asked how my leg was. Our cat was relaxed, purring behind us. Maybe it was because of the alcohol. Maybe it was because I realized he was always there to save me, but right now, the only thing I wanted was him. I leaned in.

"Kiss me." And he did, following through with the best sex I had ever had with him.

I jumped awake in bed at one in the morning because the block had worn off. I grabbed my leg, clamping my teeth.

"Grrrr!"

Andy was already out of bed, handing me a shot of whiskey, then handing me a glass of water, telling me to drink as much as I could. He massaged and flexed my foot. I don't know why because it was my quadricep that hurt. He told me to flip over onto my stomach as he stretched my leg, then brought my heel toward my buttocks. He massaged my hamstring, and around the area the bullet penetrated. Ten full minutes he worked the area. I finally began to relax with relief.

Whatever he was doing helped tremendously. He had me flip over, massaging the front of my leg. I did and then he medicated me, offering a couple of ibuprofen.

"You should be all right in a few minutes. I told you it was going to bite. Would have been worse if you stayed for the training round."

This was the part where I should have thanked him. Instead, I reminded him of how the others would make fun of me for leaving. He reassured me walking away was the wiser decision. Screw everyone else.

At some point, we fell back to sleep. His body heat soothed every inch. Awake before he was, I looked at his recent scar. It had shrunk to about an inch, right in the fleshy part below his cheekbone. There were several nicks and dents. He did not have the smooth, manicured skin of most men I knew. Every one of these marks told a story. I wanted to know them all. I could sense he was waking up, so I touched his newest scar, caressing my thumb gently over it. "It's healing nicely."

"Super glue does the trick."

"Super glue? You used super glue?"

"In my emergency kit." He opened his eyes. "How's your leg?"

I adjusted it. "Going to take it easy the next few days."

"Good. Wear your brace."

I agreed.

We took my Lexus in this morning. The plan was that when I was done with my shift he would pick me up. I liked us as a couple and this teamwork. They issued my gun back, and my uniform fit nicely. Andy had a call coming in and told me he would be in shortly. Donovan's invite stood. I walked in. Our meeting consisted of Michael, Kyle, Chris, Pete, Jason, Polack, myself, and Donovan. Andy walked in just before we started. Michael instantly objected.

"What's he doing here? You don't even work for us anymore."

Donovan answered. "He is here upon my request."

Michael sneered as I watched Andy pulling out the empty seat on my left. I turned to him, making sure Michael was off limits.

"No."

Andy turned up the right corner of his mouth in a sarcastic smile. I couldn't help focusing in on Kyle's left shoulder. My heart raced. This was my fault. I did this to Kyle. How was I ever going to make this up to him? If it wasn't for my big mouth, everything would be just like before the accident. Maybe even Taylor would have made it in the company. I looked at the recent recruits. They all brought a distinct image. If Donovan was rebranding, these were the guys to do it. They looked seasoned, and they looked tough. I leaned forward, grabbing the water bottle, cracking it open. I didn't need a panic attack right now. I was strong and in control.

Donovan asked how my leg was.

"Fine." I turned to him. Just the distraction that I needed. Not one mention of my absence from the training session.

Donovan made the introductions, passed around paperwork, and announced the teams. I thought it was going to be Chris and me. How wrong did that turn out to be?

Michael got Chris. I got Polack. Michael protested for me; he didn't like us paired up at all, arguing his objection. He even asked Donovan to give him Polack. They set the decision. Co-ed mix in both ambulances. When Michael offered to swap out of his ambulance with Polack, Donovan commented it was too late. The decision stood. They needed him as a principal driver in a senior position and working full-time. The last five people hired were all part-time.

Polack seemed to be pleased as he stared at my chest. "I've got the princess. Fine by me. You can sit back and just do your nails, honey. I'll escort you all around town. You're safe with me, princess."

Andy stood as Michael objected to his remark. I tried to pull Andy back in his seat but had to let go because I was looking too obvious. I gritted my teeth. This was going to be bad. I tried to stop him.

"No, Andy." He ignored me. Damn it. This was my fight, no one else's. I could handle this guy.

Donovan interrupted, "Mr. Wojcik, Miss Chanler is the driver, and she has seniority over you. I don't want to hear any complaints against you. We do not tolerate any inappropriate behavior. So, if you want a job here, you treat all the employees with respect."

Polack grinned, looking right at me. "I'm just trying to be nice. I can respect her, on top. I like women on top. Strong, independent. That is very attractive in a woman." Andy was standing next to him now. He grinned, looking up at Andy. "No worries, princess." Turning back to me, "You and I will be two peas in a pod. The princess and the Polack. Snug in a pod. Can't wait."

I called out, "No!" but it was too late. Andy grabbed the back of the Polack's head and smashed it into the table, busting his nose so that blood gushed down.

Everyone scrambled as Andy calmly walked away, thanking Donovan for including him. It happened so fast.

Michael stood up, pointing. "Damn straight, bastard." Totally agreeing with what Andy had just done. Andy pointed to me.

"I'll pick you up at the end of your shift."

My mouth hung open, looking at him, turning to see the damage, as he freely walked away from the chaos.

Pete asked, "Who the fuck is that guy? I'm assuming since you are letting him walk out that this is acceptable?" Donovan pumped his hands down.

"Calm down, everyone." Chris helped by rolling tissues to shove up Polack's nose, but he pushed her hand away.

"I got it! I got it. I'm fine."

Pete asked again, now directing his question right at me, "Who the fuck is that guy?"

Chris answered, "Private contractor. He had it coming. I don't blame him." She turned in warning toward Polack. "You better watch yourself, buddy. You're messing with the wrong woman."

Pete spoke up. "Are we done here? Let's go, I'm riding with Miss Chanler today. I'm your first-day rotation."

Polack pushed everyone away. "I'm fine. Get the fuck away from me."

It was a big ego crush and he was angry. There was more to discuss. I thought Donovan might have predicted this was going to happen. Polack was put in his place and Donovan didn't have to do a damn thing to correct my new partner.

Kyle walked over to me. "Well, that was interesting. Hey, if this guy gives you any trouble, just let me know. I am a press of a button away." I nodded as Polack now sneered at me. Our eyes met. He hated me. Right here, right now. I glared back with equal hate. It was now or never that he understood I was not playing this game with him. He held it for a few more seconds, before it was him breaking away from our stare.

Donovan pulled me aside. "Are you going to be okay with him? I didn't realize he was so inflated."

"Really? Why did you invite Andy, then?" The look on Donovan's face proved I was correct. "I've got it. He just needs to understand how we run things here. He's all bark."

"Tiffany, are you sure?"

"I think Andy did what you needed him to do. Oh, and don't use my boyfriend like that again. Be the leader you are supposed to be."

He narrowed his eyes at me, then dismissed the meeting. Michael walked the hall with me.

"Jesus, Tiffany. I can fight for a transfer. We can be a team again." I glanced over my shoulder; Kyle, Chris, and Pete were behind us. I turned back.

"Pete, can you grab our route and list. I'll meet you in the ambulance."

He nodded. "Will do."

"Michael, I am fine. I can handle that jerk."

Michael stopped our forward motion as Kyle stepped into the doorway we had just cleared.

"Tiffany, look, I am sorry. I'm sorry for not riding back with you and everything else."

"Michael, you don't need to apologize. You have done nothing wrong. I am probably guilty of holding you back. You deserve your own ambulance and the pay raise that comes with it."

"But, Tiff . . ."

"Michael, this isn't about you riding with me. I am a big girl who can take care of herself. Stop protecting me. I've got this."

He let go of my arm. Regret had spilled all over his face and into his body language. I reached up and gently patted his cheek, "I am good," and walked past him to my ambulance. I did a complete outer-checkpoint walk-around. Everything looked good. Pete was walking up to me with his duffel bag.

"What are you doing?"

"I'm a mechanic here, as well. Sorry, just paying attention to detail."

He grinned. "Can't fault you on that. I'll be inside."

I joined him. As soon as I buckled in, he finished looking over our orders.

"Any chance we stop for coffee?"

I turned toward him. "It's protocol. But there is only one place we stop." He set the papers in the metal file.

"Where is that?"

"Lou's café."

He rubbed his hands together. "We will get along just fine, Chanler."

Coffee and jelly donuts. This was perfect. I needed a little sugar after Andy's assault on Polack. I wondered what he was going to do with him, and if his life was now on the line. Pete seemed very curious about Andy's background. Wanted to know what he did for the company and why he was present at today's meeting.

His interrogation featured several more questions in the face of my silence. He stopped and offered that I could say it was none of his damn business. I replied that it was none of his damn business. I didn't know Pete. Information about me or anyone in my life came with privilege. He had not earned that privilege.

I turned the conversation back on him by mimicking the same questions about his family. He, too, was not forthcoming, but he caught on, telling me it was none of my damn business. That became the answer of the shift, so much so, that we said it sarcastically for the rest of our time together, even if general questions pertained to work. I liked Pete. We were going to be just fine.

Our first shift was complete. Turned out I had my permanent first shift with Pete. He only worked days. Wife wouldn't let him take a job unless it was first shift. The other three shifts were with Polack. Michael rode with Chris and

Jason. Between us we were a strong-looking shift. I needed to make sure my shift with Polack became tolerable. With his personality, I wasn't banking on it.

Michael met up with me, asking about how it went with Pete. We talked until Andy showed up, arriving in my car. The disgusted expression Michael could not hold in said it was my time to leave. I would not apologize for my boyfriend driving my car to pick me up. And he had washed it.

"Michael, he's my boyfriend. Andy is in my life to stay." He turned to me with an unfamiliar expression now.

"Boyfriend. Good luck with that. Call me if you get lonely when he abandons you. I'll be waiting."

I shook my head. This was never going to stop. I opened my back door and slung my duffel in, then slid into my passenger's seat. Oh! He had cleaned the interior. My car looked like it had come from a showroom.

"Thanks for detailing my car." He looked around, driving up the ramp.

"If you want things to last, take care of them."

I wasn't sure if that was a dig or a friendly word of advice.

"That's why I like Greg teaching me mechanics at the garage. So I can do my oil changes and know how to keep this car running smoothly." *No added remarks? He must have been just saying that then.*

"Tiffany, open the glove box and get me out the manual." I wasn't sure where he was going with this. Leaning forward, I opened the glove box and there was his gun I had taken from the warehouse. "Oh."

He glanced. "Do you have something to tell me?"

"Yes, and no."

He was watching the road and controlled this conversation.

"Let's start with the yes."

I was busted. No way of explaining this other than the truth.

"Can I wait until we are home and we have whiskey?"

His glance disapproved of my suggestion. "Then let's start with something simpler. How was riding with Pete?"

Wow, was he letting me off the hook? "Pete is good. Wanted to know all about you."

"What did you tell him?"

"Not a damn thing. I don't know him. No way is he getting anything about my life until he earns that privilege. Even then, it will only be what I choose to tell him."

"Good girl. Now about that yes question."

"Geez! Okay, fine. When I left Mildred's and all that talk about that bullet hole and the shot being meant for me, I drove to the warehouse and starting going through things."

"What were you looking for?"

"I don't know. Anything that made any kind of sense. I looked at the photos – oh, not to change the subject, but why aren't you smiling in them? Every single photo you just won your title and nothing. No happy moment."

"That wasn't a good time in my life. It was just me and Mom. Dad was gone."

It clicked. All of it clicked in my brain. His look, not of a killer but of holding in pain from the loss of his father. I stared at him. I wanted to . . . I wanted to . . . This man shut out everyone and here he was trying to let me in.

"I took the gun because I was afraid. I didn't know what to think. If you were coming back to finish the job and kill me or I don't know . . ." We drove in silence for a good minute. Then he spoke.

"That gun is unregistered. No one can trace where it is from or the owner. Be careful when you take things from the warehouse. Your car was unlocked this morning, remember. Anyone could have broken in and taken it."

I wasn't sure if he was mad or just warning me. We pulled up to the warehouse.

"Grab your duffel, Tiff."

"Should I take the gun in?"

"No, you can have it. I have a holster inside for you."

"You're giving me an unregistered gun?"

"It's your responsibility now. Don't get caught with it."

He was giving me a gun. I had my own gun now. It was illegal, but it was mine. I walked in and Kitten was there. There were roses and a bottle of champagne.

"Did I miss something?"

He took my bag from me and placed it on the chair.

"This is my life, Tiff. Everything here and all around, I earned, I bought. I want to share it all with you." He lowered on his knee. "Tiffany, will you marry me?"

Tradition. Andy, if nothing else, was traditional. My heart swelled, as did my eyes. I wanted this moment more than anything. He pulled the ring from his pocket.

"This was my great-great-grandmother's ring. It was her mother's ring, a former lady of importance in Scotland. One of the few things she had when she fled to America. One of the last things my father gave to me before his death. When I left at the beginning of the week, it was to retrieve this. It's been hidden and locked away for a long time. My mother wants this more than anything, but my father gave it to me. Grandmother didn't like Mom." He opened his hand as tears rolled down my cheek. "Tiffany Chanler, will you be my wife?" He opened his hand, and I was already nodding yes.

"Yes."

He stood, wiping my tears away and kissing me like it was our last. Andy was so happy. He fumbled getting the ring on my finger. I wiped my tears away, looking at my engagement ring.

It was small. The diamond was tiny. Andy walked past me to open the champagne. He poured us each a glass. I tried to stay in the moment, but the stone was so small. I expected bigger. I couldn't wear this ring. The comments from my mother and Hannah. Oh, I could hear them now. I knew he was on the cheap side, but he could have put better effort into my engagement ring. This was the only piece of jewelry besides my wedding ring that I was going to wear. He started talking about selling my condo and this being our home. Just one place.

I stopped looking at the ring, but my fingers were playing with it and turned it around so only the band was showing. This I could show. He looked down and fixed it, showing the diamond chip.

"I expect it will take getting used to wearing." I could feel my eyes widen, trying to agree with him as I faked a smile. I downed that glass of champagne. "How's the leg from driving all day?"

"A little crampy, but good."

"I'll start you a bath. You just relax, babe. I'm making dinner tonight, too. Make up for the past week you had to do everything on your own."

CHAPTER FOURTEEN

The negative comments about this ring were going to be a disaster. The story behind it meant nothing to me. His mother could take it for all I cared. A carat was an acceptable size for my social status. Even a flawless half-carat. But this chip? It was less. So much less. This was karma mocking me because I rejected my wealthy upbringing most of my life. My mother was going to say something insulting, and it would hurt Andy's feelings for sure. Perhaps I should tell him we needed to keep this safe somewhere and that I wasn't the engagement-ring-wearing type of woman.

I squinted down at it. Man, it was small. Andy walked in and cupped my hand between his. He grinned.

"I will call my mother tomorrow to tell her. Hopefully, you can wait, too. I want tonight to be about us." Kitten walked in purring. He glanced down. "Just us, okay?"

"Yup, just us." Good. I didn't need to tell anyone. I would take this one day at a time. Andy did all the talking at dinner. After, he shared some file about me at Angel Wings; all I heard was blah, blah, first time I saw you, blah, blah, blah. I faked a smile as he pointed to a report.

My mother texted my schedule for the next seven weeks. Hannah's important dates were underlined and had notes about what they were for. Andy took my phone when I told him what she'd sent, and he sent the schedule to his printer. The sheets printed out and he collected them, taping my schedule up in command central. He also programmed all the dates into the reminders app on my phone.

"Tomorrow morning you can tell Hannah and your mother."

I paid attention to that. "Why tomorrow?"

He gently took my ring hand into his. "Tomorrow Hannah needs you to be at the dress shop for measurements between ten and noon. You can announce it, get it over with in one telling."

I shot up and started pacing. "No. No, no, no. This is Hannah's moment. I will not take away her attention. She is getting married in seven weeks. It's all about Hannah. I am not going to steal her thunder."

He sat back. "Okay . . . I thought . . ."

"No, Andy, you don't do that to your best friend. This is something she has been planning since kindergarten. My announcement can wait until after her wedding."

"What about your mother?"

"She is so busy helping Hannah. I'd hate for her to feel guilty about not celebrating me. I would like to wait until after."

"I wish I had gauged how strongly you were opposed to sharing the news before I asked."

I felt terrible. This was a moment to celebrate, no matter what else happened in our life.

"I'm sorry. I don't mean to be like this. I'll find a way to mention it quietly to my parents."

"Good, because I already asked your father for your hand."

"*What!* When?"

"Today."

"How? I mean, did you call him?"

"Yes and visited their home."

"You showed up to their suite? Was my mother there?"

"No, she was out."

"What did you say to him?"

"Are you okay, Tiffany? You sound upset."

"I just don't want this to interfere with Hannah."

"I think you are wrong about your best friend. But Richard was home alone. He gave me his blessing and said he would leave it up to you to tell Priscilla." I let out a breath I hadn't realized I was holding. "Tiffany, come here." He pointed to the chair next to him. "I understand this came as a surprise. I realize it means a lot to you that Hannah is in the limelight. You are mine for the rest of my life. I am perfectly fine with how you need to deal. I've adjusted to the idea for several weeks now. I knew I was going to ask you. I realize we are a lot alike that way. Babe, you tell everyone when you are ready, okay? No pressure. In it together, babe." He kissed the side of my head. I nodded. "But I am still informing my mother tomorrow."

Well, that was just great. The woman already hated me. Presumably, she would try to kill me. There. Worrying about this ring? Solved. Or possibly I could bargain with her to take the ring and leave us alone. Even better solution.

I woke up exhausted. How was I going to hide this ring without insulting Andy? I was about to leave; he stopped me.

"Because we are waiting to announce our engagement until you are ready, you shouldn't be already engaged." My head tilted. He took my hand. "Let's keep this safe until you're ready to show it to everyone."

I understood. "Ah, yes, good idea. Here." I handed him back the ring.

"Enjoy your dress thing."

I grinned. "It will be more fun measuring for my wedding dress."

Andy kissed me on the lips. "I'll be taking those measurements."

I gasped, "Please don't tell me you will make my wedding dress."

He shyly laughed. "No. I'm only good at undressing you. Not covering you up."

I nodded. "Lucky thing you referred to me specifically."

He turned that shy grin up a notch with a little seduction.

"Only you."

I made my way to the address in my reminders. This was the bridal shop Hannah had picked. There were Mother and several other bridesmaids drinking champagne and being measured.

"Tiffany, darling!" Mother made her way toward me. "I realize you are working after, so yours is sparkling water in a champagne flute. I took it and shot it back like it was whiskey. She put her hand to her chest in a pleasant but shocked smile. "Is everything okay, dearest?"

I placed the flute back down on the tray. "A lot on my mind."

"Michael called; he's worried about your new partner. You know, I will never understand why you are not with him. He cares so much for you."

"Don't start." I barked out. That was one thing Michael would have gotten right. He would have bought a big rock for me. I wouldn't have had to hide his ring. I touched my finger. As much as I didn't like the ring, my finger felt naked now.

"Tiffany!" Hannah squealed from the other room. "She's here! She's here, she's here. My maid of honor, everyone." She threw her arms around me, doing a little hop.

"Okay, I'm here, you can let go now."

"Never."

"Let go."

"No, my wedding, my moment with you." She held me a little longer, making an *mmm* noise with affection. "There. Thank you. Do you want to see my dress?"

"Oh, that's right, you picked it out."

"Priscilla found it. They shipped it over here yesterday." She spun, announcing to everyone. "Shall I put on my dress?" Cheers erupted. "It needs altering, but you'll get the idea."

I poured more water in my flute. This was going to be a long morning.

Mother stood up and jerked her head for me to follow.

"Seeing all these dresses made me think about your wedding someday." Damn it! My father blabbed. "When I spotted this one, I said to myself, now this is Tiffany." She pulled a similar dress to the one I kept a picture of in my Tiffany box. Only this one was in white.

"This is Hannah's day. I don't want to talk about my wedding dress."

"Of course, but I came across this and dreamed about you."

"It's nice, but let's focus on Hannah."

"Tiffany? Is there something wrong?"

"Hannah. We are here for Hannah."

"Something is upsetting you. Did you fight with Andrew?"

"No, why?"

"You seem agitated. Don't worry. There are no expectations of you getting married. I'm simply caught up in the moment. A mother can dream, you realize."

Oh, phew. Okay, I was overthinking. Father hadn't said anything.

We were walking back in, and Hannah stood on the little stage looking down, swishing her dress, her smile a mile wide.

"What do you think, Tiffany?"

My hand covered my heart, awestruck. She was beautiful. She looked like a model for a bridal magazine. Happy, elegant, like a Cinderella at the ball.

"Wow, isn't George a lucky guy?" She reached for my hands.

"Wait until you see your maid of honor dress. Andy is going to be speechless when he sees you in it. I won't be one bit surprised if he proposes to you and we plan another wedding."

I choked on my water. My mother came at me with a napkin to cover my mouth. Hannah laughed, twirling her dress around.

Mother ordered little tea sandwiches for the bridal party, and we found a quiet corner to talk while the measurement continued.

"Washington is our destination. Your father is looking at real estate as we speak."

"So, Henshaw is Audrey's now?"

"Soon. She already has a potential merger on the back burner for when it's completed. She deserves the company. Our hearts haven't been in it for a while. As much as that contract hurt us, it has saved us."

"Washington, hum? Still getting a Bentley?"

She smiled. "Absolutely."

"Did you tell Mildred?"

Mother sighed. "Yes. Between you and her, my heart is going to ache leaving here."

I reached for her hand. "With technology today, you won't miss us at all."

"True." She nodded. "And your father is searching for a place with an in-law apartment attached, so when you or Mildred come to visit you will be in your own space."

"Nice, maybe I will spend my vacations with you."

She tapped the top of my hand with her free hand. "I would love that." She met my eyes. "Are you sure everything is all right?"

I wanted to tell her. Someone, anyone. She would understand. My mother knew me. I made a promise to her not too long ago about building our relationship so we would be closer. I blew it a few weeks ago by accusing her of wrong intentions when I found out Jordan was staying over. She deserved better from me.

Mother was the product of her environment. She continued along, playing nice, trying not to ruffle feathers. It took losing a contract for her and my father to separate themselves from the cutthroat society of which they prided themselves on being a part. They'd found new energy. I needed to be on board with them going forward, especially since they were moving in the near future.

"I have something I want to say." I heard Hannah laughing, welcoming George's sisters. I only had a minute before we had to wrap up our private conversation and join the group again. I had her full attention, like everything in the background had faded away. She was completely focused on me.

"What is it, dear?"

"Andy . . . proposed to me last night."

She gasped, her hand automatically touching her chest. I pointed my finger at her, growling in warning and serious about staying in Hannah's moment.

"Not one word. This is Hannah's time." She looked around wide-eyed, acknowledging my request with a slight nod.

"Tiffany." She whispered, taking both my hands into hers. "You said yes, right?"

"Yes, but there is a problem."

"Problem? How can there already be a problem?"

"He proposed with his great-great-grandmother's ring. It's tiny. I am being so petty, but I expected . . . more. I'm worried what people will say. I don't want him to be hurt. He is so proud."

She quieted down. "You are not petty. It's your exposure to luxury from your upbringing. You are the most unselfish young lady I know. What size is the diamond?"

"Tiny, a chip."

"What do you mean 'chip?'"

"Like, a sixteenth of a carat, perhaps?"

"Oh, I see. Not suitable in today's standards, especially since we come with money. Andrew works for himself, correct?"

"Yes."

"And he has steady income?"

"Yes, one of the best in his business."

"Investigation you said. How much do private investigators make?"

"He makes upper-six-figures, I think."

"Is he a gambler?"

I cracked a smile. "Other than taking a risk on me? No. He does not gamble, or drink, or have any other wasteful habits. I am worse than him."

"You do nothing. How can he be worse than you?"

"Exactly."

Mother gasped. "He's cheap! Oh dear, it's wise to be thrifty, but being a miser is not a good trait. Make sure you keep your own bank account. Over-spending is as bad as not spending any of the money you earn. How bad is he?"

"He's not that bad. He is thrifty. I'm the only woman he has ever been close with."

"Why? What is wrong with him? Does he have a family?"

"It's his work. He doesn't get close to people because he sees all the bad in humankind. He's military, seen a lot in his time."

"Does he have PTSD?"

"No."

"Is he an only child?"

I was insulted by the way she said that. "*I'm* an only child."

"That's why I am asking. Only children are independent."

"Yes, he is an only child."

"Are his parents alive?"

"Mother."

"Did you meet her?"

"Briefly."

"What was your impression?"

I chuckled. "She was not impressed by me."

"By you? You are lovely. How could she not fall in love with you?" She gasped. "You didn't tell her you delivered body parts, did you? I don't believe she would get your sense of humor at a first meeting. You need to stop doing that to people. Your first impression is everything."

"No, I said nothing about work. She didn't like me instantly."

Hannah called to us. I stood up for her to see me, holding my index finger up. "Be right there." She grinned and continued with her bridesmaids.

"Is he a mother's boy?"

I was sure my expression gave my answer.

"Oh dear. A penny-pincher and a mother's boy. Are you sure he is the one?"

"Mother! Yes, Andy is the one."

"Your work is cut out for you." She stood in front of me, expressing confidence. "But if anyone can handle it, it is you, Tiffany. You are strong, smart, and determined. And you will make a wonderful wife to Andrew. He will learn that he can't take money with him and to enjoy it while still living."

"I only want a ring that no one will make fun of. I'm not asking for the Hope Diamond. Just something that better suits me."

"I understand, trust me. Leave it to me. Bring your fiancé over to dinner tomorrow night. We will celebrate and bring the ring. I want to see it."

"There's a history with the ring. Andy is so proud that he proposed with it."

She smiled that confident, motherly, understanding smile.

"I will fix this with grace and decorum."

"Please don't make him feel bad."

"Trust your mother, Tiffany."

"Tiffany?" Hannah called from the other room again.

CHAPTER FIFTEEN

Not one word was spoken about my engagement. Mother kept her word, and we made this time together all about Hannah. Mother did however ask that they hold the dress she picked out for me. I saw them slip a yellow hold card on the hanger as she walked by, telling me to mind my own business. I shook my head, grinning a little, watching her play it like this was an everyday thing.

Hannah was in her happy place. By the time it was over, and we were ready to leave, I still had a few hours before my shift started. We were all invited back to her steakhouse restaurant for a proper lunch. I wanted to get a few hours in at the garage before my shift, but I played the dutiful maid of honor and followed the crowd.

Florence wanted to hear all about it. She sectioned off the back-area tables all decorated with white, grey, and violet balloons with sparkly confetti sprinkled about. The look on Hannah's face showed clearly that she hadn't told her mother of the change in location yet. Florence was grinning from ear to ear about how beautiful this restaurant was going to be decorated for the wedding.

It turned out only some of us knew of the new venue, and some meant George, his sisters, myself and Priscilla. It turned very awkward for a few moments as Hannah barked under her breath not to say anything, and she would tell her mother tonight. Mother ordered a martini, leaning into me.

"And all I have to worry about is a stingy son-in-law. Never keep things like this from me. You can see how this is going to hurt Florence, can't you?"

I whispered back. "She is going to hate you when she finds out that you were in on this and said nothing."

"I have immunity. Hannah swore me to secrecy. Besides, I'll be in Washington in a year."

"None of that is going to help you now."

My fiancé texted me that he was going to the range this afternoon to recon a new location. I wanted to go to the range and scope out whatever area he needed information on. My concerns grew about my shift. I had to establish ground rules with Polack.

Everyone was stepping in, trying to be my hero. I didn't want or need a hero. I needed him to respect me enough to know he had my back if something went down. My shift had higher than normal odds. I was a target for some reason. I assumed that was why they'd paired us up. He looked intimidating, and he acted like an ass – good deterrents in this field. I didn't need Andy or Michael or anyone stepping in. I was not a helpless woman. Yes, the guy was a major jerk, but I had him for three shifts. Time to keep this professional.

The shift started, and Michael asked how the dress fitting went. I gave him a brief synopsis. He smiled and commented that Hannah must be very excited. He was genuine about her wedding excitement. I liked that about him. I let him in on the secret that the venue had moved both in location and in date. He was invited, so this would give him time to change his day off. He deserved to be there, too, no matter what was going on between us. Hannah liked Michael; they had become friends.

Polack didn't look at anyone. I asked him to pick up the paperwork and he erupted, "What? That's my job now?"

My face scrunched. "Your job now? It's the co-pilot's job, always. We'll discuss this in the ambulance, go over who does what so there is no guessing. See you in there."

He turned and headed to the booth. I did my outside check of the vehicle. He clearly viewed it as nonsense, sarcastically asking how much longer I was going to be. I ignored him and finished when I was ready.

I told him we were stopping for coffee. Again, he gave me attitude, announcing he didn't drink coffee, instead pulling an energy drink from his bag. No coffee or donuts for him again. That was almost a good thing. I only came out with coffee. The donuts I would save to share on my days with Pete. I explained who did what on our shift. He made it obvious that when I spoke, he wasn't listening. Man, he was doing this to annoy me, and it worked.

When he was inside with a delivery, I wrote down all his duties, taping them to the dashboard in front of his seat. I titled his name in large letters across the top. When he climbed back in the cab, he looked at it and tore it off, crumpling and tossing it in the back. I didn't react in the slightest. I casually mentioned if he needed to refresh what his duties were I had them listed on the report; he could pick up a copy of it if he needed. If looks could kill, I wouldn't have to worry about my engagement ring. I wouldn't need it anymore.

Jen waited on my next dock for my ambulance to back in. It was nice to see a familiar face. After my birthday party last year, we'd become friends. She was equally happy to see me climb out. She escorted Polack in the side door, returning to catch up on the past seven months.

We picked up right where we had left off, only this time we exchanged phone numbers, promising to meet socially. Polack asked her for her number as well, leaving the both of us wearing the same look of disgust. He didn't get it and mumbled "dyke" under his breath. When he was in the cab, I clued her in on him as much as I was allowed. She told me cautiously to watch myself with him. I agreed.

Michael called halfway through, checking to see how it was going. Andy texted, as well. Other than Polack's disregard of duties and the dyke comment, the evening remained uneventful – exactly the way I liked it.

Michael was already at base when we pulled in. He and Chris wanted to hear how it went. Polack walked out after dropping our paperwork off and turned, confronting all three of us.

"If you three think you are going to gang up on me and cause trouble, you have another thing coming. I will eliminate all of you and anyone in my way. Got it? And you, princess, keep your fucking mouth closed and mind your own business. I didn't realize you and your girlfriend were in a brief love exchange. Should have pegged you for a dyke."

Michael stepped across me, backing Polack up against the wall, pointing in his chest, right in his face. Both men were breathing hard. Michael had the height advantage, finally gritting out that he had better watch his step. Chris held my arm back.

"Let it go, Tiffany. There is no reasoning with his kind. Just fill out reports. Management will be forced to deal with him, eventually."

I shifted my weight, releasing the tension from her holding me back. She was right. Start a paper trail and keep adding to it. They would have to deal with him or be sued. Michael watched for any movement from this guy in an alpha-showdown staring contest. Polack looked away first. He seemed to do that. *How interesting.*

Andy sat at his desk with all his monitors on. Kitten greeted me at the door. He swiveled his chair. "How did it go?"

"I like Pete much better."

Andy turned back to his computers and shut them down one by one. "Do you want me to have a word with him?"

I laughed. "I believe you have done enough."

He stood, walking toward me as I put down my duffel bag.

"Other than work, how was your girl thing?"

I genuinely grinned.

"My girl thing? The dress measurements turned out well. Hannah's wedding dress was there; it's so pretty. She is going to be beautiful."

He caressed my cheek with his thumb. "As will you."

"About that. I told my mother we are engaged."

He smiled. "You did?"

"She's thrilled. They would like us to have dinner tomorrow night."

He bobbed his head. "I think I can make that happen."

"Did you tell your mother?"

His facial expression became a blank slate. "Yes."

"And?"

"Not the same reaction as your mother."

My shoulders sagged. "What is her problem? I mean, really? Why can't she be happy for you?"

"She's crazy. She's not like other mothers. It's only been her and me for a long, long time. She'll come around."

"She doesn't have to. I mean, come around. I am perfectly happy with her staying away."

"I also told her we are living together."

"Is that something you needed permission for?"

I walked around him, irritated now. He let me pass.

"Tiffany, no. I do not need permission. She has old values. She's not . . . I'm not even sure how to say this."

"A prude?"

"Puritan, but only on that one value."

"Same thing. Now it makes sense."

"What does?"

I thought about her conversation, calling me a slut.

"Never mind, not worth repeating."

"What did she say to you?"

"Nothing that she probably hasn't said to any of your other girlfriends."

"She's never met anyone. I've never told her about any relationship I've had. Only you."

"Does she think you were a virgin before me?"

It was clear from his stuttering that he didn't know how to answer me.

"Doesn't matter. I won't have to see her. Let's get through Hannah's wedding without saying anything about us. She deserves to be in the limelight all by herself."

"Okay, babe. I am happy you told your mother."

"Me, too. At least I can talk to her about it. Hey, what kind of wedding do you want?"

"Whatever you want. I'm happy to go to the courthouse if you want. This is your day. Just tell me when and where. I will make sure I am there."

I laughed. "I don't know. Never thought I would get married. Mother always joked about a campfire and a bucket of beer."

"Hey, even I can do better than that."

"Hannah said I would be happy getting married on a gun range."

He softened. He liked that idea, shaking his head.

"No, too many chances of guests making you a widow after we say our vows. No guns."

"Hmm, something small perhaps?"

"I like small."

"There are only a dozen people I can think of."

"Cross Michael off the list."

"Michael, why?"

"Because it is my wedding, too. I don't want him there."

Poor Michael. "But he's my friend."

"I am sure I can dig up a girl from my past and add her to the guest list."

"But he was never my boyfriend."

"Cut the crap, Tiff. No, Michael."

This was going to hurt his feelings. "Okay."

Andy relaxed. "Come on, let's get to bed."

CHAPTER SIXTEEN

Andy and I were going in two different directions today. He was on a new job and that meant a lot of homework on his end. I planned on heading to my grappling class, then visiting Mildred because she needed to get her suspicions about Andy out of her head. I was also planning to tell her I was engaged. She was my godmother and had every right to know, no matter how much I wanted to keep this secret. Besides, it would give Mother someone to talk to or complain to about my wedding/non-wedding.

Grappling was more learning about close-contact arm ties, tangling opponents' arms and subduing them. I wish I'd learned this stuff a year ago. That staged hijacking outcome would have been a lot different if I had known this stuff. I could only bend fingers back at the time. These techniques were useful. I might even try them on Andy later.

Mildred's stop turned out not to be the joyous visit I thought it would be. She did not like Andy and asked me to think carefully about a life with him. I didn't dare mention the ring. She would have made it worse than it already was.

The garage turned out to be my source of tranquility. Greg was happy to see me, with four oil changes waiting. An hour into it, I heard someone clear their throat behind me. I turned.

"Detective Diaz?"

He looked around. "Miss Chanler. I stopped by yesterday, but your boss said you were back to driving. Congratulations."

"Thanks. How did you know you could find me here?"

"Your boss said that you would be in here this afternoon."

I was surprised he would do that. He didn't like cops.

"What can I do for you, detective?"

"This Reardon fella, when you were in your appointment, did he . . . was he off? I mean, inappropriate?"

"Yes. Had the air conditioning turned down low. I wasn't wearing a sweatshirt."

"Air conditioning?"

I looked at him with my eyes wide because he wasn't catching on.

"So parts of my body reacted to the cold?" He still wasn't getting it.

"I used a magazine to cover my chest."

Now he understood. "Oh. Oh . . . sorry. Anything else?"

I didn't want to tell him. Nothing good would come from telling him I took Reardon's phone and gave it to Andy. Besides, Andy didn't need to be involved with this shit.

"When he stepped out for a moment, I found a camera behind a picture. When I opened the door, he was standing on the other side, so I knocked him on his ass and walked out."

The detective grinned. "Receptionist mentioned that. Have you been in contact with him since?"

"No. Why?"

"He's been missing. Got a report in and it's been almost a week now. Didn't know if possibly he approached you. He has contacted others. That's why I am asking."

"I haven't seen or talked to the pervert. I intend to keep it that way."

He extended a business card. "Just in case you think of any more information."

I took the card. "Will do. Is that all, Detective Diaz?"

He looked around. "That's all. Stay safe, Miss Chanler. I don't know about this guy. He's a loose cannon and might be dangerous."

"I have nothing to fear from him."

"I . . . um, yeah. Call me with any information."

He still stood there. "Is there anything else?"

"I . . . yes, your boyfriend is Andrew McMillan, correct?" Now he needed to leave.

"And?"

"Oh, no . . . sorry. Didn't mean it to sound like that. Job hazard. I am a fan. The guy is impressive."

"I will let him know."

"Okay . . . okay . . . Thank you. Good day, Miss Chanler."

I arrived home by five. Andy texted and would be home soon. I showered and readied myself for dinner. Andy followed the same pattern when he arrived. He pulled out his family ring, smiling when he placed it back on my finger. I hoped my mother showed a good poker face tonight because I kept turning it around so only the band would show.

I checked it before we entered my parents' home to make sure I didn't subconsciously spin it.

My mother greeted us with affection and congratulations, with my father following right behind her, hugging me and shaking Andy's hand. Mother eagerly asked to see the ring that I had managed to spin between the door and here.

"Oh, just a band?"

I fixed it. "Sorry, not used to wearing a ring."

She half-smiled, I think out of sympathy for me. Andy moved right in with the history. Mother held my hand, observing the chip.

"This must have been royalty in its day."

Andy grinned. Mother asked if it had skipped his mother or if she was passing it on to Tiffany. He briefly revealed that his mother was not a favorite with his grandmother and the ring had passed directly to him. Mother asked if he had any ideas about updating the ring, showing him my grandmother's ring with added diamonds on each side, giving a more modern look, and how Richard had personalized it to show it had come from him. I didn't know her ring was a family ring. His family disapproved of their marriage, as well.

Andy clearly had not thought about altering it. He looked into my eyes as I waved it off.

"Smells good, what's for dinner?"

It clearly bothered Andy. He was quiet during dinner. Father announced he'd found a few houses in Washington.

They were flying out soon to look at them. Mother assured me everything was on track for Hannah's wedding. Florence was even on board with the change in venue, but she had made it clear they would supply the food, and that was it. I think Mother was helping with the cost. She was very carefree, talking about all the decorations and swag for the wedding.

After dinner, my parents talked about our living accommodations. Father asked where we were going to live. Andy took over the conversation, telling them we were living at his place, and most likely selling the condo. Mother interjected.

"We will buy the condo. It would be perfect when we come back to visit. Richard will still have business connections here."

I spoke up. "I'm not sure I want to give it up. Oh, we have a girl living on the second floor. She has a two-bedroom. She might sell shortly. Her mother passed away, and she inherited it."

Andy looked at me. "I suppose when I am gone for periods of time the condo is smaller and less to take care of."

"Oh, not that. It's the first place I ever bought on my own. I'm not sure I want to give it up. Besides . . . like Mother said, they can use it when they visit, or any other out-of-town guest."

His eyebrows raised. "Like my mother?"

I spread my smile. "Yes, oh yes. She can have her own place."

Father insisted. "Well, if you keep it at least let us pay for half. Priscilla is right. There will be times we have to fly back and having a place will be easier."

"I would go for half. You move some of this furniture in, I will move some of mine to Andy's place."

He thought about that. "Is there room?"

I narrowed my eyes. "Plenty. It would be nice to have a sofa."

Mother looked shocked. "You don't have a sofa? Where do you sit?"

"He has a bachelor pad. Next to no furniture at all."

Dad nodded his head. "If it wasn't for Priscilla, I would have a desk and bed."

Mother tapped his arm. "If it wasn't for me, you wouldn't even have a bed. Perhaps a mattress on the floor."

"What's so wrong with that?" asked Andy. I laughed out loud as they both turned to him.

We arrived home, and I slipped the ring off so Andy could put it away. He asked, "Do you like my family ring?"

Oh boy. "I like it."

"But you don't love it?"

"I . . . um. It's just . . . it's your great-great-great-grandmother's. I love the history it has. But it's not from you. 'Outdated' was the word Mother used. I think that is an appropriate term."

"Classic is a better term."

I smiled in empathy. "Classic. It may have come from your family, but it didn't come from you. That's all."

"I don't know what you like."

"See, you didn't ask. How are you to know when you don't ask?"

"So, you don't like it? Is that the reason you are not wearing it?"

"I never said that. However, I remember telling you that I am not taking away from Hannah's spotlight, okay? Drop it. I am not going to wear any ring, so it's moot. I've got to get ready for work." I walked past him, gathering what I needed for tonight. He was dressed to leave as well when I emerged from the bathroom. I observed him pouring two thermos containers with coffee. "One of those for me?"

"I wish you had grabbed a few hours of sleep today."

"I slept plenty."

"But you will be up all night."

"By the looks of it, so will you. Where are you going?"

"Recon a potential playing field."

"You going to tell me where that is?"

His look answered without speaking a word.

"Okay. Well, I'm in the city tonight."

He nodded. "Are they keeping you on that route?"

"I do not understand what Donovan is doing. First shift was the rural area yesterday, and tonight is city. No idea where tomorrow is."

"He swaps the routes now?"

"I know, right? Makes little sense. It's not only our shift either. He is changing it across the board. We have a meeting this Friday after our shift. Perhaps we will find out his method then." I picked up my duffel bag as Andy handed me my thermos. I grinned. "Thank you." He kissed my forehead.

"Be careful tonight. Keep alert with Bartek. I don't trust him."

"He's a colossal idiot. Needs longer to figure things out."

"Well, he better not put you at risk. That's all I am saying."

"I'm good." We walked out together before driving our separate ways.

Michael assured me he was a call away, still being protective about Polack. The good news was I connected with more friends on the docks, catching up, and none of them liked my new partner. He was condescending as ever. Didn't bother me, though, the way he thought it would. He was an amateur compared to the people I grew up with. No one was better at putting other people down than the social circle I was born into.

Maybe I had them to thank for making me tough-skinned, because Polack was bad at giving digs, making me crack a smile a few times, which pissed him off even more.

Andy texted at three in the morning. He wrapped up his evening and wanted to know where I was on my route. Burbank was the next stop and about an hour away. He replied he would meet me there. *Wow, this was unusual.* Polack went inside as Andy rounded the corner.

"Hey. What up?" I greeted him.

"Checking in before I head home. How are you holding up?"

"I'm fine. Go get some sleep. I'll be there in four hours."

"I might be gone by then."

"Gone? Again?"

"I have to go to the range. I don't like this job I took on. Too much room for mistakes."

"Then don't do it."

"I have to. Price is right. Besides, there is something I need to fix."

"Fix?"

"I'll try to wait to see you before I go, but no guarantees."

"Okay, get some sleep. I'll be there as soon as I can."

"How's your leg?"

"It's holding up. I will start walking more, build up to running again."

"Don't push it. You are back on your shift. Ease into it this time."

"Says the pot to the kettle. How are you feeling?"

He grinned. "Bullets bounce off of me."

"Yeah right. Too bad knives don't." I touched his cheek. It was healing nicely.

"And that's what happens when you let your guard down. Watch your partner."

"I will."

"I mean it, Tiff. The guy is going to attract unwanted attention."

"Unwanted attention? I'm fine. Go get some rest."

Andy kissed me swiftly on the lips, then disappeared around the corner. Polack came out with five containers. I spoke to the guard and dock nurse. "Hey, that is over our limit."

The nurse answered, "It's blood. We have a two-month blood drive going on here. Didn't they tell you to expect more containers?"

"No, but it wouldn't be the first time they forgot to tell us. Let me call it in."

Polack was on their side. "What's the big deal? It's just going to the next stop."

I walked away from him, calling base. They cleared it. I walked back with the okay and signed. They fit snugly in the cooler. I walked back to the hospital staff, waiting.

"If there is going to be more than this, we need to figure out a different transport method. This is all I can fit. If we package it differently, perhaps we can accommodate more."

The nurse responded. "I'll let them know. The blood drive just started so I expect it will be significantly more as we get into it."

"It's a possibility we can set up something additional, too. I'll speak with my supervisor. You mentioned the blood drive is only here, right? This is the main distribution site?"

"Yes. At least for now."

"Okay, thank you."

CHAPTER SEVENTEEN

Polack rambled on about the containers and what the deal was. It gave him something to bitch about. I explained that we had protocol that maintained the freezer dynamics and about the safety issues of not keeping everything at the proper temperature. They were precious products that needed to be handled with care and safety. He didn't get it. I was screwed if we got hijacked. He veered off-topic, asking about Andy. He was talking to hear himself talk because nothing he was saying was a direct question. I let him go about his tantrum but listened for any threats I needed to bank for later.

I was tired when we pulled back in. I warned Michael about Burbank's blood drive because he had the city shift tonight. I handed in the paperwork and made my way home earlier than expected.

Andy was still home. As I walked up the stairs, I heard him lecturing Kitten about catching mice and how it was time she earned her keep. I dropped my bag on the floor and looked at his on the counter.

I closed the door behind me and walked forward, tripping over my own bag, paying too much attention to Kitten and Andy as I fumbled the phone around in my hands. I caught my balance by stepping awkwardly, immediately feeling as if someone had pulled a cork out and punched the center of my wound. Streaks of pain shot up and down my leg simultaneously. I stumbled to the ground, dropping my shoulder into a lopsided roll as I grabbed my thigh and clamped my teeth.

I will not cry. I will not cry. I maneuvered onto my butt, pulled my good leg up while stretching my bad leg out, and rubbed.

Damn this hurt again. I stretched out as long as I could, rubbing my leg and rocking my upper body. The pain subsided. *Ouch.*

Andy was staring at me. "Are you okay?"

I stood up to walk it off; the steps were now an additional challenge. I took them at a snail's pace.

"I'll be fine. I'm not sure what the hell I did again, but when I landed, pain shot everywhere."

Andy watched me for a moment. "Tiffany, sit. I'll fix it in a minute." He turned back, scolding Kitten as I pulled the kitchen chair over. I heard her meow in protest. He was quickly removing the contents of the cat food can, complaining she was so impatient.

He glanced over his right shoulder to see that I was sitting, taking his hand off our very loud, purring kitten.

Andy turned away from her and walked to me.

"Wait here, babe. I have something that will help again." He always concocted something that would help. Andy kept his own triage closet. I bet he could actually perform an operation in an emergency. He came back with his medical bag, dragging the other chair over, sat down and probed around my injury. I watched as he pressed on a spot that nearly made me jump out of my skin.

My hands flailed, one gripping the edge of the table as I took as much air into my lunges as I could to prevent a scream. My body instantly broke out in sweat as I gripped the table hard from unexpected pain. He looked up, calm as could be, unfazed by my reaction. I gritted out through my teeth, "Don't do that again."

"I know what's going on. Glad I saw that, by the way. Now I know what is happening." He pulled out a sterile syringe and peeled open the wrapper of the needle. Grabbing a bottle of clear liquid, he inserted the needle and drew up about an inch of what he was going to administer in my leg. I stretched my neck, watching what he was doing.

"Is this the same stuff from before?"

He chuckled without smiling. "No."

"What is it?"

He glanced up at me and very confidently shared some long word that I wasn't even sure I could repeat. My eyebrows raised; he was speaking code. He pricked the needle in my leg, telling me to hold still from my jolt as he injected the chilled fluid. The medicine was cold at first, then it turned hot.

"Is it supposed to tingle?"

"Yes, but only for a moment. How about now? Still tingle?" He pressed the gauze down, looking up at me.

"No, it's going away."

"Good. Here, take over." He took my hand, and I nodded, taking over holding the square of gauze while he cleaned up his medical paraphernalia. "Hold it down good, babe."

"Okay."

He returned his bag to the closet. "This should relax it."

"It won't knock me out, will it?"

"Now there's an idea."

"Well, it needs to wear off by two. I'm going in the garage for a few hours."

"I wish you would sleep. You have another third shift."

"Then off the next two days."

I turned to see what Andy was looking at. He helped me up and asked me to take a few steps. It had fixed me. I bounced on my leg a little and it was fine. I didn't feel any pain and could still feel my leg.

"I have to leave."

"I know. Sorry for being such a klutz. Thanks for waiting for me and fixing my leg. I'm going to bed, and I'll text you when I get up."

"Maybe we can catch a few hours together before your shift tonight."

I wrapped my arms around him and pressed my cheek against his chest. "That will be nice. I sleep better when you're next to me."

He wrapped his arm around me. "Me, too."

* * *

I woke up with a sleep hangover. I should have just stayed in bed, but I promised Greg I would be in. Donovan would be there, too, so I could speak with him about the blood drive and cooler situation.

I texted the fiancé to let him know I was up and heading over to the garage. Nothing came back. He must have been busy. That was fine. Greg had two oil changes for me today and one full tune-up. I was moving up in the ranks. This was the first time he'd let me do one on my own. Well, almost on my own. He kept walking over to check on me. I asked him about our backup rigs, mentioning a potential use for a few months. He'd gotten in a nice, used van that he was going to convert. *Used van?* We walked over to the corner, and he showed me.

"This would actually be perfect for what they need."

"If they give me the extra funding, I can have it up and ready in two weeks."

I looked inside. "Could a refrigerator fit?"

"Different model, yes. You couldn't walk back here, but I can get one that holds the same capacity."

"I've got to go talk to Donovan. This is perfect."

It took me nearly an hour to convince Donovan this was a smart opportunity to expand Angel Wings. We worked some basic numbers, with the bottom line showing a thousand-dollar profit for our run five days a week. We could expand this service to just a blood run. We might even triple that number. The van was cheaper on fuel and we could run it with one employee, reaching a favorable profit margin. He was thinking. I could see the dollar signs in his eyes.

"I must bring this in front of the board. I like it, Tiffany. Will you be willing to crunch the numbers on a formal sheet? You have an excellent sense of business and know the language."

"MBA, duh."

"That's right, you have a Master of Business Administration. How about putting a presentation together?"

"No."

"Why not? This is your idea."

"I don't like to give presentations."

"I can do the presentation. You put it together."

"Hell no! That's a lot of work not to get credit for."

"Ah? But you said . . ."

"If I put together a presentation, I am presenting it. You'll fuck it up somehow and make it look bad."

It insulted him that I'd put it so plainly.

"Excuse me?"

"Every one of my classes I got screwed over by people in my groups. I vowed that would never happen again. I'll do it. Have them ready for Friday. Hey, what is with the change of routes, by the way?"

"We think certain shifts are being monitored. If we keep switching who is where, then it changes the dynamics."

"That's dumb. Who told you that?"

"It was a recommendation by the Risk Assessment Division from our insurance company. Would you like to tell them how dumb it is?"

"Gladly."

"No, you won't. Your last incident cost us an enormous chunk of premium. If they tell us to make changes, then we are making changes. I can't afford McMillan's services anymore. His rates are too high. I have to rely on the resources we have. Regardless, this blood bank van is a good idea. Make sure you are ready by Friday. Let me know if you need any figures from accounting."

I checked back in with Greg and updated him on the outcome. He was going to break down the cost of what he needed for expenses, including the paint job. I asked him for those numbers by tomorrow afternoon. He grumbled, walking away from me.

Hannah texted. There was one thing going smoothly in my life and that was my best friend's wedding. They were looking at a house tomorrow afternoon and she asked if I could go. She wanted me to listen for anything they might miss. That would be fun. I agreed. *Oh, damn it, I have a fiancé.* I needed to check with him. Texting Andy was useless. Nothing. Maybe he was home sleeping. My next stop was back to the warehouse.

No Andy. My phone chimed with his reply. *Sorry, babe, something has come up. I won't be back for a few days. Love you. Talk to you when I can.*

This sucked. I wondered how much he made because, whatever it was, this was not worth it. Kitten was waiting to be fed when I arrived. As soon as I took care of her, I walked around and pictured where my furniture would go. Two hours later I had it all marked out with tape on the ground showing what was going where. I liked it. This place would actually look like a home. I also liked my parents going in for half my condo. It would be perfect to stick his mother over there when she was in town. She already knew where to park.

Polack had a lot of questions about my past hijackings tonight. He almost seemed too curious. I hated the rural route. Too much time in the cab. Too many questions from Polack and the night dragged on. Michael texted me several times. I had to admit it was a nice break, having him check in on me. We talked about the new delivery van. I told him I pitched the idea and was doing a presentation on Friday after our shift. Michael being Michael said he would be there to help and support. I could always rely on Michael to be there.

I had no problem falling asleep. It was the dream of Andy's mother shooting me when I opened the door that startled me awake. I sat right up and looked down Andy's T-shirt at my hand, covering where she'd shot me. I lifted my hand. Nothing. It was clean. It was just a dream. I reached for my phone. Nothing from Andy, but Hannah had texted the address. I had an hour and a half to meet them.

Looking down at my phone and parking on the street, I saw Hannah's car in the driveway. They must have been inside with the realtor. I announced my arrival. Hannah called out that they were in the kitchen. George greeted with a warm hug. This place looked perfect. I poked around the kitchen. Hannah was smiling.

"Just look at the kitchen. It's perfect. Come, Tiff, come see the backyard."

There was a pool with a full outdoor fire pit and cabana area. *Wow.* The garden seating area was a little paradise.

"What do you think, Tiff?"

"What do I think? I'll be here all summer."

She clapped. "I know. It's perfect and only a half-hour to our jobs. Easy peasy commute."

"What are they asking?"

She lost her smile. "More than we can afford with the wedding. Looks like we will both be working plenty of overtime."

George called for Hannah while I walked around the backyard. We had a shooting range. Hannah was going to have a neighborhood. My mother would have liked this house. Speaking of which, they were sending me photos of a house in Washington. A lake house. I called as she apologized.

"Darling, I didn't mean to wake you."

"You didn't. I am looking at a house with George and Hannah."

"A house! And?"

"It's beautiful. Not as nice as the real estate you are looking at, but more than I would consider."

"You mean the one we just bought. You will love it. I love it. There is a separate area for you and Andy when you visit. The lake is enormous. They have a yacht club the next town over. Your father wants to learn how to sail."

"You really bought it?"

"Yes. I would like you to consider us going in for half of your place. Your father is going to work with Ralph Emery, his old college friend. He's bringing him on board, but there will still be a lot of business on the East Coast. Audrey will benefit from it, as well. This will be good. Get Henshaw back on its feet after losing the contract."

"You mean selling engines?"

"Some engines, but more like moving product."

"Oh."

"Ralph has another connection in Germany that may pick up a percent of the engines. We will see. That's a wild card, though."

Hannah was calling me. "Hey, I have to go. I'll talk with you soon."

"Bye, darling. Oh, tell Hannah everything is on schedule. I called around this morning."

"Will do. Bye, Mother." I turned, walking back to the house.

They'd put an offer in. Now came the waiting game to see if the owner accepted the price. Hannah was going to be a wreck for the next few days. I knew her too well. Stuff like this ate her up.

Nothing from Andy. I wondered what the emergency was. I stopped in my condo on the way back. There was no reason I shouldn't start moving some of my stuff right now. I had the time and energy. I packed as much as my car would hold. When I settled that load in, I realized I wanted it all over here right now. That was my new plan: hire a moving company this week and get all my stuff over here. I was so restless that I made a second trip. That was all I could do with my car. I needed a box truck for the rest. Everything was moving to Andy's place.

A text came through at eleven. Andy was going to be longer than expected. He would be home by Monday. Good. I could be all moved in by the time he got back. That was going to be such a nice surprise for him.

By ten o'clock, I was finishing up the presentation. Donovan was in for a treat. College had made me fantastic at this stuff. I printed out all five reports. I needed to pick up the presentation binders tomorrow at some point. We were on the city route, so that was going to be easy. Thank goodness I had Pete.

Coffee and donuts tomorrow morning were going to be my treat. It was my second day working with Pete, and I decided that I really liked him. He walked into the office supply store and helped me pick out the folders. Pete even loaded them with the reports for me while I drove. Now that was a stand-up guy. Michael, Chris, and Pete stayed during my presentation. They stood in the back, not saying a word. All the decision makers were in the room. I nailed it. They didn't even have to think about the benefits. All the figures pointed to a positive cash flow. Looked like we were hiring again.

Greg walked in, asking what the outcome was. Was he getting the van ready or not? Donovan gave him the go-ahead. That's all I could do for them. The hiring and everything else were Donovan's deal.

I drove straight over to my condo, impatient. I needed my furniture over at Andy's today. Who could I hire? Michael would help. No, I'd better not. I didn't think Andy would want him to know where we live.

It made me realize I wasn't going to have the freedom to have people over. This was going to be our next conversation. He was going to have to meet me in the middle about who got my new address. I called Hannah. Her brothers and cousins always looked to earn some extra cash, and I would make it worth their time. She called me back with eight recruits who could arrive in an hour and a half. I needed a box truck. Off to the box truck rental dealer I drove. I didn't like leaving my gun in my trunk, but there was nothing else I could do. No one had my keys, no one knew it was in my duffel, and I would be back in a few hours.

Darren brought his fourteen-year-old twins. This turned out to be perfect because they could watch the front door for me. Alexis was good about it, but Joel wanted to be part of the moving crew. I let them figure it out and, after ten minutes of arguing, they did. By nine o'clock I was back home with my car, pulling all my clothes from trash bags and sorting them back into my dresser.

I didn't want to give Andy too much of a shock, so I left his bed where it was and positioned my bed in the back corner between the windows. By eleven I was walking around inspecting the layout. I liked it. I liked it a lot. It made this warehouse look more like a home now. Tomorrow I would go back and clean the condo to get it ready for my parents to move their furniture in. I picked up my phone, smiling as it vibrated a text. *Good night, babe.* I replied. *Good night, we miss you.* Kitten was purring, sitting on the back of the couch. I hoped I was home before he arrived back. I wanted to see his face when he discovered my surprise move.

CHAPTER EIGHTEEN

Three miserable nights with Bartek. This guy was the most egotistical, offensive jerk I'd met in a long time. Perhaps I could suggest he drive the Vamp Van and give me a new partner. I told Jen and the other women to stand firm with this guy and write reports as needed. Jen empathized. He was not only inappropriate, he was being rude about it. I wrote him up when he started asking me if I'd ever fooled around with the men I worked with.

The only good thing about today was Andy would be home. It was Tuesday morning. I was tired after listening to that idiot all shift. I think Kitten loved the furniture all in one place. When I walked in, she lifted her head, almost smiling and lounging across the top of my sofa. I fed her and climbed in bed. I texted Andy: *I'm home. Going to bed. See you when you get here.*

Nothing in return.

Two o'clock my phone alarm chimed. Time to get up. A text from Andy had come in during my sleep saying he would be home around four. Good. Enough time to make myself pretty and clean this place to so it was perfect when he walked in.

Watching out the window only prolonged my anticipation. It was agony. Why torture myself? As soon as I looked away, his car arrived. I jumped from the window. "Daddy's home, Kitten. Now look your best."

She sat like a black lump on the back of the sofa. I walked toward the door, hearing him coming up the steps. The door opened. He froze, looking around. My smile covered my face.

"Hi, honey! What do you think?"

He surveys the setup, quietly. He stepped inside, closing the door behind him, placing his bag on the floor.

"How did this stuff get here?" he asked accusingly. *Oh.*

"I called Hannah and recruited her family. Some of her brothers and cousins helped." He still walked quietly, not commenting and straight-faced. "Well, what do you think?"

"It's crowded."

I relaxed some. "I know you're a minimalist, but it's only a few things. I didn't own much, and I like it. Everything fits perfect. See, now we can cuddle on the couch and watch TV together . . ."

He stared at the couch.

"I didn't wire anything up yet. I wanted to see if this is how you liked the setup. We can move things around."

He continued walking around some more. Kitten stretched up as he passed her. He looked over at command central. I didn't touch that area. He turned his head to the right and saw where I had set up my bed in the corner.

"I'm thinking we could get a folding panel and make that more private if we ever invite a guest over."

He turned back to me expressionless. "I have to go."

"What? You just got here? Where are you going?"

Andy passed by quickly.

"Andy?"

I tried to follow him to the door. No luck, too fast. I refused to chase after him. "Andy!"

He left, closing the door behind him. I watched as his car disappeared around the corner. *What the hell?* I looked around our place. I thought it looked nice. I did a great job picking where to put the furniture. Screw him. I wasn't going to wait for him to come back. I grabbed my bag and called Mother.

Both my parents were home looking at rug swatches and paint palettes, picking out the colors for their Seattle home. Eight months ago, I didn't think this would be possible, only here they were, together, moving forward into the future.

"Hello, dearest, what do you like? Its current state is all beige, but we are leaning toward moss and grey tones. It will complement the surrounding woods down to the lake."

"Woods?"

My father answered, "Woods surround the lake. The air feels clean. Quite a remarkable difference, wouldn't you say so, Priscilla?"

"Yes, I didn't realize how stuffy it is here. Clean, crisp air. Truly you can feel the difference, Tiffany. You are going to love Seattle." She glanced toward my hand. "Did he take the hint? Are you getting a new ring?"

I looked down, touching the bare skin. "No, we just put it away."

"Oh, I'll work on him some more."

"Don't bother."

They paused with the swatches, both understanding. Mother asked, "Is everything okay?"

Sighing and pulling a chair out, I sat.

"I'm not sure. I moved all my furniture over to his place. He's been gone since last week. He came home this afternoon and said nothing other than wanting to know who helped move my stuff, and then he left. Said he had to go but wouldn't tell me where."

"It was a surprise? He didn't know this plan?"

"No. I did it on my own."

Mother reached her hand over toward me laying it flat against the table. "He's in shock. He will be fine. Give him a few days to adjust. You said he never lived with anyone before, correct?"

"Yes."

"It sounds like perhaps next time you should warn him, let him have a say and be part of the plan. He is older, Tiffany. Men get settled in their ways and if he hasn't lived with anyone . . . It will be an adjustment for both of you."

Father nodded. "Picking out colors is not something I would choose, but your mother insisted we do this together. He will come around, Tiffany. Like your mother said, probably in shock."

Mother pulled her hand back and started to stand. "Let me make some coffee."

From their place, I jumped into a grappling class, but was only allowed to practice movements from my waist up. They paired me up with an older gentleman. Come to find out, this guy was retired police. He said I looked familiar, asking my name. When I answered, his expression changed. He grinned while simultaneously narrowing his eyes. He remembered me and was the cop who detained me one night when Mildred came to take custody.

That was about twelve years ago. Apparently, I was the only Tiffany he'd ever met. We shared a very nice conversation from that point on. I gave him my current status, and he had been following the Angel Wing hijackings. He asked about my leg, seeing I wore a brace. I complained that I keep re-injuring it. He chuckled, reminiscing about how I was feisty way back when, and commented that I probably hadn't changed. We finished with him shaking my hand.

"Nice training with you, kid. Watch yourself out there." And he left, headed for the benches.

No text from Andy. It was almost eight o'clock. Whatever. He had to get over it. When I pulled around, his car was back. Hopefully he was back. I walked in and he was sitting at command central. He turned. I put down my keys and bag.

"Hey," I casually greeted him.

He stood up, walking around the couch toward me. No way was I standing here idle. I walked to the fridge grabbing a bottle of water and doing my best to ignore his approach. He continued to advance.

"Tiffany, I wish you had waited for me to do this."

"Maybe I should have talked to you about it. But I was here alone. I didn't see the big deal."

"It's not a big deal. I grew up differently."

"Differently? What, you didn't have furniture?" Suddenly my heart sank. Maybe things got tough after his father died; perhaps they were homeless for a while.

"Were you poor as a kid?"

The look on his face showed slight insult.

"Poor? No. Different, yes." He stepped past me to grab water as well. Cracking the lid open, he drank. He backed up against the counter. "When my father got killed, my mother went nuts."

Oh good. There was a reason for her state of mind. I relaxed, backing against the opposite counter. If he was willing to talk, then I would listen. I gave him my full attention. He continued.

"She gave away everything that reminded her of him. I hid his guns. Otherwise, they would be gone, too." He relaxed his stance. "I came home one day, shortly after his death, and she greeted me at the door with a punch to the side of my head, demanding to know where I'd hid the guns. I blocked her blows as much as I could. I didn't know what to do, so I broke free and ran."

"Could she have wanted the guns to keep herself?"

"Guns were not safe in the house. She was in a meltdown."

"Where did you go?"

"To the woods. Stayed in there for three days. Dad and I had a secret cave. It's where I hid his guns. Where my grandmother's ring rested safely, stashed away. Everything my dad ever gave me, stashed safely there."

"Tell me again why the ring was hidden?"

"Granny didn't like Mom. The ring got passed on to me."

I completely understood that.

"I gave it a few days for her to calm down and returned. When I walked in, everything but my mattress . . . gone."

"What?"

He sarcastically chuckled. "I assumed she'd moved. There were only a few dishes, utensils, two towels, two facecloths, and our toothbrushes. She walked in behind me, informing me that this was how we were living now. We needed to forget about material things. Be ready to leave it all behind."

As if my heart could not sink any lower.

"Then my real training began."

"Training?"

"That's a story for another day." Now I knew why he reacted the way he did. "Look, babe, I don't like people here. Too much liability with the stuff I own. I'm glad you didn't ask Mike for help."

If he needed to switch gears, I could as well, sarcastically grinning.

"You mean Michael?"

"Whatever that knob's name is."

I let it go. All the negativity that was bottled inside me. His past was more intense than anything I could have imagined. Each one of the scars on his face, his body, told a different story. I knew that, and I wanted to hear every one of them.

"Andy, I wouldn't do that to you."

He relaxed his shoulders even deeper. "Sorry."

"It's fine. No worries. Now that you've adjusted, what do you think?"

"A few things need to be moved. I don't want anything behind me that looks like a home when I am on my computer system. Sometimes the video is on. I don't want anyone to see anything except me."

I nodded. That made sense. "We could hang a curtain."

His expression softened. "We could. Maybe?"

"Or we could swap your desk so the computers face the wall it's against."

He looked over to the desk. "That might work, too."

I finished my water, trying to lighten the mood. "Are you done with your tantrum?"

"Tantrum?" He was clearly amused by my word choice, showing a little lift at the left corner of his mouth.

"Yes, tantrum."

He stepped in closer. "Done."

That night, he surprised me. We slept in my bed in the opposite corner. Maybe this should be our new sleeping area and we could leave his mattress as the guest bed. Guest. The thought of his mother screamed inside my head. She was arriving in another week. My parents should have the condo furnished by then. They were showing their place today. Mildred was in charge of the real estate deal.

My mother texted at eight o'clock, asking if I was free to pick out flower arrangements with Hannah and her mother. This was last minute, and she really wasn't asking. More like,

I had better clear my schedule or there had better be a damn good reason why I wouldn't be there.

"Hey, Andy?"

He dressed in black cargo pants, a navy T-shirt that clung to his sculpted upper body, cooking breakfast. "Yes, babe?"

"What are you doing today?"

"I'm going to hook up the television and move some of the furniture. I would like to switch where the beds are. Move mine to the back corner."

Wow, well this was a better attitude. "That would be really nice. Is my bed better than yours?"

"Maybe."

"Would you consider enclosing our bedroom?"

"Enclose it? Like build walls up around it?"

"My shifts are all over the schedule. What if I am sleeping when you get home?"

"If you are sleeping when I get back then I will climb in bed with you. Tiffany, it hasn't been a problem the past six months. Let's not make it into one now."

I needed a different approach. He wasn't getting it. "What if your mother is visiting, and she's here? I might like a room that I can escape to and shut the door."

"If my mother is here, then it's probably a good idea not to be able to close the door on her."

What? "What does that mean?"

"There is no trust between you two."

"Andy! The woman is coming in a week. What is she going to do, try to kill me?"

He flipped the bacon. "No, she wouldn't do that."

Every red flag in my brain waved in alarm. "Am I safe around her?"

He turned the burner off. "Not entirely. I'll make sure she behaves."

"Then we need to put her up at my condo. She already knows where it is, and I will make sure it's furnished."

"I don't want her that far away. She will stay with us, and you will stay right here beside me."

"Then we will go to the condo. Let her have this place."

"No, Tiffany. She needs to see us together. This is how it is going to be."

"I don't like this, Andy. I may be working a lot of overtime while she is here."

"Anything she does, it's going to be right under our nose. We will do this together."

"Great. Psycho mom visit. How long is she staying?"

"She didn't say. Count on a week and no overtime. The sooner you two know each other, the easier it'll get."

"Is she safe around my parents? Because one of the nights I will make sure we all have dinner together. Mother will be mad if she finds out your mother was here visiting, and I didn't make the time for them to meet. Especially with them moving."

"So, it's definite?"

"Yes."

"Agnes will be fine. It will be good for her to meet them."

"I swear, if she does anything mean to them, there will be no holding me back."

"I will make sure she behaves. She will be fine."

"Good. At least we are on the same page. I have a change in plans today. Maid of honor duties. Got to go pick out flower arrangements."

"I thought your mother was handling that."

"They picked the flowers. Now they have to pick from different arrangements."

"Have fun." He chuckled.

"But I can help if you want to move the beds."

"I've got it. Go get ready."

CHAPTER NINETEEN

Flower arrangements were not my thing, and I pulled Mother out of her event planning duties by talking about the condo. This was Hannah's time. I needed to be patient. Florence offered my mother a job decorating the restaurants during the main holidays. That's when she broke the news that they were moving. Hannah turned to me.

"Our offer is accepted. You will always have a room in my home."

Whoa! How did this suddenly become "oh poor Tiffany?" I cracked a grin. It was time to reveal a little information.

"I am living with Andy now. Mother and Father are keeping my condo for when they are here visiting."

Mother added, "There is a separate wing for Tiffany and you when you come out and visit."

Hannah beamed. "Road trip!" She wiggled her eyebrows up and down.

The flower arrangements took longer than expected. I was itching to get to the garage and help with the Vamp Van. Parts were starting to come in and Danny was back doing the rebuild. Hannah let me off the hook.

"I know we all have a lot going on this week. Let's raincheck lunch. I need to get the realtor paperwork. She's going to put my condo on the market, too. Neither George nor I need to keep our places. Besides, it will help keep the cost of our mortgage payments down. Thank you all for taking the time out for me today. Love you."

When she hugged me, she held on a few seconds longer.

"I want the 411 on everything. You are leaving holes in your information. I just know it." Not much got by Hannah.

"Fine!"

She separated us. "I'm serious! Don't tell me I can't get his address out of Darren, either. He will sell you out for free beer."

I laughed. "I'll come see you. I promise."

She pulled me in again. "Good. Love you. Stay safe. No hijackings until after the wedding."

I smiled. "I don't have that kind of power."

"Well, make sure Andy steps up his game. Otherwise, he will answer to me."

I nodded. "Okay, fair enough."

Mother walked out with me. Her driver was waiting.

"Maybe you should start practicing driving, Mother."

"I will when I have my Bentley."

She made me snicker. "Maybe denting this car will lessen the pain of denting the Bentley. You know, make your mistakes here?"

"I am a very good driver. Stop assuming I am going to get into an accident."

"I'm just saying. A little practice won't hurt. Oh, Andy's mother is coming next week. Perhaps dinner one night?"

"Of course. Let me know the date as soon as you can. My calendar is filling quickly. Also, I want to know if she has any dietary restrictions."

Hmm. One way to get rid of her. "I will."

I spotted Danny. He was deep into welding. All the guts to this van were spread out in orderly fashion. Greg stood there tapping his watch and looking at me. I shrugged.

"Sorry, best friend is getting married and I am the maid of honor."

He waved his hands at me as if that was a lame excuse. My list had two oil changes and a swap out of a set of tires. Andy texted me. *What time you home?* I estimated how long this would take.

I replied: *5:00*

He responded: *I am taking you out tonight. I want you to meet some people.*

I didn't know why my stomach fluttered, but it did. Warmth filled my heart. He was introducing me to people from his circle. I whipped through my list. I needed to get home and get ready.

I rushed through the door. "What do you want me to wear?"

"Wear? Ahh . . . usual clothes."

"Dress? Dress pants? Jeans?"

"Jeans."

"Is that what you are wearing?"

He looked down. Then back up at me. "Yes?"

I smiled. "Just need to shower, thirty minutes tops."

"There is plenty of time."

I kissed his cheek and closed the bathroom door.

I wasn't taking any chances even though he looked casual. Andy wore the same clothes everywhere, the range, work, my parents' house. I knew he owned a tux. He had broken it out one night and surprised me. Almost saw him in it twice.

I wore the same outfit I met Audrey in the last month. It was casual, but my shoes brought it up to cover any social occasion. Andy complimented my choice of outfit, adding that I looked beautiful.

He drove my Lexus. I brought up the fact that, with my parents buying into my condo, we could afford a new car for him. He shot that right down with "My car is fine."

I soon discovered the reason we took my car. He was registering it to have a special sticker for the base. I now had access. I was one of them. The soldier at the gate shook Andy's hand as he quickly introduced me, still in my seat with my seatbelt on.

We were eating on the base tonight. He drove to the back where a long, low building stood. "Is this a hotel?"

He glanced at me. "Yes, also serves as a function hall. The restaurant is good."

He parked, and we walked toward the entrance. He opened the lobby door for me. Heads looked up, watched us for a moment, then went back about what they were doing.

Andy, with his hand resting on the small of my back, led me to the lounge. I heard people talking. It was busy in here. Lots more heads looked up and watched as he guided me to a table in the far back corner. Five men were talking over each other, drinking beer. One of them shushed the others as they all watched us approach. Andy introduced me, "This is Tiffany, my fiancée. Tiffany this is Troy, Richie, Harry, Sahil, Vic."

Harry slapped his hand on the table. "God damn it, she does exist."

Sahil laughed "Pay up. I told you. Come on." He tapped the table. As they reached in their pockets Andy pulled a chair out for me.

"Want anything from the bar, babe?" I scanned the restaurant.

"Water with lemon." He nodded, looking over the table. "What about you clowns?"

Richie pointed, circling another round. "Sahil just wiped us out."

Andy turned, walking toward the bar. Richie leaned in.

"You really going to marry that guy?"

I adjusted in my seat, sitting taller, making sure I looked confident. This was a table full of alpha males. I needed to stand my ground.

"That's what 'yes' generally means."

Troy sat back, amused. "Oooo, you just got burned, Richie. I like her." He grinned, picking up his beer.

Richie turned back, grinning as wide as Troy. "Then that makes you as insane as the rest of us. Welcome to the cross court . . . Tiffany, is it?"

Troy smacked Richie's shoulder. "Yah, you know, like that big fancy store." He leaned into the guys. "I bought my wife a bowl from there for our seventh anniversary. It arrived bigger than I expected. I wanted something nice for her to put cereal in. Turns out it's a serving bowl. Beautifully handcrafted, though. She breaks it out on the holidays."

Vic's face soured. "Okay, Martha. Don't give yourself an erection now."

I tried hiding my amusement.

"What? I am just saying, Tiffany's carries quality stuff."

Harry hit Richie. "Don't egg him on, next he'll be saying the word 'pottery.'"

Troy looked around to the guys. "This is why none of you are married."

Vic seconded Troy's observation. "No woman is going to take my balls. Single forever."

Troy pushed his hands at the air like he was pushing them all away. "Don't listen to them. They don't know what they're missing."

Andy returned, placing water in front of me. "They behaving?"

All the guys quieted down, whistling, looking around, innocent as could be. I smiled. "Yes."

Sahil leaned in, glancing at the men. "We have a problem, chaps. She must be renamed. Little Suzy Homemaker, over here," he shook his thumb at Troy, "has a shopping addiction. We can't have him jumping online every time we say her name."

Troy defended himself. "It was one time."

Sahil turned to me. "I've got it. Since he's Mulligan, we will call you Gilli."

I scrunched my face. "I think I like Tiff better."

Vic leaned back, laughing, pointing to me. "There's your challenge."

They all joined in, laughing, agreeing with my new name. Andy leaned over. "Golf terms."

I looked them up on my phone. Mulligan meant a do-over, a second chance to make things right. Was that why they called him Mulligan? Andy *was* the type to fix what needed fixing.

Gilligan was a challenge to do something amazing a second time. I wondered if there really was a way for me to fit into the incredible life he'd already built.

Andy settled them all down. "You wish you could be as good as me."

Harry picked up his beer. "What? You're going to break out in song now?"

I listened to their banter. Okay. I got it now. The beer round arrived. Andy drank with the rest of them. Food came around and all went quiet while we ate. They talked about current affairs. Every one of these guys knew what was happening everywhere, anywhere in the world it seemed.

They talked about "hot spots." Vic stopped the conversation, pointing directly at me. "Is this cool, man? I don't even know her."

Andy nodded. "She knows what I do."

His eyes shifted from me to Andy. Alpha males didn't trust easily. I brought Vic's attention back to me.

"What? He's saved my ass several times."

Troy pointed in the center of the table, laughing. "That's two of you. Any more takers?"

Vic sat back, unamused. Sahil lightened the tension. "It took three months for them to relax around me. I don't know why they stopped. I take their money every chance I get."

Andy brushed my arm. "I don't give a fuck what they think. I'm still marrying you. Remember, you are my Gilli now."

Troy added, "I don't have any problems here. I think Vic was unloved as an infant."

"Fuck you, Pottery Barn."

Harry laughed. "He definitely wasn't breastfed."

Vic stood up and threw down his fork, walking behind Sahil and to the bar. I watched wide-eyed.

Harry asked, "Anyone bring a pacifier?"

Sahil leaned in, "He's insecure. Nothing against you, Gilli."

Troy looked from Richie to Harry to Andy and sat up. "I'll go talk with him."

Andy held his arm out. "Just let him calm down. He will come back. This isn't about us. Something else is preoccupying him."

They looked over to him and went back to eating. I asked, to keep the conversation going, "How did you all meet?"

No one wanted to start this conversation. Andy answered for the group. "Ten years ago."

Troy interrupted, "Eleven."

Andy paused. "Do you want to tell the story?"

"No, you can't track time for shit."

He raised his eyebrows. "Eleven years ago. We all did a job together. We accomplished something few men could do. Since then, we have racked up some more events, and we are a team."

Sahil added, "We came together organically."

Richie looked disgusted. "Why do you have to bring sex into it? Sounds like we are gay."

Troy held his hand up as Sahil kept repeating "organic."

"Organic, Richie, like naturally. Not orgasmic. That's something I do with the wife, not you guys."

Sahil said, "Organic, stupid."

Richie finally got it. "Oh, yah. Okay. Yah, we just worked good together, Gilli. Had that flow going." Troy slapped Richie on the back,

"That's right. We flow."

Vic finally walked back to throw a fifty on the table.

"I gotta bounce."

Troy smacked his arm and spread his arms apart. "Sorry fellas, something has come up. Nice meeting your girl, Mulligan." And he turned and left.

Sahil shook his head. "Street Rat is running for the cheese." They all nodded, agreeing.

"Street Rat?"

Andy leaned in, his eyes narrowed, speaking softly. "Later."

I found out that none of them lived here. They were scattered all over the map. They were only here to help Andy during the next few days. He needed troubleshooting for this new job. It wasn't coming together for him. Too many holes, he kept saying. I think the reason Andy wanted me to meet them was because they were all staying in our home for the next two days. Yup. Andy tucked me in, saying goodnight and he'd see me in the morning.

I had all six of them in full camo walking into the warehouse telling me I had better have saved some hot water, while Andy started cooking. Troy liked my furniture. Sahil and Harry flipped a coin for the spare bed. I was dressed in my uniform and Troy whistled.

Harry pointed, "You let her out with that peashooter? You should be ashamed, Mulligan. That won't even break the skin."

I looked down at my 9mm, grinning. "It's all they allow us to carry."

Andy walked over, kissing me. "Have a good day, babe. We'll be gone before you get back. The guys are staying another day. We won't be back until the morning."

"Should I buy food for tomorrow?"

"Yes. Steak and eggs."

Sahil called from the back. "And vegetables for an omelet." These guys heckled each other with fantastic one-liners. I didn't want to leave. I grinned, listening. Sahil shouted, "Thank you, Gilli!"

Andy swiftly kissed me again. They all called a goodbye, except for Vic, who watched me as he closed the door. I heard Troy telling Andy I had improved the place. He liked my style of furniture. Andy agreed with him. *Are you kidding me? He had a meltdown when he first saw it. Men!*

I was stumped looking at the parking situation. It didn't feel right: six burly men, all their gear, but just two cars, one of them being Andy's. I drove to the corner, halting in amazement. I shifted my car into park and stepped out. There was a camo-painted, full-size Suburban, an old Chevy blazer, and an old Cadillac with horns on the grill. I looked on in awe. Turning back to my car, I noticed a small helicopter on our warehouse roof. Yes, a helicopter. I wanted to take a picture but didn't dare. My fiancé had very cool friends.

CHAPTER TWENTY

A helicopter. That's what I'd heard while I was blow-drying my hair. Pete said my name. "Tiffany?"

I glanced over to him. "Ah, yup?"

He grinned. "You okay?"

I nodded. "Yes, why?"

"Because I asked if we were stopping for coffee three blocks ago and now we just passed Lou's."

I slammed on the brakes, pulling off onto the next side street. Coffee and jelly donuts were a must. I put an order in for two dozen for when I was done my shift. Lou told me he would make them fresh. Had to feed my boys tomorrow morning. Perhaps I could win over Vic with a jelly donut.

Michael even asked at the end of the shift what was distracting me. I rattled off, "Wedding, parents moving, father losing his company."

He chuckled. "Okay, okay. I get it. How's your mom?"

"Call her."

He narrowed his eyes slightly. "Are you okay?"

"I'm fine."

"You're good with me calling her?"

"Yes. I forced you to talk to her so many times, it's only natural you have a friendship. They just bought a house in Washington."

"They bought it?"

"Yup. Even picked out the new interior color palette."

"Wow, that was fast. I didn't expect them to find something right away. I am really going to miss Priscilla."

"They will be back and forth. They bought my condo."

"What?"

"They wanted to downsize, and since I moved in with Andy . . ."

"You moved in with Andy? You mean moved in, moved in?"

"Yes. It's official. All my stuff in one place now."

Michael was lousy at hiding his emotions from me. "Well, isn't that just great?"

"Thank you, Michael. I need to go. We have company coming over later."

"Hope you didn't move too much over. I give it another month. He'll fuck it up somehow. Just remember I always have room. You are welcome over anytime."

"Michael!"

"Just saying, Tiff. How well do you really know him?"

"See you tomorrow, Michael." I dropped our reports and headed to my car.

This was exciting to me. I loved meeting Andy's friends. I shopped and stocked the fridge with man food, plus Sahil's veggies, then slightly cleaned up our place.

For six men staying here, there wasn't one trace of them or even Andy here today. Our bed was made, everything was in order. How the heck could they do that?

I texted Andy: *Any chance of meeting up?*

Instant reply: *No.*

I stared at the big fat "no" he'd typed. He let me meet them. Why couldn't I hang out at a work site? I knew what they all did. I started to get mad looking at the "no." Fine.

I texted Hannah I was coming down. At least there was someone who was safe to tell about my meeting Andy's friends. Florence greeted me before walking in.

"Tiffany, your mother is very talented. I can see why Hannah asked her for help."

I wasn't sure if she was complimenting me or not. "What do you think about the botanical garden?"

"It's Hannah's wedding and, truthfully, I can't blame her for choosing a different location. She lives in this place enough."

I hadn't considered that. Hannah practically lived here. No wonder she wanted a garden wedding. "Hmm, that makes sense now that you said it."

"I am also grateful it only seats a hundred and seventy."

"I understood she was scaling back because of the new house and now they need to pay for the venue."

"I am not sure your mother knows how to."

"Would you like me to say something?"

"Tiffany, when is the last time you spoke with your mother about the wedding?"

"Few days ago. Why? Has something changed?"

"Yes, please call her but not in front of Hannah."

"I'll talk to her. I know how over-the-top she gets. Don't worry, Florence. I've got this."

She nodded to me then looked past to acknowledge the couple standing, waiting their turn.

With the bar still temporarily empty, I secured my seat next to the pickup area. Hannah saw me and walked over with a water filled with lemons.

"Nice. Oh, you make it look so pretty."

She grinned. "No skimping for my maid of honor."

"Perks. I like it."

"I'm glad you're here. I have the countdown list we need to go over. One month, Tiffany. I can't believe it."

"A month and three days."

"So much is happening."

"Then take a moment for yourself."

"I can't. Not with the house. *Oh!*" She held out her hands. "We close two days before the wedding."

"Wow. Okay, we've got this. Calm down."

"Your parents are flying back that Friday."

"What? Like from Washington, or to Washington?"

"They close on their house the week before and are setting up the construction for remodel. What if something happens and their flight gets delayed or cancelled?"

I reached for her hands. "Stop worrying. They know enough people. Someone has a private jet somewhere."

"I can't do this without Priscilla. She has been my fairy godmother through this."

"Hannah? What are you so worried about? This isn't like you."

"Did you get your invitation yet?"

"No, but what address did you use?"

"The only one I have, Tiffany. Your condo."

"Oh. Okay. I live with Andy now."

"I know that! I don't have the new address."

"I think we have a post office box. I need to ask."

"I asked my brothers, but none of them knew. They just followed. They said it is in a remote part of the city. Are you living in the slums?"

I laughed and shook my head. "No."

"Why the big secret?"

"It's not . . . well, maybe? Andy likes his life private."

"You have friends and family. Are we not allowed over?"

"Of course you are. I just moved. Let me settle in and I will check my mail when I leave here. Did you get any replies?"

"Not yet."

"When did you send them out?"

"Two days ago."

"I'm not sure the mail is that quick."

"My sister called me earlier. She received her invitation today."

I tried to keep my amusement in. Hannah clearly didn't see this irrational expectation. "You know what? I bet mine is in my mailbox. You can confirm two from me."

"Not the same. Fill out the RSVP and you need to check off what you want to eat."

"Is it sit-down plated? I thought you decided on the stations."

"We did, but plated is easier for my parents' catering. There's a small kitchen, so everything has to be timed right."

"What are my choices?"

"Steak, pasta or vegetarian."

"Two steaks."

"Tiffany!"

"I'm just saying?" I tried to lighten her mood. "Hannah, they just went out. Give everyone a few days. How many are invited?"

"We cut the list to one-sixty."

"Okay, that is good. When do our dresses come in?"

"Next week."

"And your dress is here? How are the alterations coming along?"

"Fine?"

"See, we have the guy, the dress, the wedding party dresses, the invitations are out, flowers are picked, menu is planned, and you have a house to come back to." She sighed. "Where are you going for your honeymoon?"

"We decided not to go on one since we bought the house. We are moving in instead."

"Hannah, are you sure about that?"

"We are already over budget. The house is something we both want."

"What about going away some place local?"

"I want to be in my house."

"Okay, so later when things settle down. Or you can make it your first anniversary/delayed honeymoon."

"Possibly? But it doesn't matter. I am having the wedding I want, the house both George and I want, so the honeymoon doesn't matter."

"Hannah. Your bridal shower?"

There was relief in her eyes as her face relaxed. Is this what she was getting at?

"I don't care if I have one." Only, her tone said different.

"Tomorrow . . . no, I can't do tomorrow. Saturday . . . um, dang it. I don't know how long everyone is staying."

"Everyone?"

"Andy has some longtime buddies staying over. I don't know for how long."

"He has friends over and I can't even have your address?"

"Stop that. I will clear this up. I promise."

She checked on her customers with a few more coming in. I called Mother.

Apparently, I sucked as the maid of honor. Mother already had a surprise bridal shower planned, and those invitations were being mailed as soon as the RSVPs came back. This event was being held at Hannah's family's Italian restaurant, where Hannah barely spent time anymore. Florence was in on it. Maybe that was why she asked if I'd talked to Mother lately. I hung up, speculating about the next few days. Hannah came back briefly. The place started filling up.

"So, Monday I will be coming off my third shift. Give me until two to sleep. I won't put in for extra hours at the garage. You and I will go pick out your bridal registry."

Hannah bit her lower lip. "Um, I was going to go this weekend with George's sisters. They wanted me to start picking out stuff for the wedding since our offer is accepted on the house."

"Oh. Well, yes. Okay, that settles that."

"Thank you, Tiffany. I know how much you hate shopping. Just you being willing to make that sacrifice means the world to me. Wait here. I've got to make my rounds."

I finished my water and threw down a five. At least I felt like that covered the lemons she sacrificed. I caught her attention and signaled to call me later. She waved, giving in. I turned, heading for the entrance. Oh, mother of God. Not now. Blake Montgomery, walking, talking on his phone, heading right at me. And now our eyes met.

"You're fucking kidding me. Call you right back." He grinned ear to ear. "Tiffany Chanler. Hear you are broke now."

"Heard wrong." I faked a smiled.

He stopped. "No, really, if you need some money, I know of a couple of guys who would pay for you." I tried to walk by him, only he was blocking me. "Lots of men like your daddy want a girl like you."

"Last time you tried to block me, you ended up in the ER." I stretched up, examining his face. "How's the nose?"

"Fuck you."

I stepped back. "Can you afford to be in here? Or you going to do what your parents usually do and leave before paying the bill?"

He stood his ground, narrowing eyes on me. "You might be able to save your parents from poverty with that body, but you should practice not speaking." He nodded his head, eyes crawling all over my figure. "Did you know my mother started a charity funding page for your family?"

Okay, now this hit a nerve. "What?"

"Even she has taken pity on your family."

"Stay out of our fucking lives."

"Would love to, but you just keep popping up in places you don't belong."

There was no talking to him, and a good chance of round two happening. I walked around him.

"Blake, nice ankle bracelet by the way."

He looked down. "Fuck you, Chanler."

I waved my middle finger at him in a goodbye.

My leg twitched with small muscle spasms, causing me to walk oddly. Why did I let him affect me?

As soon as I slid into my car, I searched on my phone. That son of a bitch was right. Clarissa did start a funding page for my family. I called Mother immediately. This was a disaster.

I stopped at the condo on my way home. I needed to check the mail more often. Hannah's wedding invitation was there, as well as a few packages. I checked on my nearly empty condo, filling Hannah's RSVP out immediately and writing a little personal note on the back. There, that would make her smile. I opened my packages. A pair of new jeans and two short-sleeve dress shirts. I stuffed the trash in a small bag and headed back out, dropping the RSVP in the mail. Robin walked in. Shirt torn, she looked like she had gotten into a fight. She smelled like pot.

I stopped. "Robin, are you okay?"

She did not stop, just flipped me off. "Mind your own fucking business, warden."

Half of me understood her attitude. I had one similar at a younger age. But it was up to me to protect this community. My parents were going to be living in this complex at times. There were several single women and older tenants.

"Hey! I don't give a flying fig about what you do or who you do it with. Just don't bring it back here. I care about the residents, and if you bring harm to any of them . . ." She stopped, turning slightly.

"I took care of it. No one is in danger here." She turned back toward the door, disappearing up the stairs.

She took care of it? What the hell did that mean? This girl was trouble. I needed to tell Mildred.

I threw my trash out and walked toward my car, making my way to my parents' place to see what damage the funding page had caused. Never had I witnessed my mother so irate. Audrey arrived minutes behind me with a counterattack plan. Clarissa had raised sixteen thousand dollars so far. Not one of my parents so-called friends told them about this. Mildred arrived shortly after Audrey had gotten set up, initiating contact with the funding source to say this was a hoax. The embarrassment factor was the biggest blow. Mildred didn't know about this. I know she backed off from the group when Mother left. Mary wasn't on social media, so I doubt she even knew about it. Father walked in to see the chaos. "What's this about?"

Three women answered him in unison. He didn't know who to listen to. He picked Mother. "Priscilla, what is going on?"

My father didn't understand the negative effects this was having. He even considered it an olive branch coming from Clarissa. This made my mother angrier. Audrey calmed her down, explaining to Father how it was set up as an insult, disguised as a gesture of kindness. He slowly began to see the ill effects it was having on Mother. He didn't fully understand, but he sided with her anyway.

I took Mildred aside, telling her about the odd behavior going on with Robin. She had been toying with the idea of a security system. The annual condo association meeting was coming up. Perfect time to list it on the agenda.

Audrey pulled me aside. "I heard you are back driving?"

I nodded. "I am. I don't like my main partner, though. He calls himself 'Polack.'"

"Does he know that is an insult?"

"Ex-prison guard. Dumb as a bag of rocks. I think they fired him."

"Just be careful. I still love you, you know."

"I know. How's the company?"

"Richard has set up ten percent of the engines to be sold through an old friend of his. We are making progress. The numbers are recovering slowly. I think I'm going to be okay."

"Are you glad the company is now yours?"

"Not mine yet. Few more months and the transfer is final."

"Can you fix this social media funding embarrassment?"

"I just did. It's shut down. Someone needs to talk to the woman who initiated it."

"Mildred." I called Mildred over.

"Yes?"

"Can you speak to Clarissa about the social media funding page?"

"Gladly." Audrey explained what she did to end it and how they would be contacting Clarissa about the scam. Mildred learned what she needed to say to approach her on this. Mother complained that this was a social lowball, even for Clarissa.

Everything seemed to be in a calmer state, and I wanted to get home. There were six hungry men arriving in the morning. I needed to be prepared.

Father pulled me to the side. "What is your day like tomorrow?"

"I'm busy in the morning. Why?"

"What about Saturday? We can meet early."

I ticked off my plans in my head. "I believe so, but it all depends on tomorrow morning. Can I call you when I know more?"

"Of course."

"Is everything okay?"

"Yes, a few things I want to go over."

"Okay, I'll let you know as soon as I know."

"Drive safe, Tiffany."

"I will, Father."

Audrey hugged me. "Come by the office."

I quickly grinned. "I will."

Mildred and Mother walked behind me.

"We'll straighten this out, don't you worry," Mildred stated. Mother was keen to hear about anything that would distract her. I interrupted. "That new tenant at the condo. She's fine, just needs to learn the rules."

"Yes, the biggest problem with living in such a close community," Mother answered, knowing of issues she had to deal with living here. "Goodbye, darling. Drive safe."

"I will, Mother. Bye, Mildred. You know I'm working when you have the meeting, right?"

"I am aware. I will make sure you acquire the results."

"Good." I turned, closing the door.

I texted Andy I was heading back home.

Nothing.

CHAPTER TWENTY-ONE

Andy hooked up the television for me. All the electronics worked. Kitten sprawled out behind me across the sofa as I flipped through stations. There was a thud against the wall outside in the hallway and Kitten leaped off the sofa. She was already crouched down, aiming her body right at our door. I muted the TV and quietly made my way to our bed. I pulled out the .38 revolver, releasing the cylinder. Five bullets.

I crept toward the front door; we listened. I watched Kitten's ears that were much better equipped for picking up sound. They twitched a little with her sniffing under the door. She didn't make any alarmed motions and then lost interest, walking away. I couldn't imagine anyone being out there. Who would have a key to our outside door? She would have stayed sniffing if it was someone unfamiliar.

I listened with my ear against the door. I heard something that sounded like wood creaking under a footstep, triggering my heart to double its pace so it was pounding against my chest. There was no damn light in the hall. Why didn't we have a light in the hallway? That needed to change. I gently stepped away from the door, tiptoeing to my duffel for a flashlight. Found it and turned our light off.

Damn it, the TV was still on. I practiced how to hold the light alongside my revolver. This was how they taught us to hold it in training, but I remembered some of my cop shows and they held it like this. I liked this way better. I'd have to ask Andy which was correct. I listened, reaching for the doorknob. Nothing. Then I slowly cracked the door, swinging it open to scan the stairs down to the right, because that was the angle I was coming from, and up to the left.

Nothing. I listened. Still nothing. Slowly I crept down to check the door, tugging it. Secured. Nothing.

I made my way up, Kitten running ahead of me. She stopped, the hair on her tail puffed like a toilet brush. My heart pounded in my ears. She crouched slowly, moving ahead. I stepped behind her, matching her speed. She bolted ahead, my flashlight following. A mouse squeaked, scampering across the floor.

"For the love of Christ!"

I grabbed my chest as I leaned forward, letting my butt rest against the wall and supporting myself with my left hand on my knee. I stood in this position, getting my composure back. I walked the inside perimeter as a precaution. When all-cleared, I grabbed Kitten and walked back inside, locking the door. I watched out the window; all was quiet. I wanted Andy to put up some exterior lights, as well. Time for bed.

Andy texted me at five in the morning: *Heading home. Be there in forty-five minutes.*

That was my warning to get up and shower. Not sure what the men had planned, I waited before starting breakfast. They all piled in wearing full camo makeup and fatigues. Andy placed his bag down.

"Moring, babe." He kissed me like he always did and right in front of the guys. I had to say, I liked his camo stripes across his face.

Troy called out. "Damn straight, fellas. That's why we marry them."

Vic responded, "Not in my fucking life. They are a distraction. Another thing that's going to get you killed."

Andy smacked my butt. "I will die a happy man."

Troy dialed his wife as he walked out the door. "Hey gorgeous, I'll be home about three." He closed the door behind him.

Richie started pulling food from the fridge. "At least she knows how to pick a good steak."

Sahil grabbed pans out. "Richie, take out the vegetables like a good soldier."

Richie's arms were filled with the steak packages. "Get your own damn rabbit food."

Sahil opened the fridge, pulling out the items he'd requested. "Thank you, Gilli. These are perfect."

"No problem." I walked over to everyone. Harry was already sprawled on the bed in the back. Andy grabbed clean clothes and headed in the bathroom. Troy slipped back in announcing he was hungry.

"What's taking you damn people so long?" Richie had steaks sizzling in the pans. Sahil asked if I wanted an omelet with him. His looked good. I wanted one. Oh! I had donuts.

"Jelly donuts right from Lou's café. He made a fresh batch for me yesterday afternoon." Troy picked one up and nearly ate it in one bite.

"Mmm."

He gave me the thumbs-up. Richie held a hand out for one while he flipped a steak with the other. He, too, moaned with delight. Troy shouted to Vic, who declined, sprawled out on the sofa, hat pulled over his eyes. With four steaks done and two to go, Troy swapped out with Sahil, cracking eggs in the pan. I set the table and pulled all the extra chairs over. Sahil put our omelet plates down.

"You know what I want right now?"

I grinned. "What?"

"Crepes."

"I like crepes."

"I'll ask your husband if we can fly to France tonight."

I laughed. "Ah, no. I have to work. Seriously? You have a craving and just go to that part of the world?"

He shrugged. "Yes? Don't you?"

"Um, no."

"Your husband does. Why not you?"

"We are not married yet. Besides, I have a job. I can't just pick up like that and go."

"Poor Andy. No more bratwurst adventures."

"Bratwurst?"

Andy appeared behind me. "Sahil . . . are you telling on me?"

"A little. Well, Gilli, perhaps you should put in your resignation now."

"What? I'm not quitting my job."

Andy touched Sahil's shoulder. "Zip it."

Troy walked over with the plate of steaks and salt and pepper. Richie followed him with the plate of eggs. "Eat it while it's hot, bitches."

I pulled the orange juice from the fridge. Richie asked, "Got any vodka for that?"

I was about to say sorry when Andy spoke up "Hang on. I got that bottle of Goose from the last crepe escape."

Richie rubbed his hands. "Nice, straight from the old country."

Troy spoke up. "Coffee for me. Got to get home to the wife after this."

It took the smell of food to lure Harry from his twenty-minute power nap. Vic stood at the kitchen counter, eating, doing something on his phone. No one asked him to come over. I felt bad for him standing there alone. I leaned over to Andy. "Should I ask Vic to sit?"

Andy glanced over to him. "Nah, let him be."

"Sahil, this is delicious. I mean fantastic."

"Thank you, beautiful Gilli. At least one of you enjoys the art of French cooking."

Richie spoke up with a mouthful of steak, "You can keep your delicate cooking. Nothing beats a side of cow and eggs. American food."

Troy finished, bringing his plate to the sink. He washed it, dried it, and put it away. Same with the pans we used. He poured another cup of coffee and pulled a jelly donut out, biting it as he made his way back.

"Hey, where did you get that?" Harry asked, pointing.

"Gilli picked them up for us."

He finished eating as well and did the same with his plate. He lifted the box lid and took two donuts, coming back to sit. I mentioned the noise I heard last night. All of them froze, looking at me as I told the story. All eyes were now on Andy. I asked him if we could install a stairway light. He said we would talk later. Troy grinned.

"You ought to give her some night vision training." Sahil started shaking his head side-to-side repeating, "No, no, no, no."

Richie laughed. "Gilli is a long way from night training."

Harry looked over to me. "You work a fair amount of nights, right?"

I glanced from Harry to see that Sahil was still objecting, shaking his head from side to side.

"Yes, two second shifts and one third."

Harry focused on Andy, putting his utensils down.

"I'll think about it."

Sahil stopped moving his head, looking straight at Andy. "Bad idea."

Andy pumped his hand down gently. "She'll be fine."

Troy grinned ear to ear. "You're gonna have some fun, Gilli."

Sahil spoke out again. "I must protest."

Harry seconded it. "No worries, Sahil. She can handle it."

Richie leaned in. "I'm not saying a fuckin' word."

Vic cleaned his plate now. "I gotta go. I'd like to say it was fun, but you guys are a bunch of assholes." They all stood up, each one clasping his hand with a brotherly shoulder hug.

"Be safe, brother." Troy let go of Vic's hand.

"See you cats in the alley." He waved, leaving.

Troy stretched. "I gotta hit the road." They were all leaving. I wanted to walk out to see who owned what transport. Andy reluctantly walked with me. Harry was the one who had the helicopter. Richie drove the Caddy, Troy the Bronco, Sahil had the economy sedan, and Vic the Suburban. Watching them go was as exciting as their walking in this morning. I waved goodbye and we walked back in.

Andy could not appreciate my enthusiasm. He finished cleaning up, and I poured another cup of coffee. He asked what I was doing today and that landed me back in bed with him for a few hours.

My alarm chimed at one. I needed to get up and get ready for work. Andy slept right until the moment I had to leave. I tried to convince him to stay in bed, but he needed to get up and do something. I left before him and as I drove past the empty lot, I couldn't help but smile, thinking about the guys.

Bartek was especially observant tonight. He asked a lot about this route. He asked if it stuck to this pattern every time and what was going on with the new blood-delivery van. I encouraged him to put in for the route. He replied that there was no money in it.

I laughed. "It's the same pay as this." He didn't see my amusement at all. Oh well. I called Father when Bartek went in to exchange a delivery. We planned to meet for breakfast tomorrow morning. I knew he wanted to talk to me about something, and they were flying out to Washington Tuesday.

He reminded me to bring them my extra set of condo keys. They had arranged to have furniture moved over there.

Mother called an hour later. "Darling, your bed will not fit in our condo. I just remembered that we bought a queen-size for you. Would you like your bedroom set? I ordered an adorable cottage-style set for your father and me. He is going to love it. Two dressers, two nightstands. We have a matching bench for the end of the bed. He likes his bench. That is a must."

"Let me get back to you on that. I have to check with Andy."

"Oh, right. Has he adjusted to the furniture?"

"Yes, and I know he will like my other set. It's king-size and the area where it will go should fit perfectly. I just need to let him decide."

"Yes, I agree. Good plan of action. Let him decide. Okay, give me notice as soon as possible. Hannah will take it if you don't. They have that big house to fill."

"I'll ask him tonight. I'll have an answer tomorrow morning."

"Bye-bye, dear."

I hung up. Bartek was walking out with the first load. They installed temporary coolers for the extra blood. Vamp Van was almost complete. The back boxes were a little more complicated to maneuver around inside.

Michael was texting me, asking how the wedding plans were going. How did he find out? How could Michael possibly know Andy proposed to me? Mother! She must have told him. I had to wait a whole stop to call her out on it.

When we finally arrived, Jen was waiting outside, busy on her phone. She tucked it in her pocket and walked toward me.

"Hey Tiff, how goes the battle?"

"Long. But I refuse to complain. At least I am finally back at work."

"How's your leg? I see you still favor it."

"That's not because of the original injury. I keep fucking it up. As soon as it seems better, I overdo it. Vicious cycle."

"You look good. I would have gained twenty pounds." She looked me over, leaning in, whispering "bitch" in a playful tone.

"Oh, I gained weight, all right. I became a mad woman with cardio when I tried on my uniform and could barely button it. This is the cause of my gimp walk now."

Jen laughed. "Good to hear you are like the rest of us." She handed me back my clipboard, waving Bartek to follow. I called Mother.

"Hey, did you tell Michael I am engaged?"

She sounded confused. "No. Why are you asking me that? I said I would keep it hush-hush."

"He texted me, asking how my wedding plans were coming along."

"Your wedding plans? Are you sure he was not talking about Hannah?"

Right at that moment I felt like an idiot and sighed. "That is probably it. Sorry about that."

"Tiffany, slow down, dear. We all have so much on our plate at the moment. Although, I can see this is going to eat you up. Tell Hannah. She will be excited for you. It will not affect her wedding."

"No. I can wait. It's only a month."

"Dresses come in this week. And don't forget to let me know as soon as you can about Andrew's mother. What is her name again?"

"Agnes."

"That's right. Such an old name. You don't hear that around much. Like Mildred."

"Don't even think of inviting her. I want you and Father to meet Agnes first."

"Mildred is your godmother."

"Mother, please, just us. You will see why when you meet her. Mildred will get a chance another time. Not now. I only want us."

"What is wrong with the woman, Tiffany?"

"Plenty, but I can't get into it now."

"Okay, you can tell Mildred if she finds out."

"I will handle it."

"Fine. You better prepare me for his mother. I don't like surprises."

"I will. I gotta go."

"Tiffany."

I hung up.

Jen walked back to me. "How can you stand that guy?"

I looked toward the door. "He is of no importance to me."

"He's so creepy."

"I get that, too. I'm hoping, as time goes on, he will get better."

"You know when you look at someone and think, 'he's got people locked up in his cellar?'" I laughed. "That's your partner."

"He probably does."

"Tiffany, be careful. I mean it."

"Thanks, Jen." She walked back in to check on things. I looked around and back at my phone. Michael's text was still on the screen. Hannah's wedding. I replied, *Busy. Did you put in for the time off?*

Michael replied, *Yes.*

I wasn't sure how he was going to be with Andy there. I replied, *Nice.*

He texted, *How's Bartek? Is he still being a prick?*

I grinned. *Yes. I like it when he's quiet.*

Didn't know he could be quiet. I couldn't shut him up the days he rode with me.

Maybe it's because I'm female. Or "bitch" as he likes to say.

If he is calling you that then you had better log it into your reports.

I was already on it. *I am. No worries.*

Tiffany, I'm sorry. I should be with you.

I shook my head. Not when he found out I was marrying Andy. *You deserve your position. And see? We still get to talk.*

Michael replied, *Gotta go.*

Bartek and Jen were walking out. I signed the inventory while Bartek stored it in the back. Jen separated her sheet.

"See you soon, Tiff."

I grinned. "Next week."

She tapped my arm, walking back in the hospital. Bartek sealed the doors. I noticed his body reacting in a sudden jolt of panic as his hand clearly felt under the handle. The tension released as he removed his hand, leaving me curious. Did he have something under there?

I continued walking toward the cab. We both climbed in and proceeded to the next stop. He jumped out first, opening the doors and collecting what this hospital needed. The blood moved in first. I did what I normally did, waiting for him to come back out for the rest of the delivery. When he cleared the door again, I touched under the handle. There was a bump. I slid my phone under to take a picture. What the hell was that? I slid my phone back under the handle and took more photos. I coasted away, examining them. I wasn't sure what this was, and it was only under the one handle. Was this on all the ambulances? I texted Andy. He asked me to send the photos. Andy called.

"Anything for me to worry about?" I asked.

"I'll pick you up tonight. Is your bag in the ambulance or your locker?"

"Locker. What is it, Andy?"

"Tracking device. How did you come to find it?"

"Bartek closed the doors and panicked at the last stop with his fingers behind the latch. He was feeling for something and relaxed, I guess when he felt it again. He's not aware that I was paying attention."

"Good, keep it that way. We have to make sure your car doesn't have one."

"What?"

"Tiffany, the best thing you can do right now is pretend you don't know it's there. Keep your eyes open, though. I'll pick you up, okay?"

"We will leave my car tonight?"

"Yes."

"I am meeting my father for breakfast."

"You can take my car."

I sighed. "Fine."

"What's wrong?"

"Nothing."

"Okay, see you at eleven."

It was possible Andy and I were overthinking this. What if our company installed these on all the transports? It could be I was being paranoid. I wanted to ask Michael to check his doors, only that would pull him into my potential trouble.

I could check them tomorrow after I met my father. Patience. The one thing I was terrible at. If the company didn't do this, then it was pretty clear Bartek was up to something. I suddenly really disliked him and wanted to find out about his past.

We were back in the truck, two more stops and done. I broke the silence.

"So, you were a prison guard?"

"Fifteen years. One guaranteed job when you get out of the reserves."

"Oh, what branch?"

"Army."

"What did you do in there?" Military people loved to talk about themselves back in the day. Well, most of them did.

"MP."

"Military police, really? Why didn't you become a cop?"

"They gave me prison guard."

I was clearly prying. I backed off. That was enough information for tonight. He was ex-military and prison guard. Never made it to a cop post in civilian life.

I didn't expect him to ask about me.

"What's your story, princess?"

"You can stop calling me princess."

He chuckled. "It fits you."

"No. No, it doesn't."

He looked around. "Look at you. What's a pretty little girl like you doing working here?"

"I like my job."

"Heard you are college-educated."

"Yup."

"And you drive an ambulance for a donor service?"

"Yes."

"Who are you running from?"

"No one. I like what I do."

"Do you have a criminal record?"

I shook my head. "No."

"Do it for the thrill?"

"I do it to save lives."

"Doctor would be more appropriate."

That was all I was going to answer. He hopped out at our next stop, opening the doors.

CHAPTER TWENTY-TWO

Andy waited in his car at the back of the parking lot. Smart move. I didn't want Bartek to see we were together. Last time they met Andy bounced his head off the meeting-room table. Michael saw Andy's car.

"What's he doing here?"

"Giving me a ride home."

Michael turned, concerned. "Something wrong with your car, Tiff?"

"Yes, gonna look at it tomorrow."

"I could have driven you home."

"Thanks."

"You know I am always here for you, right?"

"I do, Michael."

Bartek was leaving. I handed my reports over and signed out. Andy watched me as I entered his car.

"Well, he likes to talk about himself. Found out the guy was an MP in the army. Been a prison guard for fifteen years."

Andy corrected me. "Army Reserves, seven years. He's forty. Ex-wife, no kids."

I looked over. "Thank god for that."

"They fired him from the prison for selling drugs inside. He smuggled them in and distributed them on his rounds."

"Wow. Guy's got balls."

"Prisoners liked him. He's gotten some good outside connections."

"Why the tracking device?"

"It's military."

"You think he is going to set up a hit?"

"I think he is capable of it."

"What about my car?"

"I'll take care of it in the morning. You drop me back here, meet your father, and I will swap vehicles with you."

"Thank you."

He turned toward me, watched the road again, and cupped my hand. We were holding hands. When we were almost to the warehouse, he announced, "Mom's arriving Thursday."

Well, isn't this just great?

"How long is she staying? Mother wants all of us over for dinner."

"Plan for Friday or Saturday night."

"Okay. Narrow that down so I can tell her."

I loved morning snuggles with my mercenary, neither one of us making the first move that would end the moment. His phone didn't care, though, blaring like an air-raid alarm. It was a severe alarm. Both of us sat up and I asked, "Who's calling?"

He grinned. "Mom."

I rolled my eyes, throwing the blanket off. "How appropriate."

"I changed it for you, so you would know."

"Thanks. I'm gonna jump in the shower."

He nodded, answering his phone. "Hello, Mom."

I caught my reflection in the mirror. Oh, I needed to relax when she called.

Twenty minutes later, there was fresh coffee, our Kitten eating happily, and my soldier standing there playing with what looked like a walkie talkie. I asked, walking toward him, "What's that?"

"A jammer."

My eyebrows lifted. "What is a jammer?"

"It blocks GPS."

"Oh?"

"It sends out the same frequency as the tracker, thus blocking the signal."

"Where is it going to go?"

"In your bag. I'm giving you a backpack to carry. Keep it in the ambulance on your shift."

"Okay. That should be fine. Chris brings a backpack with her. So do some of the guys."

"Only problem is, it works on all the frequencies. That means all the phones, everything in the truck."

"What if someone is tracking Bartek?"

"I'm working on that hiccup."

"You won't know where I am either."

Andy placed the jammer on the counter, frustrated. "I can override your phone, but I don't know what he has."

"We know about the tracker. Let's find out why it's tracking. I mean, maybe this isn't him. Angel Wings could have done this."

"I doubt it."

"I am going in for a few hours after meeting Father. I can snoop around."

"If Angel Wings is part of this, why the reaction from Bartek?"

"That's been bugging me, too. So, if Angel Wings has the vehicles equipped for tracking, we would place them in the same spot on all the vehicles, right?"

"If Angel Wings was tracking vehicles, then the devices would be under the dash on the driver's side. That's where there is a plug-in. They would not bother hiding it."

I just realized they could track my jelly donut run with Pete. Bummer.

"What is it, Tiff?"

"There goes my coffee and donut stops."

"Seriously?"

"Hey, it's the little things."

"They allow you to stop for breaks."

That made me happy. "Good. I can only go with Pete."

He picked up the jammer again. "Then I will put this in your car."

"Is there something that will detect if there is a tracking device?"

"Yes, the Lexus has an advanced computer system. I don't want to fry it."

I nodded. "Yeah, let's not do that. I was thinking more like those metal detectors."

"I will have to hand-search."

"Oh, I don't mean to change the subject because I forgot last night, but Mother wants to know if we want my king-size bedroom set from her place. It's too big for the condo, and she's already picked out new furniture. If we don't take it, she is going to offer it to Hannah."

"We'll take it."

Wow, that was fast. I didn't expect him to answer so quickly.

"That means more furniture in here."

"We can put it in the back corner."

"Where your bed is?"

"I can make that a closed-in bedroom."

"Can you do it by the time your mother arrives?"

"Yes."

This was a change of heart. "Great."

He looked at his watch. "You better finish getting ready. Drop me off at Angel Wings first."

I agreed, turning to finish my morning ritual.

We swapped driving positions as Andy slid into the Lexus. "I'll be about an hour with this. I will call you when I am close."

"Okay."

"Tiff, tell your father we will pick up the set tomorrow."

"Tomorrow?"

"Yes."

"All right."

I did not like driving this hunk of junk. I was meeting Father at his favorite breakfast spot down at the wharf. I never realized he liked this place because of the boats. I assumed it was because of the scenery. He showed me photos of the boat he was going to buy. The only thing I knew about boats was that they named them. I asked what he was naming his. He grinned.

"I have a few ideas kicking around." Hmm. He wouldn't say. "We will fly you out for the christening."

"Keeping it a secret until then?"

"Yes."

"Andy will probably be with me."

And right then, I found out the reason for our breakfast.

"Yes, about your fiancé."

The way he said it sent a shiver up my spine.

"What about him?"

"Your mother said nothing the other night because of her respectful manners but both of us noticed. He clearly was in a fight."

"Some guys jumped him."

"Are you safe around him?"

"Safer than the president."

"Mildred said he was part of your last hold-up. Evidence says he tried to shoot you."

"Look, if he tried to shoot me, I would be dead. He saved my life that night. It's been becoming a habit."

"Is he the reason Audrey only received half a liver?"

"Audrey is drinking again. I'm not sure she even deserves half."

"Tiffany!"

We both looked around. No one paid attention to us.

"He takes jobs from some not-so-desirable employers. By your and Mother's standards, so do I."

"We just want better for you."

"Like Blake Montgomery? Andy is an angel compared to half the men in your social circle."

"He's not right for you. He is ten years your senior."

"How old is Mandy Stone?"

"Enough, Tiffany."

"No, Father, you sit up on your high horse and point. Andy is a good man, he makes a decent living, he treats me well. Besides, I love him. I will marry him."

"What is his income?"

I paused. I didn't know. "We haven't talked about that."

"You haven't talked about income? Is he marrying you for your money?"

I quickly thought about his warehouse, his car, his lack of furniture . . . and shrugged.

"Maybe? I'm happy to share it with him."

"You need to see my lawyer about a prenup."

"Did Mother sign a prenup?"

He stared hard into my eyes. "She didn't have to. We both started the same when we married. No help from our families."

"Isn't this becoming a pattern?"

Father sighed, sitting back, both palms on the table. "You're right."

"Excuse me?"

"I am doing exactly what my parents did."

I wanted so badly to react with sarcasm but held my tongue. He leaned over, picking his coffee cup up. "I . . ." He was reflecting. "Tiffany, I'm sorry. I am told his mother is coming for a visit."

"Yeah. Oh, tell Mother Friday. She is arriving Thursday."

"We look forward to meeting her. I'm sure she is a lovely woman."

And then every inch I just gained erased in my head. I was so screwed. She was not a lovely woman, and she told me I was a whore to my face. We finished eating. Andy arrived, swapping our keys. Father studied him like a lab rat. Andy kissed the top of my head, confirming the rest of how our day was playing out, insisting I be home before five. Andy reminded me of my third shift tonight, and I needed sleep before I went in. With a respectful greeting to Father, he left. I turned with a raised eyebrow. Father remained quiet.

CHAPTER TWENTY-THREE

There was a full list of things that needed to be done. Greg walked in as I zippered up my mechanic suit.

"Hey, I'm really sorry about not being able to make it down here as much. It's been busy for me outside of work. My girlfriend is getting married and my parents are moving to Washington state."

He grumbled, "I get it."

"I'll do what I can today but the next month is going to be limited."

"We'll figure it out."

"How's the Vamp Van coming along?"

"Kid's been working hard. Just needs the paint job and she's ready for duty."

"Wow, really? That was fast."

"Been a week."

"Already?"

"The oil changes are priority. Anything else is a bonus, Tiff." He hesitated.

"Are you okay, Greg?"

"Why don't you put in as driver for the blood-mobile?"

"Because I like driving the big rig."

"It will give you regular hours. More consistency."

"I like my schedule. What's going on?"

"It's the guy they have you with. Cousin of mine knows him from around. The guy's garbage."

"He's all talk. Hey, do you know of any company tracking devices on the vehicles?"

"I can't even hire a steady part-time guy in here. They are paying Danny minimum wage as a freelancer. The only reason he working this is I let him borrow tools whenever he needs them."

"That's a no then?"

"Cheap-ass company. Talk a lot. Just never do it."

"I'll get on those oil changes. First I want to check out the Vamp Van."

I walked over to the blood bank van. Danny was inside testing the cooling units. My eyes went wide as I looked at the transformation from the past week.

"You are so talented, Danny."

"Tiffany, I've been hoping to see you. Uncle Greg said you used the organ armor."

"I did, during my last hijacking. You saved a life, Danny. I would not have gotten that liver to the patient without it."

"Epic. Never saved a life before."

"I carry those in my ambulance. They are there if needed."

"Heard you got shot."

"Yup. I don't recommend it."

He turned up a dry half-smile. "Don't plan to. Come up here. Let me show you what I did. Who's driving this rig?"

"We don't know yet. Hey, are you painting it?"

"Yes. Going in the tent tomorrow."

"I've been calling it the Vamp Van."

He squinted his eyes. "Vampire?"

I cracked a slight smile. "Yes, transports blood."

"I get you."

"Can you paint a small set of fangs somewhere? Nothing noticeable, just as an inside joke for us."

"That can be arranged."

Danny gave me the full tour of our new blood transport wagon. He'd used every square inch efficiently. I finished the oil changes, then helped Danny wrap the last part of the van for paint. He was coming in early tomorrow. It was Sunday and Greg closed the garage down so he could set up a temporary paint shop. Michael walked in dressed for work. I realized I was late. He walked toward me.

"I wasn't sure if you were here or if your car didn't move from last night."

"Are you working a double?"

"Yes, with your partner."

"You and Bartek?"

"Yes. Kyle called; shift opened up. Your guy has been grabbing every opening this past week. Requested as much overtime as allowed."

"Are you using my ambulance?"

"Yes."

"Son of a bitch."

"What's that got to do with anything?"

"You in the city?"

"Yes, but you have the rural route tonight."

"Watch your back with him. There is a lot we don't know yet."

"That's why I took the shift, Tiffany. I don't like him. I want to find out more so I can protect you."

I sighed. "I am fine, Michael. But I appreciate anything you can find out." I didn't want to discourage him. He might find something that Andy couldn't.

"Tiffany?"

"Yes?"

"I miss you."

"Michael."

"No, I miss hanging out with you."

"I know, I miss hanging out with you, too."

"Maybe you can call me sometime, go to the gym, Hannah's bar?"

"I have, you turned me down."

"Sorry about that."

"Next few months are tough. Wedding duties, parents moving."

"I understand. Glad it isn't your wedding."

He said it. I could either get this over with right now or keep pretending I was not engaged. "Michael."

He narrowed his eyes. "What? You're marrying that maggot!"

I reached for his arm. "Shh, Michael. He asked. I said yes." At the horror on Michael's face, my heart sank deep in my chest. "We are not announcing it until after Hannah's wedding. Say nothing. I don't want to steal Hannah's spotlight."

He turned. "Whatever, Tiff. Good luck with being married to that scum." He quickly headed out the door. Out of the nine people who knew, I had two that were for it: Mother and Troy. Several were against it, and Richie, Harry and Sahil were neutral. A campfire wedding was probably appropriate. We were going to have, like, a total of a dozen guests when our announcement became official. Maybe the new lake house would be an option.

I cleaned up and crossed what I had accomplished off my list, leaving it out for Greg to add or subtract from. Kyle was in the dispatch box for another few hours. I poked my head in. "Hey."

He turned. "I don't like the Polack."

"I think it's unanimous."

"Why did Donavan hire him?"

"I'm guessing his training and low pay grade."

He looked at my brace. "Leg holding up?"

I leaned on the doorframe. "I keep pushing it and fucking it up again."

He chuckled. "Yah, sounds like you. I have a name of a good physical therapist."

"PTs are cruel."

He chuckled. "With zero sympathy."

"You just want to see me suffer."

He snapped his fingers together, pointing at my leg. "Always." He made a clicking noise from the corner of his mouth. "Seriously though, Tiffany, are you okay with that jerk?"

"I'm fine. I don't trust him. Keeps my guard up, and hopefully one step ahead."

"You're with that private contractor?"

"Bartek doesn't know that."

"The way he hopped the Polack's head off the table it's a good thing he doesn't know he is your boyfriend."

"I've got to go catch a few hours of sleep before my shift. Kyle . . ."

He answered Michael's question on the scanner, then turned back to me. "Yes?"

I looked down, then back up. "I'm glad you're back."

He nodded. "So am I."

I tapped the doorframe and opened my hand in a parting, small wave before heading for my car. I texted Andy I was on my way.

When we arrived home, he had the back corner of the room framed and ready for phase two. He was serious about making this place more like a home. One juicy burger later, I was ready to nap.

My alarm chimed at nine fifteen. Andy was sitting at his computer station, looking over to me as I sat up, now awake. Ugh. Time to get up.

I just remembered I'd told Michael about the proposal.

"Tiffany, I've been thinking about the jammer. I don't want you to use it yet. I'm going to track your route the next few nights."

"Okay. Hey, I forgot to tell you that Michael knows we are getting married."

He stood up, carrying my phone over. "You told him?"

I threw off the covers. "Kind of. He mentioned that he misses hanging out with me. I said that I did, too, and, with Hannah's wedding and my folks moving, we'd figure it out and get back on track like how it used to be."

Andy said nothing, but I saw his jawline tighten. "Anyway, he made a comment about how at least it was Hannah getting married and not me."

Andy stood like a statue. "And?"

I took my phone from him. "And I thought that was the perfect opportunity to tell him."

"What was his reaction?"

"Hurt, I think. He will get over it and accept the fact that we are together, and nothing is going to change that. The sooner that sinks in the easier it will be to hang out with him again."

"I don't want you hanging out with him."

I tilted my head to the side. "Why? He's no threat to you. Michael is a respectful guy. Once he accepts us, then it will be back to the way it used to be."

"Like hell it will."

"Andy, you cannot think of Michael as a threat?"

"He's not a threat. He's an interference."

"He's my friend."

"I don't care what you call him. I don't like him, and you are not hanging out. Those days are over, Tiffany."

"What do you mean those days are over?"

"I mean you will be my wife. You are not hanging out with men anymore."

"What about Troy, Harry, Richie, and Sahil?"

"They are different."

"Why because they are your friends? What about Vic? I don't like him. You can't hang out with him anymore!"

"He's part of the team I need occasionally. If he makes you uncomfortable, I will fix that."

I stomped to the bathroom. "You are not telling me who I can and cannot hang out with. You have a problem with Michael, get over it!" I slammed the door shut. *Who does he think he is, telling me who I can have as friends?* I showered and pretended he wasn't here. He was equally mad. When I was ready to leave, I picked up the backpack.

"Am I taking this or not?"

"Leave it," he barked back.

I did, walking out the door.

CHAPTER TWENTY-FOUR

Both Michael and Bartek were coming from their prior shift. Michael didn't have anything to say to me. I could tell he was avoiding me. Bartek met me at the ambulance as I did my regular outer-shell inspection. I decided to have a little fun as I messed with the back handles.

"What the fuck are you doing?" he asked.

"Same thing I always do, searching for anything that will compromise our safety."

"Just get in the damn vehicle and let's go."

"My truck, my rules."

"You're wasting company time." I ignored him, continuing my inspection. "I said, get in the damn truck."

"You seem to have it backward, Mr. Wojcik. I'm the queen; you're the worker bee. You do not tell me what to do. I tell you what to do. Wait in the cab."

He threw down our clipboard and stormed back in the building. I finished when Jason walked out. "What's going on?"

"I'm riding with you tonight. The Polack just made a scene inside with the wrong people. He's with Michael for the night." Jason picked up the clipboard. "We are swapping locations. We have the city; they have the rural run. I'll be right back."

I hopped in my ambulance. Michael and Bartek entered Michael's rig. Bartek slammed his door closed as Jason took his seat.

"Okay, Tiff, lets rock and roll." Heading for my first stop, a text came in from Andy. *Where are you?*

He damn well knew where I was.

As soon as Jason was inside, I answered: *Bartek had a meltdown when I did my shell inspection. They swapped Jason to my truck and Bartek back with Michael. They gave me the city route.*

He replied: *Okay*

That was it. Fine by me.

Jason was a good guy, about the same size as me. I think that's why I had Bartek. If Jason were bigger, I would have gotten him. Too bad. I liked Jason. He even opened up, talking about some of his work experiences with Kyle. Apparently, I could ruin entire shifts he worked. One part of me felt bad, the other part laughed out loud at his stories. Michael texted halfway through our night. *Whatever you did to the Polack, he is feeding on pure hatred for you.*

Technically, I didn't do anything.

If he calls you a dyke one more time, I will dump him in the middle of nowhere.

I texted back: *That's just prison talk. Don't let him get to you.*

He replied: *Never again am I going to do a double with this idiot.*

I felt bad: *Sorry, my fault.*

Michael gave me some sarcasm: *Well, at least he's keeping me awake.*

I grinned: *Then you are welcome.*

At least Michael and I were back on the same page. Andy was a whole other kettle of fish.

Bartek wouldn't even look at me when we pulled back on base. Jason said goodbye as Michael walked me to my car.

"That guy is not right in the head, Tiff. I don't expect he likes women."

"You think he's gay?"

"No, my guess he likes to put them down . . . abusive even. I'm serious. He's the type that would sucker punch you in the face."

I knew where Michael was going with this. He watched his father beat his mother throughout his childhood.

"Tiff, let me talk to Donovan. I think this guy should run the blood bank van. He can be alone and none of us have to be in danger."

Perhaps Michael was right. "Okay. If you go to Donovan, I will back you up."

His shoulders dropped. He sighed as he held both my shoulders.

"Thank you."

I nodded. "I'm not stupid, you know. I don't want trouble."

He grinned. "I know you don't want it, but trouble is good at finding you. Get some rest. See you tomorrow." He let go, turning to walk to his car.

I walked into the warehouse and opened our door. The back area was lit up more than the outside. Drywall was up. Andy had installed different wood flooring in there. He had hung a door, and was installing a doorknob. I dropped my bag and walked toward him.

"Wow, this looks fantastic." I checked my watch. "Nine hours and all this? You have no excuses in the future when I ask you to do something."

"I have motivation."

I squatted down next to him. "Look, you need to relax about Michael. There is nothing but friendship between us. You are who I want my future with."

His eyes darted to mine, and then back on the screw he turned.

"I'll try."

I gave him a slight grin. "That's all I am asking. Thank you."

I settled in bed before he did, but we woke up together around three in the afternoon. Our first stop was Mother's house.

They gave us the big news as we walked in. They had sold the place, with incentive to be out in three weeks. We gave her Andy's set of keys to the condo as we walked past all the furniture with color-coded tags. White was going to the condo, green to Washington and pink was ours. *Pink. Figures she picked that for me.*

There were a few pieces Mother couldn't decide on. One was the dining room table. Apparently, it was too big for the new house, and it was way too big for the condo, so she asked Andy. I was bracing for him to say no. Instead, he surprised me, accepting the offer.

My mouth fell open as I pointed, stuttering, "But, but, but —"

His eyebrows raised. "What? It fits in our place." A small plane could fit in our place. That was not what I was getting at. "We will need a bigger moving truck. And more help."

Mother smiled, delighted we were taking it, as they taped a big pink tag to the side along with all twelve chairs. My old room was simple. King bed, two nightstands, two dressers, two lamps. That was it. Andy tested the bed. I looked down at him. He gave a quick grin, then went serious. "We will never get rid of the guys now."

I chuckled; he was being cute. "Where is your bed going?"

He answered with his eyes closed. "Upstairs."

My eyebrows scrunched together. "In the gun room?"

"Yup."

I instantly realized that would be a brilliant place to stick his mother. I grinned, delighted by the idea.

Mother walked in and asked Andy what time he would be coming tomorrow. He looked at his watch. "I will be here around noon."

I interrupted. "That gives me three hours to sleep?"

"No, you will be sleeping. I have a few men helping. We will be back around two when you wake up."

"You don't want me helping?"

"I want you to sleep. We can handle this."

Mother smiled. "That's what I like to hear. Tiffany thinks she has to do everything. See, dear? You have a man now who wants to take care of you. Let him."

I turned. "Fine." It was a lost argument at this point. I knew what battles to fight. This wasn't one of them.

When we were sitting in my car, I couldn't help myself. "So, you have a meltdown because I moved my bedroom and living room set in; now you get offered a monstrous dining room table and you're all 'yes, we will take it?'"

"I am part of the decision. There is a difference. You moved your stuff in, bypassing that step. I don't like surprises."

I slowly shook my head. "Whatever."

We stopped at the paint store and picked out the new bedroom's wall color. We both liked the slate gray. Since that room had two gigantic windows and lots of light coming through, we went with a darker color to contrast with the natural light. I also found curtains that would work out perfectly. They could be Andy's next project while I was working tonight. At least I could help him prep the work area.

Thinking about the work at home reminded me they had painted the blood-mobile. I had to sneak in and see where Danny had added the fangs. I didn't care how Andy had overreacted when I brought up Michael. I still shared what Michael had said to me this morning about Bartek. I figured this was desensitizing. The more I said Michael's name, the sooner Andy would stop reacting like a child.

Who Andy really didn't like right now was my work co-pilot, Bartek. He handed me a pocket-size Taser gun along with a boot knife, making me practice pulling it from my boot for half an hour. He already had me tracked by GPS, but insisted I call him at every stop. Because of last night, I wasn't sure what route we would be on.

Bartek remained quiet tonight. He didn't utter any comments about my vehicle precheck and climbed straight in the ambulance with our clipboard for our runs. We were back on the city run. I texted Michael with an apology for having to do two rural night-shift runs. He texted back to call him if there was any sign of danger from Polack. *The Pol-...Screw it. I just couldn't do it.* I didn't like using that term and I couldn't call him that even if he preferred it. Bartek is his name and that's what I am sticking to.

Audrey texted me: *Check out last night's closing stock prices.*

It was two in the morning. She was burning the candle again. I knew for a fact the doctor told her to get regular sleep.

I guess I didn't answer her quick enough. She sent me a screenshot. Henshaw Logistics was up four dollars from the bottom six dollars it fell to when the government pulled the contract. I texted her back: *That is wonderful news. Go to bed.*

She replied: *I am in bed, Mother!*

Then go to sleep.

She sent me a string of dollar signs with the text: *Sleeping is for pussies. Besides, I will get plenty when I am dead.*

I couldn't help it: *Given the way you drink, that should be soon.*

A tongue emoji instantly appeared. Where did she find that?

I texted I would stop by and see her tomorrow afternoon. Andy sent me photos of the fresh paint job. I was supposed to call him. He answered with, "Every stop, babe. It's not too much to ask, given the instability of your partner."

"I'm sorry, Audrey distracted me. Stock is up at Henshaw. Looks like she turned the company around."

"That's excellent news."

"Yes, but I knew she would, especially now that it's hers."

"I thought it didn't change ownership for another thirty days."

"It doesn't, but all the bigwigs know it's a done deal. She's worth investing in. She will far surpass my father."

"How's your schedule going?"

I turned to see if Bartek was coming back yet. Nothing. "Quiet. I like quiet."

"Good. Next stop, call."

"I will." The side door opened. Bartek was walking back with the guard and nurse.

"Gotta go." I hung up.

Bartek secured the boxes, and I signed the paperwork. Another ambulance pulled in next to mine. I didn't have a clue who this was. This was a delivery dock. Not a human drop-off. They made no move to exit their cab. "Pearson Ambulance" was written on the side of the van.

The nurse spoke up. "Oh, that must be the transport waiting for the guy to get out of surgery."

I stepped around to get a better look at their rig.

The guard chimed in, "Here's as good a place as any to wait."

I turned. "I suppose."

Bartek spoke. "We don't own the fucking dock."

I liked him better not speaking. "See you guys next week," I said to end our conversation. The guard tapped the back of my ambulance. I looked over to the two EMTs on their phones, while a blueish light illuminated their outline.

I secured my seatbelt before driving away. Our night turned out to be uneventful, just how I liked it these days. I also looked up Pearson Ambulance Service. They were legit.

I arrived home to see our new back room looking beautiful. I wanted Andy to frame our bedroom in now. This open warehouse was shaping into a nice home. He could frame in the entrance to be a nice mudroom, with wooden shelves for our shoes and hangers for our coats. This place had so much potential.

CHAPTER TWENTY-FIVE

I awoke at two o'clock to Andy calling to me from outside. "Come on, babe. Get up." He was alerting me to the moving crew waiting outside. I sat up, stretching.

I slumped over, sliding out of bed. I yawned and scooped up Kitten, walking right into the bathroom and locking the door. By the time I finished showering everyone had left and our house was fully furnished. The table fit nicely in here. Andy walked back in the door.

Wow. This place was ready for company. I turned to watch Andy's reaction as I spoke.

"I would like to have Hannah and George over; my parents, too. If this is where we are living, people should feel welcome to visit anytime."

Andy stiffened, just as predicted. The thought created tension. I knew this was going to be an issue.

I stepped closer. "I know you have been alone for a long time. Nobody comes over unannounced. My schedule is crazy. Everyone already learned a long time ago to call first. Andy, I won't share this address without approval, but I want your approval."

Andy remained quiet for a moment, glancing around at all the changes in here. There were a lot. This was a new place, a new atmosphere, even for him. I observed Andy's lengthy, slow exhale and took it as a good sign.

"Parents and girlfriend. I can handle it if that's it."

I added. "George, too. It's a package deal now."

"Fine. George."

Damn, I forgot Audrey. "How about Audrey?"

Andy tilted his head, considering. "Not yet. She knows too many hacking tips."

"Computer?"

"Yes."

"Okay, I can live with that. You did an outstanding job with the guest room."

"It looks decent, right?"

"This is fantastic. If you want another project, ideas are flowing."

"Not right now, but what are you seeing?"

I took his hand and dragged Andy to the front door. "This area could use shelves and a six-foot wall extension to hang coats."

He studied. "Not a terrible idea." I nodded, happy that he agreed.

"I hope Agnes likes the new room."

"Don't expect compliments on any of this. She is a minimalist."

"Good to know. I won't take offense from complaints." I looked over to our bed. "Any chance you can build our room with walls so I have someplace to get away?"

Andy cracked a smile. "We could always take the backroom and give up our bed." I actually liked the idea.

"Deal." Andy bent down to smack my butt, then kissed me. This man looked more relaxed than I had ever seen him.

"This is really feeling like a home, Andy. Thank you."

"I like it, too."

We were heading in separate directions for a while. I stopped by the condo to pick up mail. All was quiet in the neighborhood. I stopped in to visit Audrey, who was downsizing the company and getting the first level of Henshaw Logistics available to rent. "Trimming the fat," she said over and over. I supposed, since everyone was on her payroll now, it had to be done.

Audrey was thrilled to share all the changes being implemented. No wonder the stock was rising again. Audrey was a smart, savvy, ruthless businesswoman.

I peeked in to see how Mother was doing. Everything waiting to be moved into the condo was neatly lined up in the foyer. Right then I realized Andy's mother was supposed to be coming here for dinner. "Hey, Mother?" I called.

She was busy packing her fine china. "Over here, Tiffany."

I walked through the now empty area that the table had occupied for decades.

"Did Father mention Friday dinner?"

Mother suddenly stood straight as a board. "We will just have to move dinner to your house. I can still cook. Father and I will bring the food."

I shrugged. "Perfect." I wrote the address down and programmed it into her phone, warning her we lived in an old warehouse and not to worry if she thought the GPS was mistaken.

She reminded me, "Tiffany, dresses are in. Tomorrow is the fitting. Ten o'clock. Don't be late."

There goes grappling tomorrow.

Speaking of grappling, I had a few hours free, so I stopped in on a class. My head instructor was working with two men around my age. I watched, taking the bench. These guys were fierce. The takedown power the smaller guy had was a force to be reckoned with. My instructor gave a half-wave to acknowledge I was there.

They stopped, talking the sequence through before performing it in slow motion to work out the mistakes. The instructor had them stand ready and blew the whistle. I actually stood up, amazed at what I was seeing, but he clearly did not like what they had done because he made everyone take a break. I walked toward him as he turned to me.

"You holding out on us?" I accused.

He wiped his forehead. "How's the leg?"

"Better. I'm taking it slow this time."

He chuckled. "I give it another week before you do something stupid again."

I scrunched my face. "Hey!"

He half-grinned. "You are the most impatient person I have ever met."

I shrugged. "I'm getting better."

His lip shot up. "Yeah, okay."

"I wanted to come in tomorrow, but I have maid-of-honor duties."

"Who stuck you in a wedding?"

I smacked his arm. "I can do the dress, thank you. My best friend is getting married."

"Just kidding, Tiff."

"Listen, I have a new partner. He sort of hates me."

"Who could hate you, Tiffany?"

"I know, right? I think it's women in general he just doesn't like. I was wondering if I could stop by after my appointment and get a few tips for close-contact situations."

"Are you worried about this guy?"

"I'm worried about anyone. But this guy is a higher risk factor than most of the others."

"Swing by tomorrow. I'm here all day. I'll show you some stuff."

I let out a breath. "Thanks. Those guys are good."

"They are fighting dogs."

I tilted my head, having never heard that expression used for humans. "Code for something?"

"Think with their dicks. If they slowed down just a little to look in the other's eyes, they would know not to react so violently and more skillfully. Right now, it's a challenge for first, not to ultimately win."

I sat down. What he just said hit like a brick to the side of my head. I was both of them, trying to be first. I always wanted to be first to the takedown. First to complete the maneuver.

I turned my head, looking up. "That's me?"

He grinned wholeheartedly. "That's exactly you, Tiffany." Cupping my knee with his hand like we just had a major breakthrough, he added, "We might actually get some work done tomorrow."

Did I carry an attitude here? I knew sometimes I came in pissed off, but, all in all, I thought my head was in the game. I wasn't going to question it any further. I wanted to see what tomorrow would bring. "I need to be an equal player."

"Then let's make you one."

I stopped by work because it was across town. I wanted to check out the Vamp Van. Danny was peeling back the final sections. I watched in awe. This kid had more talent than anyone I knew.

For a quick moment I wanted to take this solo transport on. What a beautiful rig. He made the W in "Angel Wings" the fangs. Perfect!

I walked into headquarters. Donovan was easy enough to find. I asked, "Who are you appointing for the blood wagon?"

Donovan looked up while holding a stack of papers, deciding whether to drop them or keep holding. The papers shifted as he struggled with them. "I am appointing Allen." He stared, waiting for a reaction.

Who was I to counter his decision? It was the right call. Truth be told, I would have done the same. Allen was a perfect candidate. He obey the laws, and his paperwork and reports were always in order. He was perfect for the runs.

I nodded, agreeing. "Wise choice."

I was so screwed. Something bad was coming. I could feel it in my bones. I turned, walking out the door. It was time to get serious.

I called Andy. No answer. I texted him about moving dinner to our place and Mother bringing the food. Surprisingly, he replied, *That's fine.*

Wow, my man was coming around. He texted again to say he would be home around two in the morning.

I popped the trunk. My gym bag was in the back. Okay, it was exercise time. I texted Michael. *Heading to the gym. Just saying. Never say I don't invite you.*

He texted back. *Already here, lazy.*

I snickered as I replied, *On my way.*

I found Michael easily enough. We worked out on the elliptical machines. It was a little strenuous on my leg, but I lightened the tension and discovered working it out this way was actually really good.

I broke the news that Donovan gave the blood wagon to Allen. Michael complained some, then let it go, knowing there was nothing we could do.

It was seven o'clock by the time we finished. I was hungry and Hannah was working tonight. I invited Michael to tag along, and he gladly accepted.

CHAPTER TWENTY-SIX

The bar area was nearly empty, which wasn't out of the ordinary for a Monday night. Hannah usually used Monday evenings to catch up on paperwork. She looked up from her stack of papers. "Well, I'll be damned."

She came around the bar and ran into Michael's arms, hugging him and kissing his cheek. "I miss you. I miss you. I miss you." He wrapped his arms around her tight, grinning with both eyes closed, holding her against him.

I smiled as he lowered Hannah back down on her feet. She released him, playfully slapping at his arm. "Why haven't you come in to see me?" She pointed a finger to me. "This one has been making the effort. Why not you?"

Michael apologized, promising to be around more often. Hannah walked with us to the bar. Michael and I took our seats as she walked behind the bar again, making my extra-lemon water and asking Michael what he wanted. He looked at the water and cringed. "I'll take a screwdriver."

She smiled. "Coming right up." While she made his drink, Hannah reminded me about tomorrow's dress fitting. Michael asked what the dress looked like, giving Hannah an excuse to pull out the bridal bible and go over everything. Andy texted, asking where I was.

I told him I was at the bar with Hannah and Michael. I refused to lie or cover up something that I should not have any guilt over.

He replied to text when I was on the way home. Oh boy. I had the feeling Andy wouldn't be overcoming his dislike of Michael anytime soon. Hannah and Michael stared as I put the phone on the bar.

"What?" I asked. Michael took a long sip from the glass, placing it back on the bar. "Must be your fiancé."

I wanted to kill him!

Hannah looked from me to Michael. "Fiancé?"

Michael instantly realized what he had said. "Tiff, I'm sorry. It just . . ."

I turned my focus to the look of shock on Hannah's face.

"Did Andy propose?" she asked.

There was no getting out of it now. "Yes, but I didn't want to say anything until after your wedding." I glared at Michael. "Jerk!"

He cringed. "Sorry, that just slipped out."

Hannah shook off her shocked reaction and squealed. "You're getting married? You're getting married! Oh, Tiffany! I am so happy." She ran around the bar again, latching on with a tight hug.

I patted her back. "Okay, okay, you can let go now." She separated from the embrace. "Why were you keeping that a secret? Where's the ring?"

"This is *your* wedding celebration time. Mine can wait."

"Oh, that's crap. I am so happy for you. Oh my gosh." She threw out her hands as if bracing herself. "Yup, the Earth stopped moving. I felt it."

I brushed her away with a wave. "Hilarious."

Hannah laughed. Michael remained quiet.

"Tiffany," she said, "don't hide big announcements like that ever again. Oh! Tomorrow we can look at dresses for you."

"I'm all set. Tomorrow is your day."

She made her way behind the bar again. "Our day." And pulled a bottle of champagne out. "We are having a glass. This is on the house."

Michael downed a whole glass in one chug. Hannah filled it again. "I'm sorry, Michael. We will find you a beautiful bride. Oh, my cousin Emily! Right, Tiffany? They would be perfect. I will make sure she is at your table."

Michael chuckled. "Yeah, sure Becca will love that."

"Who are you bringing?"

"Rebecca."

"Oh, that girl from the gala?"

"Yes."

"Are you two a thing?"

"A thing?"

"Like, are you a couple?"

He shook his head. "No."

She reached over, patting his hand. "Then leave Becca home and meet Emily."

"All set, but thanks."

"Fine, you will see. I'll tell Emily not to worry about Becca."

Hannah turned. "Did he get you a ring?"

Oh boy. This was going to happen. "Yes, his grandmother's."

She made a sweet face as her hand covered her heart showing George's ring like a disco ball. "Aww. That is so sweet, I didn't realize how sentimental he is."

My head screamed "cheap."

"You better wear it tomorrow. I want to see."

We ate, and I ordered takeout for Andy later. I texted him when I left and added that Hannah now knew we were getting married.

He texted back: *Ok babe.* Wow, that was an easygoing response. I suspected Andy was happy about everyone knowing. He woke me up at two, showing just how pleased.

My phone alarm chimed at eight. It was dress-fitting day. As much as I wanted to hang out in bed with my mercenary, I had to shower and shave to get ready. I even styled my hair and put on makeup.

Andy handed off the coffee, kissing me affectionately before he let the mug go in my hand. "You look beautiful." He took my hand and slipped the ring on. "No reason to hide this anymore." I looked down. *Damn it.* Whatever. It was what it was.

I mustered a slight smile. "What are you doing today?"

"I've got some surveillance."

"Surveillance?"

"Yeah, a potential problem."

"Everything okay?"

"No, but it will be."

"What time will you be back?"

He picked up his coffee. "Dinner time."

I narrowed my eyes. "That's anywhere from four to eight?"

"Six-ish."

I nodded. "Want me to cook?"

He laughed. "Bacon and eggs."

My eyebrows shot up, delighted by the suggestion. "All day, any day."

He placed the cup on the counter. "Good thing I love breakfast food."

I stepped into him. "Yes, good thing."

Andy's phone rang with the siren tone he had assigned to his Mother. I stepped away. *Ugh, the witch is arriving in two days.* He answered, letting me finish my coffee. As I washed the mug I flicked water at Kitten, who jumped off the counter.

I packed my bag for a private training session with my instructor. Andy, still on the phone, told Agnes to wait as he asked about my day's schedule upon seeing the bag.

I quickly went over the itinerary, then kissed my man with the thought of his mother calling me a whore running through my head. As soon as he uncovered the mouthpiece, I loudly professed that I loved him again. *Take that, mommy dearest.*

When he replied, "Love you, Tiffany," I froze in my tracks.

His mother heard that, making my heart flutter with an overwhelming feeling of joy. I had won, right here, right now. I turned to head out the door. This was my turf. I looked forward to Agnes visiting now.

I walked in for the dress fitting to find more champagne flowing. Only now Hannah added that we had more reason to celebrate, announcing my engagement and scolding me for having kept the news myself.

It was the moment I had dreaded, as everyone asked to see my ring. There were quiet murmurs, stuttering responses, *hmms* and fake, "Oh, that's lovely."

Mother took hold of both my shoulders. "It's Andy's great- great-grandmother's ring. I'm working on him to jazz it up a bit. Bring it into this century."

Hannah sighed. "Andy can do better than that. You, for heaven's sake, are a Chanler. He needs to step up."

I lowered my hand. "It has great sentimental value to him."

She handed me a glass of bubbly. "Then he can wear it."

All these ladies understood. Why didn't he? I took one sip of the alcohol and put my glass down. I was training after this, I couldn't drink.

Hannah had me go first, and I slipped my maid-of-honor dress on. Mother gasped, bringing her hand over her mouth, with tears swelling her eyes. She pulled a tissue up from the box. "You look ravishing, Tiffany. That color. You should wear more clothes in violet."

I watched Hannah instruct the seamstress about the length at which she wanted the dress to fall. They hemmed to tea-length. Hannah walked out with shoes. "Slip these on, chickee." I secured the fancy satin shoes, and wow, just wow. She and Mother snapped photos. Mother complimented Hannah on her style. They finished pinning me, and I slipped out of the dress.

Hannah made me try on three wedding dresses before I was handed back my street clothes. One was the dress mother had on hold. I loved it, only it was too white. I still had the dress I wanted with the product number and designer in the box, and I should have brought the picture with me. *On Friday I will show her when they come for dinner.*

Mother remembered something she wanted to tell me. "Tiffany!" I pulled the curtain back enough to see her. "Tiffany, do you remember that man, repulsive little man, trying to pass himself off as a psychologist that one time?"

I tilted my head. "The guy I had to do the questionnaire with?"

Her hand shot out, showing her excitement that I had remembered. "Yes."

"What about him?" Mother had my full attention.

"Does he live in the condo complex?"

"Absolutely not! Why?"

"I thought I saw him get into a van and drive off."

"What? Are you sure?"

"I think so. Small, greasy-looking man. Quite a similarity."

"That was a while ago, Mother. Are you sure you remember him?"

"One notices and remembers people, especially in negative situations. He tried to pass himself off as a doctor. The nerve of him. And he purposely pronounced our name incorrectly."

"There is no reason he would be at that complex. Besides, he's in a bit of trouble with the law."

"How do you know this?"

"A detective came by work a few weeks ago. They seized his files. Asked about my visit. My guess is several people complained about him."

"Serves him right for being an imposter. Maybe it was just a
similarity. It was a brief look."

I didn't like that there was even a chance he could have been
at the complex. "Are the cameras up?"

"Next week."

"Did you move everything in?"

She smiled. "Almost. The place is adorable. Father loves it. Reminds us of our first apartment. One bedroom, cozy. This condo is bigger, though, and I like that it's on the ground level. We will install a patio fence to have a little more privacy. It's perfect for what we need here."

Hannah walked back in with one more dress.

I protested, "No."

"Yes. Just let me see this on you. Please! It's my day. Do as I say." She extended the dress toward me as I grumbled, reluctantly grabbing it.

CHAPTER TWENTY-SEVEN

I called Andy on the way to grappling. He didn't answer and it went straight to voicemail. I knew he was in the woods somewhere. I left him a brief, detailed message about Mother's possible sighting at my complex, anticipating any questions he might want answered.

I arrived to find my instructor holding a bar with what looked like leather cuffs on the ends.

I raised an eyebrow. "What is this?"

He grinned and gave a slight laugh. "It's called a spreader bar."

I did not share his amusement. "And?"

"And I want you to practice moving from down on your knees standing back on your feet. Balance is most important."

"What does that thing have to do with balance?"

"You'll see. Shoes off. Attach these to each area above the ankle." He adjusted the width, locked the length, and handed me the bar, which was about as long as the width of my shoulders. I strapped the cuffs around and he lowered onto his knees. I immediately was off balance on my first step, stumbling. He held his hands out, "Tiffany, slow. Okay, roll over and adjust your knees, soften. Stop resisting."

I cleared my mind. Slowly adjusting to this restraint and made my way on knees to mimic his posture and complimented.

"Good. Now I want you to practice moving around the mat until you don't even notice it's there anymore."

I tilted my head, looking back at the bar. "Is that even possible?"

"Watch." Spreading his feet about the same width as mine, he maneuvered around the mat with ease, somehow managing to look graceful. He pointed out when lifting his knee, the opposite foot matched the same distance, move for move.

Okay, that was very cool. He had the special distance the same. "How is this going to help in close-contact fighting?"

He stood up, looking down. "When you don't have to think about where the other half of your limbs are, the ones you are using will be more effective." He turned to address another student before adding, "One hour, Tiffany. Stop resisting. Start acting with one flowing movement."

One flowing movement that wanted to rip these things off and throw them across the room. Twenty minutes in, one of the guys I had seen in the group before walked over. "Close your eyes."

I narrowed my stare. "What?"

He squatted down. "It helps to close your eyes."

"How so?"

"Trust your instincts, takes away from worrying about who is watching. Do you have something to cover your eyes?"

"No."

"I'll be right back."

He ran over to his bag, pulling out a bandana and jogging back. He folded it the long way before handing it over. "Here, it's clean."

I took it from him, looking around to see who was watching.

He grinned, looking around. "We are all here for similar purposes."

I glanced back up. "I know."

"Okay, you can keep that. If you've moved up to the bar, then you will need it for a while."

I raised the bandana up. "Thanks." He trotted away.

My instructor observed me from the side of the room. As soon as our eyes met, he turned his head away. I looked down at the bandana. *All right, I'm willing to try this.*

I secured it around my head. Andy had done training with me blindfolded before. I understood the concept. Now I just needed to concentrate.

I pulled my right leg over slowly, feeling the restraint from my left. Okay, learning to stand up and kneel down without falling would be my first goal.

As soon as I was on my feet, I heard my instructor yell, "Tiffany, remain on your knees. I don't want you above waist level."

I lifted the bandana. "Why?"

"How many times do you stand up in your cab?"

Oh, excellent point. I pointed, grinning. "And that's why you get paid the big bucks." I lowered to my knees, tipping to the side and rolling over on my butt, securing the bandana when I stopped.

He let me take the bar home, with instructions to practice for an hour tonight.

Andy arrived home shortly after I did. I was cooking breakfast for supper, plating the food. "Perfect timing." I grinned as he stopped advancing. He looked down at the bar laying on my bag.

I asked right away. "Do you think it's possible that Mother saw Reardon?"

He picked up the bar. "What are you doing with this?"

I brought dinner plates over to our new, monstrous table, shaking my head from the very frustrating practice. "Oh, that. My instructor says it will bring up my skills in close altercations. I need to practice for an hour tonight."

Andy stood there grinning, adjusting the bar.

I tried to stop him. "I'm not sure what he had it set on but that was the distance he wants me to practice."

Andy gave me a sultry look.

I asked, not sure what was going on, "You hungry?" I turned to get water. Andy grabbed my arm, stopping my forward motion, pulling me toward him. I figured he wanted a kiss and this would be a nice way to greet each other. He smelled of earth and pine.

The way he kissed me made me grin, as I began to get the hint about how he was feeling.

"I guess the recon was successful."

His tone dropped low and soft, "How long did he tell you to practice with this on?"

I looked down at the bar in his hand, still not fully understanding. "Um . . . an hour."

He lifted me over his shoulder. "I can help with that."

I screamed from the surprise. "What are you doing?" I laughed.

"Making sure you follow through with training."

That's when I learned the other use of the spreader bar.

The food was cold, though neither of us cared. The conversation finally came back around to Reardon. Andy was going back out tonight. He wanted to look around my condo complex. He played on his computer for an hour while I cleaned up. Andy then changed into night-gear clothing, kissing me.

"I'll be late. Keep up the training, babe. I like your homework. Big fan."

I smiled, almost embarrassed about what he'd done.

"Go. Find out about Reardon."

Andy kissed me goodbye. "I'll find that trash and burn him."

I tapped his face. "Good. I don't want that creep around my parents."

He turned and walked down the stairs. How was I going to strap that bar on now without thinking about sex? It was hopeless.

I awoke later to the feeling of Andy climbing into bed, him tucked against me. I moved to turn into him, and he held me in place.

I relaxed into his hold and asked, "How did it go?"

"Reardon won't be bothering anyone."

Now I wanted to turn. He let me up. "Did you find him?"

"Yes, not at the condo address."

"And?"

He propped up on an elbow. "I'm tired, Tiffany. I need a few hours before I have to be on the range."

"So, you took care of him?"

"He's taken care of."

I could see he looked exhausted. I wanted to know more, but this wasn't the time. I understood getting no sleep, double shift, all of it. I slid back down, returning to my original position. He placed his arm around me, his body tucked against mine, and I could soon hear him lightly snoring over my ear.

Andy must have been exhausted. He didn't wake up once while I got ready for work. I quietly packed my bag and snuck out.

It was a Pete morning. I loved working with Pete. He noticed I wasn't favoring my leg as much, reminding me to keep taking it slow. Slow and steady was the way to build it back up.

Pete asked about Bartek, referring to him as The Polack. I wanted to say what I really thought, but I had too many people already concerned. I gave a generic answer like anyone would.

"He's a jerk. Heard he got fired for selling drugs at his old job."

"I didn't know that."

"Hey, you're ex-state police. Any chance of looking him up?"

"I'll see what I can do."

"Any information will be helpful since I am stuck with him."

"Don't worry, kid, just stick to the job and everything will be fine."

"That's what I'm trying to do, but he keeps doing odd stuff."

"Like what?"

"He argues about everything and questions procedure, stuff like that."

Pete laughed. "Probably isn't used to taking orders from a woman."

I turned into the hospital. "Perhaps."

Michael asked what I was doing after work. Then he saw the ring. He picked my hand up, squinting. "Is that?"

I pulled my hand away. I had expected this exact reaction.

He looked into my eyes. "Please tell me that is not your engagement ring."

"It's his great-great-grandmother's."

He pointed. "So, give it to her. You mean he didn't even buy you a ring?"

"This is fine."

"Tiffany? Come on. That's fine in the early 1800s. Not by today's standards."

I turned, walking away. "It's fine, Michael. Drop it."

"I thought he made good money sleeping in alleys. I guess he really is homeless."

"Enough, Michael."

"Tiffany," he pulled my shoulder to stop me. "You deserve better."

"Okay, this wasn't what I was expecting, but this is what I got. I'm not marrying him for the ring. I am marrying him because I love him."

Michael softened, looking as though he was about to say something. Instead, he turned and walked away. I refused to go after him. I walked straight to the Lexus, heading to the grappling studio.

I adjusted the spreader bar back to about where it was before Andy found a different use. My instructor watched as I buckled the cuffs around my ankles.

"It should be the width of your shoulders." That was all he said before going back to watching two young guys grapple. I adjusted it outward one notch.

Andy was out when I arrived back home. I opened a can of cat food and fed Kitten. Andy's mother would arrive tomorrow. Our house was clean and ready for company. I texted Andy to see what time he would be home. I smiled when Andy texted back to say he was on his way.

He walked in with purpose, right to the computer system. Something was wrong. I followed. "What's going on?"

"Tiffany, I need everything quiet for about an hour. No TV, no calling my name. No coming near the station, okay?"

I nodded, pointing toward the door. "I'll go for a run."

He turned sharply. "No, not from here. Go to the gym."

"I can do that. I'll be back by seven."

"Sorry, babe. Have a good run."

He sat down and plugged his headphones in. "Here." He spoke into the mouthpiece.

The gym was a good idea, but Hannah's bar was better. I walked in and took a seat. She grinned. "We have a dress code."

"I know. I was heading to the gym, and I realized you were a better idea."

"I don't see you forever and now it's almost daily."

"Your bridal shower is Sunday. Perhaps I should go shopping instead."

Hannah grinned. "I am so excited!"

"Mother said we have the entire bar area."

"Yes, Sunday afternoons are quiet there."

"I'm decorating Sunday morning."

"Are you working Saturday night?"

"Yup."

"Tiffany, get some sleep. We can handle it."

"I'll grab sleep after, no worries."

"Well, should be done by three."

"I'm fine, Hannah. Monday's a day off. Besides, less future mother-in-law to deal with."

"Future mother-in-law? Is Andy's mother coming?"

"Tomorrow."

"Tiffany, you must bring her."

I shook my head from side to side. "No, no . . . no. Not a good idea. I'll be happy to get away from her."

"But it will be rude of us not to include her."

"Hannah. From what I am learning . . . the way Andy makes you feel uncomfortable . . . it comes from psycho mommy dearest."

"No?"

"I met her for like 20 seconds. She called me a slut, a whore, and other stuff. She scared me."

"What? She said that to you?"

"Yes. I hid out in my condo for a few days."

"Why didn't you say something to me? When was she here?"

"Couple weeks ago. Now I live at Andy's and she is staying with us."

"For how long?"

"I hope only a few days. I think Andy is trying to do the right thing, but this woman is a lunatic."

"My condo is a mess. But you are always welcome."

"Mother furnished the condo. I can go back there in an emergency."

"I think Priscilla said they are moving in there this weekend."

"Movers are coming Saturday. Father's flying out Monday."

Hannah poured us both waters. "This is so crazy. All of us in new places. I'm getting married in three weeks, and you . .

. When are you tying the knot?" She reached over and took my hand. "Have you thought about a wedding?"

I exhaled. "I'll wait until everything settles down. Maybe we will get married in my parents' new back yard. They said the view is amazing. Mother's expecting a campfire wedding, anyway."

"I'll need plenty of notice."

"No worries. It won't be like this speedy wedding."

"Hey, I've got the venue I wanted, the man I want. It is meant to be."

"Well, you better not tell me you're pregnant."

She chuckled. "No. Three years is the plan."

"You will be thirty. That's cool."

"Yeah, give us a chance to enjoy each other for a few years. You know, practice with the nieces and nephews first."

"I like it."

Andy texted: *FUBAR. I have to go. See you in the morning.*

I didn't like this text. I hoped it didn't have to do with Reardon.

I placed the phone down so Hannah couldn't see.

"Is everything all right?"

"No, something is going wrong. He won't be home tonight." I turned my phone over. "Looks like I am going shopping. What are your top five from the list?"

Hannah said gift card, and I said thank you. One four-hundred-dollar gift card for one awesome friend. This should cover a few items on her list.

I stopped in to check on Mother. She had a team of eight women and Jordan there packing and labeling boxes, going from room to room. Three color-coded notebooks were spread open on the kitchen counter, labeled "Hannah Wedding," "Hannah's Bridal Party," and "Condo/Seattle Move." Father's plane ticket was labeled and tucked in the clear sleeve with everything in order.

I looked around, understanding where some of my organizational skills had come from. "Very impressive, Mother."

Mother closed the cap to a marker as she walked over. "This one is finished. Hand me a black marker, dear."

I opened the box, handing one fresh marker over. She grinned. "Don't worry, everything is on schedule. What time will you be at North End?"

"Right after my shift, about 8:30."

Mother walked over, flipping the page and marking off 8:30 a.m. "Is dinner still six on Friday?"

"Yes."

"There is a change. I'm cheating. Mary is cooking chicken and dumplings with vegetables. I'm bringing wine and dessert. I just can't cook a meal right now."

I smiled. "Phew. You are human. I was going to say I will cook but screw it. Mary's chicken and dumplings . . . yum!"

"Go talk to her. Mary offered to come to you and cook there."

I went to find Mary.

CHAPTER TWENTY-EIGHT

It was seven a.m. and Andy still wasn't home.

I texted him: *What time is your mother arriving?* He replied that he would be home within the hour and Agnes would arrive at ten.

My stomach hurt right until the moment he walked in. He had time to shower, with me following right into the bathroom. There was no way was I facing this woman alone.

I talked to Andy about Mary coming over to cook dinner. He thought that was a little over the top until I mentioned what she was making. He gave in and accepted her cooking here.

The hour approached ten. I wished I were at the garage. Andy sat at the computer station. I was pretty sure this guy hadn't slept since yesterday.

We both heard the car door close. My heart pounded harder at the sound of footsteps on the stairs. My ears followed the sound of anything I could pick up from this woman, as my body stiffened at the knock on the door.

Andy stood up, walked over, reaching for my hand. "Everything is going to be fine, Tiff."

We walked toward the door. Andy reached for the knob and my eyes widened, watching it twist in slow motion.

There Agnes stood, wearing a black and white, plain, military-issued pantsuit. The door opened wider to reveal a duffel bag hanging over her shoulder.

She almost smiled while looking at Andy, then her eyes shifted to me and beyond, into the room.

"What in the name of God?" Agnes barked. "What is all this sinful waste?!"

Andy pulled me into him, securing an arm around my shoulders.

"Tiffany is all moved in, and we picked out some pieces from her parents' place. You have a separate room now."

She scanned the area, her eyes shifting quickly around and her lips pressed in a hard line.

"What did I teach you about material objects?"

"We are getting married, Mom."

Her eyes shifted straight to my ring.

"Ciara ring?" she asked, pointing like an angry deity.

I folded the left hand into my right. Andy grinned. "Fits her perfectly."

I thought steam would start leaking from Agnes's ears. "Your father said he lost it."

"No, he gave it to me. Come, let me show you your room."

Her icy stare into my eyes sent shivers down my spine. I imagined I would probably lose this finger, with her biting it off in the middle of the night to get the ring.

She walked slowly past, eyes dropping on my ring. *Holy smokes, I'm shaking. Physically shaking.*

Andy headed to the back room, with her slowly walking, scanning the new furnishings. Her head turned toward our bed. Then to the sofa and television. I watched as her head shifted left to right until reaching the back room. Andy walked her in, closing the door. Oh, that was a dangerous sign. They were in there for twenty minutes. I packed my bag for second shift, thinking of any excuse to get out of here.

Andy exited the room alone, walking toward me. He stopped a few feet away, reaching out for contact. "She'll be fine. This isn't just her world anymore. She needs to adjust. Don't take what she says personally."

"I'm not going to take insults from her."

He nodded. "No, neither will I. This is your house now. Yours and mine.

"She hates the furniture."

"Doesn't matter. I like it. I like sleeping in a comfortable bed, sitting in a comfortable chair, the sofa, the television . . . everything." He turned to the dining room table. "Blueprints are no problem on this table."

That felt relaxing to hear. "Blueprints? What do you need blueprints for?"

He said it so matter of fact. "Strategic mapping."

Then I remembered about last night. "Hey, did you straighten out last night?"

His mother now opened the bedroom door, with both of us turning to watch her approach. "This is ridiculous clutter. All of it. This is going to make you soft and lazy. She is going to get you killed."

"You only live once, Mom."

"If she needs all these material possessions, Andrew, she is the type of woman who will drain your bank account. Look at her. You work hard for what you have."

He released his hold on my arm. "She has her own money. Tomorrow we are having dinner with her parents. Here. Tiffany has a friend coming over to teach her how to make a particular chicken dish."

"She doesn't know how to cook?"

I interrupted. I was done listening to her speak as if I wasn't here. "I can cook. Mother is actually French-trained. She originally planned on cooking for everyone, but a change in circumstances pulled her attention to more important issues. Our family friend is from the South. She volunteered to make our meal extra special for our first meeting here. It will give me a chance to learn how she prepares it. Andy is going to love it and I want to make sure I get the technique right so I can duplicate it in the future."

She narrowed her eyes directly at me as if I were not permitted to speak. This woman was far worse than Clarissa Montgomery. Agnes continued looking around the place in disgust. "Andrew, what time does she leave?" She was talking about me.

Andy answered, "Fourteen hundred."

My mind shouted: *Right now, leave right now!*

"I suppose you will make me wait in this clutter until she goes?"

I turned my head up toward Andy. "Wait for what?"

"She has a few people over at the base who want to speak with her."

"Or, I can go now and you come when you are done babysitting." She raised her eyebrow to challenge me.

"Excuse me?" Did she just say that?

Andy cupped my bicep. "Mom, enough. I will not stand for you being rude to my fiancée."

"This is not me being rude; this is pointing out that you obviously like adolescent girls. I didn't realize your taste was so juvenile."

"Tiffany is only ten years younger."

"I guess a mature woman wouldn't put up with your failures. Her naivete will complement your ego, Andrew."

I felt his hand tighten around my arm. I turned my head to him.

"Maybe your mother should go on ahead. Meet there when I leave. Hey, don't they have a hotel on the base? She might be more comfortable staying there."

His grip softened. "Excellent idea, babe." He looked over at his mother. "Why don't you go on ahead. I'll be over after I make sure my woman is all set for her shift. Also, think about where you want to stay. If our home is too cluttered, then I will pay for your room at the base."

She looked from me to Andy and back in a hard stare. I tried to raise my eyebrow in a cocky look, but my lips were pressed tight, trying not to show the tremble. This woman was going to be my mother-in-law.

I was not going to take anything she said personally, because no matter who Andy hooked up with, she would hate them just as much. I turned toward Andy, who gave his full attention to me.

"Hey, I can fiddle in the garage for a few hours before the shift. Greg will appreciate it. I haven't been able to put much time in there lately."

Andy softened. "Are you sure?"

I gave a brief smile. "Yeah, I'm good." He looked tired. I wanted him to get a few hours of sleep. "Or I can stay and make you sleep for a few hours."

He rubbed my arm. "I'll get enough when I am six feet under."

Agnes commented. "I am sure that will be soon. She is ruining you."

"Mom, I'll catch up with you later. Go ahead to the base. I will call when I am on my way."

She scowled. "Fine." She marched past us and out the door.

I needed to find out. "Is she always like this?"

He sighed. "Pretty much. It's just been the two of us for a long time. Mom will adjust."

"What was she like with your father when he was alive?"

"Dad? Well, Dad was fun. He knew how to redirect really well. She is extremely competitive actually, to a fault."

"Well, I have no intention of challenging her to anything, so she can relax."

"Mom will find something."

"Great. But since she is gone for a bit, why don't you take a quick nap."

He stepped into me, resting his hands on my waist. "Only if you lie down with me."

I checked the time. "Okay."

Sleep was the farthest thing from his mind. He managed to get me to sleep for a few hours. *There goes my garage time.*

Bartek texted a lot that night. I thought he timed our stops, as well. I thought I saw him set his stopwatch on his phone. I almost asked him, but Andy texted to ask how my night was going. I filled him in on my suspicions. He texted that he would follow my ambulance for a few hours.

I didn't want to but out of curiosity asked how his mother was doing. Andy told me she was staying at the base. It felt like a weight lifted from my shoulders, leaving a sense of relief. I didn't want to come home to her. I couldn't even imagine what she would say seeing Andy and me in the same bed. At least tomorrow I was covered with allies, between Mary and my parents coming over.

CHAPTER TWENTY-NINE

I felt some of the tension release at the sight of Andy's car as I pulled into my parking spot.

I walked in to find him sitting at command central, playing with the computers. He called for me to come over. Kitten intercepted, attacking my feet, making me bend down to scoop up one very fluffy feline. I continued walking toward Andy with a loudly purring kitty in my arms.

Last night, Andy had filmed a few stops on my run, keeping the camera focused on Bartek. "I don't like it, Tiff. He's on someone's payroll."

"You think? The guy's as crooked as they come."

"I haven't picked up any interest in particular on the market. I don't see what his angle is."

"You said he was a drug dealer in prison? Could he be setting up drugs? Could be he knows someone in the hospitals who has access."

"That's good logic, Tiffany. I'll look into it."

"Well, if it's quiet in the underworld again, that's the only other corrupt thing I can guess. Makes sense with him, right?"

"Beautiful, sexy and smart. I am one lucky man."

"And, as your mother pointed out, a cradle-robbing man at that."

Andy grinned. "That, too."

It was three in the morning when my eyes popped open at the sound of a gun cocking. I sat straight up. Andy wasn't in bed, but I heard him quietly shush me from close by.

My eyes adjusted to the darkness as I watched him step silently toward the door. I slid out of bed and onto the floor. My bag sat close by, containing my 9mm. I peeked out the window to see if there were any vehicles outside.

Andy slipped on his night vision goggles, then carefully opened the door. He entered the hallway with Kitten running after him, but he managed to shut the door in time, so she didn't escape.

I reached for my bag, pulling the gun out. My heart pounded. Perhaps his mother was here spying on us? I couldn't hear anything, and I knew Andy would be mad if I left the room. He didn't need me screwing things up, so I stayed put.

Whatever was going on seemed to be taking forever. I peeked at my phone and saw the time was three-thirty. *Where could he be?*

At the sound of the doorknob turning, my heart sped up. A figure walked in. It was Andy.

"Tiff, all clear."

I turned the light on to see him removing his goggles. "What happened?"

"I'm not sure. I heard something, enough to wake me up."

"What did it sound like?"

"Like someone walking around upstairs."

"Find anything?"

"Nothing."

"Maybe it was your mother."

"That's what I'm guessing."

I holstered my gun, snapping my head up. "Seriously?"

"Wouldn't be the first time for her."

"Then she needs to stay here so we can keep a closer eye on her."

"You know, babe, I actually like that she's at the base."

"Yeah, but not if it's tempting her to come here and wake us up in the middle of the night. Do you have cameras up around here?"

"Some, but there will be more tomorrow."

"Okay. Let's try to get a few hours of sleep. I have third shift with Bartek tonight and I need to stay alert."

Andy returned to bed with me but, when I woke again, I found he had already left. I grabbed my phone to check the time again. It was 9:11. The sun streamed and I raised my hand to block the rays while checking to see if his car was still here.

It was, so he was somewhere on the property. I thought about last night and wondered if he was installing more cameras. I texted him: *What about some breakfast?*

He texted back: *I'll be there in fifteen.*

I pulled out eggs, bacon, and a loaf of bread, his mother's insults funneling through my head. *"Can she cook?"* . . . *I can cook, lady.*

I plated our food and brought it to the big table. Kitten lounged across the back of the sofa. Andy must have fed her earlier. I retrieved the orange juice and poured a cup of coffee for myself as I listened to Andy's gait coming up the stairs. He walked in wearing camo fatigues with a gun strapped to his side and black stripes on his face. He dropped his maintenance bag.

"Smells good, babe. Perfect timing." He leaned in, swiftly kissing me on his way to the sink to wash up.

I stood, holding the back of the chair. "What were you doing?"

"Cameras. Someone entered here last night, and not my mother."

I stiffened. "Really? How can you tell?"

"There's a few boot prints. Someone scaled the back side of this place."

I turned to see the back area was now covered by walls. The back room was enclosed now to make a private bedroom. "So, they have an easier entry with the back area walled off?"

"Not anymore."

"This is crazy. Who knows you are here? I mean, it can't be random."

"It's not random."

"Who then? And why?"

"I will find out."

I drove to my grappling studio, then practiced for two hours. My instructor shared some new techniques for breaking free from an attacker's grasp. From there, I worked out on cardio for forty-five minutes, then headed to the garage for the afternoon.

After my second oil change, it was time to wrap up. I needed to meet Mary and show her the way to the warehouse. Andy called. "We have a few more joining us for dinner. Make sure you have enough to feed everyone."

"Who?" I asked. It wasn't like Andy to suddenly add more guests for a special meeting with the parents.

"Harry, Troy, and Sahil."

I grinned. This would be a welcome, not an intrusion. "Got it. I'll be back in an hour or so."

"Careful, Tiff. Watch your six."

"That's your job," I said, still grinning into the phone.

"Gladly."

I smirked. "See you soon." I hung up.

Mary had a list. I knew we were going shopping. I didn't want her to cook and buy the food, too. We met at the Price Rite grocery store. I informed her of the extra company, so we tripled the list. Mary talked excitedly about the extra people, saying it had been a long time since she had cooked for a crowd. I insisted throughout the trip that she stay and eat with us.

Soon after we returned, the pleasant scent of home cooking permeated the warehouse. Mary had even baked an almond pecan sheet cake.

Agnes arrived, going straight to the back room. Mary gave a startled reaction, so I whispered, "She doesn't like me."

Mary's expression changed from bewildered to appalled, and she whispered back, "What? She just doesn't know you yet. You will win her over, Tiffany. I'm sure of it."

Next, we both turned at the noisy commotion out in the hall, making its way up the stairs. It would have sounded like there was a brawl in the hallway, if not for all the laughter.

Andy and Sahil fought to enter the door first. Sahil pushed Andy away, closing it shut on him and bracing against it so he couldn't enter. Sahil continued laughing as he spotted us. He stood up, stepping away from the door. "Hello, Gilli."

Andy opened the door, grinning. "Hi, babe. This must be Mary. Welcome."

Our warehouse began to shake. Dishes bounced. Windows rattled. Mary held onto me looking all around. I didn't understand what it could be. Andy and Sahil remained calm as could be amid the sudden chaos. I didn't know what to do. "Andy?"

He pointed to the ceiling, yelling, "Apache. It's all right."

Mary was frightened. "What is Apache?"

Sahil walked over to us, yelling, "Helicopter. He will shut it off in a minute." He caught a glass bouncing off the counter and held the pot on the stove. "Smells good, what's for dinner?" he continued yelling.

Mary answered, still holding onto me. "Chicken and dumplings." The noise died down and the shaking ceased. "Heavens to mercy. Someone is landing a helicopter on your roof? Is it safe?"

I looked over to Andy. He stepped forward. "Oh, yes. I have a landing pad up there. Reinforced steel in the structure."

"Really?" I questioned.

The noise stopped and Andy walked out of the house. Sahil asked, "Do I smell cake?"

Mary smiled. "Yes, a little Southern sheet cake."

Sahil stepped over, hugging her. "I don't know you, but I already love you. This smells like home." He let her go, opening the oven to peek in. Mary didn't know how to react. She looked both surprised and proud.

"When did you get in, Sahil?" I asked as he lifted the lid, inhaling with pleasure.

"Beautiful, may I taste?"

Mary handed him a spoon as he dipped it into the gravy, blowing on it and bringing it to his mouth, moaning as he savored. "Just like Momma's."

Andy returned with Troy and Harry. Troy had a bag. Harry did not. Mary looked bug-eyed as they piled in.

Troy commented. "Damn, smells like good cooking to me." He smiled, glancing over to Mary. I introduced everyone. Mary stood, only greeting in vowels.

Sahil was next to her. "She cooks like my Momma."

The men reacted like they were in for a treat. I guess they had all met Sahil's mother. Andy now made his official introductions. Mary blushed, staring at me. "He's very handsome, Tiffany. You will make beautiful babies." All the men remained silent.

Troy spoke up, "Want to see my two rugrats?" He pulled out his phone, showing us two boys, one named William, who was ten years old, and the other named Shane, who recently turned seven. They were both on dirt bikes. Andy smile when Mary said they looked like handfuls.

Troy laughed. "Just like their daddy."

Harry slapped Andy on the back. "You're next, brother." Agnes walked from the back room to join us. "You better not have impregnated the girl and that's why you feel you need to marry her."

All the men looked elsewhere as Mary gasped at her bluntness. I turned, hearing Mother call out from the hallway.

Andy walked to greet them at the door. Father pointed upward with an amazed expression. "You have an Apache helicopter on your roof?"

Andy grinned, pointing to Harry. "It's his. This is Harry, Richard. He dabbles in the stock market. You two should have a lot to talk about. Priscilla, this is Harry, Troy, and Sahil."

Mother looked in awe from man to man to man. Suddenly, Andy's mother stepped forward.

"Priscilla, this is my mother, Agnes McMillan. Mom, this is Priscilla and Richard Chanler."

Agnes did not try to shake their hands. Mother read her thoughts right away.

"It's a pleasure to meet you, Agnes. I hope you are enjoying your stay. You have an advantage. This is my and Richard's first time visiting here."

Troy stopped the conversation. "Allow me to show you around, Priscilla." He took my mother's arm to escort her around. The sight was almost comical, as Troy stood six-foot-five on a bad day.

He towered, all beefed up in his T-shirt, looking like a force of nature. Father took over the conversation. "We originally planned on hosting you over at our place, but we recently sold it. We are moving to the West Coast. The movers are coming tomorrow."

Agnes studied Father. "Unexpected, I take it?"

Father smiled. "It is a delightful change for us. Been a long time coming." He turned to Mary. "Mary, it smells divine. Thank you for stepping in and helping."

She adjusted her hands to wipe them on a dish towel. "My pleasure, I should leave you all to talk." She brought her watch in front of her face. "I should be going."

I stopped her. "No, stay, I mean it. Unless you have to go." She looked from me to Richard. "Please stay, Mary. We can leave together and make sure you get back to the city safely."

She turned to Andy. "Please stay," he sincerely asked. Sahil seconded the request.

Mary blushed. "Okay, let me call my husband. I think he has a dinner meeting, anyway." Mary pulled a flip phone from her purse and walked to the back of the kitchen.

Mother and Troy returned from their tour. "I love this place," she said. "Big, open floor plan. The bedroom set fits perfectly in your guest room. Andy, I can't get over the fact that you framed that room in one day."

Sahil tore a piece of bread off, dipping it in the gravy. "You should see what he can do in the wilderness. Once we were dropped in the middle of nowhere –"

Andy gave Sahil a look that stopped him from talking.

Father asked, "You guys were in the service together?"

Troy walked by, heading toward the food. "Still are. We meet up for jobs here and there."

Father pointed to the roof. "Is that why you have that?"

Harry grinned. "No, I bought that last year when some of my investments climbed."

Father reasoned. "That's a forty-million-dollar machine up there."

Troy turned, bringing the bread to his mouth. "He bought it at a discount."

Mary became comfortable enough to shoo them away from the pot. "Why don't we bring this to the table and start eating."

Mother had brought wine. She and Father were the only ones drinking. I had to work tonight, Harry was apparently only here to drop Troy off and eat, Sahil and the boys had an evening planned, and Agnes turned her nose up, saying it was the devil's water. If I weren't working tonight, I would have poured a full glass right in front of her.

Harry and my father talked business. Harry had heard of Henshaw Logistics. Father explained they were ahead of the game until the government pulled their contract.

Mother, trying to include everyone, asked Agnes what she did. "Government contracts," was all she said. The table went quiet. Mother ignored the silence, asking what kind of contracts. Agnes answered, "Construction."

Harry said he might have another connection to sell engines. Father perked up, interested.

Mother tried to engage Agnes in conversation, but it was clear she had nothing to say to any of us. Andy filled in and talked with Mother, as did Sahil. As soon as Sahil mentioned Paris, she lit up. From then on, those two talked about practically nothing else.

Mary was in her own conversation with Troy as he showed her his family and places he had been. Mother spoke up that they had imported this very table from France.

With 9:30 p.m. fast approaching, I had to get ready for work. I excused myself while Sahil finished the last of Mary's cake. Andy followed me into the bathroom and attached a hidden wire to my bra. We heard Mary telling the story about how Troy and Harry's arrival had made the entire room shake. At ten o'clock, Father and Harry exchanged business cards, shaking hands, and wishing each other a good night.

Everyone piled out except for Agnes. I packed up to leave, Mary was leaving, and my parents were leaving. We all walked out, and Andy warned them about the soon-to-be whooshing air.

Harry started his helicopter. He turned all the lights on for show and lifted off. Mary, Mother, and Father were excited to watch him leave. They stood there talking about it for another few minutes.

Andy kissed me goodbye, telling me he would not be far tonight. Andy, Troy, and Sahil walked back inside.

I had to admit, seeing Harry take off was exciting, and this was going to be my life with Andy.

It turned out Agnes left shortly after I did. Sahil followed the ambulance all night, and Andy and Troy staked out the perimeter of the warehouse. If anything happened tonight, they would find out who was behind it.

CHAPTER THIRTY

I felt a little safer knowing Sahil was somewhere nearby. Bartek asked if I knew anything about the guy in the meeting who'd smashed his head into the table. I told him he worked for Angel Wings as a private contractor, trying to get Bartek to talk. Bartek asked if I'd ever been tempted to make more money.

There was one way to answer this, and it would shut Bartek up from making any further conversation. We had an illegal tracking device on the back of the truck. Bartek had been timing the runs. I wanted to find out what he was up to.

I answered simply that I had never been approached. I considered that was a safe, cautious answer that left room for more conversation. He talked about how much debt he owed. His ex-wife had cleaned him out, and he was set up to take the fall at the prison. He didn't like being so poor.

I let him keep talking, but decided to be very careful with my responses. This could be a setup.

He confessed he grabbed all the overtime he could, and it still wasn't making ends meet. This guy had money issues and was looking to grab any open shift. Right then, he was fishing to see if I was an asset or liability.

Bartek pointed out the ring on my finger. I shrugged, saying it was my grandmother's ring and had been in the family for generations. He laughed, telling me a guy would never give a ring like that if he wanted to get laid. I said nothing. I knew this was being recorded. Eventually, we finished up our shift, and I had to admit it actually hadn't been so horrible.

Michael met up with me at the office and asked when our next gym session would be. I replied that this weekend was out, and weekdays would probably be better.

He turned and looked me right in the eyes. "Tiff, thanks for letting me back in. I miss hanging out with you."

I nodded. "Me, too, Michael."

He smiled. "You'd better take care of the leg. I plan on spinning you around the dance floor at Hannah's wedding."

I laughed. "We'll see."

He stepped closer, speaking in a low voice. "How was riding with Polack tonight?"

"Interesting. The guy opened up a little."

"He's been grabbing every shift he can. Something is up. I don't trust him."

I agreed. "Something is definitely going on."

"Is your boyfriend looking into his connections?"

"Fiancé, Michael."

"Whatever."

I slightly shook my head. "He's looking."

"Good. Clue me in if he finds anything. Perhaps I can help."

"Get some rest, Michael."

"You too, Tiff."

I walked to my car. Bartek had his hood up, apparently dealing with car trouble.

"Greg will be here in about an hour if you need anything," I offered.

"Can you give me a ride?"

"Um. I have an appointment, sorry."

"Just down the street."

I was stuck. If I said no, then we were going back to square one. "I can look. I'm getting good with cars."

He blocked my way. "Fuse blew. There's a parts store down the road. They opened at seven."

"Which fuse? I can grab one in the shop."

"Or maybe it's the battery?"

"We have a battery pack in the shop to give you a jump."

"Never mind, I'll call my buddy."

"No one is allowed in here without clearance."

"Not even if my car is down?"

"We have a garage. They can fix it. And you can be picked up from outside the gates."

"So that's a no on the ride?"

"Sorry, I gotta go. But check inside. Michael is still here. Maybe he can help."

"Forget it. I'll figure it out."

I started my car with uneasy suspicion. I pulled out and drove away, then turned my car around in the garage to see if Bartek's car trouble was a setup. Five minutes later, there he was, coming up the ramp in his car, which was running fine.

What the hell was that all about? Tonight we were scheduled to take the rural route together. I called Michael. He hadn't left yet, and I told him where I had parked in the garage. He pulled up three minutes later. I explained what had just happened.

He didn't care if there was fallout later and insisted we switch routes tonight, last-minute, so no one would know until it was time to leave. I agreed, comfortable with the swap.

I arrived home and Sahil pulled in behind me. I grinned. "I expected you would already be here."

"Mulligan said to stay with you. So, I stay with you."

"Oh, sorry. I didn't mean to take so long. Something strange happened."

"I know. I heard. Glad you didn't let him in your car. The guys need to listen to this."

Andy and Troy were inside going over camera footage. They did not appear happy. Sahil shouted to them he had material. They waved him over. He looked at the footage they were inspecting. I stood next to Andy. I couldn't see a thing.

Sahil leaned in. "No."

Troy sat back. "Yes."

Sahil turned to Andy. "Shit."

Andy stood up. "Who's hungry?"

We all walked to the kitchen. Andy made breakfast. I asked.

"Who is it?"

No one answered.

Sahil pulled the recorder out, playing it back. I still had my wire on. "I'd better take this off."

Andy lifted my shirt, not flinching one bit, he pulled my wire off. I didn't care if the boys saw my bra. Heck, I had changed in the open at my grappling class when I ran late.

Troy cleared his throat as I looked over to see him grinning and Sahil looking away. "What? It's a bra. I'm sure you fellas have seen your fair share."

Andy chuckled, pulling my shirt back down.

They listened to Bartek's conversations. I pointed out that I finally got him talking. Then, Sahil crushed my hopes, telling me the conversation was completely rehearsed. They now knew who they were dealing with, and Andy needed to find out why. None of them would tell me who was behind this.

Troy agreed that staying on the city run was a good idea, enough to throw them off their game tonight, and Andy would have two more days to find what he needed.

Andy and I grabbed a few hours of sleep while Sahil took the back room and Troy kept an eye out. They had swapped at some point, because when I woke up Troy was in the back room sleeping and Sahil was sitting at the table, saying good morning to me. I slipped on a sweatshirt and walked over to him.

"Your husband makes the best coffee known to man."

I pulled a mug off the hook. "I know, right? No matter how many times I try, I just can't perfect it the way he does."

Sahil patted the table for me to sit. "While we will do everything to protect you, there are some instances where we won't be able to get to you. How are you protecting yourself?"

"I have been taking grappling classes on and off for about five years now. I have two black belts and my instructor is working with close contact maneuvers."

"Show me."

"What, right now?"

"Show me right now."

My brain planned for a moment. Sahil put his cup down, and I smiled, pondering what I should show him. Before I knew it, the last of his coffee splashed in my eyes, and I landed on the floor with his knuckles against my throat. It left me coughing and gagging.

He helped me up. "You cannot take time to consider what you want to do. Logic will get you killed, Gilli. In the brief time I have known you I can see why Mulligan wants you all to himself. You are part of my family now. You must do your job to stay part of it. Now let's try this again. No thinking this time."

Andy stood in the middle of the room. I was straddling Sahil on the floor between the dining room table and the kitchen, pulling back a punch as he flipped me off him and dumped me on my back.

"What the–?!" Andy grabbed Sahil around the neck as I shouted to Andy that he was teaching me how to fight. Andy looked down, releasing his grip, and Sahil burst into laughter. "She's got some power behind her punch."

I needed this break, panting frantically to catch my breath. Sahil, meanwhile, breathed with ease. "She's got to get her cardio up."

Andy raked his hand through his hair. "Her leg has been a setback. Bullet penetrated the muscle."

Sahil reached out for my arm to help me back on my feet. He tapped Andy on the chest. "It's your duty to teach her. If she is becoming part of the family, she needs training."

His head dropped down. "I know, didn't see this happening so soon."

I felt a sweaty mess. At least I stank like coffee. "What came so soon?" I asked, looking at Andy.

"You're being set up."

I walked by, tapping his arm. "Tell me something I don't know."

Sahil said it. "It's one of us."

One of us. That stopped me in my tracks. Sahil, Troy and Harry were all here last night, enjoying the company. "Richie or Vic?"

Sahil answered. "Richie is in Spain."

I shot my glance to Andy. "Vic."

The expression on Andy's face was disappointment. None of us said another word. I turned to Sahil. "How long are you here for?"

"A week, little sister."

"Can you work with me until you have to leave?"

"As much as you can handle."

Andy put his arm on Sahil's shoulder. "Thank you, brother."

"One condition."

I took a step toward Sahil. "What?"

"You bring my adopted momma back to cook. I need nourishment."

I grinned. "Well, you can start by being my date tomorrow at a bridal shower for my best friend. Mother will be there; she is the wedding planner. I am the maid of honor."

"Yes. I will be honored. I need proper clothes. Mull, take care of our bijou. I need to shop."

Andy smiled. "With pleasure."

Sahil cleaned up in the bathroom while Andy and I sat, talking on the couch. He asked what Sahil and I had covered, and over the next half-hour I showed him in slow motion.

Andy looked concerned.

"What?" I asked.

"Sahil has done a far better job in a half-hour with you than I have done in two and a half years."

I sat closer. "No . . . no. I shoot better because of you. I am so much better all-around because of you. I love you, Andy."

He held up my ring finger. I smiled. "And we will have a great life together."

He shifted his gaze, looking into my eyes. "I don't know what I would do now if you were not part of my life."

I reached up to touch his face. "Then let's make sure we never find out."

CHAPTER THIRTY-ONE

It was moving day for my parents. I called Mother to see if she needed me to do anything for Hannah's bridal shower tomorrow. It was just like her to have everything in order.

I needed to pack an outfit to take because I planned on going directly to the restaurant after my shift. I glanced through what I had, and the teal cocktail dress I wore to my birthday seemed like it would be appropriate, if it still fit me. I tried it on. A little snug, but it was the right length to cover my bullet scar.

I walked out, with Troy now awake and whistling at me. I grinned. "Where's Andy?"

His head tipped to the side. "In the garage."

I questioned. "We have a garage?"

Troy looked confused. "You've never been in the garage?"

I must have looked as confused as I felt. "No?"

Troy sounded curious. "Hmm. That's interesting."

"Is it here?"

He pointed. "That building."

"He owns that building, too?"

"He owns all these buildings."

Clearly my shock was apparent. "What?"

Troy sat forward. "Oops. You two need to talk."

"Yah think?!"

Andy was walking back in, his eyes on me.

"Where are you wearing that?" He pointed to my dress.

"You own all these buildings?"

He glanced from me, to Troy, and back. "Um, yes . . . why?"

"I thought they were abandoned buildings."

"Tiffany, I have a gun range over there. Did you assume I could do that without owning the area?"

I considered his statement. He was right. "What else do you own that I don't know about?"

Troy smiled widely. "Dude, you haven't shown her the collection?" Andy stared hard at Troy. "Oh, come on, buddy. You guys are getting married."

Andy turned back to me. "Go change. I want to show you some stuff."

I changed into jeans and a T-shirt and followed him across the lot to the building the boys had all parked in front of. Andy opened the door and flipped the lights on. Troy walked in behind us. There were motorcycles, a Jeep, Hummers, off-road vehicles, and a tank.

"What is all of this?" I walked around, taking in the vehicles and equipment that were all in pristine condition. "This is yours?"

He shrugged. "Yes."

"Are they in working order?"

Troy laughed. "Dude, I can't believe you didn't show her this."

I walked in awe, with Andy following behind me. "How much is this stuff worth?"

Troy answered for him. "Couple million, right, brother?" Andy must have not liked his answering. I heard Troy say, "Oh, sorry."

I chuckled sarcastically. "And you get pissed at me for spending a few hundred on stuff from the shopping channel?"

Troy stopped walking. "Right. See you guys back inside." He turned and walked straight out.

I stared right at him. "Seriously? Why did you keep all this from me?"

"I wasn't keeping it from you. I just didn't get around to showing you yet."

"That's a load of crap."

He said nothing, so I continued. "The buildings are all yours? I mean, I moved in. You threw a tantrum about my furniture. I told you how much my parents gave me for the condo. For Christ's sake, Andy, I even tell you about hanging out with Michael." I looked around again.

"Does your mother know about all this stuff?"

He looked confused. "Not all of it, but some."

"So, is this why she thinks I'm after your money?"

The look on Andy's face made it clear he hadn't considered that. I spread my hands open. "Might as well get it all out now. How much money do you have, Andy? You know my worth."

He looked around for a few seconds as I folded my arms, growing more agitated by the moment.

He stared at me. "Eighteen million."

I uncrossed my arms. "Eighteen million. Eighteen million dollars?"

I didn't get it. He drove a piece-of-crap car. He lived in an unfurnished warehouse. But he also had a building loaded with toys and owned an industrial park, with god knows how many acres.

I looked down at my ring, then surveyed the vehicles around me. *Seriously?* I took my ring off and threw it at him.

I was furious. Mad that he kept all this from me. Ticked off he had money and didn't tell me about it. Pissed that he had given me a chip of a diamond.

I marched right past him and out the door. This was crap.

Troy tried to smooth things over. I didn't want to listen to any of it. I packed my bag for tonight, stuffed my outfit in, and left. I called Mother to tell her I was heading to the condo. They were already there and had just bought Japanese food.

The place looked completely different. My parents were at the table, with another plate out for me.

Mother could tell I was upset. "Come sit, darling."

I took a seat, filling a plate. Father commented that today was a success, and he would be flying out on Monday to meet the movers arriving mid-week.

I ate, but Mother couldn't stand it anymore. "Tiffany, what happened? You are not wearing your ring and you seem very upset."

I sat back. "I'm not upset. I am angry."

She poured more wine for herself and Father. "What happened?"

"Well, I just found out he owns that entire industrial park we live in."

"Oh? That's quite a piece of real estate. No wonder he can land a helicopter there." Father pointed out.

Mother knew this was not the issue. "Go ahead, darling. What happened?"

"That building before ours is filled with motorcycles, off-road vehicles, classic cars, military vehicles. He has a damn tank!"

Father sat forward. "A tank? Really? I would like to see that."

Mother touched my father's arm, then turned to me. "Okay, so he is a collector. It's nice to have a hobby. Why are you upset?"

My father piped in. "What kind of tank?"

"Richard." Mother shushed him.

I added, "He has eighteen million in the bank."

Father smiled. "Good, that makes me feel better. I had apprehensions about him. Audrey couldn't find much. I knew he had some fortune with the way his men were talking at the table. So, he must be Mulligan Travel."

I looked at Father. "What is Mulligan Travel?"

"It's the name the industrial park is owned under."

Now that made complete sense. "His buddies call him Mulligan."

Father and Mother chuckled.

"They gave me a nickname. Gilligan. They said we're two of a kind."

Mother perked up with an ah-ha moment. "I thought I heard Sahil call you Gilli."

"Yeah, he shortened it."

"Dearest, don't be upset with Andrew. Money is sometimes hard to talk about."

"Really, he knows all about my money. I put it out there. It wasn't a problem for me."

"That's not really the issue, is it?"

"He complains if I buy stuff on the shopping channel, meanwhile he drives a crap car, his place had a desk and a bed when I moved in. That's it! And on top off all that, he gave me a cheap-ass ring that he didn't even buy!"

Father excused himself to the living room, turning on the stock report. Mother looked sympathetically at me. "I can see why you are upset. You know he can afford a grand ring for you and he gave you his family ring."

I stuffed another piece of sushi in my mouth, crunching it so I didn't have to speak.

Mother took a sip of wine. "Tiffany, it is possible that ring means more to him than any store-bought ring does? Perhaps that is why he gave it to you. Was he close to his grandmother?"

"I don't know. His mother wasn't, I know that much. And his Dad got killed on duty when he was fifteen."

"Agnes raised him?"

"Yes."

"She is a very stern woman."

"She hates me. But I don't care."

"Tiffany, when she said she worked in government contracts, I had a fleeting moment in which I considered she might be the one who pulled the Henshaw contract out, but then she said she is in construction. That was a relief."

Mother's words sent my mind racing. What if Agnes did have something to do with pulling Father's contract?

Just then, a text from Andy came through: *I am following you tonight. Sahil wants the address of the restaurant. He will meet you there at 8:00 a.m.*

I sent the address.

CHAPTER THIRTY-TWO

I didn't care where Andy was. I still had steam to let off.

He texted me on the way in and told me to meet him on level three in the garage. He had that Honda he had made me drive for a while. I met him so he could tape my wire back on. We said nothing to each other about what happened this afternoon. When he finished, I pulled down my shirt and walked right to my car.

Michael did exactly as we planned and handed off the city route to me last minute, alerting dispatch we were switching. They didn't seem to mind. Josh rubbed his hands together. "Nap time for me between runs."

Bartek suddenly realized what was happening. "Hey, that's our run tonight."

I turned my head and, in my most authoritative voice, announced. "I changed it."

He stared back at me. "You can't do that."

I corrected him. "I can do anything."

While I conducted my outer-shell check, Bartek sat inside the cab, talking on the phone. When I was done, I hopped in.

He immediately commented, "You know, you don't own this fucking place. You are not the boss."

"Actually, on night shifts I am. I have the highest-ranking status and seniority. That makes me the boss. What's the big deal, anyway? What difference does it make if we are in the city or the backwoods?"

He said nothing and sat fidgeting with his phone. It wasn't until three in the morning, when we were halfway done, that he demanded we pull over in a deserted parking lot. I refused, reminding him we were almost at the hospital.

When I drove past the lot, he looked at his phone and grabbed my steering wheel, shouting for me to turn around. I punched him in the ear, managing to take back control.

I watched him, and he watched me. "You fucking touch me or this steering wheel again I will have you arrested and fired so quickly you will have bigger troubles than making ends meet."

"Fucking bitch." He threw his phone on the dash.

Andy drove in ahead of me. There was that other ambulance at the docks. As soon as Andy walked in front of the headlights, the other ambulance pulled away. Andy opened Bartek's door, pulling him out of the ambulance. He had him restrained and immobile within a minute.

Andy ordered me to call the police. I did. He called base on the handheld, asking for a replacement, explaining that Bartek just attacked me. My phone lit up like Christmas.

Michael called immediately. I answered to tell him I would call back in a bit. Andy and the hospital guard stood watch while I did the delivery, explaining the story over and over.

A nurse leaned over, telling me Bartek grabbed her butt last week and that she hadn't been planning to report it. Now, she said, she definitely was. *Great, I wonder how many others are going to file complaints now.*

The cops showed up, and I had permission to travel to the next hospital with another police escort. Andy disappeared for a while after I told him about the parking lot where Bartek wanted me to pull over.

At my next stop, Chris was dropped off by a state trooper. As I finished up, she shook her head while waiting on the dock. "Damn, woman. Trouble just loves to follow you."

I checked the handle of the back door. The transmitter was gone. Maybe Andy removed it. I thanked the cop, and Chris hopped in the passenger seat. "Tell me everything."

Michael called Chris after hearing she was with me. They talked for a bit, and we arrived at our next stop. She hung up. "If it doesn't work out with you and your contractor, I believe Michael would like a chance."

I shook my head. "He's a friend. That's all he will ever be."

She opened her door. "That's a shame. He's a nice guy."

"No chemistry."

She nodded. "I get that."

Donovan stood outside the office entrance. I parked with Chris, who reassured me she would handle all the paperwork. I thanked her, and Michael drove down the ramp. Donovan asked, "Jesus, Tiffany, are you okay?"

"I'm fine."

"Let's go to my office."

Michael ran to catch up. "She told you how dangerous he was, as did I and everyone else."

Donovan turned while asking me to have a seat. "I know. This is my fault. I need to talk with Miss Chanler. Mr. Wojcik will not be returning."

Michael was still angry. "If you had listened in the first place none of this would have happened."

"I will speak with you next. I need to talk with Miss Chanler." Donovan walked into his office and closed the door. This was not entirely his mistake. Michael and I had taken it upon ourselves to make the route changes. The bottom line was Bartek was fired.

I warned Donovan about the sexual-harassment complaint the nurse was planning to file, and a whole new set of stress lines formed across his face. He thanked me for being so professional and said he assumed I had asked Andy follow us because of my own suspicions about Bartek. That wasn't really the case, but it closed the matter without further questions.

I met Andy in the third parking level to remove the wire. We were talking more but still angry with each other. He told me he was going to bed and Sahil would meet me at the bridal shower.

When I arrived, Sahil had already parked and was waiting for me, looking as dashing as ever in his blue, power suit. *Wow, what a handsome man he is all dressed up.* I pulled my cocktail dress from my bag, all scrunched up, and grabbed my shoes.

He pointed. "No, no . . . put it back. I heard about that dress. Not appropriate for a brunch bridal shower. Here, Troy and I rummaged through your stuff. This is better. It was my black, yellow, and white sundress. He handed me the shoes Mother bought in France. Then he handed me my makeup bag.

I looked at my makeup in his outstretched hand. "Who are you, Makeover Man?"

"Gilli, there is not enough time this morning to make you into a fairytale princess. We will have to settle for something less."

I grabbed the bag. "Hey!"

"Come on, just do your best."

"I just worked a third shift and I was attacked."

"You have very limited supplies. We will go shopping to fix this."

"Don't judge. I'm not a fan."

"You and Mulligan both. I expect he still has his tux from Troy's wedding. It took three of us to drag him in there to get fitted. No worries, though. They will be looking at me, not you. Come on."

I walked in with Sahil. Mother was delighted to see him. He shooed me into the bathroom to get ready, telling Mother I needed a makeover.

"I heard that!" I yelled.

They ignored me. Hannah walked in as I began applying makeup. "Sahil? Where have you been hiding him? He is incredible."

"Andy's friend. You should see the one I left back at the house."

"Should I make room for them at the wedding?"

"No, they are only here for a few days. Sahil is a darling, but I'm changing my opinion. He says I need a makeover."

She laughed. "You do. I like him even more now."

Sahil and Mother decorated and placed things just so. I was in charge of the balloons and setting the tables. To say Sahil was the son my mother always wanted was an understatement.

I realized she was openly willing to trade me right now. I had never seen my Mother so happy around another person before in my life. They spoke back and forth in French, discussing the placing of some of the games. He poked through the prizes, loving what she had put together. Little did Mother know he was a trained killer.

Oh, good lord, I wanted alcohol. And that was a first.

Hannah changed into a pale-yellow sundress. She looked gorgeous. Mother slipped a tiara on her head and the festivities began. George arrived at one to help open the presents. Sahil liked the doctor, telling me the importance of having a doctor in the family.

Then he sat with me for a moment, telling me to not be so hard on Mulligan. This was new to him, he explained. Andy never had any kind of long-term relationship before, and his mother always made sure she was front and center.

I was a big deal, Sahil said, explaining that Andy was changing because of me. Then he dropped the hammer, telling me Agnes was the one I needed to worry about and to not let my guard down.

Great, I had my own monster-in-law from hell.

Three o'clock rolled around, and I was fading. The party was just wrapping up when in walked Andy and Troy. Andy wore black cargo pants and a black T-shirt, with Troy sporting a nice, button-down, short-sleeve shirt and dress pants.

Hannah smacked my arm to get my attention. "Is that?"

I nodded. "Yup."

"Make them stay for my wedding."

Mother walked over, greeting Andy first, then Troy. All the women stared.

Sahil scolded Troy. "You couldn't dress him better?"

"He's got nothing except the tux he wore at my wedding."

He gave up. "The two of them were made for each other."

Troy smiled at me. "Gilli, looking good woman. I like that much better than the teal evening dress."

Fashion tips from mercenary killers. What next?

Mother introduced Andy around as Troy filled a plate of food. I walked over.

"Looks like it was a nice party." Troy said as he looked around.

"It was. What are you guys doing here?"

"Mulligan was worried about you driving. You haven't slept in a while. I'm here dropping him off so he can drive you home. Sahil and I can help with the cleanup. You know, give you both some time alone." He winked and nudged me.

"That won't be necessary."

"Awe come on, Gilli. This stuff is new to him. Give the guy a break. He loves you."

"Love has nothing to do with it."

"Love has everything to do with it. You have a lifetime to get to know one another. What counts is you treat each other as if neither one of you is replaceable. You do that, and your life will be easy."

"Is that how you treat your wife?"

"Hell yeah. I rely on her for everything. When I come home, it's my job to take care of her."

"That's really nice, Troy."

He put a few more lobster bites on his plate. "These are good."

"Everything is good. Eat up."

Andy broke away from my mother. "Are you ready to go, babe?"

"Do you want something to eat?"

"No, I'm not hungry."

Sahil walk up behind me. "Go get some rest. Troy and I will stay and help clean up."

I nodded. "Thanks."

Hannah and Mother walked over. Sahil volunteered to clean up with Troy. Hannah grinned, and Mother leaned in to hug me. "Get some rest. You look exhausted."

Andy was parked a few cars back from mine. We took his car home. Andy transferred my work bag, and apparently Troy already had my keys. The ride home remained quiet.

Back at the warehouse, I changed, and Andy climbed in bed with me. Neither of us said much. He tucked me into him with his arm around me and I fell asleep.

CHAPTER THIRTY-THREE

I awoke to the sound of Andy's voice.

"She left the base."

I sat up and scanned the room to find the men happily eating leftovers from the party. Reaching down for a sweatshirt, I slipped my arms in and walked toward them.

Andy stood, walked to the counter and poured me a cup of coffee, meeting me at the table. I picked up a tiny sandwich, thanked Andy for the coffee, and asked, "Are these all the leftovers from the party?"

"Hannah is really nice. She made the waitstaff pack all this up for us," said Troy between bites.

"Her family owns the restaurant. Plus a few others in town."

Troy nodded. "Good food. I'll have to bring the wife if we are ever back here together."

I picked up Andy's phone to check the time, grumbling after seeing it was nine p.m. I was going to be up all night.

Sahil pushed his chair away. "I'm going to get some sleep."

I followed him with my eyes. "You were a big hit today. Thank you."

He cupped my shoulder, walking by. "Goodnight, Gilli."

Troy brought my attention back. "Agnes left the base."

"Left to go where?"

He turned to Andy instead of me. They knew something. "We don't know."

This felt very confusing. "She just up and goes without saying bye?"

"Yeah."

"You may be used to that, but she's a jerk."

Andy's face hardened. I leaned in closer to him. "You, her only child, announced that you are getting married, and she decided to stay elsewhere without giving me the chance to get to know her. Then she left without a goodbye. That's rude. I will not excuse her. Maybe you should start telling her how childish she is acting."

"Tiff, I don't excuse it. I can't control it, either. She is who she is. I told you, she's not like other parents."

"You're right, she's an ass. I want more control over her visits. I will not allow her to do what she wants in my home. She will not make me feel inferior or not good enough. I am good enough. I'm better."

Troy interrupted, "You know, no one can make you feel like less of a person without your consent."

My mouth dropped open. "What is that, mercenary psychology 101?"

He sat a little taller. "Ah no, Eleanor Roosevelt."

Who is this guy? I wondered how a guy like Troy got so philosophical before my thoughts returned to the matter at hand. "Anyway, I mean it, Andy. I understand there are friends of mine you do not want around here. I deserve the same respect."

He tilted his head. "We'll talk about this later."

I felt satisfied that I was getting somewhere. "Now, what about Bartek, did you find anything?"

My sleep schedule was completely off.

On Monday morning, Sahil shadowed me to my grappling class. He met my instructor and observed. The final half-hour, my legs were cuffed, and I was back on my knees working on becoming one with my movements. Sahil watched for a minute, then asked, "What are you doing?"

"Learning to move my body without thinking."

He walked over on the mat, reaching his hand out. "Get up, this is ridiculous." He walked away and grabbed a pair of chairs. "Here, this is about how far apart your seats are, right?" I looked, and he was about right. "Do they have chalk here?"

"I don't know."

"Never mind. He removed his shoes and placed them a few feet in front of the chairs. "Marginal line. Now sit. You're driving. Pretend you are on your route." I held my hands up to my imaginary steering wheel. "Now this entire right side is exposed. You being right-side dominant is a problem. Look, I can disable your leg, arm, any part of your right side. What are you going to do to protect yourself?"

I let go of my imaginary wheel. "Put you into a tree."

He grinned. "I like it, but no. What you are going to do is learn to sacrifice something on your right to disable him with other parts you can use. Now, the guy grabbed the steering wheel, correct?"

I thought about what happened for a second. "No, Bartek grabbed at my wrist holding the steering wheel. Then grabbed the wheel with his other hand."

Sahil leaned over. "So, something like this?"

I observed. "Yes."

"Gilli, stare at me. Where am I vulnerable?"

I looked him over. "Chest, private area, legs."

"Typical female."

"What?"

"Gilli, my neck is right in front of you, so are my eyes, ears, nose. All those areas are target shots. You will change a fight to your favor if you can disable any of those areas."

I knew this. Why was I being so stupid?

"You know, Gilli, I am going to tell you a little secret about your husband."

"We are not married yet."

"Shut up; just listen. Don't tell him I told you, either. When he first met you, it was love at first sight."

"What?"

"He was doing a job and Richie and I were at the base for other reasons. Well, he came back telling us he had just met the woman of his dreams."

"Seriously?"

"He walked into your ambulance. You had the guy on the ground with you finger up his nose and your hand clamped on his face."

I chuckled. "Yes, that's how we met."

"He said you were the most beautiful woman in the world, and you know what he said to us?"

"No?"

"That woman is going to be the death of me, and I am going to love dying."

A smile spread across my face. I couldn't stop it, then I blushed trying to hide it. "And you want to hear what else, Gilli?" I covered my smile with my hands, looking at him. "After meeting you. Now I realize why. I'm serious, you need to protect yourself better. You are family now. There are few people I would take a bullet for. You are not one of them yet."

"Hey!"

"When you learn to fight for your own life again, and not be the victim like you did that day Mulligan first met you, then you will have that respect. If you are going to work in a field where danger lurks, then you'd better toughen up. Otherwise go work in an office or be a telemarketer, a profession where you only have to use your voice and your wits. You are in a physical profession. Time to take it seriously again."

"But my leg keeps setting any advancement back."

"Then change professions."

"No."

"Then stop making excuses."

I had seen Sahil shirtless. He had bullet scars, knife scars, all kinds of scars. He was right. I had gotten soft. "You're right."

He grinned. "Nasty habit of mine."

I asked the guys to leave Andy and I alone for a bit before I sent them over to Hannah's steakhouse for lunch on me. I walked into the warehouse. Andy looked up from his computer station with his index finger to his lips, signaling for me to be quiet.

It still wasn't right between us yet and probably wouldn't be for a while. There were a lot of things we needed to talk about. I walked toward him, removing one article of clothing at a time catching his attention. One by one I watched him watching me.

He ended the conversation he was having. I removed my underwear and stood next to the bed, naked, watching him stand and walk toward me.

I lifted the covers and slipped under them. He stopped next to our bed, removing his clothes and sliding in next to me. It was going to be awhile for us to get back. But right now, for this moment, we were the two people who fell in love at first sight.

CHAPTER THIRTY-FOUR

Pete wanted details, right down to the moment when Andy pulled Bartek out. It was understandable, given his past experience as a state trooper. I didn't tell anyone about the tracking device.

Job postings were out for new hires. My shift turned to overtime for any takers until they hired a replacement. Kyle was stuck chasing people to fill it. Previously, Bartek had been eagerly taking all the overtime shifts. Now we were thin on manpower.

Everything seemed to settle back down at home. Harry picked up Troy, and Sahil stayed longer, spending time with Mother. I focused back on training and catching up in the garage for Greg. I figured with Andy's warehouse full of toys, I'd better start learning to help keep them maintained.

It was Friday and the last day of my shift. I was starting my third oil change when I heard a familiar voice call out my name.

"Miss Chanler."

I stopped, giving Detective Diaz a moment of my time. I straightened up as he approached, curious about the reason for his visit. "Detective?"

"You are one hard lady to track down."

"Not really, what's up?"

"I need you to come down to the station with me."

"Why?"

"I have a few questions."

"So, ask them?"

He looked around. "Not here."

Greg walked over from across the garage.

"I have a busy afternoon, Detective Diaz."

"You may want to reschedule your plans."

"What is going on?"

"I will tell you everything at the station."

"Am I under arrest?"

"I hope not, Miss Chanler. Come with me, please."

Greg tried to stop him. "What's this all about, mister? Tiffany is not going anywhere."

"We found Reardon's van. Although there is no body as of yet, there is blood and brain matter all over the front cab. Miss Chanler's address was written on a file resting on his dashboard."

My heart pounded. "Okay. Let me change."

He agreed. I texted Andy, telling him that Detective Diaz was here and I was going to the police station for questioning. I asked him to call Mother. The detective let me drive my own car and follow him to the station.

Diaz led me to a room with a big table, covered with photographs from the crime scene. I picked up a photo of the van. It did look familiar. I think Mother was right, I had seen this van at my condo complex.

Diaz asked where I had been the past few days. I told him the truth, that I had moved out a few weeks ago and my parents were now living in my condo.

I told him I could pull up their bank transfer dates in my checking account and show that their names had been added on the deed. He had to release me unless he was going to make an arrest. Everything was about to end here.

Mother and Audrey arrived, and Diaz moved all of us to his office. I could not give him any more information. I didn't know anything else.

He placed a photo of Reardon's van on his desk. Mother pointed, telling me, "I told you I recognized him at your place. That's the van I saw."

Now Mother was being held. She gave Diaz everything she knew.

Audrey argued with the detective until there was nothing left to say. He tried to remove her, but she fired back at him with a list of her legal rights as long as the Constitution.

The facts were, Reardon was confirmed alive a few weeks ago. None of us was being arrested, so Diaz sent us on our way, telling Audrey not to come back.

That didn't sit right with her, and she served him another two-minute lecture about her right to be there or anywhere else she pleased. She finished by saying that unless we were suspects, there was no reason to waste taxpayer dollars to have us watched.

I did have to give Diaz my new address. I was hoping to avoid that, but Audrey reminded him with her final outburst.

Andy was not going to like this.

Sahil and Andy met us back at Henshaw Logistics. The building was practically empty. Audrey openly gawked, with flirting smiles at Andy.

"You a Ranger?" She inquired.

"Once," he answered.

"You ever kill anyone?"

Mother was appalled. "Audrey! Stop that."

Audrey purred. "I bet you have skills."

I moved in front of Andy. "Stop ogling my boyfriend."

Andy corrected me. "Fiancé."

I turned, searching his expression. I was going to marry him someday. I corrected myself, "Fiancé."

She put on her pouty face. "You guys are no fun."

Audrey gave the security guy orders to accept the delivery for the food, throwing down some tip money and telling him to ring her when it arrived.

We all piled into the boardroom. Mother was on the phone with Father in Washington. Andy questioned what I saw from those photos and what happened at the station. It was only last week that he had seen Reardon.

Why was there a folder with my address on his dashboard? Surely Andy would have seen that. There were so many questions in my head. *The phone. What did Andy do with it, what information did he have, and who did he give it to? What did he find when he found Reardon? Where was Reardon? Did he kill Reardon?*

Sahil spoke French over the phone with someone. Andy excused himself to walk over to Sahil. He must have known who he was speaking to.

Audrey called over for me to sit with her. "How was dinner the other night?"

"Intense. Andy's mother is mean."

"Richard mentioned she's in government contracts."

"Yeah. Different department, thank goodness. This is crazy, but I had a fleeting suspicion that she tampered with our company. She is in construction, though."

"What's her name again?"

"Agnes McMillan."

Audrey shook her head. "No, Margaret Hamilton is the bitch that dropped it."

Audrey played with her computer. Mother walked over to us, taking a seat. The security guy called. Andy left to get the food.

Sahil hung up, then joined us. "This is a nice building."

Mother smiled. "This used to be my husband's company. Audrey here remarkably salvaged it and bought us out after we lost a devastating contract with the government."

"What was the contract, logistics?"

"Engines."

"Engines? What kind?"

"Semi-trucks, green clean engines. We are about ten years ahead of regulations."

Sahil nodded. "Who dropped it?"

"It was an entire program, budget cuts."

"That's tough."

"Who were you dealing with?"

"Ross Turner, Carl Nichols, Jermaine London, and their department head, Margaret Hamilton. It was Ross, mostly. We never met the others."

Sahil rubbed his face, sighed, and stood up. He strode to the other side of the table and answered his phone. We all resumed talking. Mother walked to the sideboard, opening the cabinet, pulling out plates and bottles of water. Andy returned with two big bags of food.

Sahil called Andy over, then stood close in front of him as the two spoke in low tones. I pulled out the food, watching them. They stood there talking for a bit. Mother called them to come over and eat.

Sahil began to walk over, but Andy grabbed him by the arm, looking angry. Sahil tapped Andy's bicep. "I got it. She'll be safe."

Andy called me over and led me down the hall. "I have to go. I don't know how long I will be. Sahil will be with you. I'm calling Troy back. You won't be able to get in touch with me. But as soon as I can, I will call."

"What? What happened? Hannah's wedding is a week from Sunday."

"I will do my best to make it back. Watch your six."

"Andy?"

"I mean it, babe. Watch yourself."

There was no kiss. No nothing. He turned and disappeared around the corner.

I walked back in. "Sahil? What's going on?"

"Not sure. He's going to find out, though."

It was my last shift of the week. Sahil followed me all night. By the time we pulled in neither one of us had gotten any sleep since yesterday.

I walked into the house and nearly jumped out of my skin. There were Troy and Harry sitting at my table. Sahil walked past me. "Did you get hold of Richie?"

"He's on a plane."

I followed Sahil with my eyes. "You knew they were here?"

He stopped at the fridge. "Yes."

"Well, next time tell me. Jesus, my heart."

He shrugged, pulling out orange juice. When I calmed down, my body reminded me that I urgently needed sleep. I put my keys on the table, then realized I didn't see any vehicles or air service. "How did you guys get here?"

"Uber."

Troy shocked me with that casual answer. "Uber?"

Harry has his bird over at the base. We hitched a taxi over here."

"Well, here are my keys if you need my car."

They both looked up and said "thanks" at the same time.

Troy commented about how he liked my Lexus, and from there car talk dominated the conversation. I changed and slipped into bed, listening to a testament of how nothing dominates like a Shelby Cobra.

Sahil sat at my side of the bed, nudging me. He was talking on the phone.

"I am. She's like a hibernating bear." I felt him nudge harder. "Gilli, LEO's here."

"What?" I stretched.

"Gilli! Police are here. Go see what they want. Don't tell them I am here."

I went from sleep to wide awake, sitting straight up. Sahil squatted to the side, and I knocked him off balance when I swung my feet over. "She's awake," he repeated into his phone as I caught him and kept him from falling over.

"You're like a bull in a china shop."

"Sorry." I let go. "What are the cops doing here?"

He stood up. "That's what you are going to find out. Here, put this on."

He handed me Andy's blue sweatshirt. I opened the door, yelling, "one minute," at the sound of constant knocking.

I ran down and opened the door. Two men showed their badges. Detective Diaz stepped out of his car behind them, looking up at my building. "You live here?"

"Yes?"

"It's an industrial park."

"Yah, so?"

"You moved from a condo to this?"

"What's this about?"

"We found Reardon's body."

"Am I under arrest?"

"No. Mind if I come in?"

Diaz signaled to the two cops. "You guys can go. Miss Chanler, I have some information that you might be able to help me with."

I looked around. "Wait here. You woke me up. Let me get dressed."

"Sorry about that."

I closed the door and darted up the stairs. Sahil complimented me and told me to invite the detective in. He would be listening from upstairs. I changed and brushed my teeth, returning to let Dias into our home.

"Wow, this place is deceiving. Nice home."

Kitten walked by him as if he didn't exist. "I hope you're not allergic to cats."

"No, not allergic, just superstitious. My mother never liked black cats."

I laughed. "Well, she will probably be all over you then."

He backed up while I made coffee. "Okay, so let's say I'm allergic. Can you put her in a room?"

"You're in her house."

"I'm allergic."

I scooped up Kitten and put her in the back room, closing the door.

"Thanks."

"We have ghosts in here, too." I laughed.

He looked around. "I believe it."

"Coffee?"

"Nah, all set. You here all alone?"

"No. Boyfriend, remember?"

"Yeah, that's right." He looked around.

I checked my phone. It was two o'clock. "I'm on five hours' sleep in two days. Let's drop the chit-chat."

He pulled out some photos. "How are you with DB shots"

"DB?"

"Dead body."

I shrugged. "Guess we're going to find out."

"They found him in the lake a few miles out. Autopsy will have a report in a few days, but we're pretty sure the bullet in the head is the cause of death."

I looked. Dead center, forehead. "Do they know what kind of gun?"

"Not yet."

"Why are you here, detective?"

"Your boyfriend. His name Andrew McMillan?"

"You tell me."

"Your fella, I hear he's a pretty good shot."

"Award winning, but you already know that. What are you getting at?"

"Just thinking. This guy Reardon was a perv. I have over three-dozen confessions of some of the things he did. Some girls under eighteen. You said he was a scumbag. Did he try anything on you?"

"He didn't try, but he set it up to try. I figured it out real quick and knocked him on his ass. That was the first and last time I ever saw him. I told you this, remember?"

"Why do you think he had your address?"

"I cannot even begin to guess."

"Maybe you humiliated him. You know, the one that got away."

"That doesn't even make sense. I saw him one time."

"Miss Chanler. Are you telling me everything? Why would he try to go after you?"

"I don't know. I can't tell you what I don't know."

"Did McMillan know about him?"

"What are you getting at?"

"I mean, if my girl was indecently propositioned, I would have a score to settle."

I shook my head. "Are you saying that if your girlfriend came to you and said, this guy didn't touch me or hold me hostage and I walked out on my own free will and knocked him on his ass when he stepped in front of me, that would justify murder to settle the score?"

He didn't answer, so I did. "I feel a lot safer with guys like my boyfriend carrying guns, than I do you carrying a gun and walking the streets."

"I... I."

"Are we done, detective?"

He put the photos in his pocket. "We are done. Thank you for taking time to speak with me. I'll be in touch with any further questions."

"I'll walk you out." I let Kitten out first.

What an ass. He left, and I looked up as Sahil walked down the steps. "Well handled, Gilli. By the way, that bullet hole is right against the forehead. Andy didn't shoot him. If he shot the guy it would have been a work of art. Clean, smooth. That was a panic shot."

It was my day off and I had men to feed. I shopped, stocking the fridge with everything I thought they would eat. Harry and Troy were due back at seven and I thought burgers would be a good choice.

Sahil fit in another close-combat session, setting up a marked-off area we were training in. Four times he had me right down on my ass. The next three I started catching on.

I slipped up, though, trying to anticipate what he would do during the next run-through. He changed his tactics and quickly immobilized me, straddling atop me, triggering a torture tickle session. I was screaming uncle for him to stop, laughing so hard. When finally up, all three men were standing in the kitchen looking down at us.

"Having a laugh, are we?" Harry commented. Sahil reached his hand out, helping me up.

I punched his arm. "Jerk."

We all ate. Richie was briefed on what had been happening. He shook his head upon hearing about Vic going rogue.

I filled everyone in on my schedule. They all knew exactly where I had to be and when for the next week. They even made a backup plan for who was taking me to the wedding if Andy didn't get back in time.

Sahil secured that spot, having already befriended my mother and Hannah. Troy added his wife would kill him if he went to a wedding without her.

Richie was a boxer on the side. After dinner, he taught me ducking and weaving. Sahil drove to my mother's, and Troy and Harry were outside.

I wasn't sure about Richie in the beginning. As it turned out, I really liked him. He was a city boy. He could break into anything, pick any lock, and had a dry sense of humor.

At ten o'clock, Sahil rolled back in. "Tomorrow we pick up your dress. They open at eleven. Priscilla wants you to buy pantyhose. I'll add them to the list. We are meeting Hannah's in-laws for a garden party at three. Oh, Richie, I got a text from Mulligan. He wants you to follow Bartek Wojcik for the next few days. Here's his address. Harry, if you can tap his line, here. Troy, Vic is in Washington."

I jumped up, panicking. "That's where my father is."

Sahil raised his eyebrows. "D.C. Washington D.C."

My heart slowed. I needed water. "Anyone want water?" They all said yes.

Richie left. Troy took the back room and Sahil the couch. Harry worked at Andy's computer, and I slid into bed.

Sahil woke me up, not with a nudge, this time, but instead with a big slap on my thigh. "Shower. Come on, we have a big day."

I left my bed, and Richie took my spot, saying, "Someone wake me up at two."

That was fine. He was on top of the covers and on Andy's side.

Sahil and I picked my dress up right at eleven. I had everything I needed until Sahil spotted a peach garden dress. He found it in my size and made me try it on. Then he found a red dress that had roses stitched on the shoulder straps. He made me try that one on, too.

"What the hell?"

"You have two other engagements this week. Look the part."

White sandals went with both dresses, so I only had to buy the one pair of shoes. He found a necklace, bracelets, and a few hair accessories. Four hundred dollars later, we were back in the car.

"I'm doing your hair when we get back."

I shook my head and texted Andy: *Help . . . Sahil is dressing me and styling my hair.*

Nothing.

I let Sahil do my hair, but I put my foot down on him doing my makeup. I needed a haircut. I looked like a 1950s pinup girl.

When I walked out of the bathroom dressed and with modest makeup on, all the men commented that I looked good. I didn't understand all the fuss. Sahil took a picture. "Your fiancé will be pleased."

"Really? Because he likes the fresh-out-of-bed look."

"Come on, we'll take your car. I'm driving."

CHAPTER THIRTY-FIVE

Michael was next to Mother. Father wasn't due back until Wednesday. Sahil navigated us right toward them. He leaned in.

"Is that the guy from your work? Michael, is it?"

"Yes."

"What is he doing here?"

"Friend of Hannah's. He will be at the wedding."

Michael had not seen Sahil yet. I hadn't said anything to him about Andy's friends. Michael gave Sahil a quick glance, but he couldn't take his eyes off me.

Mother gasped in delight. "Tiffany! That outfit, it's gorgeous. Where did you find this dress? Who did your hair?"

Sahil took full credit. Michael tried following along with their conversation. "Wait, wait, wait. Who is this guy? He's living with you, Tiff?"

"Oh, Michael, this is Sahil. Andy's friend."

"Brother." Sahil corrected me.

"Brother. He's here to keep an eye on me while Andy is away."

"Keep an eye on you? Like a bodyguard."

I liked that explanation. "Yeah, like a bodyguard."

"You know, Tiff, you could have asked me."

"I didn't ask anyone, so cool your jets. Andy didn't like what happened with Bartek, so he asked Sahil here to come stay for a few days."

"Brother? What, adopted?"

Sahil walked my mother away by the hand. "I am going to go say hello to everyone. I think you're safe, Gilli."

Michael watched, his mouth hanging open, as Hannah gave Sahil a hug. "How long has he been here?"

"A little while. He met Hannah last week."

"Well, Priscilla seems very comfortable with him."

"Yeah. He goes to France a lot. She loves that."

He stepped closer to me. "What the hell is going on, Tiff?"

"Nothing, Michael." I looked for the bar and made my way toward it.

"Lemon water, please."

Michael was right behind me. "Tiffany. Come on. It's me you are talking to."

"Reardon's dead. They found his body in the lake on the south side."

"Did your boyfriend kill him?"

"Fiancé. No, he didn't."

Michael ordered a beer. "That dress is pretty, by the way."

"Thanks."

Hannah darted over. "Oh, my god! Tiffany. Love, love, love this on you! Sahil said he found it at the bridal shop. I love it, and your hair! Come on. I've got people for you to meet. Come on, Michael, you too."

We met the groom's family. Hannah's brother asked me if I was all settled in, which took Michael by surprise He couldn't believe I hadn't asked him to help with the move.

Michael curiously asked if I had any updates on Bartek's break in at Angel Wings. I did not. Didn't even know about it, but it had apparently happened yesterday.

Hannah rejoined us and asked where my ring was.

At my response of, "I don't want to talk about it," Michael's mood transformed from grumpy to cheerful in an instant.

Mother and Sahil joined us as the party began to die down. Mother finalized the rest of the week's schedule. Sahil had already confirmed his extra duties and noted them on his phone, and Father was flying in on Wednesday.

Hannah, who had a little too much champagne, giggled when George scooped her up and kissed her on the mouth in front of everyone. The love between them and their playfulness forced a smile on my face, thinking back to when Andy scooped me up like that on my previous birthday.

Sahil wished everyone a good night, then drove me back to our empty home. All the guys were out. Now I remembered.

"Hey, did you hear that Bartek tried to break into Angel Wings yesterday?"

"Yes."

"So, you knew?"

"It's our job to know, Gilli."

"Well, is it your job to let me in on it?"

"No."

"What?!"

"He's a petty drug dealer. He has someone on the inside of a few hospitals."

"What does that have to do with Angel Wings?"

"He was probably using the canisters to smuggle his drugs."

"What? And you don't think I should have been aware of this?"

"He can't do it anymore."

"Exactly! He can't do it anymore, so if none of us knew about it what's to say the operation isn't still going? Maybe that's why he tried to break into Angel Wings."

"He broke in to look at paperwork. He claimed he was making sure his hours were recorded."

"And you don't see him as a threat?"

"No. If you want to open those containers and find some pills, tell your little detective buddy, and bust his operation. By all means, go right ahead. He's not what we are looking for."

"What are you looking for?"

"Bigger."

"Is there something bigger brewing?"

"Always something bigger."

I hung my dress. "Hey, Sahil?"

He looked up from Andy's computer.

"Thanks for today."

"My pleasure, Gilli."

*　*　*

I woke up at five in the morning to get ready for work. There was still no message from Andy. The way he left, the secrecy of it all, was really starting to get to me.

When I was done in the bathroom, Richie stood waiting. "Come on, cupcake, you're not the only one who lives here."

He was right. I had four other men living here for the time being.

"Sorry, Richie. You guys are so quiet, sometimes I forget you're here."

"It's all good. I grew up with three sisters. Mulligan needs to get the other bathrooms functional."

"Oh yeah, there's one upstairs."

"There are three upstairs. No reason not to get one of them working as backup."

I grinned. "Want some breakfast?"

"I'm good. Just going to shower and get some shuteye."

"Okay, hey, thanks for doing whatever you're doing."

"Mulligan's always there for us. It's what we do."

When I arrived at work, everyone was buzzing about Bartek's break-in. Technically, he didn't actually break in. He walked in and rifled through paperwork, not at all hiding what he was doing. The way Sahil explained it, the stupidity of the move was obvious.

Pete and I were on the same page. I did want to tell him about the suspected drugs. I could imagine him being really pissed off if something happened and he got caught in the middle. He was an ex-state trooper. He could tip off someone to take care of it.

We stopped for our coffee and donuts. When we were back on the road, I brought him on board.

"Pete, I got handed some information last night about Bartek."

He laughed. "What else did the Polack do?"

"He's been acting irrational. I found a tracking device on the back of my ambulance."

"Tracking device?"

"Yeah, hidden up under the handle. He must have put it on."

"Why?"

"No idea. But then he started timing the runs."

"Timing, you mean keep track of the stops?"

"Yes. At least it looked that way."

"You are very observant."

"When you've been attacked as many times as I have, little things start to stand out."

"Good to know I'm safe."

I chuckled. "Anyway, I wanted to see what he was up to. That's why I didn't report it."

"Ah, you're one of those thrill-seeking women. Looking danger in the face. Now I see why you've been hijacked."

"Trust me, I'm not looking for that kind of adventure."

"So, what do you think he was up to?"

"There was that night last week when Michael and I switched runs last minute. He was furious, and in the middle of the run demanded I turn into an empty lot."

"Is that when he grabbed your steering wheel?"

"Yeah."

"So, what's the info?"

"I think he's smuggling pills in our cargo."

Pete laughed. "Seriously?"

"He was fired for dealing in the prison. I think he may have some people on the inside of the hospitals."

"Tiffany, I doubt it. First, he's dumb as a bag of rocks. Second, I heard he's piss-poor. I don't think he would have risked his job like that. There's lots of overtime available. This is an easy gig."

"I want to check."

"The tubs are sealed."

"That's right. I can ask the dock nurse for some tape. We can seal them in front of her."

"And tell her what? We think there is drug trafficking? Let me think about this without setting a whole system in lockdown. I can make some phone calls and get an investigation going quietly. I'd rather not spend my afternoon under a microscope. Besides, I'm playing golf with the fellas. Don't ruin a man's leisure afternoon."

I nodded. "Okay, but don't say I didn't warn you if something happens."

"Nothing's gonna happen. I've been in this game for a long time. Besides, this isn't his shift."

He was right. This wasn't Bartek's shift. "How long were you on the force?"

"Too long. The shit I have seen . . . glad it's behind me. I'm taking the easy life from here on out."

"I wish you worked second and third shift."

He laughed. "Not if I can help it. Part-time first shift is for me."

Sahil was calling me. I answered, "Hello?"

"Harry is taking over. I have to go run an errand."

"Okay. Do you want me to cook dinner?"

"No. I'm dining with Priscilla."

"You and Mother are really hitting it off."

"Your Mother is an exquisite woman. We share a similar taste. She is refreshing to be around. You need to get your cardio up. Richie's going to work with you this afternoon."

"Good to know. Glad I didn't make plans."

"You don't make any plans without checking in with me."

"Yes, mother."

"Straight back, understand? Harry needs sleep."

"Straight back, got it." I hung up. Wow, I just realized Sahil was the mother hen of the group.

We made it back. Richie stood at the stove, shirtless, cooking breakfast food. Harry walked in behind me, announcing he was taking a shower. I figured Troy must be on watch.

Tuesday and Wednesday were quiet shifts. Father arrived home, but I still didn't hear directly from Andy. Sahil could reach him on occasion, which sort of bothered me. I wish I knew how to run his computer program. All the guys could easily enough, but I would screw something up, so I didn't even try.

Tonight was my last night at work before three days off.

Kyle walked toward me as I shut the hood on the ambulance. "Tiffany, I wouldn't ask unless we were desperate. I know you have the wedding on Sunday, but can you work Saturday night?"

"Really?!"

"We're in a jam."

"Didn't Donovan hire two new guys?"

"They start Monday."

"Which shift Saturday?"

"Grave digger."

"Route?"

"Rural."

"Who are you sticking me with?"

"Allen."

"Geez, you really must be desperate."

"He's still kicking and screaming."

"Did you ask Michael, or was I first?"

"Michael's pulling a double. Friday night and Saturday morning. Technically, I can't pull him in."

"That's fine, I get it. Yeah. I'll take it, but I can't give you a double. I am in the wedding party."

"I know. Everyone is sick of me calling. I think they are trying to avoid me now. Lucky you're here, though."

"Yeah, lucky me."

"Thank you."

CHAPTER THIRTY-SIX

Sahil lectured me all the way inside. "There is no reason for you to be changing oil the day before the rehearsal dinner. This is a reckless decision."

"Don't worry, I'll stick my hands in bleach."

"I don't understand. Priscilla is top of her class, your father distinguished, and then there is you. What happened?"

"Life. This is where I belong, here with Andy. Did anyone hear when he's coming home?"

"No."

I stomped my foot. "Is he going to make the wedding, at least?"

"Don't know."

"Great!"

"I will be with you if he is not back."

"I want my fiancé. Is this what our life is going to be like?"

Sahil softened, Richie laughed. "That's why I'm single, baby. No one to worry about but me." He looked around. "And you clowns."

He sat on the sofa, making Kitten lift her head. "This is a cool cat. Never liked cats until this one." He reached up and pet her.

"The good times are far more memorable than the missed ones. So, he misses a wedding. It's not his wedding, so it's good. He has me as a replacement, which is even better. I'm far more handsome and dress better."

"I disagree. I want Andy back."

"Get through tonight, Gilli, and the next few days you can celebrate Hannah's rite of passage. This is a big moment for her. Just like it will be for you soon."

"Oh, yeah . . . um, my schedule. I took another shift."

"No."

"Yes."

"Un-take it."

"I can't. I said I would help."

"What did I tell you about checking with me first?"

"Saturday night, third shift. I have plenty of time to get ready for the wedding."

"No wonder Mulligan mutters to himself about you."

"They are desperate. Bartek being canned has made it difficult to fill all the shifts. Look, they hired two more guys. They don't start until Monday, but then everything will be back to normal."

Sahil threw up his hands.

"What?"

"Nothing. We will figure it out." He walked away. I grabbed a shower now while no one needed the bathroom. Four hours of sleep was a good thing.

Michael stopped me inside the office. "Tiff, third shift right before the wedding?"

"You're pulling a double. Besides, Kyle was desperate."

"I know, but . . ."

"But nothing. I'm running the rural and it's easy-peasy. I'll even give them all a heads-up tonight, tell them to make it easy for me."

"I suppose. You all set for the rehearsal dinner?"

"Yes. See, I'm not missing anything."

"What about a bachelorette party for Hannah?"

"She said no. Tomorrow they sign on their new house, we have the rehearsal dinner, and Mother has hired movers for them Saturday as their wedding present."

"What about a honeymoon?"

"They are going to wait."

"I guess the house is a big deal."

"It is to them. That's what they want."

"To each their own."

My shift was simple and uneventful, just the way I liked it. The only thing bothering me was still not having heard from Andy.

Sahil styled my hair again. He stared at my chest. "What are you looking at?"

"Nothing."

"Fuck off." I pulled up the material to cover myself up more.

"It's that scar Tiffany. You are far from earning those wings in this group."

I glanced down, but my hand beat my eyes, covering the burn mark that looked like a phoenix.

"I'm not looking to earn anything in this group. Andy is all I want."

"Cherie, it's a package deal. We are a family. Even Victor."

"What's his problem anyway?"

"Stubborn. Quick to overreact. Like you. Both of you need a time out."

I resented that sharply tilting my chin upward to stare at him in the eyes making the brush tangle in my hair as he held it firmly. "Ouch." I grabbed my hair trying to set it free. I bet Sahil could kill a person with a hairbrush. He released the tension and went right back to styling. "Like you."

This time he styled it with an edge, looking retro, with a black flower clip on the side. Red made my eyes pop. It was another color I tried to stay away from. He wore black with a red handkerchief in his pocket. Another new outfit, I noted.

Richie, Harry, and Troy wore black camo. This time they brought out the big guns. "What's going on?"

Troy smiled. "Target practice tonight, Gilli. Go have fun."

I pointed. "That's not target practice."

Richie answered. "Since when have you been to target practice with us?"

"Never."

"There you go. Someday when you're not playing the socialite, we may bring you."

Troy shot out his finger. "Oh, wait a sec, wife wants to see a picture of you." He snapped a photo on his phone. So did Sahil. Troy tapped and grinned. "She looks forward to meeting you. Says you look beautiful and to have fun tonight. Oh, and she says to smile."

"Does she know about the rehearsal dinner?"

He grinned. "She knows everything."

"Well, at least one of you tells your woman what's going on."

They all moved toward the door. "Come on, time to move out."

There was a military Hummer parked next to Sahil's car. "Where did you get that?"

Troy laughed. "Your garage. Don't tell your old man." They all piled in, laughing.

I raised my hands. "I don't want to know."

Sahil removed the backpack from my back seat. "There is a jammer in there. Andy put it in."

Sahil handed it to Troy, passing it back to Richie. "I know. Get in, Gilli." Troy handed Sahil a bag.

My door was still open. Sahil walked over. "Throw your legs out for a second." I did, and he pulled out what looked like a brace.

"My leg is fine."

"Good to know." He put on a thigh brace, then pulled out a small pistol, tucking it in the side sleeve. "Now, the object is to be able to walk like there is nothing there. Don't bump into anyone. Know your personal space."

He pulled out another brace and strapped it to my other leg. For this one, he inserted two knives. "You don't have to think about this leg. Everything is flat."

I realized my eyes were bugging out of my head. "Why am I wearing this stuff? It's Hannah's rehearsal dinner."

"Just a precaution."

"Are they in danger?"

"No."

"Am I in danger?"

"No."

He slipped on a double holster, inserting a gun in each, then put on a suit coat. "Legs in."

I swiveled as he closed my door. He slid in with the bag between us.

"I'm serious Sahil. My family is there tonight. Are they in danger?"

He started the car. "Not on our watch."

CHAPTER THIRTY-SEVEN

I was accustomed to wearing the brace for my leg, but the gun strap and knife straps took some getting used to. I had seen a lot of movies with the heroine in exactly my getup.

The dress flared out perfectly to keep anyone from being suspicious. I was part of the covert team. Why there was one in the first place at my best friend's rehearsal dinner, they were not disclosing.

My outfit was once again well complimented. The nice thing about this being a private estate was Hannah had use of it all weekend. The tables were set up generally how it was going to be. The garden was lit through to where the wedding would be held. Some chairs were out.

It was theater-style seating. The justice of the peace arrived shortly behind us. Sahil checked the place out completely and then inspected the garden. I didn't see him again.

Mother organized the helpers to set up tomorrow. Everything was checked and rechecked.

Hannah would be meeting the movers at her and George's condos, then George would join them at the house. I was on deck to be with Hannah tomorrow.

Her parents catered the rehearsal meal. We had lobster, crab, and pasta. It took me a while to notice, but there was no alcohol here. I pointed that out.

Hannah laughed as Mother answered, "We have a one-day liquor license, and we can only serve beer and wine."

"Yikes, why?"

"The estate's rule. And the alcohol must be on the tables. No bar setup."

I shrugged. "That's not bad though, right?"

Hannah shook her index finger in the air. "To get this place… small sacrifice." She looked around. "It's so pretty here."

Mother stood up. "Just wait until you see it Sunday morning."

"Tiff, what time are you arriving Sunday?"

I cringed. "About that. I have to work 11-7."

She shot up. "What?!"

"It's really tough right now at work. I promise I will be here on time. I'm bringing my stuff to work and I will drive here right after."

"What time will that be? I'm getting married at eleven."

"Plenty of time. I'll be here by nine."

"You better be."

Mother touched my shoulder. "Tiffany? Are you sure you can't get out of it?"

"They are really stuck, Mother. They have Michael working tonight and the morning shift."

"Hannah, I am with you tomorrow. We will make sure everything is perfect."

She looked me over again. "I think I like your hair the other way for the wedding."

I grunted. "Talk to Sahil, my fashion designer and hair stylist."

"He has a very good eye for style. Where is he?"

"Around, someplace."

"Did you lose weight, Tiffany?"

"Not that I'm aware of?"

"You look as if you have. I hope the dress still fits right."

"It's been like three weeks. Of course, it does."

"Two more days and I will be Mrs. George Paris. What is Andy's last name?"

I smiled. "McMillan."

She rolled it over in her mouth. "Tiffany McMillan, Tiffany
McMillan. It sounds like a detective's name."

She made me chuckle. "I'm not sure I will take his name."

"Really? But I should have figured that. Typical of you. Non-traditionalist to the end."

"That's not it at all. I like Tiffany Chanler. It's who I am."

"You can be Tiffany Chanler as Tiffany McMillan."

"Okay, stop. It's not even worth talking about right now."

She looked at my hand. "You're still not wearing your ring. Something's up. You better tell me tomorrow."

"Nothing is up. Father, how is Washington?"

Everyone knew what they were supposed to do. We went through the ceremony three times because of the bridal party. Their final decision was to have everyone stand in three rows until Hannah was at the altar, at which point the full wedding party, except for me and the best man, would sit in the front row. On the last attempt, we got through it successfully.

It was approaching ten o'clock. We all had a big day tomorrow. Mother confirmed once again who was doing what, and that they were meeting back here at eleven.

Hannah turned to me. "My condo by nine. The movers are arriving about ten. I have everything packed. Once they load up my place, we are bringing them to George's. His condo is small, so I can't imagine we will be there for long."

"Then I have to get home and grab some sleep."

"Damn it. I was hoping to take you to the spa."

I shook my head. "Sorry. I don't want to fall asleep in the middle of eating."

"Fine."

Sahil walked in. "Gilli, time to go."

Mother and Hannah tried to approach, but he excused himself, telling them he was working tonight and would see them soon. They didn't know how to react. He rushed me out, just like a bodyguard under high alert.

Straight in the car and on his phone, he spoke, "We're moving."

"What's this all about?" I didn't like this game anymore. "I've located the tracking device on your car. Same one that was on the ambulance."

"Then should we go home?"

"Yes."

"But they will know where we live."

"Home advantage."

"This is not a home advantage. Do you know who wants to know? What if there are dozens of people? What if this is a whole operation and Andy walks into this shit?"

"He's trained to walk into shit. We all are. You have the A-team here, Gilli. We know what we are doing."

"Now, when we get to the warehouse we are going to walk in together. I am going to change first. Then you. I am heading out. I want you to sleep on the couch tonight. Grab your pillow from the bed and a blanket. Turn the television on and stay put.

"Mulligan said you shop on a home network channel. Tonight, you have all access and can buy what you want. Don't open the doors for anyone." He turned, looking right at me and nodding once. "Understand?"

"Yes."

"How well can you sleep?"

"I don't know."

"Have you ever taken anything?"

"I have pain pills from these scars last year. I didn't take them because I didn't like the way they made me feel. But I did take a half one once to knock my ass out."

"Did it work?"

"Yes. Andy couldn't even wake me up."

"Take a whole one tonight. It will be better for all of us that we know you are passed out on the couch."

"Are you telling me I am only effective sleeping?"

"Yes."

"Jerk!"

"I don't expect you to understand now. Someday you will look back and it will all make sense."

I didn't talk to him for the rest of the ride home.

CHAPTER THIRTY-EIGHT

We arrived, and I did just as I had been told. I took a whole tablet and hit the couch, spending as much as I wanted on the shopping network.

I heard Troy's voice. "Damn, she's a lightweight."

"Gilli. Gilli, wake up. You have to be at Hannah's."

I swished my arms around for all of them to leave. Next, I felt arms on me. I was dragged up into the upright position and cubes of ice were dropped down my back.

My eyes flew open and I jumped to my feet. "What the fuck?!" I screamed.

"Works every time." Troy laughed.

I shook the ice out, looking at my audience. "What was that for?"

Sahil slapped my arm. "Shower, you need to be at Hannah's in an hour."

"Crap!" I grabbed my phone. It was eight o'clock. Richie was asleep on my bed. Sahil asked if I wanted coffee.

I closed the door and jumped in the shower. It was definitely a jeans and T-shirt type of day. I was out within fifteen minutes and grabbed my bag, the coffee in the traveling mug, and my keys.

I looked back to Sahil sitting at the table. "Well, aren't you coming?"

He didn't even turn. "No."

"So, you took care of what you needed to last night?"

"Almost."

"And I am good to just go?"

"Go."

"Do I need anything like that gun or knives?"

"No."

Oh, what the hell? "Fine. I'll be back."

"Bye."

Whatever. I didn't have time for this nonsense. My car was the only car out front. I jumped in and drove right to Hannah's, arriving only a few minutes past nine.

She opened the door. "Ugh. I can't wait for this week to be over."

"When will the movers be here?"

"They just called. About an hour."

I looked around. There were boxes everywhere. She was ready to go. "Did you put your condo up for sale yet?"

"Monday. I can't thank Priscilla enough for hiring a moving company for us. This is so much easier. I think I am going to head over to the hall after we finish here."

I plunked down on her chair. "I think that is a bad idea."

She curled up in the opposite one. "Why?"

"Because, you should keep it a little surprise for yourself instead of seeing it being put together. Save it for tomorrow and enjoy the finished product."

"I can't see George, I can't see my function hall, I can't work, you have to go home and sleep after. . . . What the hell am I going to do? Oh, by the way, I'm really mad at you for taking that shift tonight."

I grunted. "Get in line. I thought the girls were getting together for a manicure party?"

"That's not until six. And let me see your nails." She leaned forward, grabbing my hand. "Yuck. You're the one that needs it most and you're not going to be there. I have my nail kit. I'll be right back."

The movers came just as she finished shaping my nonexistent nails. They did the job in an hour, when Hannah was done with my first coat of polish.

We packed up and drove to George's place. She was right. It was small. He kept the bare minimum of furniture. I wondered if that was just a guy thing, and it wasn't only Andy.

There was enough time for her to apply the second coat of polish. My nails were completed. The movers closed up and drove to the new house.

Hannah and I sat on the floor of George's place. I looked around. "This place is going to sell as soon as you list it. Great location, perfect for someone who is single."

"I know. We are going to list it for a few thousand more than the recommended price. I want it to cover the cost of the wedding."

"Is that setting you back?"

"Twelve thousand."

"Does that include the food?"

"No, that's just the cost of the location."

"Wow? Isn't that a little pricey for a hall?"

"No, we have it for the entire weekend. All ours."

"I suppose."

"Tiff, what happened between you and Andy? Why are you not wearing your ring?"

I looked at my phone. "I better be going."

"Tiffany!"

"It's just a learning curve. We are still getting to know each other."

"I heard his mother is a jerk."

I sneered. "That's putting it mildly."

"So, what's up with Sahil?"

"He worked last night. He's grumpy when he's on duty."

"On duty? Where was he working?"

"Local. That's why he dropped me off."

"Oh . . ."

"And he needed to get back to work, that's why he rushed me."

"Okay. I was wondering what the deal was. He was so personable before. Is he coming to the wedding?"

"Not sure yet. I am hoping Andy gets back." I turned up a smile. "I can't believe you will be married tomorrow. No longer mine."

She leaned back on her elbow. "I'll always be yours and you will always be mine. That's what best friends forever are. No, George or Andy will ever come between us."

"I hope so."

Hannah cupped my knee. "Tiff, what is it? Something is bothering you."

I sighed. "Do you think you know George well?"

She sat up. "Yeah? Why you ask?"

"I . . . I don't . . . Not sure."

"Don't you know Andy? I mean you guys have been pretty much living together for the past half-year."

"That's just it. When I think I've figured him out, I find something I didn't know."

"Like his buddies? To tell you the truth, Tiff, I'm glad he has friends. It makes him more normal now."

I snickered. "Yeah, his friends."

She wiggled to sit straighter. "George is easy. Besides, what I don't know, his sisters tell me. I mean they tell me everything. They will rat him out for any reason. They love me and they love telling on him."

"Andy doesn't have family except his rotten mother."

"Don't worry, I think men in general hold things in. He loves you. No doubt about that."

"What makes you say that?"

"Just the way he looks at you. The man is smitten."

"Michael looks at me, too."

"Yes, he does. You gotta deal with that. Michael is going to be in love with you forever."

"I wish he would move on."

"Then you have to let him go if you want him to really move on."

"I'm not holding on to him."

"Yeah, okay." Hannah stood up.

I followed her. "Why do you say that?"

"I know you. Whether you are aware of it or not, you are still holding onto him."

"You're nuts."

"Fine, just stay in denial."

"What am I doing that is making me hold on?"

"Well, when Andy isn't around Michael is."

"That's because you're always working."

"You become very sarcastic when he mentions his girlfriend."

"That's because she was a bitch to me at the gala on our first meeting."

"Tiffany, you are going to find an excuse in everything I point out."

"No, I'm not."

"Okay, let's just drop it." She looked at her phone, smiling, flipping it for me to see the picture. "Debbie has pre-wedding, girls-only drinks. I just found something to do."

I checked the time. "I have to get some sleep."

"Don't be late tomorrow."

"Don't be hungover tomorrow." I pointed right back to her.

Harry was sleeping in the back room when I arrived. I gathered my stuff I needed for the night and all my wedding attire. With everything set, I picked up Kitten and climbed into bed.

Sahil was the only one there when I woke up. I showered again and filled my thermos with coffee. He had me wait as he strapped a gun to my ankle.

"What's that for?"

"Anything."

"It should be pretty quiet tonight."

"It should be quiet every night, but sometimes that's not the case. I need you to pull your shirt up."

"Why?"

"Wire."

"This seems a little over the top for tonight."

"Shirt."

I lifted my shirt, and he taped the wire. "Just talk how you normally would. We will hear everything."

"Are you following me tonight?"

"Not me."

"Who?"

"One of us."

Whatever. He was being uncooperative. I grabbed my dress. "I will take that, Gilli. You will have it."

"You don't trust me with my dress?"

"You will just throw it wherever and it will be a wrinkled mess. I will get it to you."

"Fine. Okay then, I guess I'm all set."

"Have fun."

"You, too." I didn't understand and gave up.

My car was the only one out front again. I looked up to our living area, then opened my back door to throw my bag in. Hannah was sending me photos from earlier. Drunk-women photos. At least their nails looked nice.

Chris and Allen were in the office. She looked up. "Hey, I'm just getting off a double. Sorry I'm not riding with you. I would have liked that."

I gave a slight grin. "Yeah, me too. Instead, I'm stuck with this guy."

Allen turned his head. "No, you're not. I took second shift. Someone else is with you tonight."

I tilted my head. "Who?"

"John."

"John who? Do we have a John working here?"

Chris looked back up. "Yeah, he's the ex-trooper I mentioned before."

"This must be him?" A heavyset guy walked down the hall toward me.

"Chanler?"

"You must be John?"

"I'll be right out. I have to change."

"Okay. We'll head out in fifteen."

He nodded, walking past. I looked at Chris. "That him?"

She didn't care for him. "Yup."

"Great. I guess I'll get my ambulance ready."

"Good luck tonight."

"Thanks." I headed to my truck.

CHAPTER THIRTY-NINE

John carried the paperwork and hopped inside. He didn't say anything about my ambulance precheck. That was a good sign.

Halfway out to our first stop, he chuckled out loud. I turned toward him. "Something funny?"

His finger brushed over his lips. "Pete said you were a looker. Damn, why are you doing work like this?"

"I like doing this. Helps people, saves lives."

"Yeah, that's what I used to think being on the force. People don't fucking care, though. They only like you when they need something from you."

"So why did you take this job?"

"It's easy."

"Not always."

"Yeah, I heard the Polack gave you a bit of trouble."

"He was nuts."

John laughed. "Okay, we are about thirty minutes out. Wake me when we get close."

"You're not supposed to be sleeping."

"I've been doing this route since I started. Nothing happens."

I shook my head disapproving. Whatever. He leaned his head back and shut his eyes.

I called his name when we were close to our first stop. He woke no problem, grabbed the clipboard and got his papers in order. He pulled the paper he needed and waited for me to back in before handing me the board.

He wass polite and matter of fact. That was fine.

He pulled the containers off and walked in. I didn't know this dock nurse, and she kept looking back at me. One thing about John was he was slow in there. Just like Allen. I bet he was talking the nurse's ear off.

He finally walked back out with her. She signed, and he loaded back up. Again, he rested his head back and closed his eyes.

Our night continued this way until he asked me to go in at the halfway point. He had to use the bathroom. We locked the ambulance up and I made the delivery.

I remembered one of the old-timer guards. He smiled, delighted to see me again. I glanced at the time. I had been in here half an hour.

The nurse came back through, unrushed. She pointed out I had an extra container that needed to be brought to two hospitals over. It was blood supply that they needed. Something had happened to someone.

It wasn't an unusual request. These kinds of things happened now and then. We just filled out the extra paperwork. It was a bigger hassle for the hospital than for us.

John was there on the dock, doors open and waiting for me. He took notice of the extra and asked me about it. Both the nurse and I answered. He shrugged, not really caring. There was already an Angel Wings approval code.

He delivered the next stop, again taking forever. When we pulled into Seven Hills Hospital, there was a correctional officer squad car parked. I asked the nurse about it when she checked our containers, and she held the one filled with blood bags. "We have an inmate cut pretty bad. That's what this is for. He was depleting our supply. All set now, but we don't like being so low this close to the prison."

I nodded. John followed her in. There was someone in the squad car. I couldn't tell if it was a man or woman.

Finally, John walked back out, chatting with the nurse. She seemed to like John; there was a little flirting going on.

One more stop, and then the long ride back to base. We pulled in and John requested again that I take the product inside. He put his hand on his stomach, saying it must have been something he ate. We locked the ambulance up again, and I went in for him.

Another half-hour wait. I asked the guard if tonight was unusual. I didn't remember it taking all this extra time. I was going to have to break some speed limits to get back in time.

We walked out. John was in the ambulance moving things around. This was our last stop. The next shift had these containers to swap out on their first stop. "What are you doing?"

"Oh, I clean up on this stop. Make it easy for the next crew. I'll take those." He took the hand cart from me, loading them in backwards. "Why are you doing that?"

"OCD. When they stack them back on the cart, the top one will be at the top again."

"You know it doesn't matter what order they are in."

"It's just my thing. Oh, and invoices out of order. I hate that."

He was nuts, but okay. I could live with this quirk.

"Come on, we gotta fly. I have a wedding this morning."

He finished up. "A wedding? You know what the one food is that ruins a sex life?"

I didn't know where he was going with this. "What?"

He cracked a grin. "Wedding cake."

"Hm, I would have guessed baby food."

John shook his finger at me. "I like it. Want me to drive?"

"No, I got this."

"Okay, boss, let's go."

"I know a lot of guys, feel free to test the limit."

"Good to know."

We were on a good stretch of road for the next twenty minutes. There wasn't much around here to get in our way. I did see a few deer on occasion, but that was rare.

John sat back in his usual manner and closed his eyes, saying. "Wake me up when we are close."

I glanced in all the mirrors and nothing was around. "Okay."

I pushed sixty in a forty-five zone. I was driving an ambulance, for heaven's sake. Who was going to stop me?

A few minutes down the road I saw a car in my side window. I slowed down some. It was a cop car. They were going faster than I was.

The lights turned on and I slowed way down. Crap. I didn't need this right now.

I tapped John, who opened his eyes. "What?"

"I might need your credentials."

The vehicle came flying up and around us. It wasn't a cop car, but instead a corrections department car.

I glanced at John. "Oops, sorry."

He tilted his head back and held the seat. I put my foot down to accelerate and the corrections department car slammed on its brakes. I hit my brakes hard and swerved off the side of the road, smashing through bushes as I fought to bring the rig to a halt.

Finally, we stopped. John had hit his head and was unconscious. I grabbed the handheld. "Accident! Tiffany Chanler. We are on the southbound side, Route 140, twenty minutes from last delivery. Ambulance off the road. Partner unconscious."

"Tiffany, are you hurt?"

"Minor. John is coming to."

"Help is en route. ETA eight minutes. Stay put."

I saw a guy approaching from behind. "Someone is here."

I unbuckled, pulling my gun. My door opened. It was a guy in a corrections officer uniform who yanked me hard from my seat. I fired my gun, shooting him in the leg. He yelled, grabbing my gun from my hand and throwing it off to the side.

Another guy grabbed me, head-butting right against my skull. "Hello, princess." It was Bartek.

He threw me on the ground, kicking me in the stomach. My insides shattered. Never had I felt a pain like this.

"Think you're all high and mighty now, don't yah? Look at you. Nothing but a whore. Only thing you should be doing is spreading your legs."

I heard John yelling from the cab. "Leave her alone."

He stopped and turned. "I'll be back, bitch."

He climbed in and the guy I shot stood on his feet. "Hurry up, we gotta get out of here." He looked over at me, pointing. "Fucking cu– "

His body jerked back once, then a second time. Blood seeped through his shirt around his chest as his legs buckled, making him drop.

Bartek climbed out of the driver's side holding a container, seeing his buddy lying on the ground.

I pulled the gun from my ankle as Bartek looked right at me.

"You're gonna fucking die, bitch."

He reached back and pointed a gun at me. He stood there motionless as the side of my ambulance sprayed with red. All his movements relaxed, dropping the container then falling straight to the ground.

I heard sirens in the distance. John was still in the cab.

"John!" I yelled. Nothing. My head was pounding, I made my way over to him, gun still in hand. He was slumped over against the door.

"John?"

He started to come to. "Jesus. Are we in a ditch?" he looked over to me. "Tiffany, you're bleeding."

I holstered my ankle gun. The real cops arrived, two cars and an ambulance all making their way toward us.

"All clear," I yelled.

They rushed down the little incline, guns drawn, taking in the two dead bodies. I stated my name with my hands visible. We were here on the side of the road for forty minutes. Another truck from Angel Wings was en route to collect the containers.

One of the cops came back to the ambulance where John and I were being patched up. Officer Wright had the lid off the container, wearing gloves. He asked what our cargo was. John said the clipboard should be on the dash. He showed us the open container that Bartek took. It was filled with pills in bags.

"What's this?" I asked.

John knew what it was. "Prescription drugs, from the look of them."

"Were you aware of medication in your transport?"

"We don't transport medication. We are blood and donor organs."

"Well, it looks like someone's been a bad employee. What do you know about the DBs?"

"The guy next to the ambulance is Bartek Wojcik. He was my former co-pilot until he attacked me on our shift two weeks ago. I knew he lost his job at the prison for selling drugs."

Officer Wright nodded. "Explains the uniform, also the extra layer with the shooter. I think we have a drug ring gone bad."

"How much do you think that's worth?"

"Street value, ten grand. Prison value, double."

"Really?"

He nodded.

I was still wearing the wire as the EMT asked if I was struck anywhere else. I lied. I had to. No way was I going to explain why I was wearing a wire. I checked the time. "I have a wedding at eleven. Any chance of wrapping this up?"

"You're going to miss it. "

"I can't miss it. I am the maid of honor."

John backed me up. "We told you everything. This is no reason to hold her. I can stay. I'm sure she can give you her contact info and sign a sworn statement right here."

I added, "We don't know what is in the containers. They are sealed inside the hospital. We only have the paperwork that goes to each container and there are double signatures from the hospital and us. Did you open that container?"

"No, it was opened."

"Bartek must have opened it in the ambulance."

"Can't wait to see the paperwork on this one."

"Can I make a phone call?"

"Who?"

"Someone who can pick me up so I can get to the wedding."

It was eight o'clock before the Angel Wings transport arrived. Jeff walked over. "Tiff, are you okay?"

"I'm fine."

Officer Wright followed someone to secure the containers in my ambulance. There were about fifteen people here taking pictures and combing through the crime scene. The medical examiner arrived.

"Hey, why is that cop carrying a container . . . opened?" Jeff asked.

"It's filled with prescription pills."

"What? We don't transport medication."

"Well, apparently we are the transportation for some drug ring."

"Donovan is going to flip."

"I think it was Bartek's deal."

"Everyone's been talking about that scum. Never worked with him, though."

I laughed. "Yeah, so much for changing the company image. Angel Wings rebranding at its finest."

Jeff walked down to my ambulance.

Ouch. My ribs hurt.

I called Sahil. "Hey, I need a ride."

"Mulligan will be there in twenty minutes."

"Andy's back?"

"Yes."

Tears moistened my eyes. This was no time for getting emotional. I fought to keep my composure.

An officer returned with the containers. Jeff had the clipboard under his arm. "Hey, Tiff, I don't see any paperwork for that container."

I removed the ice pack from my head. "It was there. We signed for it."

Jeff motioned to Officer Wright to check Bartek's body for an invoice. The state police pulled up. John walked over to the trooper as he exited his car. They smiled, greeting each other. The trooper smacked John's arm and gestured at the mess.

Officer Wright briefed the trooper and the other cop before sending them to follow our Angel Wings ambulance. They were going to open the containers at the hospital. There was nothing left for the EMTs as we signed our releases.

The tow truck arrived to bring my ambulance and the corrections car back to where they were continuing their investigating.

By nine o'clock, Andy pulled over, black tux and all. He wore his shades. He talked to the officer for a few minutes. Officer Wright nodded. Both men walked over.

"Miss Chanler, we are releasing you to Major McMillan. He will bring you in tomorrow to go over the report. I need you to sign an official statement, something better than this scribble."

I agreed. Andy shook the officer's hand. They found my gun and took it as evidence. I was still wearing my ankle gun. Boy, they missed a bunch of stuff. Andy walked me over to his car, helping me in. I told him my ribs hurt as he gently assisted getting me in his car.

"Hold it in, Tiffany. We will be cleared soon."

I ignored the pain as he walked behind and slid into his seat, started the car, and drove away. We drove for forty minutes, arriving at a coffee shop just down the road from Hannah's wedding venue. The Hummer was parked here.

Andy helped me out as Sahil and Troy exited the vehicle. Andy grabbed his medical bag. We walked in and took over the ladies' room. Sahil had my dress as I stripped down. Andy removed the wire and examined where Bartek kicked me. He cleaned the area and stuck a needle in. There was already a bruise showing.

"I think it's just bruised, but it's still going to hurt like hell, babe." He wrapped them and checked my head. "Nice egg. That's going to be a hell of a headache later. Here, take these."

Sahil was getting impatient. "She needs to get dressed."

"She needs to be okay first."

I touched Andy's shoulder. "I can get dressed."

Andy stepped aside, helping me. Fifteen minutes later, he was answering my phone for the eleventh time, trying to calm Hannah down. Sahil took the phone from him as he talked to Hannah, assuring her we would be there soon.

I applied a little makeup. Sahil styled my hair quickly to try to hide the bump that was already bruising up nicely.

We left the bathroom and headed back into the car. Sahil and Troy jumped in the Hummer. Andy opened the trunk, and there was his rifle case and green camo as he threw my uniform on top. We arrived twenty minutes to eleven.

Andy stopped me from getting out. "I have one final thing for you to put on." He handed me a velvet ring box.

I looked, taking it in my hand. I opened the lid, as the sunlight hit the ring, filling the car in tiny, white sparkles.

Andy leaned in. "I have been thinking. My grandmother's ring needed a personal touch. I added the diamonds."

I pulled it out. The chip was in the middle, surrounded by four triangle diamonds about a third-quarter carat each. It looked like a flower made of diamonds. It was absolutely beautiful.

"What do you say, Tiff? This is my do-over? Will you marry me?"

Tears streamed down my face and I nodded as he slipped my ring on.

Sahil opened my door. "Come on, Gilli. Hannah's waiting."

BOOKS BY SUZANNE EGLINGTON

High Priority: A Tiffany Chanler Novel

Priority Suspect: A Tiffany Chanler Novel

The Dating Policy

The Marriage Policy

The Baby Clause (coming soon)

Inceptions: The Kate and Robert Chronicles

You and I: The Kate and Robert Chronicles

Beckham 101: The Kate and Robert Chronicles

She's Got the Jack: The Kate and Robert Chronicles

Suzanne Eglington
FILNE

www.suzeglington.com
Amazon
GoodReads
FaceBook
Twitter